THE *Heart's Stronghold*

Virginia Company Bride ©2020 by Gabrielle Meyer
Embers of Hope ©2020 by Kimberley Woodhouse
A Treaty of Tulips ©2020 by Angie Dicken
A Promise for Tomorrow ©2020 by Amanda Barratt

Print ISBN 978-1-64352-311-8

eBook Editions:
Adobe Digital Edition (.epub) 978-1-64352-313-2
Kindle and MobiPocket Edition (.prc) 978-1-64352-312-5

Scripture quotations are taken from the King James Version of the Bible

This book is a work of fiction. Names, characters, places, and incidents are either products of the author's imagination or used fictitiously. Any similarity to actual people, organizations, and/or events is purely coincidental.

Cover Photography: Stephen Mulcahey / Trevillion Images

Published by Barbour Books, an imprint of Barbour Publishing, Inc., 1810 Barbour Drive, Uhrichsville, Ohio 44683, www.barbourbooks.com

Our mission is to inspire the world with the life-changing message of the Bible.

 Member of the
Evangelical Christian
Publishers Association

Printed in Canada.

The *Heart's Stronghold*

4 *Historical Stories*

Amanda Barratt
Angie Dicken
Gabrielle Meyer
Kimberley Woodhouse

BARBOUR BOOKS
An Imprint of Barbour Publishing, Inc.

Virginia Company Bride

by Gabrielle Meyer

Dedication

To my elementary schoolteachers Roxann Ree, Rhoda Trafas, Arlene Walen, and Stephanie Doty. Thank you for never giving up on my atrocious spelling and for encouraging my love of reading. May this book show you that your work as teachers has had an eternal impact and that I am forever grateful.

Chapter 1

James Fort, Virginia
October, 1608

*A*nne Burras thought it a shame that her mistress had endured months of ocean travel just to die before reaching Virginia. Now, as the sun baked the parched ground and the men lowered Mistress Forest into her shallow grave, Anne almost wished it had been her. Instead, Anne was the only European woman in a fort with more than two hundred men.

"Lord, we commit Mistress Forest to Thy loving arms," the priest said in a solemn voice. "Ashes to ashes and dust to dust. Amen."

"Amen," the others echoed.

Anne's "amen" was a mere whisper, indistinguishable among the deep voices of those around her.

Instead of walking away, the men lingered, their gazes on Anne. Some jostled, some whispered, and others nodded in her direction. A few looked as if they might approach her.

A more terrifying prospect, Anne could not imagine.

"Everyone back to your work," President John Smith called out to the men. "The *Mary Margaret* must be unloaded and the cargo dispersed to the guardhouse or storehouse—immediately."

Slowly, the men began to leave the tight cluster around the dusty grave, though some did not go far. Only the priest, Master Forest, President Smith, and Captain Newport remained with Anne under the vast blue sky.

Tears threatened to fall as the reality of her position washed over Anne. Mistress Forest had been the only motherly figure in her short life, and now she was gone. She was the one who had insisted on bringing Anne to Virginia, knowing Anne had no one else in the world. Though Anne was just a maid, Mistress Forest had educated her and provided her with a good life. Her husband, Master Forest, had protested every step of the way. He had never liked Anne and often told her so. Now he glared at her from the other side of the grave, accusation rolling off him in waves of hatred. Somehow he would find a reason to blame Anne for his loss, though she had done everything in her power to make her mistress well.

Panic threatened to overwhelm Anne, so she lifted her gaze off the grave and tried to focus on what was real and tangible.

From every angle of the small fort, men watched Anne. As they unloaded cargo, stood guard at the bulwarks in their metal armor, or chopped firewood, they kept one eye on her every move. Not that she was moving. She hadn't moved an inch since she had come to stand before the grave.

"We must discuss the glaring issue at hand," President Smith said in a quick, no-nonsense voice to Master Forest and Captain Newport. "The girl will be a distraction and a hindrance we can ill afford in the fort."

Anne could not bear to look directly at President Smith. His reputation as an adventurer and explorer had made him famous all throughout England. His account of the first year in Virginia, which he had spent with Captain Newport the last time the captain had been to James Fort, had been published, and everyone had been talking about Captain John Smith—now the president of the colony. Anne had both dreaded and longed to meet the famed hero.

But here he stood, clearly angry at Anne's presence.

"Master Forest gave very generously to our cause," Captain Newport said with a tight mouth, nodding toward Anne's employer. "When he requested we bring along his wife and she requested we bring along her maid, how could I say no?"

"It's quite simple." President Smith's chest rose and fell impatiently. "You simply say no." Smith was the first person Anne had ever encountered who made no attempt to pacify or please Master Forest. But the older man was so grief-stricken, Anne doubted he was listening to the argument.

"What will we do with her until you return to England?" President Smith asked.

Captain Newport paused. Anne had liked him from the start. He wasn't a young man, but his features were boyish and handsome. He loved the sea and loved telling stories about his many adventures. He had been kind to her and had paid her attention, making her feel noticed and appreciated. Now his face was sad and his eyes were heavy as he looked upon her. "What would you like, Anne Burras?"

Anne sucked in her breath and blinked several times. Never once, from the time she had been orphaned at the age of two until this moment at the age of seventeen, had anyone ever asked her what she wanted. It was such a foreign concept to consider, she was truly stunned. "I—I will do as my master commands," she stuttered as she nodded in deference to Master Forest.

The men turned to her master, and President Smith crossed his arms. "What would you like done with the lass?"

Master Forest's face was set like stone. "I don't care what becomes of her. She was my wife's maid. I do not want her."

The words, though true enough, stung Anne's heart and solidified the truth of her position. Once again she was unwanted, unneeded, and unloved.

President Smith growled and threw up his hands. "I have no time for this, Newport. There is not one decent dwelling in this desolate place that would be proper to keep a young woman. And, more importantly, we have more pressing matters to discuss—namely, the ridiculous letters you brought from the stockholders, as well as the outlandish gifts King James expects me to take to Chief Powhatan." Smith's voice had become more and more irritated.

"President Smith, a word?" One of the older gentlemen who had been standing nearby stepped forward. He was dressed impeccably, from his ruffled white collar down to his polished black shoes. A pointed goatee and a curled mustache completed his look. Anne had once seen a picture of a peacock, and that image came to mind again.

"What is it, Master Caldwell?" Smith asked impatiently. "If you have a suggestion, out with it."

Master Caldwell's jaw clenched and his dark eyes narrowed, but he bowed slowly and deliberately before President Smith. "My home, though modest and far beneath my standards, is clean and acceptable. I have a young servant boy who could use some help and act as chaperone. It would not be ideal, nor proper by English standards, but it might be the best we have to offer the girl until Captain Newport returns her to England."

Smith rubbed his hand down his face and growled again. "Fine." He looked directly at Anne, forcing her to stare back at him. "But I do not want any trouble from you, do you understand?"

Anne's eyes grew wide. It had been her lifelong goal to stay out of trouble and go unnoticed. Nothing good came from getting attention, especially negative attention. It had been the death of her mother and, if Anne wasn't careful, it could kill her too.

She nodded quickly. "Aye, sir."

"I want you to work hard and keep to yourself," Smith continued. "You will draw a great deal of attention among the men, but I do not want you to pay them any mind. I fully expect you to return to England when the time comes."

The idea that she would continue to be the center of attention in the fort made her skin crawl. She would avoid it, if at all possible. "Aye, sir," she said again.

"You'll stay at Master Caldwell's home, but if you have any trouble, you will need to speak to me." Smith nodded firmly, as if this matter was settled and he could move on—which he did.

As President Smith turned away, Captain Newport walked to Anne's side, sadness still deep within his kind eyes. "If you need anything, please let me know. We will return to England as soon as possible."

She was not prone to questioning her superiors, but she needed to know what to expect. "How long might that be, sir?"

Captain Newport sighed and glanced at Smith's retreating back. "I had hoped to leave here within a fortnight, but I'm afraid we have much to accomplish before we can sail home. It might be six to eight weeks, if it be God's will."

Six to eight weeks? The same sense of panic again washed over Anne.

"I will do all in my power to make it as short as possible," Captain Newport said with an encouraging smile. "Will you be well enough?"

"Aye, sir." She would have to be.

"Anne Burras," Master Caldwell said as he approached. "This way, please."

Captain Newport nodded encouragement as Anne turned to follow her new employer. She refused to look back at Master Forest, though she suspected he was watching her. It would be a relief to be out from under his disapproving glare.

"I think you'll find my accommodations acceptable," Master Caldwell said as he began to lead her away from the grave.

Anne finally had a chance to take in the full scope of the fort—and found herself greatly disappointed. She didn't know what she had expected, but surely it had not been what lay before her.

The fort was shaped like a triangle, enclosed by rough-hewn palisade walls. To one side of the fort was the James River and to the other two sides were swampy woodlands. At each angle of the fort, bulwarks jutted out and sentinels stood guard with muskets and cannons pointed toward the woods. The inside of the fort could not be more than one acre, with seven thatch-roofed buildings laid out in systematic order. Along each side of the fort, three long buildings, each two stories high, made up the living quarters. In the center were three smaller buildings. One looked like a storehouse, the other a guardhouse, and the third was the church. To her, the church was the most beautiful of all with its large cross proclaiming the fort's dedication to God.

Scattered between the stick buildings were workstations under canvas awnings, suggesting the fort housed a blacksmith, a silversmith, and carpenters. Glassblowers and other artisans had come over on the *Mary Margaret* and would soon be put to work as well.

"Each of the communal living quarters is shared by two or three dozen men," Master Caldwell explained to Anne. "I am one of the few men wealthy enough to have two private rooms all to myself."

As they passed the carpenter's tent, a tall, broad-shouldered man glanced up from where he stood inspecting a pile of shingles. There had been many men at the grave, but she didn't remember this one being there. If he had been, she was certain she would have noticed him, since he stood so much taller than the rest and had the most piercing blue eyes she'd ever seen.

Instead of staring at her, he simply returned to his work as if seeing a woman in the fort was commonplace. His response was so different than that of the other men, it made Anne pause.

"Here we are," Master Caldwell said, pushing open a heavy wooden door at the end of one two-story building. He bent to enter and Anne followed, trying to forget about the shingle maker to focus on her new job. She did not want to disappoint Master Caldwell.

The room was dark and Anne's eyes took a moment to adjust. A hard-packed dirt floor gave off a musty smell, and the stick and mud walls crumbled in places. Though the room was rustic, the furniture was remarkably ornate. A large wooden table with four chairs, a tall sideboard, a sturdy cabinet, and a massive fireplace made the small room feel even smaller.

But it was the thin boy of maybe ten or eleven who captured her attention. He sat in a chair by one of the glassless windows holding a shirt in one hand and a mending needle in the other. When he glanced up and saw Anne, his mouth fell open and his eyes grew wide.

"This is Daniel," Master Caldwell said to Anne. "Daniel, this is Anne Burras. She will reside with us until the supply ship leaves."

"How do you do?" Anne asked.

Daniel couldn't seem to find his voice.

"I sleep in the next room," Master Caldwell continued impatiently. "Daniel will sleep on a pallet on the floor in there. You will sleep on a pallet in here."

Anne nodded as she noticed the clay pots and cups sitting on top of the sideboard and the dirty tin plates and silverware resting on the table. There were a few melted candles in the dusty room, but none were lit this early in the day. Other sundry items hung from the walls and the low wood ceiling overhead. Cobwebs clung to the corners, and though the floor was dirt, it looked as if it hadn't been swept in some time.

"There is much to be done here," Master Caldwell said to Anne. "And I'll expect you to do your share." He nodded. "Now I must go see about your rations." Without another word, Master Caldwell left the room.

Daniel still stared at Anne as she stood and clutched the one small bag she had brought with her from England. More than anything, she wanted to cry. But she didn't give in to the desire, afraid if she started, she might never stop.

John Layton hadn't wanted to believe the others when they said a young woman had come on the supply ship. He'd even ignored the funeral and kept busy making cedar shingles as long as possible to deny the truth. But now that he had seen her with his own eyes, he could no longer lie to himself or pretend she wasn't there.

With nearly two-thirds of the colonists dying within a year of arriving at the fort, John was certain the last thing they needed was female distractions—and he should know better than anyone else. Nothing good came from being distracted by a pretty woman—hadn't he learned that firsthand? Wasn't that why he had signed on to colonize Virginia, because he'd been told there would be no women in America?

Throwing down one of the cedar shingles he'd been inspecting, he wiped the dust off his hands and strode across the busy fort toward President Smith's new quarters.

Early that morning, Captain Newport had arrived on the *Mary Margaret* with more supplies and seventy new settlers. While John appreciated the arrival of the ship and all the necessary cargo the captain had brought, he loathed the new mouths to feed. John had been one of the first colonists to arrive at James Fort in May of 1607. By January the next year, only 38 of the first 104 men were still alive. Since then, there had been two new waves of settlers, though many of them were already buried.

Death was such a common occurrence in the fort that John did not allow himself to befriend the new colonists. Most people died of disease and hunger, while others died of accidents and Indian attacks.

The biggest threat to life in Virginia, though, was laziness and ineptitude. Instead of laborers and craftsmen, the Virginia Company continued to send gentry to James Fort—wealthy second- and third-born sons who didn't know how to fell trees, plant crops, or even hold muskets. They were just there for adventure and entertainment, eating precious food supply, while men like John worked to keep everyone alive.

Now there was a woman among them to complicate matters. The knowledge made John's temperature rise as he strode across the fort.

Smith's door was closed, so John tapped on it before someone called for him to enter.

"Goodman Layton," Smith said with a nod. "I was just about to send for you."

The president's quarters were some of the nicest in all of James Fort because the previous president had spent most of his time furnishing it while Smith had been exploring Chesapeake Bay. When Smith had returned in September and found the fort in a state of turmoil, John had been one of the first to demand President Ratcliffe resign. After he left, the men nominated Captain Smith to fill the role. Smith wasn't happy to take the job, but he couldn't see any other way—and neither could John.

"Have a seat," Smith told John.

Captain Newport extended his hand to John. The other men in the room were Newport's first mate and the four members of Smith's council. John had been asked to be on the council but had refused his nomination on several occasions. He much preferred taking orders instead of giving them. It helped him to sleep at night knowing he wasn't making decisions that might ultimately lead to more deaths.

"Unfortunately, Newport brought some unsettling orders," Smith said to John before he was settled into his chair. "They are placing demands upon us that we cannot possibly meet."

"I'm certain you're under great pressure," John said respectfully. "But that's not why I've come."

Smith's eyes grew hard as he seemed to prepare himself for yet another blow. "What do you need?"

"I am concerned about the woman."

Smith slammed his fist onto his walnut desk, and the other men jumped. "I have more important things on my mind."

"But she'll be the death of us, I'm convinced," John said. "It's hard enough to get the men to do their work. With another distraction amongst us, it will be almost impossible."

"Newport has brought letters from the company demanding we fill the hold of his ship with gold or the lost colonists of Roanoke." Smith lifted one of the offensive letters and let it float back to the surface of his desk. "At the very least, they want proof of an inland route to the Pacific Ocean. Since we have none of these things, they are demanding an account of our efforts here. I've tried to tell them it will take time, but they need money to pay for this venture—and they need the money to come from Virginia."

"I tried to tell them myself," Newport added, "but they do not understand what it's like here."

"Since we have no gold, I plan to fill the hold with cedar shingles," Smith told John. "It's not what they want, but at least they can sell them and recoup some of their cost. I want you to put thirty of the new arrivals to work felling the logs and making the shingles. We must have enough to fill the cargo hold before Captain Newport is ready to leave."

It wasn't a request, but a demand, and one John was willing to oversee. They would have to work night and day to fill the hold, but it could be done. "Of course."

"We also need more shelter for the new arrivals to live in," Smith continued. "See that you put twenty men to the task of erecting a two-story structure about thirty feet long and ten feet wide."

John stared at Smith. "Where? There is no room."

Smith rose from his desk and strode to the window to look out. "It's past time we add on to the fort."

The council members looked among themselves with questions in their eyes.

"I want to add an addition to the eastern side." Smith turned and met John's gaze. "Extend the palisade about sixty feet from the southeastern bulwark and about forty feet from the northern bulwark. It will create a five-sided fort, instead of three-sided, and will add enough room for us to build more housing."

John nodded. "Now that we have two hundred men in the fort, we should have no trouble getting everything accomplished."

Smith sighed. "You'll only have about eighty men to do all this work."

"Sir?"

"Newport and I will be taking about a hundred and twenty with us to visit Chief Powhatan at first light."

"What?" John looked from Newport back to Smith, incredulity marring his voice. "Why?"

Captain Newport appeared exhausted and probably wouldn't get any rest for many weeks to come. "King James has requested that we make Chief Powhatan an honorary member of royalty. He has sent several gifts, including a golden crown and a four-poster bed. He has asked that I deliver it to him immediately and in person."

Smith's complete disdain for the idea was evident in his scowl. He paced across the small room looking out one window and then the next. "It's a ridiculous gesture and will probably anger the chief—not to mention it's a waste of our time and energy."

"I have brought a three-piece barge to transfer these goods up the James River to the chief," Newport said to John. "It's being assembled as we speak."

"We could have used the space in the cargo hold for more supplies," Smith said with contempt. "Instead, the king sends a barge and a four-poster bed."

Newport held his peace, though he looked as if he wanted to make a retort. The men generally got along, but John sensed Smith's impatience with Newport. The captain was the only liaison between the colony and those back in England. Smith sent letters and directions with Newport, but he clearly was not being heard or understood.

John hated to bring up the young lady again, but he couldn't hold his tongue. "And what of the woman? How will we keep her from being a distraction?"

President Smith stopped his pacing and leveled a glare at John. "If you are so concerned, I will make you personally responsible for her. See that she is safe and that she does not keep the other men from their work." Smith waved John away. "Now go see that my orders are fulfilled."

John just stared. The last thing he wanted was to be responsible for the only woman in the colony.

"She's a kindhearted young lady," Newport said to John with deep affection in his voice. "She won't be any trouble."

With a groan, John pushed open the door and left the president's quarters. He wished he could believe Captain Newport, but his experience with women had proved that there was no young lady exempt from trouble.

Chapter 2

She'd been in the fort for only one day, and already she felt as if she had met all two hundred men who lived there. Of course, there were those who had come on the supply ship with her, but she and Mistress Forest had spent most of their time in their cabin, and Anne had met only a handful of them before arriving in Virginia.

"May I carry your water for you, my lady?" one of the men asked Anne when she stepped outside Master Caldwell's rooms and into the dying light of day. Her cheeks warmed at being called "my lady." She was anything but a lady.

"Would you like me to fetch more water for you?" another asked with a wide, toothless grin.

Anne held a bucket of dirty water she had used to wash all the beautiful wooden surfaces in the home. "No thank you," she said as kindly as possible.

"May I walk with you to the well?" asked a third, this one with hair as yellow as the sun.

The fort's well was only a stone's throw from Master Caldwell's door, but Anne just smiled, not wanting to be rude. "Of course."

Four other men appeared at Anne's side, their dirty hair combed and their faces shining, while a dozen others watched from the shade of one of the buildings.

"Pardon me," Anne said to two of the men standing beside her. When they moved, she tossed the water into the dusty yard.

"You are a sight for my sore eyes, Anne Burras," one of the men said to her, his eyes aglow. "I'm so tired of smelly men and rotten food, I could vomit."

Anne tried to appear unaffected, while inside her stomach turned at the thought. She had tried to go about her business as President Smith had advised, yet every time she turned around, there was a man at her elbow. Even while she worked in the cottage, as she had come to think of Master Caldwell's rooms, she had looked up to find men standing at the windows watching her.

Anne did not want to encourage these men, so she simply tried to ignore them as best she could.

"Would you marry me, Anne Burras?" one of the other men inquired.

"I already asked," said the first who had come to her door.

"What did she say?" asked the other, as if she were not standing there.

He sighed, his voice dripping with heartache. "No."

Anne started toward the well, her wash bucket now empty. But before she could reach the wooden structure, three more men beat her to it and started to turn the crank to bring the bucket up from the water below.

"I am quite capable," Anne protested.

"You're no bigger than a flea," said a short man with wiry

whiskers. "This is hardly nothing for me, but it'd be too much for you, I think."

Trying to keep her patience in check, Anne allowed the man to assist her. She had never had help a day in her life, and she found she didn't enjoy it as much as she'd always thought she would.

"Everyone back to your work," growled a man as he strode toward the group.

It was the carpenter she had come to learn was John Layton.

The group of men scurried away like mice running from a hungry cat.

Goodman Layton stood a head taller than everyone else and it was clear he had some sort of authority over the men.

Anne paused, quietly transfixed by the mountain of a man before her.

"Captain Newport promised me you wouldn't be trouble," he said with a scowl on his handsome face.

"Trouble?" Anne asked, confused by his accusation. How had she caused trouble?

"The men." He waved at the whole lot of them, most having not gone far. "Winter will be upon us before we know it, and they all have work to do. They cannot be toting your water nor doing your chores."

"I didn't ask—"

"Leave them be, or I'll have to put you on house arrest."

Her mouth fell open at the threat. "I have no wish—"

"Just do your work and let them do theirs."

Indignation rose in her chest. "You are making false accusations and are not allowing me to defend—"

"I have no time for your defense." He took a step closer to her, and she had to look up into his face. His blue eyes were more startling than she recalled, especially now with fire in their depths. He could only be in his midtwenties, but the hard lines around his mouth and eyes spoke of experience well beyond his years. "I am one of the few men who have survived this place, and I have done it by sheer willpower. There is no nonsense to be had here, no time for debate, argument, or frivolity. We either work or we die."

His words hit their mark and she swallowed hard. "I do not wish to die."

"Nor do I. And I do not wish for these men to perish either. So they must do their work."

"But that's the trouble," she said, a bit of spark returning to her voice, willing him to understand. "I am not encouraging these men to do my chores. On the contrary, they will not let me alone."

The man turned and faced the others who were still listening. "May it be heard," he said loudly. "Anne Burras is not to be bothered or harassed. Leave her to her work. If she be in need of assistance, she will come to me."

Several men cursed, and a few spat on the ground. Others simply turned and walked away, their shoulders bent.

"And who might you be?" Anne finally asked, though she already knew. "Whom should I inquire after, should I need assistance?"

He wore no hat on his curly brown hair, and his clothing was clean and well fitted. He wore dark breeches, tall stockings, a linen shirt, and a leather vest. Though he was not dressed as well as Master Caldwell, he still bore himself like a gentleman when he bowed before her. "John Layton, at your service."

Anne didn't know why heat warmed her cheeks or pleasure swirled within her stomach. The feeling was entirely unfamiliar, and though she enjoyed it, she did not understand it.

John straightened and met her gaze.

The feelings only intensified, so she took hold of her bucket, which had been filled just before John approached, and clutched it in her two hands. "I—I must see to our evening meal."

Without another word, she walked away from John Layton, toward the cottage. When she turned to close the door, she looked back to where he had been standing and found he was already gone.

Daniel knelt before the hearth and blew on the coals to catch the kindling on fire.

Anne closed the door, thankful for the relative privacy of the room.

"Anne?" Master Caldwell called from his chamber.

"Aye, sir." She set her bucket on the table and walked to the open door.

A large four-poster bed with dark red curtains stood in one corner, a desk in the other. Master Caldwell sat at his desk, a quill in one hand, a potato in the other.

Before him on the desk was a pile of potatoes and a small sack of corn.

"We will have several guests for supper this evening," he said without looking up at her. "Friends of mine who have requested an audience with you."

Anne frowned, recalling John Layton's threat, as well as President Smith's warning. Would they be angry if Master Caldwell allowed men to visit her? But who was she to question her master or tell him what he could and could not do in his own home?

He finally looked up at her, a frown between his dark eyebrows. "Do you understand?"

"Aye, sir."

"I expect you to make them a nice meal. Daniel will fetch you sturgeon, turtle, or oyster to make a stew. He will also go to the storehouse and get our daily ration of corn, which you can use to make corn bread or mush. There might also be some root vegetables to be had from the supply ship."

Anne's gaze drifted to the potatoes and corn on the desk.

Master Caldwell shifted his position to try and shield them from her view. "You will leave this food alone."

Nodding, Anne took a step backward and returned to the main room of the cottage.

"And close the door," he called out after her.

She did as he commanded, curious about the food he had on his desk. There was no other food stored in his home. All the food in the colony was kept in the storehouse and rationed out by the storehouse keeper each day.

Daniel rose quickly from his place near the crackling fire. "I can see about an onion if you'd like. There aren't many in the fort, but the keeper might give me one if I said it was for you." His gaunt cheeks filled with color.

It was evident that the young boy wished to please her, but she didn't want special treatment. "I can make do without one."

The look of pleasure slipped from his young face, and Anne's heart broke just a little.

"Unless," she said quickly, "it wouldn't be too much trouble."

Without another word, he left the cottage so fast he forgot to close the door behind him.

Standing outside the cottage were half a dozen men. They snapped to attention when she walked to the door.

How would these men get anything done if they lounged about waiting for a glimpse of her all day?

More importantly, how would she convince John Layton that she wasn't encouraging them?

The sun peeked over the eastern horizon as John stood at the riverside gate and watched the barge move upriver with Captain Newport, President Smith, the priest, the physician, and over a hundred other men on board. Almost everyone had come to send them off. There was no way to know when the barge would return. After they delivered their gifts to the chief, President Smith planned to spend time exploring further upriver to see if they could find a passage to the Pacific Ocean, which the Indians claimed was just over a small mountain range to the west.

Now that the barge had departed, the remaining men stood about talking to one another.

It was time to get busy, and no one would be exempt from the work.

"Everyone to your posts!" John called to the men. "Thatcher's group will head to the eastern tip of the island and fell cedar trees, Hanover's group should start digging holes for the eastern palisade addition, and Meacham's men are in charge of preparing the site for the new living quarters."

No one seemed to hear John's commands, or if they did, they simply ignored him.

Anger rippled under his collar.

"You'll only frustrate them further with your ire," William Cole said to John, coming up alongside his friend. "Your only hope is to convince Caldwell to put them to work."

Edward Caldwell stood just inside the fort's gates, his pristine white collar like a beacon for an Indian's arrow. Though he and President Smith did not always see eye to eye, Smith had placed Caldwell in command of the fort until his return. John was convinced the only reason for Smith's decision was because Caldwell was well liked among the men and would have the most influence over them.

It couldn't be because Caldwell was known as a hard worker; the opposite was actually true. He was a gentleman adventurer, the third-born son of a lord. His wealth in England had left him completely bereft of skills, and he was good for almost nothing in Virginia, except eating precious stores of food. But he did have a charismatic personality, and if John could convince him to rally the men, they might fulfill President Smith's orders before his return.

But before John could approach Caldwell, another distraction drew his attention.

Anne Burras appeared outside Caldwell's house with a basket of wet laundry, which she carried to the clothesline on her hip. She wore a dark burgundy gown, which was snug at the waist and full at the hips. Upon her head she wore a white cap to secure her dark brown hair, but tendrils escaped and blew in the wind, softening her already attractive features.

Without speaking, about half of the men moved in her direction and made a semicircle around her to watch her work.

"I wonder how long it will be before other women arrive," William mused as he crossed his arms and stood transfixed by the woman.

"This one is one too many, in my opinion," John said through gritted teeth.

Caldwell noticed the commotion Anne had caused, and he too turned toward his maid. But instead of breaking up the group who had gathered, he quietly moved among them, his hands outstretched.

Frowning, John left William and crossed the fort to speak to Caldwell. He must do something and soon, or nothing would get done. They didn't have a moment to spare.

Anne glanced over her shoulder as she hung each piece of

clothing on the line that ran from the building to the palisade wall. Her cheeks were pink and full of health. When she caught sight of John, she quickly lowered her brown eyes, as if she'd been doing something wrong.

Though Anne made a pretty picture, it was Caldwell that held John's attention. He was collecting kernels of corn from each of the men, putting them in a small burlap sack.

John frowned. What was the man doing?

"Master Caldwell, a word?" John asked.

Caldwell continued down the line until he finished collecting from each man, and then he closed the small bag and motioned for John to join him in his home.

Without trying to be polite, John pushed his way through the crowd of men and entered Caldwell's rooms.

John paused, surprised at how clean the room looked. The furniture, which John had built for Caldwell's home over the winter, gleamed. Had Anne done this?

"What do you want, Goodman Layton?" Caldwell asked.

John had little time for small talk. "Why are you taking corn from the men?"

"As payment for watching Anne."

John's mouth fell open, appalled and disgusted by Caldwell's admission.

"You do not approve of my actions?" Caldwell asked John as he jiggled the bag of corn with a satisfied grin.

"Of course I do not."

Caldwell shrugged. "It matters not to me." He turned and entered the next room.

John followed.

Setting the bag on the desk, Caldwell took a seat and dipped a quill pen into the inkwell before adding several marks into a ledger. "I do not plan to starve this winter," Caldwell said to John. "Though I owe you no explanation, I will give you one. Anne is my servant, and as such, I am at liberty to use her in any way I see fit. I could keep her locked up in the house all day or allow her to work out of doors where others can enjoy her presence. If they do, they pay me."

John gripped the back of the extra chair but refused to take a seat. "The men need to work. I cannot stop you from what you are doing, but I can implore you to put them to their tasks. We have a quota of shingles to fill by the time Smith and Newport return, not to mention all the other tasks the president has assigned to us. We must work diligently to accomplish them."

"And accomplish them you will," Caldwell said patiently as he scratched a few more lines in the book. "As soon as I fill my own quota."

"Which is?"

"More food."

John briefly closed his eyes and rubbed his hands over his temples, trying not to lose his temper. "You would take the only food these men have and benefit from their hunger?"

"I could care less about their hunger," he said. "It is my hunger I am concerned about."

Frustration swelled in John's chest. "You have your payment for now, so please tell the men to go about their work."

Caldwell sprinkled sand on the ink and then lifted the book and tapped the sand onto a piece of paper before closing the pages. "Very well. I'll go now."

He stood and ran his hand down his goatee.

John followed him, and they emerged into the sunshine once again.

"Attention," Caldwell called out to the men. "Goodman Layton has assigned each of you a job. It is time to get to work."

A general cry of disappointment arose from the group, and John shook his head. How did these men think the work would be done? Did they not think about the future? About the winter that would surely leave them all sick and starving once again if they did not take action now?

Anne finished hanging the clean clothes and quietly picked up her basket. She moved toward the house where John stood just outside the door.

He had to move aside for her, which he did, but not before he noticed her look at him with apprehension.

She was close to him, so close in fact, he could smell the scent of soap on her hands from the washing. "I did not encourage them," she whispered for his ears alone and then walked into the house and closed the door.

As the men moved away, guilt pricked at John's conscience for the way he had treated her yesterday. It wasn't her fault she was the only woman in the colony—and it wasn't her fault that Caldwell was encouraging the men. He should have been more patient with her. It was his own fear that had driven his anger.

As the men dispersed to do Caldwell's bidding, John walked to the well for a drink of water.

"What she needs is a husband," William said to John as he met his friend at the well. "If she was spoken for, the others might leave her alone and do their tasks."

"A husband?" John shook his head as he turned the crank to bring up the bucket. "A husband would keep her in the colony."

William shrugged. "And what's the trouble with that? If she married, the others would leave her alone. Soon more women will follow. I heard that Captain Newport is trying to convince the stockholders to send brides. He said the colony wouldn't be civilized until there were families about—and how can there be families without women, I ask?"

John shuddered to think about a colony overrun with women and children. It was hard enough to keep a group of men alive.

He took the cup from the peg and dipped it into the bucket of cool water.

"What do you have against women?" William asked John, crossing his arms and leaning against the well. "You haven't had a positive thing to say about them since we came here."

Without warning, John's thoughts returned to the night his mother had been accosted by their creditor and his brother had struck the man for taking advantage. The creditor had died, and John's brother had hanged for manslaughter. Weeks later John's mother had died of a broken heart, and it was all because John hadn't been there to help. Instead, he'd been in town flirting with a young lass. His mother had often warned him that he was spending too much time carousing when he should be home working hard to pay off the debts his father had left.

Just before his mother died, she warned John that if he didn't curb his wild ways, he'd find himself no better off than the lecherous creditor who had accosted her. The very thought had made John swear off women altogether.

"Women aren't the trouble," John admitted, almost to himself. "It's the men who cannot control themselves where women are concerned that bothers me most."

He tossed the remaining water back into the bucket and then lowered it into the well.

If he was honest with himself, Anne Burras wasn't the problem.

It was men like John, before he was reformed, who were too foolish to know when enough was enough.

"You might be right," John said. "Maybe someone does need to stake a claim on Anne Burras so the others leave her alone and get their work done." And that someone should be a man who had the willpower to send her back to England where she belonged—instead of marrying her and keeping her in Virginia.

Unfortunately, from the looks of things, the only person in the fort who had that kind of willpower was himself.

Chapter 3

There's an illness, Anne." Daniel entered the cottage and set a bundle of shirts on the table. "Two have taken ill in the east quarters and three more in the west building."

Anne removed the bundle from the table and set the dirty shirts in the basket by the door. Master Caldwell had agreed to let her take in extra laundry as long as she completed all the tasks he assigned to her first. In payment the men were offering English coin, which had little use in James Fort but would serve her well when she returned to England.

"What ails them?" Anne asked as she stirred the pot of oyster stew. It was her second evening in Virginia, and Master Caldwell planned to entertain more gentlemen that evening.

"Ague." Daniel took a seat on a low stool near the door and picked up one of Master Caldwell's shoes to polish. "They're just off the ship, and they're miserable. Some have asked for you."

"Me?" Anne shifted the pot out of the heat. "What would they have me do?"

Daniel shrugged.

"What about the physician who came over on the *Mary Margaret*?"

"He went with President Smith."

Anne wiped her hands on her apron. She had little experience with illness, but there had been ginger root in the storehouse when she had gone there earlier. Maybe she could make them ginger tea to help with their fevers.

"Go to the storehouse and fetch me some ginger root, please," Anne told Daniel. "Tell Master Riddles it is for those who are ill."

Daniel set down the shoe and jumped to do her bidding.

While he was gone, Anne set a pot of water to boil over the fire. It didn't take Daniel long to return with the ginger root, and when he did, Anne cut off a piece and boiled it in the hot water.

"Will you come with me?" she asked Daniel. "I may need help."

Daniel nodded and took the clay cup Anne retrieved from the sideboard.

"Show me to the men in the east building, please," Anne directed.

He opened the door, and, as always, a group of men were lounging around, waiting for her to appear.

Ignoring them, she followed Daniel across the fort to another two-story building. "In here," he said, opening the door.

Anne entered the building ahead of Daniel. The stench assailed her nose as her eyes adjusted to the dark. Unlike Caldwell's rooms, this room was bigger and housed several bunks. A single fireplace against the inside wall was all the room boasted. There were no chairs, no tables, and no bureaus. Just dirty, smelly men.

She found it difficult to assess who was sick because half a dozen men were lying in their beds. As soon as Anne entered the room, though, all but two of them jumped up at the sight of her.

"Who is ill?" Anne asked, holding the steaming pot of tea.

The men took a moment to come to their senses. Clearly they were startled to see her there.

"Ross and Peter," one of the men said as he pointed to the two still lying in their beds.

"Will the rest of you leave us?" Anne had no wish to be watched as she took care of the sick men—and she didn't think Ross and Peter would like to be watched either.

"As you wish." The man who spoke to her ushered the others out. They protested all the way.

With Daniel's aid, Anne helped the sick men drink the tea, though one had already succumbed to delirium. There was little she could do to help.

"These men are very sick," Anne whispered to Daniel after she had ministered to them for a while. She picked up the pot of tea to leave. "I wish the physician were here to see to their needs." She didn't like their color or their high fevers.

"There are three more men in the other building," Daniel reminded her.

"And they have the same complaints?"

"Aye."

Anne sighed. She would need to make more tea.

They stepped outside and found a group of men waiting.

"I'm not feeling well, myself, Anne," said one of the men who often waited outside Master Caldwell's cottage to get a glimpse of her. "Could I see you alone as well?"

The man, whom she'd learned was named Albert, looked healthier than any of the other men in the fort.

"And me," said another. "I'm feeling a bit poor."

She didn't even bother to answer them.

"Here comes Goodman Layton," said a third, a warning in his voice.

The group of men dispersed, and Anne sighed with relief before bracing her feet and squaring her shoulders in preparation for John's rebuke.

He strode up to her, wood chips clinging to his shirt and hair.

Instead of scowling, as he was prone to do, concern softened his eyes. "Are they bothering you?"

Anne glanced at the men who had gone their separate ways and shook her head. "No more than usual."

He had a metal tool in his hand, and he grasped it now, looking around at the departing men. "I saw you from my work area." He nodded toward the awning where she had witnessed him making shingles. "What brings you to this side of the fort?"

Lifting the now-empty teapot, she indicated the building where she had just exited. "Some of the men are sick with ague. I brought them—"

"You went into their quarters? Alone?"

"With Daniel." Anne motioned to the young boy who stood quietly waiting.

"You may not go into the men's quarters." John shook his head, a bit of the ire returning. "It's not decent."

Anne wanted to laugh. "Decent? I hardly have to worry about decency around here."

"That may be so, but I don't want you tending to the sick."

"Because it's not decent?"

"Because it's not safe."

"I'm perfectly fit. I haven't been sick in years."

"This isn't England. There are diseases here that I've never

36

witnessed before." Real concern filled his eyes. "I've seen a robust, healthy man hard at work in the morning, as weak as a newborn calf at noon, and dead by nightfall."

Again, his words sobered her. "The doctor has gone with President Smith, so who will see to the men?"

"They will have to see to themselves." He took the teapot from her hand and began to walk toward Master Caldwell's cottage. "We were doing just fine before you or the doctor came."

Anne followed John, wondering at the hard edge to his words. "You've lost two-thirds of your colonists. Maybe the doctor and I are needed here, after all."

He snorted.

Did he not want her at the fort?

She could have carried the teapot back herself, but she allowed him to do it for her. His help was different than the others. Instead of treating her like she was a queen, he treated her like she was a pest. For some reason, she actually found it refreshing that he didn't fall over himself to please her.

The walk back to Caldwell's cottage didn't take long. John followed Anne and Daniel into the main room and set the teapot on the table. Thankfully, Caldwell had gone with the men to the east end of the island, so his overshadowing presence was absent.

"Daniel, will you fetch more water from the well?" John asked the boy. "After Anne makes another pot of tea, I will personally deliver it to the other sick men."

Taking the water bucket, Daniel left the cottage without a word.

"I might not like you tending to the sick," he said at her questioning gaze, "but that doesn't mean that *I* cannot see to their well-being."

He turned away from her probing gaze and made himself busy examining the room.

Anne only smiled to herself, thankful that someone would take care of the men.

John tried not to appear uneasy as he stood in Anne's presence. It was the first time he'd been alone with a woman in years, and he was very aware of her every move.

"The rooms have benefited from a woman's touch," he mused, admiring the polished wood and the clean hearth.

She didn't comment as she lifted the lid off a pot and began to stir the contents.

He couldn't ignore the delicious aroma wafting from the stew. "Oyster?"

"Would you like to try some?"

His stomach growled and his insides hurt from hunger. He cooked at a communal pot each evening and his diet had been wanting—not only from lack of food, but from lack of imagination as well. He wanted to refuse her offer, but he couldn't help himself.

"Aye," he said.

She took a small mug and ladled a bit of stew into it.

"It's not much," she warned. "Just a few things I was able to mix together."

She extended the mug, and he took it from her. Their fingers brushed, and a tingling sensation raced up his arm. It took him by such surprise, his back went rigid.

Anne looked up at him, her large brown eyes soft in the firelight.

"Thank you," he managed to say around the sudden lump in his throat.

"You're welcome." Her voice was gentle and calm, and it wrapped around John in such a way that the room suddenly felt warmer than it had been a moment before.

He didn't wait for a spoon, but sipped the stew. It slid over his tongue in a surge of flavors he hadn't tasted in years. Instead of satiating his hunger, it only made him long for more.

"This is good, Anne." He shook his head in astonishment. "Very good."

A beautiful smile lifted Anne's lips.

John's knees went weak, and he had to chastise himself for his reaction. He was no better than all the other men who waited around for a glimpse of her. He'd seen pretty girls before—so why was he reacting this way now?

The reminder of his earlier conversation with William returned to him. If he was going to stake his claim on Anne, he would need to do it soon and do it right. To make the others believe it was authentic, Anne would have to believe it too. He wouldn't make any promises he didn't intend to keep, but he would show her he was serious.

A part of him felt guilty at the possibility of making her think he was falling in love with her, but the other, more practical side told him it was for her own good and for the good of the colony. She would probably appreciate having more privacy and less attention, and soon she would be on a ship back to England, where she belonged.

John finished his stew and handed back the cup. If he was going to start, he'd have to start now. "This is the tastiest stew I've had in a long while, Anne."

Her cheeks blushed at the compliment.

"I haven't eaten anything like this since I was in England." He pulled out a chair and took a seat.

She looked at him with questions in her eyes but didn't say a thing.

"I've been eating out of a communal pot for so long, I forgot what a real meal tastes like."

"You're welcome to more."

He watched her move around the room, her feminine form reminding him of why he had enjoyed the lasses back home. Now that he had given himself permission to flirt again, his pulse quickened and all the old feelings stirred to life again. "I might take you up on that offer." His words were smooth, and the memory of how he had charmed the ladies back home returned with ease.

Picking up the ginger root, Anne took a knife and began to cut off pieces of the plant.

If he wanted to win her over, he would need to know more about her. He didn't remember a single lass who didn't like to talk about herself. Settling back into his chair, thankful Daniel was taking his time and Caldwell was out of the house, John allowed himself to enjoy Anne's company.

"Did you leave a family back in England?" he asked.

She stopped chopping the root, her hand pausing as she looked straight ahead at the wall. "I have no family," she said quietly.

"I'm sorry to hear that." He leaned forward, his heart heavy for her. "I don't have any family left either."

Anne turned, her eyes sad. "Now I'm sorry."

He shook his head. "That's why I came to Virginia." He studied her for a moment. "Why did you come?"

She shrugged. "I had little choice. My mother died when I was two, and Mistress Forest took me in, sparing me from the workhouse. When she decided to accompany her husband to Virginia, I was told to come along."

"Now she is gone and Master Forest has no need for you." He stood and took a step toward her. She was so dainty, yet she was hearty and hale. If Virginia was going to be colonized by women, Anne Burras would be the kind they would need. "What will you do when you return to England?"

Taking a step back, she looked him over from head to foot, and he realized, too late, that his height might make her feel intimidated. He retreated, putting a little more space between them.

"I–I'm not certain," she said quietly.

"Surely you considered what you might do if you were free from your mistress."

She set the knife aside and lifted her apron, wiping her hands on the coarse material. She held it a bit longer than necessary as she kept her eyes down. "There are precious few options for an unmarried woman in England."

John's heart began to beat a little faster. "Do you wish to be married, Anne?"

She swallowed and still did not look at him. "I—I haven't given it much thought. As Mistress Forest's maid, I didn't have time for such things. I imagined I'd be her servant for the remainder of my days."

"And now?" He leaned on the sideboard, consciously aware of the intimacy of the room and the growing darkness outside.

"Now?" she glanced up at him and clutched her apron tight. "Now I'm not sure what I want."

"Anne." John needed to make his intentions known so the others would soon know as well. "I—"

The door creaked open, and Caldwell appeared over the threshold, his unsuspecting gaze turning from surprise to anger.

"What's the meaning of this, Layton?" Caldwell asked. "What are you doing here alone with Anne?"

They were standing closer than necessary, and John knew how it must look. "We are waiting for the boy to bring back water. Anne has been making ginger tea for—"

"You are not welcome here when I am not at home." Caldwell stepped into the room, his overbearing presence drowning out everything else. "I am responsible for Anne, and it's not proper for her to entertain gentlemen when I am not at home."

John straightened his back. "President Smith asked me to keep watch over Anne while he was away."

Anne glanced up in surprise at the announcement.

"I will see to her welfare," Caldwell said.

"But you were away," John explained, "and she was in need of assistance."

Caldwell's lips pinched and his eyes narrowed. "That is all well and good, but you have no business being here alone with her."

Daniel appeared at the door, the bucket of water weighing down his slight frame.

"And where were you?" Caldwell grabbed Daniel's ear and hauled him into the room.

John flinched at the look of pain on Daniel's face.

"I went to fetch the water, sir," Daniel said in a weak voice.

Caldwell pushed him away and Daniel fell to the ground, the bucket of water sloshing onto the dirt floor, instantly turning it to mud.

"Now see what you've done." Caldwell stared down at the boy. "I told you to stay with Anne every moment."

"Aye, sir." Daniel rose on shaking legs.

Anne stood silently near the hearth, her eyes downcast.

John clenched his fists, hating to see the power Caldwell wielded. He had never liked the man and had even less respect for him now.

"I have guests coming," Caldwell said to John, disdain dripping from his voice. "If you'll kindly depart."

John hated to leave Anne in a house with Caldwell, but it wasn't his house and Anne wasn't his servant. He had no right to stay if he wasn't wanted.

John moved toward the door, his heart heavy. "Good day, Anne."

She lifted her gaze but did not respond. No doubt she was afraid to anger Caldwell further.

"And stay away from Anne," Caldwell said, coming to the door, his bulk filling the frame. "If I see you bothering her again, I'll be forced to take matters into my own hands." He paused, his eyes taking on a gleam. "That is, unless you're willing to pay like the rest."

Clenching his jaw tight, John stared at the man. How could he stomach the idea of taking food from men to spend time with Anne? "What's your price?"

"For you? Two cups of corn."

Two cups was half of John's daily ration. He shook his head. "What you're doing is ludicrous."

Caldwell began to close the door.

"Fine." If it meant winning over Anne, he would pay the price, but there had to be a better way.

Chapter 4

*J*ohn wiped his brow as he helped lift a tall log into place along the palisade wall. Progress had been slow, and he wondered if they would have the annex finished by the time President Smith and Captain Newport returned.

The log fell into its hole, and John stepped back to assess the stability.

"How many logs have been prepared for the wall?" John asked Timothy Hanover, the foreman he'd put in charge of the fort addition.

"About half of what we'll need," Hanover admitted as he ran his sleeve across his sweating hairline.

"I put you on the task a week ago." John frowned. "Why aren't the logs ready?"

Hanover was one of the three dozen men who had survived the first year, and that was why John had assigned him the job. "Very few of these highborn men know how to handle an ax, and even fewer have built a wooden structure before. When they do work, I spend most of my time fixing their mistakes."

John sighed. "Those who do not work do not eat." It was something President Smith had often told them that first year. "Hold back their food rations if they do not complete their daily tasks."

"Aye." Hanover nodded, his face solemn.

After seeing that the log was secure, John stepped away from the wall and looked out over the open expanse of land they had cultivated to grow their corn. Over a hundred acres had been painstakingly broken, but the crop had not grown well. Inadequate rain had led to a poor yield, making them all the more dependent on the supply ships.

In the distance, a movement caught John's eye. Ever on guard from attacks, he was motionless as he watched and waited. The threat of Indian and Spanish invasions was always present. Guards stood watch over the fort night and day around the clock. Each man was required to take his turn on the bulwarks for a twenty-four hour shift, and even now there were men standing watch as the others worked on the fort expansion. Three times a week they conducted practice drills in the fort yard, and daily John took groups of men to the guardhouse to show them how to load and fire a gun. Not only were the men inept at building, but they were just as inept at warfare.

A sorrier lot of colonists John had never seen.

Satisfied that his eyes had played a trick on him, John finally let out a breath and entered the palisade. He needed to return to the men he had put in charge of making shingles. If he left them for too long, they would find an excuse to take breaks or bother Anne.

Thinking of Anne, frustration built in John's chest. He had gone to Caldwell's home five evenings in a row, sacrificing his precious food supply, but had not had a chance to spend time alone with her. Caldwell entertained his friends every night, demanding Anne wait on them, and by the time she was finished with her chores, she was exhausted. John didn't want to force her to keep him company, so he had left each night with nothing to show for his time there.

And the men had increased their ardor, if that was possible. Several of the highborn men who spent time at Caldwell's had shown serious interest in Anne. Two had even proposed marriage. They were men of wealth and standing in England, and if she said yes, she would want for nothing back home. But she had refused them, and each time she had, John had felt a weight lift off his shoulders—which surprised him. If she married someone else, wouldn't that eliminate his need to pursue her? He wondered why he felt relieved that she wasn't married to someone else, and the only reason he could surmise was that he didn't like any of the men who had made offers. And, besides, if she married someone in the fort, it would mean she would stay in Virginia, and he was still convinced it would be better if there were no women in the colony.

John strode back into the fort, determined to see Anne now, before she was busy catering to Caldwell's friends. But first he stopped at the storehouse to get his daily ration of corn.

The sun beat down on his back, unseasonably warm for October, and it only made his temper rise higher.

A group of at least a dozen men—most of them assigned to making shingles—sat in the shade of a building within eyesight of Caldwell's rooms.

The sight of them was the fire needed to set off John's fuse. Not one of them looked concerned to meet their obligation—and the threat of starving didn't seem to alarm them either.

"I will personally stand guard at the storehouse," John roared, "a musket in hand, and prevent each of you from receiving your daily ration if you do not get to work immediately." His voice had reached a pitch uncommon to him, and it caused his throat to strain. "Now!" he thundered.

The men hadn't seen him coming and jumped at the sound of his voice. They bumped into each other in their haste to get away, two of them falling back into the dust.

"If you are not at your station within a minute," John growled, "you will lose tomorrow's ration as well."

Anne stepped out of Caldwell's home at that moment, her eyes wide at his outburst.

He stood in the dusty yard, breathing heavily, with a small sack of corn in one hand. She must think he was mad! Would she shy away, afraid of his temper, or would she be thankful he'd sent the men away?

She simply looked at him, a brow raised, and then went to the side of the building to take clothes off the line.

John took a deep, steadying breath and tried to compose himself before he approached her.

"Good morrow, Anne."

"Good morrow, John."

It seemed ridiculous to be holding the corn, so he set it down on a nearby bench and went to stand beside her.

She glanced at him, a bit of laughter in her eyes.

"What is so funny?" he asked.

"I've never seen a group of grown men move so fast before."

"Aye?" He took a shirt off the line and set it in her basket. "And I've never seen a more slovenly group of colonists."

Her smile faded and she frowned. "Have you heard the news? Three of the men who took ill last week have died, and four more are sick today."

He had heard—had actually helped bury them just beyond the

fort. "Aye." Death had become such a part of life at James Fort, he hardly took notice.

Fear pinched at the corners of her mouth as she set her hand upon a shirt to remove it from the line. "I've sent Daniel for more ginger. I cannot abide seeing the men suffer."

John set his hand over hers, fear gripping his heart like never before. "Stay away from them," he said. "You'll do no good if you get sick."

She moved her gaze from his hand to his face, her eyelashes lifting gently from her cheeks. "Are you worried for me?"

It felt good to touch her, and if his instincts were correct, she liked it too. Was he winning her over?

Or was she winning him over?

He pulled his hand away, realizing he was worried about her, far more than he should be. Hadn't he convinced himself he was the only man in the fort strong enough to capture her heart and then let her go?

"Aye." He nodded at her question, probably more surprised than she was at the admission. "I do not want any harm to come to you, Anne."

She studied him for a moment. "No one has ever worried about me before."

How could that be true?

A commotion tore his gaze from Anne.

Two guards opened the west gate facing the river to allow visitors into the fort. It couldn't be people who posed a threat, or the guards would never willingly allow them to enter. But it probably wasn't one of the colonists either. They usually entered through the east gate, facing the fields and the side of the island where they were cutting trees.

Three Powhatan girls entered the fort, baskets on their hips.

Anne stood still as she watched the Indians. They were probably the first she had seen since arriving in James Fort, and no doubt she was curious.

"Those are some of Chief Powhatan's daughters," John told Anne as the girls began to speak to the men who were gathering around them. "They come to the fort from time to time to trade with the men."

"What do they trade?"

"Food."

"And what do the men give them in return?"

"Beads, cooking utensils, cloth, sewing needles." John turned from Chief Powhatan's daughters and smiled at Anne. "Would you like to meet them?"

Anne's eyes grew wide, but she nodded.

She stayed close by his side as they walked toward the Indian girls.

One of them caught his eye and smiled.

"John," she said, her accent still foreign to his ears. Her gaze shifted to Anne in curiosity, though she didn't seem surprised to see a woman in the fort. Perhaps word had already spread about Anne's presence on the island.

"Anne, this is Chief Powhatan's daughter, Pocahontas."

"How do you do?" Anne asked the girl, who was no more than thirteen.

The other two Indians stopped speaking, and all three studied Anne with deep, probing eyes.

Pocahontas nodded, a smile quick to appear on her face. "How do you do?" she asked Anne in return.

"And these are Pocahontas's older sisters, Matachanna and Namontack."

"How do you do?" Anne asked the other two.

They were quieter than Pocahontas, who had become a popular and frequent visitor to the fort.

"You are *woman*?" Pocahontas asked, trying the word on her tongue.

"Yes." Anne's gaze wandered over the Indian girls with the same interest they showed for her. She did not seem afraid, but merely curious. "I'm Anne."

"Anne." Pocahontas repeated her name with a nod. She extended the basket to Anne, revealing squash, beans, and corn. "You like?"

Looking up at John, Anne questioned him with her eyes.

"Pocahontas is offering to trade her food with you."

Anne shook her head. "But I have nothing to offer."

"A gift," Pocahontas said. "To Anne."

"A gift?" Anne continued to shake her head. "I cannot acc—"

"You'll insult her if you do not," John warned quietly.

Anne swallowed, her smile wobbly. She reached out her hands to accept the gift. "Thank you."

Pocahontas handed her two handfuls of beans, which Anne cradled in her apron, a large squash, which John accepted on her behalf, and several ears of corn. All the while, Anne thanked her profusely for the offering.

"I will give you a gift the next time you come," Anne promised Pocahontas.

Pocahontas simply smiled and then continued her trading while Anne and John brought the food back to Caldwell's home.

"I cannot believe her generosity," Anne said. "I must make her a gift as well. Maybe a cap or a pair of mittens?" She looked at John expectantly, but he simply shrugged. He didn't know what Pocahontas might like.

"Thank you for introducing us," she said as she set her bounty down on the table in Caldwell's home. "I thought I would be afraid to meet the Indians, but they seem very nice."

Pocahontas was nice, as were her sisters, but not all of them were kind to the colonists. Many were hostile, angry at the intrusion, and still some were quietly watching and waiting to see what would happen.

"Do they live far from here?" Anne asked.

"Aye. But they come often, leaving early on foot." John frowned, confused by their timing. "I am surprised Pocahontas is not in her village, since President Smith and Captain Newport are visiting her father. She and President Smith are good friends."

Anne didn't seem to notice John's musing, and he decided to drop the subject so she wouldn't become concerned.

The weather had turned cool, and Anne was especially thankful for the warmth of the fire in her kitchen as she set the corn cakes in the small oven at the back of the hearth. Master Caldwell had taken a contingent of men to the east side of the island to cut more cedar, offering Anne and Daniel a bit of space to breathe. While her master was charming and gregarious with his friends, he was sullen and demanding with his servants. Even so, Anne couldn't complain. She was warm, well fed, and safe for the time being.

A knock at the door sent Daniel to his feet.

A familiar male voice greeted the boy. "I've come to see Anne."

Her heart sped at the sound, and she couldn't stop the smile from lifting her lips even if she had wanted to. John had come again.

Every day for the past week, since Pocahontas had come to visit, John had stopped by the cottage to collect the daily pot of ginger tea—despite Master Caldwell's threats. It was the very least Anne could do to help those suffering from the mysterious disease that had plagued the colony for two weeks now. The men continued to ask for her to nurse them, but John had refused to let her. Instead, he brought her gift of tea to them. They had already lost seven men, and another group had taken ill yesterday.

It was time to face reality. She was running out of ginger—and it didn't seem to be working anyway.

John had to bend under the lintel to enter the cottage, and when he straightened, he caught her gaze and returned her smile. His eyes were so brilliant and smile so bright, she caught her breath and had to force herself to put one foot in front of the other as she moved to get the tea.

"Daniel," John said to the boy, "could you please retrieve my daily ration for me?"

The boy grinned and slipped out of the cottage, closing the door softly behind him without asking a question.

Anne didn't say a word, but she was secretly happy that John had sent the boy away. John had taken to the habit of asking Daniel to run errands for him when he came to visit, and Daniel often stayed away much longer than necessary.

The first two times John had sent Daniel away, she had thought he was simply asking the boy for his help. But by the third day, she had started to suspect that he was doing it intentionally to have privacy with her. At first she wasn't sure how she felt about that, but by the fourth and fifth day, she had come to look forward to the few stolen moments she had in John's company, away from prying eyes. He was a gentleman in every way and didn't spend the time flirting with her like the others. Instead, he had been getting to know her, asking her questions, genuinely listening to her answers, and then sharing things about himself.

"Will you have a seat while you wait for Daniel?" she asked John.

He stood with one hand behind his back while the other held his hat. Something about his stance made him seem apprehensive and a little embarrassed.

"I brought you a gift, Anne."

She turned from the teapot and gave him her full attention. Heat filled her cheeks at the way his voice had dipped with intimacy when he said her name.

"A gift?" She wiped her hands on her apron and dropped her gaze. Should she take a gift from him? But how could she not? He had been so kind to her these past two weeks, keeping the men at bay and helping her with the sick. She should be giving *him* gifts.

He slowly pulled his hand into view and presented her with a green glass jar. "It's the first jar the glassblowers have made here in James Fort."

It was a beautiful piece of glass, perfectly shaped, with a wide mouth.

Anne stayed near the sideboard, both embarrassed and honored that he would bring her this valuable gift.

"And there's more," he said, walking toward her. He lifted the jar for her to inspect the contents.

"Why—"She looked up at him, her eyes large."It's a honeycomb."

"One of the men found the beehive when they were felling trees yesterday and brought it into the fort." John smiled and his cheeks deepened with dimples. "I was able to convince the storehouse keeper to give you the first bit."

He took another step toward her and placed the jar in her hands. She wrapped her fingers around the cool container, and he wrapped his hands around hers.

He stood so close Anne could smell the scent of cedar and woodsmoke on his clothing. His hands were rough from work yet as gentle as if he were holding a newborn babe.

Her stomach fluttered and her skin tingled at his touch. She had never felt such a rush of joy or anticipation as she did in this moment. She loved when he touched her, spoke to her, and made time to see her. He was well respected in Virginia and worked harder and longer than any other man in James Fort. Having his attention was a gift even greater than the one he presented now.

"Thank you," she whispered, uncertain what else to say and afraid her voice would not work if she tried to say more.

He ran his thumbs over the tops of her knuckles in a feather-light touch. It sent a shiver up her spine and made her knees grow weak. There was no telling what this man could make her think or feel if he continued to caress her.

Needing space, she gently pulled away from his hands and turned back to the sideboard to set down the jar. "I made an extra corn cake for you," she said, just as gently as before. "Would you like me to serve it to you now?"

He hadn't moved and was still standing close behind her. Every inch of her body was aware of his nearness. She longed for him to stay—but she also wanted him to leave. She couldn't think straight when he stood this close.

"Aye," he said and finally stepped away to take a seat at the table.

Anne took the cake from the oven and set it on a plate. Without looking his way, she knew he was watching, and the knowledge made her hands tremble.

Picking up the jar of honey, she tilted it to drizzle a bit over the cake, and then she turned and met John's gaze.

The space between them was filled with attraction, as if they were being pulled together by an invisible string. It both frightened and exhilarated her.

She set the plate before him and placed a fork on the table.

"Thank you," he said. "But you didn't need to use your honey for me."

"You appreciate my cooking more than anyone else," she said. "Why waste it on someone who doesn't?"

He grinned and used the fork to cut into the steaming yellow cake before lifting it to his lips.

She watched the fork as it entered his mouth and came out clean. John closed his eyes and uttered his appreciation with a sound in his throat.

"It's even better with the honey," he said as he opened his eyes and found her admiring him.

She turned, embarrassment warming her cheeks at being caught, but he reached out and took her hand in his, stopping her from walking away.

"Anne." He gently tugged her to come closer to him, and she was forced to meet his gaze. "I haven't spoken so plainly with you before, but—" He stood, so they were face-to-face. "But I've come to—"

The door opened and Daniel entered.

John dropped Anne's hand and resumed his seat at the table.

Anne took a giant step away from him and went to the sideboard, placing her hand on her cheek to try to cool the skin.

"Master Forest is here to see you, Anne." Daniel opened the door wider to reveal the man who had brought Anne to Virginia. He stood in a dark coat and a ruffled collar, a black hat sitting high on his head.

Anne's insides began to quake for an entirely different reason, and she swallowed the fear racing up her throat. Master Forest entered the cottage, his brooding eyes sweeping over the scene in one quick perusal.

John rose from the table and bowed to the gentleman. "Good day, Master Forest," he said.

"Goodman Layton." Master Forest nodded but did not smile. He looked from John to Anne, his frown deepening.

Anne had hoped Master Forest would leave her alone—and so far he had. She hadn't seen him once in the two weeks she'd been at the fort. She had heard he stayed in his room, but she had been too afraid to inquire after him for fear she'd draw unwanted attention from her former master.

"I've come to speak to Anne," Master Forest said to John and Daniel, his voice stern. "Privately."

It was John's turn to frown as he probed Anne with questioning eyes. She knew he was asking if she wanted him to stay—and the truth was, she did—but she did not want him to hear what Master Forest might say.

So she simply nodded at John that it would be fine for him to leave.

He left his cake on the table and rose. "Come, Daniel, we will wait outside."

Anne was thankful he would be within calling distance, though she didn't think she'd need to worry about requiring assistance. Master Forest would not harm her—at least not physically.

John ushered Daniel out of the room and closed the door behind him, but not before offering her an encouraging smile.

Her heart warmed at his thoughtfulness but cooled the moment she met Master Forest's hard gaze.

"I think you know why I've come, Anne." He didn't take a seat but stood in the center of the room and stared at her.

She wanted to play naive, but she did know why he'd come, though she would never admit it to him. Instead, she clasped her hands in front of her waist and lowered her gaze.

"I never approved of my wife taking you in," he said, just as he'd told her a dozen times over the course of her life. "And when she insisted you come to James Fort, I knew from the start you'd only bring us trouble." He choked on his emotional words. "I tried to refuse her, but she insisted. Now she is dead and there are others who have died as well."

Anne swallowed hard. He had a wild look on his face, and she could see by the bags under his eyes and the lines around his mouth that he had not been well. His grief hung from him like a black cape, engulfing him in sorrow.

He took a step closer to her, and she forced herself not to cower. She didn't want to show fear, nor did she want to seem prideful. She had danced this dance all her life.

"I know what your mother was, and I fear that she gave you her powers before she was hanged. But my wife did not believe me." His voice shook with the force of his convictions. "Have you cast a spell over this fort? Have you put sickness upon these men?" His face grew red as his accusations increased. "I've heard you concoct a drink every day to be administered to the men. Is it a potion?"

Anne shook her head, tears threatening to fall.

"Did you kill my wife, Anne?" He took another menacing step closer to her, and she had to turn her head away from him. "Are you a witch, just like your mother?"

"No." She continued to shake her head, panic making her tremble. "I am not." And neither was her mother, she was certain. Though she couldn't remember her mother, she was convinced she could not be what others had accused her of. Nearly a hundred men and women had been killed in North Berwick, her mother being one of the last, before the witch hunt had ended. King James had personally been at the head of the investigation, convinced a local coven of witches had conjured up a storm that had prevented him and his new bride from traveling home from their wedding in Norway.

"I fear I have brought witchcraft to North America by allowing you to come." He shook his finger in her face, his voice so loud, spittle flew from his lips. "I am watching you, Anne. I cannot prove anything now, but if I see you doing something suspicious, I will accuse you for what you are."

The door flew open and John appeared over the threshold, fire in his eyes. She had seen the look before and watched it make lesser men cower before him. "I believe you are finished."

Master Forest tugged his coat down and pinched his lips together. He did not say another word but left the cottage, pushing past John as he went.

"Did he hurt you?" John asked her.

Anne shook her head and tried to compose herself. She did not want John asking any questions. It was better to say nothing, to keep to herself and stay unnoticed. Nothing good came from being the center of attention.

Nothing.

Chapter 5

John had spent two days trying to get Anne to tell him about Master Forest's visit, but she kept to herself and refused to engage with his questions. He did not know what the man had said, but he had heard the tone of his voice and saw the look of fear on Anne's face when Forest had appeared.

Clouds covered the vast sky and weighed down John's mood. From where he sat making shingles, he had a good view of Anne's front door. He also had a good view of the men who lingered near her house longer than necessary, trying to get a glimpse, a smile, or a conversation from her. It still angered him whenever he caught the others lounging about, ignoring their duties.

"One would think you'd be whistling while you work instead of frowning," William Cole said to John as he tossed a shingle onto the growing pile at their feet.

"Whistle?" John set the froe against the edge of the cedar log and raised a wooden mallet. He struck the metal froe, and it sank into the wood. Setting aside the mallet, he turned the log and pressed against the froe until it split the shingle away from the rest of the wood. The smell of fresh cedar filled the air around him. Tossing the shingle aside, he did it all over again without thinking. "What do I have to whistle about?"

William struck his froe and grinned. "I've heard word that you've won over Anne Burras."

John stopped his work and gave his friend his full attention. "What have you heard?"

"That you plan to marry her."

"The others are saying this?" Was that why fewer men had been stalking around Anne's home like hungry wolves?

"Aye." William nodded. "And I've helped along the rumor."

So John's plan was working. Good. He wanted it to keep working.

"If you want the others to believe the rumors are true"—William struck the froe—"you'll need to look a little happier."

John wanted to be happier, but he couldn't deny the feeling that Master Forest had hurt Anne and now she was pulling away from John for fear that he might learn what had transpired. He hated the idea that someone would intentionally hurt her—but he also hated the idea that she was hiding something from him. He just wished she would trust him.

But why should she? Wasn't he trying to trick her into believing he loved her so the others would stay away?

Guilt washed over him like the brackish water in the James River.

"Indians!" A call arose from the eastern bulwark. "Ambush!"

Immediately, John rose to the alert, his heart pounding and his pulse thrumming through his veins. He, along with all the other men, ran to the guardhouse where two guards were always on duty, ready to arm and assist the fort.

Armor stood at the ready, and John grabbed a musket, a bandolier, and a dagger.

One of the guards who had been standing on the bulwark rushed into the guardhouse, breathing heavily. "The call came from Goodman McIvey who was working with Master Caldwell felling trees." He bent over to catch his breath. "He saw the Indians attack two men before he ran toward the fort to call for help."

John slipped the bandolier belt over one shoulder, ready to fight.

A second guard ran into the guardhouse, breathing just as heavily as the first. "Master Caldwell and his men are rushing to the fort. There appears to be no Indians following them."

John pushed his way past the guards and into the open yard. Several men were entering the eastern gate, sweating, out of breath, and wild with fear. Caldwell walked in behind them, a little less ruffled, though visibly upset as he strode toward John and William.

"We were ambushed by Powhatan Indians," Caldwell said to John. "Two of our men were killed, others wounded."

"Powhatan?" John shook his head. "Why would Chief Powhatan send warriors to ambush our men while Captain Newport and President Smith so recently visited them?"

"Mayhap he has sent them because he knows our numbers are low." Caldwell wiped his brow with a handkerchief he pulled from his pocket. "Over a hundred men were with Smith and Newport. If Chief Powhatan was angry over their gifts and he wanted to retaliate, now would be the time to strike."

A more disturbing thought came to John. "What if he killed Newport and Smith, and now he's coming here to kill the rest of us?"

William and Caldwell were quiet for a moment, and then Caldwell set his mouth and shook his head. "They could have been hunters sent out by Powhatan, and they decided to scare us. It wouldn't be the first time."

Caldwell was right. Over the past eighteen months, there had been dozens of isolated incidents. But that didn't mean this one was isolated. Only time would tell.

"I want double guards on the bulwarks for the next few days, just in case," Caldwell ordered. "For now, we will continue as usual."

John wasn't certain it was wise to continue their work, but what choice did they have? They had stockholders in England demanding a product from the colony.

Returning his weapons to the guardhouse, John stepped out into the cold afternoon air and caught a glimpse of Anne dumping a pail of water.

He wanted to go to her and reassure her, but what could he say? The fort was a dangerous place to live, and they had no certainty that they would survive each new day.

The very thought of losing Anne, the way he'd watched others suffer and die, was enough to convince him he needed to find a way to make her promise she'd be on Newport's ship when it left James Fort.

Not only for the colony's sake—but for her sake as well.

The room felt colder than usual as Anne stood by the hearth and stoked the flames. Master Caldwell had not yet risen from his bed, and Daniel was fetching the morning water.

Anne stood and slipped her cape over her shoulders, trying to brace herself for the cold lying just beyond the door. With a deep breath, she opened the door and stepped outside.

A thin strip of sun peeked over the eastern horizon while a few morning stars sparkled in the west. Ahead of her, the James River flowed toward the ocean and a home that was quickly fading from memory. What would await Anne when she returned to England? What kind of life would she have? She had no family or friends to greet her or offer a warm place to live, and no guarantee of employment, especially if people learned about her mother. If it hadn't been for Mistress Forest, Master Forest would have abandoned Anne years before their arrival in Virginia. As it was, his threat still lingered near, taunting her with its implications.

What would happen if he accused her of being a witch? Would the men turn on her? Would they hang her as they had hanged her mother? She had learned from her mother's experience that all it took was a simple accusation, a few twisted half-truths, and a heavy dose of fear to turn a group into a lynch mob.

Anne shivered at the thought and closed the door behind her.

She went about her morning necessities and brought in a heavy armload of wood. Daniel had gone to the storehouse for their daily rations and was already grinding the corn for their breakfast when she returned.

Despite the warmth of the fire, Anne could not shake the chill that had come over her. Though she had slept well the night before, exhaustion overtook her and she struggled to complete her chores.

The room began to spin, and she grabbed the back of a chair to keep from falling. Her legs had grown weak and her stomach started to turn.

"Are you well, Anne?" Daniel asked, coming to her side.

She managed to pull a chair away from the table and sat, her head in her hand. "I will be fine in a moment."

Daniel hovered near her. "Shall I get you something?"

Her throat had grown sore, so she nodded. "A drink of water, mayhap."

He rushed to do her bidding just as the door to Master Caldwell's bedchamber opened.

"Why is my breakfast not on the table?" he asked.

"Anne is not feeling well, sir." Daniel came back with a mug of cool water, which he placed in Anne's shaking hand.

Master Caldwell took a step back, his pointed goatee resting against his broad chest. "You're ill?"

Fear seized Anne's chest as she tried to stand and prove that she was well—but the room spun so violently, she fell back into her seat and dropped the mug. It hit the dirt floor and splashed its contents onto her boots.

"Daniel, set out Anne's pallet again."

Daniel did as he was told and brought Anne's straw mattress out of the rafters, placing it in the corner of the room where she slept at night. He also took out her blankets, which she had recently folded and put into the cabinet in the corner.

"Lie down, Anne." Master Caldwell gave his orders from near the door, not getting closer to Anne than necessary. "I know nothing about illness. Is there someone who can assist you?"

His voice held true concern, and Anne fleetingly wondered if he cared about her or if he just cared about the extra rations she brought in for him.

"I will be fine," she said, praying it was true. The reality that she might be ill with the same disease that had killed the others gripped her throat with panic. Would she die?

"Goodman Layton has been assisting the others," Daniel said to Master Caldwell as he helped Anne to her pallet.

She was shocked at how weak she'd already grown as she was

forced to lean her weight against the small boy. It took all her will-power to reach down and try to remove her shoes.

"Allow me," Daniel said to her, his voice soft and gentle though it was filled with fear.

Caldwell simply stood near the door, his eyes hooded as he watched. "You've been seeing quite a lot of Layton, have you not, Anne?"

Anne closed her eyes, pain starting to pound in her temples.

"Anne?" Caldwell demanded.

She blinked, realizing she'd almost fallen asleep. "Aye," she whispered, uncertain what it was that he had asked.

"The others are talking," Caldwell said. "Do you plan to marry Layton?"

"Marry?" her throat hurt so badly now, she could hardly speak.

"Do you plan to marry Layton?"

She mustered all her strength to shake her head, sadness mixed with longing and fear. "I'm returning. . .to. . .England."

If she lived.

Forty-eight hours had passed since Daniel had rushed into John's quarters and told him that Anne had taken ill—the longest forty-eight hours of John's life.

John sat against the wall in Caldwell's main room and leaned his head back to rest. A fire smoldered in the hearth while Daniel slept in the next room. They'd both been awake through the night, seeing to Anne's needs, and Daniel had finally passed out, exhausted. John had lifted the thin boy in his arms and brought him to his pallet.

Caldwell had left the house an hour previous, scowling at John as he left. The man had not been happy to send for John and was even more upset that John had insisted on staying until Anne regained consciousness, even abandoning his own duties to see to her needs.

She moaned beside him and tossed her head on her sweat-soaked pallet.

John moved away from the wall and sat beside her on the floor. He took her hand in one of his and smoothed her brow with the other. She had become delirious in the night, calling out wild things he couldn't begin to decipher. Something about her mother and Mistress Forest. When "Master Forest" came off her lips and she began to call out for him not to accuse her, John had sat up straighter to listen, but then she had fallen into mumbling and he could not make out her words.

"Anne." John whispered her name now, leaning down to speak close to her ear. "Wake up, my love."

The words slid off his tongue and startled him.

But once he spoke them, he realized that somehow, in such a short time, they were true. He had fallen in love with Anne Burras, despite his efforts to hold his feelings at bay.

Yet how could he not love her? In the few weeks he'd come to know her, he had held a great deal of admiration for the beautiful, hardworking woman. Not once had she shied away from a task, not once had she spoken ill of her master or her circumstances, and not once had she failed to make John feel appreciated. Everything within him wanted to protect her, cherish her, and make her happy.

In a land where life was short and precious, he'd found that love grew quickly.

From the few things she had shared, he surmised that her childhood had been difficult, though it had not broken her spirit. What might it be like to be the man who could finally offer Anne what she deserved—what he knew she longed for? What would it be like to love her with complete and unconditional love?

Any man would be blessed to have Anne by his side, and for some reason, God had allowed him to be that man—at least for the moment. Overwhelming gratitude filled him, even while fear held a grasp on his soul.

A knock came at the door, and John stood. His back and legs ached, and his head pounded. He hadn't slept for more than a few minutes, in short, uncomfortable naps, throughout the long two days he'd spent by Anne's side.

Cold air seeped into the room as John opened the door and found William standing on the other side, his face grim. "There was another ambush at sunrise, this time on the palisade addition. One man was killed and three more injured."

John's senses snapped to attention. "Why wasn't I sent for before now?"

William looked away, moving uncomfortably. "We knew you were busy with Anne—and it all happened so fast, it was over almost before it began. A handful of men are trailing the Powhatans, but they won't go far before they turn back."

Running his hand through his hair, the exhaustion returned and John leaned against the doorframe. "What about the others who are harvesting trees?"

"We sent a runner out to warn them." William moved restlessly on his feet. "We could use you now, to settle the panic."

Anne moaned again and John's heart squeezed. How could he leave Anne when she needed him? What if she awoke and was only coherent for a few moments before returning to delirium, or even worse? He didn't want to miss the chance to talk to her.

But what about his men and the fort he had defended with his life for the past year and a half? They also needed him right now. What if the Indians returned and he wasn't there to lead the men in fighting? Most of them were fresh from England, and though they had been drilling for three weeks, they were not ready to face an attack without experienced men in command.

"We need you," William said. "At least until Caldwell returns."

John hated to leave Anne, but he had little choice. If the fort came under attack, they would need every able-bodied man available. He could not protect Anne if he was sitting by her bedside. "I'll be there soon."

William nodded once and left.

John closed the door and walked across the room to wake Daniel. When the boy was roused, John returned to Anne and knelt beside her again. He took her hand and lifted it to his lips. "I'll return as soon as I am able. Get well, Anne."

She appeared to be sleeping peacefully, so he rose and set his hand on Daniel's shoulder. "Take good care of her."

"Aye, sir." Daniel nodded. "I'll do my best."

He knew the young boy would try. He just hoped it would be enough.

In less than an hour, Caldwell returned with the men he'd taken to the woods. Again, they were shaken, but this time there was talk of refusing to return to their work.

Within three weeks of the new settlers arriving, they had lost nine men to illness and three men to Indian attacks. John saw the fear in their eyes and knew that most of the men had not been prepared for the realities of colonial life.

He was still getting used to it himself.

"Quiet!" Caldwell called to the men as he took the steps up to the bulwark, his wide girth making it harder for him to mount the raised platform. "I need quiet," he shouted again.

The sixty or so men who were left standing all quieted to listen to their commander. John waited patiently to see if Caldwell would rise to the occasion, or if he'd be like so many other leaders who had failed James Fort these past eighteen months.

"There is no need to panic," Caldwell said to the colonists. "We have withstood greater attacks and will stand to fight another day."

Murmured complaints filled the air.

"There is talk of abandoning our tasks," Caldwell continued. "But I will not hear of it. President Smith left me in command, and he gave me a job to do. We will fill his order for shingles, finish building the addition to the fort, and assemble another building for housing. We cannot allow our enemy to prevent us from attaining our goals."

More complaints rang through the group, this time louder.

"How are we to build a colony if we are afraid?" someone asked.

Caldwell lifted his hands to quiet the group. "We must persevere, come what may."

"But we're losing our men," shouted Hanover. "How will we defend the fort if we're out in the woods when our enemy attacks?"

The other men echoed Hanover's question. Everyone seemed to be talking at once.

"There are only thirty men inside the fort during the day," shouted another. "We could never withstand an attack with those numbers."

Caldwell lifted his hands again to bring the group to order. "I will not be swayed on this issue."

John, listening as the men argued with Caldwell, felt torn. Caldwell had a good point. They needed to persevere, regardless of the risk. But the men also had a good point. Without Newport and Smith and the 120 men with them, it would be difficult to defend the fort against attack from the Indians—or the Spaniards. Shouldn't they stay in the fort and finish making shingles from the logs already there?

What if Smith and Newport were already dead and these two small attacks were just a precursor to ones yet to come? Staying together would be wiser than spreading out their defense.

"I will hear no more of this." Caldwell shook his head. "I am through talking. We will resume our duties at sunrise tomorrow morning. Use the rest of this afternoon to drill and practice loading your weapons." He left the bulwark and started toward his house without another word.

John raced to catch up to him and intercepted him before he entered the building.

"Master Caldwell, may I have a moment of your time?"

Caldwell sighed and turned to face John. "Has Anne died?"

A weight dropped in John's gut at the very thought, and suddenly he wanted nothing more than to go to her side and see how she fared. "I pray God not," he said. "It is not Anne but the men I want to discuss with you."

"A disagreeable lot."

"I think they may have a point. Until Newport and Smith return, it might be best to keep our defense together in the fort. It can't be much longer, and we have plenty of cedar to continue making shingles for a week or more."

"And what of the palisade? Shall we stop work on that too? And the additional housing? When Smith returns, we'll need all the space we can get for the men he took with him."

"We've slept in tents before, and we can do it again." John was not one to suggest avoiding responsibilities, but there came a time when common sense should prevail.

"No." Caldwell shook his head. "We will continue to work and show no fear to our enemies." He started toward his home again, but John followed.

When Caldwell reached the door, he turned and faced John. "Do not tempt me to arrest you, John Layton. I'm exhausted and irritable right now. I do not want to hear one more word about the unrest."

John held his tongue, knowing he would have to follow Caldwell's orders whether he agreed with them or not.

"I would like to come in and see Anne," John said.

"I'll have Daniel see to her needs." Caldwell opened his door and stepped over the threshold, barring John from entering. "Your interest in her has cost me dearly. She has not had a visitor in over a week, and if she regains her health, I will insist you stop seeing her so the others return."

Caldwell was losing his source of food income.

"I need to know if she is better or worse." Panic tightened John's chest at the thought of not being by her side.

"Good day, Goodman Layton." Caldwell closed the door in John's face and secured it from within.

John stood for a moment in the cold and tried to reconcile the fear and longing he felt in his heart for Anne. How had he come to care for her so completely in such a short time?

With nothing left to do, he returned to his work, praying like never before that Anne would live.

Chapter 6

The sky was gray and overcast and the air was as cold as December, though the calendar claimed it was still the end of October. John clasped his hands together and blew warm air into them before rubbing them briskly to return a bit of life into his fingers.

A few flurries fell lazily from the sky, swirling in wisps on the hard-packed earth as men moved around the fort.

Two days and nights had passed since John had last seen Anne. Daniel had snuck away on several occasions to share her progress, but when John tried to see Anne for himself, Daniel told him he wasn't allowed to let John enter or Caldwell would have John arrested for trespassing. Since John didn't want to get Daniel in trouble as well, he stayed away and waited impatiently for the reports.

Picking up the froe, John set it on top of the cedar log and then lifted the wooden mallet and forced all his frustration into the blow. The shingle split away from the log in one smooth motion and John felt a measure of satisfaction, though it didn't lessen the ache in his chest. All he could think about was Anne.

"You've lost your heart, I'd wager," William said as he worked alongside John once again.

John chose to ignore his friend.

"I've seen it before," William said with a sad smile. "Does she love you?"

Did she? John had no way of knowing. He had sensed her attraction to him, but he didn't know if she loved him. She would probably think him mad if she knew how he felt.

"Will you ask her to marry you?" William could be persistent.

"My plans for Anne Burras have not changed," John said simply. He landed the mallet on the froe again, sending a shingle flying across the workspace.

William raised a brow. "Is that so?"

"James Fort is no place for a woman," John insisted. "If she survives this illness"—he swallowed hard, trying not to think about losing her to death—"I will make her promise to return to England."

"And what happens if Newport brings a bevy of women with the next supply ship? Will you regret sending Anne away?"

"No." John shook his head decisively. "I cannot abide watching her suffer here in Virginia. Others may come, whether I like it or not, but at least Anne will be in England where it is safer."

"*Is* it safer?" William asked as he set his froe upon his log. "There is not a place on this earth that is safe from death." He shrugged. "How are we to know the future? She could set sail with Newport, only to be shipwrecked on the high seas. Or she could return to England, only to be struck down by a runaway horse. There are no guarantees."

The thought of Anne staying and of him making a life with her as man and wife tantalized his senses. His willpower to live and to fight and to work would only be strengthened if he knew he was doing those things for Anne.

But the thought of her lying on her pallet on the verge of death, only to be revived and faced with the threat of an Indian attack was too much for his weary soul to envision. No. It would be far safer for Anne to face the known enemies of civilization than those that were less familiar in the new world.

Daniel suddenly appeared. His eyes were huge as he wildly motioned for John to come.

John dropped his froe and mallet and leapt over the pile of shingles. He was at Daniel's side in a heartbeat. "Is it Anne? Has she died?"

"Come with me." Daniel didn't answer him but started to run toward Caldwell's rooms.

"What's wrong?" John asked, passing the boy as he raced past. "Has something happened to her?"

John didn't wait for the boy to answer, nor did he care if Caldwell would arrest him when he learned he had entered his home. He pushed open the door and skidded to a halt.

Anne sat on her pallet, her back resting against the wall, a steaming cup grasped in her pale hands.

"Anne." John cried out her name as he fell to his knees beside her.

Her eyes were large in her thin face, made even more prominent by the dark circles beneath.

He took the mug from her hands and set it aside, then her took her hands in his and kissed each palm, praising God that He had spared her tender life.

"Anne, Anne," he said over and over as he pressed his lips into her hands. "I feared I might never see those beautiful eyes again."

She dropped her gaze, clearly embarrassed by his show of affection, but he didn't care. She hadn't pulled away, and that was all that mattered.

"How are you feeling?" he asked.

She finally lifted her lovely face to meet his gaze. "I am well. Daniel says I owe my life to you."

He still held her hands, pressing them to his cheeks, loving the feel of her—alive and well. "Daniel has been with you night and day from the start," John said, finally letting her hands go. "He deserves your praise—and my undying gratitude."

She smiled, her eyes shining with the gesture. "You act as if he did it for you."

Love swelled in John's chest as he lifted his fingers to her cheek and caressed the silky smooth skin with his thumb. "He did."

This time Anne didn't lower her gaze but stared at him.

"I'm a fool, Anne Burras." He shook his head, needing to tell her the truth, realizing life was too short to keep things hidden. "I've fallen in love with you, when all I intended to do was monopolize your time so the others would leave you alone."

She lifted her eyebrows, a myriad of emotions fluttering across her face. "Y–you love me?" she finally whispered.

"I do." He couldn't stop himself from smiling. "More than I thought possible—and now that you're well, I'm more convinced than ever."

Anne closed her eyes and lowered her chin. It quivered as if she was about to cry.

John pulled his hand away, afraid he'd said too much too soon.

Anne's body trembled at the weight of John's words.

He loved her?

No one loved her.

"Have I upset you?" he asked gently.

Tears gathered in her eyes, and when she finally opened them to look upon his dear face again, they spilled onto her cheeks. "You have not upset me."

A hopeful smile tilted his mouth as he reached up and wiped away one of the tears. "Then why are you crying, my love?"

She rested her hand upon his. "Do you truly love me, John?"

"I did not think it possible so soon—but I do."

His blue eyes, which were so clear and bright and full of love, shined upon her and she couldn't deny what he said—nor how she felt. During her illness, when she had moments of lucid thought, all she could see in her mind's eye was John and how much she wanted him by her side.

And he had been there, at least until Caldwell had banned him from his home. But more importantly, he was here now, proclaiming a love she had never thought possible.

"I love you too," she whispered.

He took her into his arms then and held her close against his broad, strong chest. She'd never felt so safe or complete as she did in that moment. It felt as if she could do anything and she'd succeed because John would be there to offer his love and support.

"Anne." He pulled back and looked deep into her eyes. "I must ask you to make me a promise."

She would promise him almost anything in this moment. "You need only ask."

Fear tinted his gaze. "Promise me you'll be on Captain New-port's ship when he leaves Virginia."

Confusion made her frown. If he loved her—didn't that mean he wanted to marry her? Or had she misunderstood? "Y–you don't want me to stay?"

"I do." He ran his thumb along her jawline and down to her

chin, resting it just below her bottom lip. "But the colony is not safe. I couldn't bear to watch you suffer and die the way so many have gone this past year."

"But if I leave, I'll never see you again." The thought of being separated from him—now that she knew she loved him—was more than her weary heart could handle.

"I have signed a three-year contract with the Virginia Company," he said. "I've already fulfilled half of the agreement. When I have completed the rest, I will sail back to England to be with you."

A year and a half? So much could happen in that amount of time. Keen disappointment tightened her throat, and she was afraid she might start to cry for an entirely different reason. "What shall I do until you come for me?" He knew, as well as she, that an unmarried woman had little to no protection against the world. "Where will I live and work?"

He ran his thumb along her bottom lip, sending a spiral of heat through her middle.

"I have a small savings account in London, and I have an annual wage allotted to me from the Virginia Company." He studied her for a heartbeat, as if weighing the wisdom in his next statement. "Before you leave Virginia, I'd like to make you my bride. You will arrive in England as Goodwife Layton and will have access to what little I have to offer."

He was proposing marriage, after all? She didn't want to be separated from him, but the prospect of returning to England to wait for him was not as daunting if they were man and wife.

"I will do what you think is best," she said.

John's smile returned, and he could have lit the sky with it. "If you promise to go, I will promise to come to you as soon as possible."

"Healthy and well?" She didn't want to think about all that he might face here in the colony over the next eighteen months. She couldn't, or she would be a puddle of tears.

"God willing." He continued to caress her cheeks, her chin, her lips. "You've made me the happiest man in North America," he said with a beautiful grin. "I will make you my bride as soon as the priest returns to do the honors."

She leaned into his touch, yearning for more, yet uncertain how to encourage him.

Her simple movement seemed to be all the encouragement he needed, because he pulled her closer and laid a sweet kiss on her lips.

Anne melted into his arms, drawing strength and comfort in his embrace. She met his kiss with a passion she did not know existed, and deepened the kiss until she was breathless.

John took his time kissing her, allowing his hands to explore her back, her neck, and then her arms.

"What's the meaning of this?" Master Caldwell's voice scorched Anne's ears a moment before the door banged against the wall. He clutched the back of John's jacket and tried to haul him away from Anne.

Master Caldwell was no match for John's strength and size, but John did not fight his superior, nor did he seem repentant in the least. He simply stood and faced Master Caldwell.

"What are you doing?" Master Caldwell demanded. "I warned you not to enter my home again."

"I love Anne," John said plainly. "I plan to make her my wife."

"You will do no such thing."

"She and I are free to do as we please."

Master Caldwell's face turned from pink to fiery red. "I am her master."

"Anne is a freewoman, not indentured or contracted to you. If she so chooses, she is free to marry me."

There was a moment of silence as Master Caldwell's chest rose and fell in sharp, short breaths. "I may not be able to stop you from marrying, but I can arrest you for trespassing, as I warned."

John took a deep breath and nodded. "You have that right—but I will be more beneficial to you if I am free."

Anne clutched her blanket, her energy drained. She was so exhausted, her eyelids hurt from trying to keep them open, but she couldn't sleep now, even if she wanted to.

Master Caldwell's gaze was shrewd and calculating as he studied John. "Mayhap you're right, but you are also no good to me if you are keeping the other men from coming to see Anne."

John took a step forward. "I will insist she is not bothered by the other—"

"Since you cannot marry until the priest returns, she is still my maid and under my care. You will insist upon nothing."

"I will tell the others she is spoken for."

Caldwell lifted a shoulder, as if he were no longer worried about what John would do.

"I have returned early because there was another death today." Caldwell spoke so calmly about the incident Anne would think he had lost all ability to empathize. "An arrow, through the heart."

John's mouth grew tense as his eyes narrowed. "We need to stay inside the fort until Newport and Smith return with reinforcements."

Master Caldwell went to the sideboard and opened it. He pulled out a bottle of wine he kept hidden in the back corner. Uncorking the bottle, he poured the red liquid into a clay goblet. "I don't think that's the best course of action."

"President Smith would insist—"

"President Smith is not here." Master Caldwell took a sip, and a smile tilted his bewhiskered mouth. "But I am, and I will decide what's best."

"It will only continue."

"I know." He pulled a chair out from the table and took a seat, his goblet in hand. "But I will not need to worry, because I will no longer be in the woods."

Anne clutched her blanket and John crossed his arms.

"Starting tomorrow morning, you will be responsible to take the men out to fell the trees. And because you're so eager to work, I will insist you double the amount of logs harvested or face more severe consequences."

John stared at Master Caldwell, his eyes hard with loathing.

"Please," Anne begged her employer, fear making her throat tighten. She wanted to rise to make her case, but she was too weak. "Don't send him because of me."

Master Caldwell didn't acknowledge her. "Leave," he told John. "And do not come back until you've done as I've commanded."

John let out a deep breath and then walked to Anne. Thankfully, Master Caldwell did not stop him—but he probably knew he couldn't stop John even if he had wanted.

Crouching down to be closer to Anne, John took her hands in his. "I will marry you as soon as the priest returns." He lifted her hands to his lips. "Be ready."

Tears stung the back of her eyes. "Don't go, John. You may be killed."

His shoulders were set and his jaw was hard. "I have no choice."

She closed her eyes and shook her head as the tears fell.

He leaned down and placed a kiss on her forehead. "Knowing you are waiting for me will be all the strength I need to do my job."

He let his lips linger, warming her skin with his breath. "Pray for me," he whispered and then stood and left the cottage.

Anne fell against her pallet and wept until unconsciousness overpowered her.

Chapter 7

With the threat of more attacks, Master Caldwell had posted double guards on the bulwarks. Anne watched two of the men change shifts as she walked to the well a week after John proposed.

Her strength had quickly returned, and she gave the credit to John's proposal. His love was like a balm to her soul, healing the wounds she had carried since she was a child. She had not told him about her mother yet, but she planned to one day soon.

Master Forest had stayed in his room as always. Anne wondered if he'd heard that she was sick and if it made him rethink his accusation.

Anne turned the crank on the well and watched the rope as it slowly wrapped around the wooden wheel.

There had been no more attacks, but John and his men had come across evidence that someone was watching the fort. He had shared the information with her the second night he'd returned from harvesting trees and said she must always be on alert. He didn't know when Newport and Smith would return, nor did he know why Powhatan's warriors were targeting the fort.

Wind blew against Anne, fluttering her cape and pulling at her hair, which was neatly secured under her white cap. The weather had turned mild again, though it was not warm. It no longer nipped at her cheeks and nose when she went about her chores, and she was thankful her cape was enough to keep the chill at bay.

She turned the crank and brought the bucket to the surface. A group of men watched her work, but they no longer pestered her like they once had. She didn't know if John had told them they were engaged or if they just guessed, but they gave her a wider berth and no longer came to the cottage to see her. It angered Master Caldwell, but Anne didn't mind. She had never liked that he profited from her presence in his home, but she hadn't been able to stop him.

Anne poured the water from the well into her bucket and paused to check her surroundings. John should be returning at any moment, which is why she had come to fetch water. Daniel could have accomplished the task, but she wanted to be there when John entered the fort. She longed to speak to him before she returned to the cottage under the watchful eye of Master Caldwell.

"Visitors," one of the guards called.

A guard jumped off the bulwark and went to the gate to unlatch the bar holding it in place. He made a slight bow as Pocahontas entered the fort.

Anne's pulse sped at the sight of the Indian princess. She wore a buckskin dress with cloth leggings and a cloth undershirt. Her black hair was worn in two long braids that hung over her shoulders and lay across her chest, almost touching her waist. John had told Anne more about Chief Powhatan's favorite daughter and how she had spared President Smith's life the first winter they were in Virginia. Since then the chief's respect for President Smith had never been in question, though Anne sensed that John was uncertain of it now, with Smith and Newport not yet returned.

"Anne?" Pocahontas saw Anne standing by the well and came to her, a smile of greeting on her beautiful face. Under her right arm she carried a basket filled with more food. "How do you do?" Pocahontas asked in short, practiced tones.

"I'm well," Anne said with a smile in return.

The chief's daughter looked closely at Anne and her smile fell. "You've been ill?"

Anne touched her sallow cheek, surprised that the girl could see her illness, even now, when she felt so much better. "Yes."

"I bring medicine next time," Pocahontas said slowly.

Anne suddenly recalled the present she had made for the Indian girl. "I have a gift for you."

Pocahontas nodded, though Anne wondered how much the girl understood.

"Come," Anne said to her. "It's in my room."

The younger woman followed Anne to her quarters and hesitated just outside the door.

"Would you like to come in?" Anne asked.

Looking around the room without entering, she just smiled and shook her head.

Anne went to the cabinet in the corner where she kept her bedding and removed a pair of white knitted gloves that she had made since Pocahontas's last visit to James Fort. They were not decorated or adorned, but they had been a painstaking task that Anne had fit into her busy days.

She walked across the room and met Pocahontas at the door, a little bashful to hand over her creation. "For you. A gift."

Pocahontas reached out and took the gloves. They were long,

meant to be worn up to the elbows, and were a beautiful comple-ment to her dark skin.

The girl looked at them in awe, and then she lifted her gaze and smiled. "Thank you."

Anne simply nodded, unsure how to proceed.

"I bring more food." Pocahontas reached into her basket and pulled out a large orange squash.

Taking the offering, Anne smiled back at her new friend. "Thank you. I think I will make this into a pie with the honey from John."

"John." Pocahontas's smile fell and she looked toward the gate where she had just entered. "Danger in wood."

Fear clutched at Anne's chest as she nodded. "I pray for his safety."

Pocahontas's eyes filled with concern. "I pray too."

The simple statement was just as precious to Anne as all the gifts the girl could give.

"I trade." Pocahontas indicated the other side of the fort where the men were gathering.

Anne reached out and touched the girl's arm. "I look forward to seeing you again." It was nice to see another female after so many weeks of only men.

Pocahontas simply smiled and moved on.

The gate opened again, and this time the tired crew of men under John's command entered the fort. John was at the front of the group, and Anne breathed a sigh of relief.

He caught her eye at the same moment, and though he looked exhausted, his countenance lifted.

She met him in the middle of the fort, near the pretty chapel he had built that spring and summer after the first one had burned.

"How are you feeling today?" he asked her before they came to a stop in front of each other.

"I am well." She still held the squash that Pocahontas had given her. "A friend stopped in to see me."

John grinned and touched her arm in a brief but meaningful brush of his hand.

"And how are you?" she asked, wanting to rub away the worry lines around his eyes. "Did you meet your quota for the day?"

He sighed. "Aye."

"And did you see any more signs of the enemy?"

"No, thanks be to God." He motioned for her to follow him into the church. "I need to rest for a while. Do you mind sitting with me?"

She shook her head, happy just to be with him. Master Caldwell did not like John in his home, so why not spend time somewhere they were both wanted?

John pushed open the door of the chapel and held it for her to enter.

The room was a bit musty and cool. Rafters overhead held lanterns made in James Fort by the silversmith. They were unlit and full of cobwebs. A dozen or so wooden benches, hand-hewn by John, lined the building. He indicated the one at the back, closest to the door, which he propped open for propriety's sake—as well as for light.

Anne took a seat and set the squash beside her. John sat on her other side. He lifted her hand in his and traced his finger against her soft skin. "I think of little else but you all day," he said quietly. "Your eyes, your smile, your hair." He looked up and let his gaze roam over her features. "I think about how beautiful you are and how much I want to kiss you."

Her cheeks warmed at the admission, and it made him chuckle.

"Do I embarrass you, my love?" he asked.

"You know you do."

He captured her mouth against his, and she leaned into him, thankful for one more day in his arms.

Pulling away, he wrapped his arm around her shoulders, and they stared straight ahead at the chancel. It had been made of cedar, with a cross in the center and a large pulpit off to the side.

"President Smith might arrive back any day now," he said to her. "And then we'll be married."

"Will Captain Newport leave immediately?" she asked reluctantly.

"I believe he will. It's getting late in the season."

It was a bittersweet idea. The sooner Captain Newport returned, the sooner Anne would be a bride. But it also meant her time with John would be at an end—at least for now.

She wouldn't even think about the possibility that it could be the last time she'd see him.

"Are you ready for the wedding?" he asked.

"I am." There was little to prepare, though she had been rationing her corn to have enough to make extra cakes for their wedding celebration.

He rubbed her shoulder. "I will speak to President Smith and ask for the use of his quarters for our honeymoon."

Anne's cheeks grew warm again at the mention of their wedding night.

"Though I do not know how long we'll have together before you leave," he cautioned. "It might just be one day."

"Let's not talk about me leaving." She fought back the tears that threatened at the very thought of saying goodbye to him.

He kissed the top of her cap. "What would you like to discuss?"

"Anything but our separation." She looked up at him, savoring the look in his beautiful blue eyes.

"As you wish." He winked at her. "Would you like to discuss our honeymoon again?"

She buried her face against him and relished the laughter rumbling in his chest.

A month had gone by since Anne Burras had arrived in Virginia, and John was surprised at how much his life had changed since that fateful day. He never would have believed the first time he saw her that he would be anticipating their wedding any day now.

John worked with the energy of three men as he and a crew of fifteen others cut down the beautiful red cedar trees they used to make shingles. The trees were large but not unmanageable, and the most difficult part of their task was hauling them back to the fort with carts.

For the first time in weeks, the sky was bright blue and the sun was shining. The air was still crisp, but it felt good against John's hot skin. Thoughts of Anne were always close at hand, though he kept an ever-watchful eye on his surroundings.

The men rarely spoke as they worked. John wanted them to concentrate on cutting trees and watch for trouble. Both activities, if not done diligently, could lead to someone's demise, and John had no wish to add to their growing death toll.

Two more men had been buried early that morning before they'd left the fort.

John was so thankful it hadn't been Anne.

As the afternoon wore on, John left his crew to search for the next tree they would cut. While he walked through the woods, within shouting distance of his men, he kept a vigilant watch for signs of Indians. They hadn't seen any for days now, but he wouldn't let his guard down for a moment. He kept his hand on his dagger at all times but knew that if an arrow caught him unawares, he would have no need for the dagger.

A crack behind John made his heart leap to action, and a second later a sharp blow to his head turned the world dark.

The first thing John became aware of was the pain. It radiated from the back of his head and wrapped around the sides, making his temples feel as if they might explode.

He moaned as he tried to move, but a hand held him down.

"*No te muevas.*" A stern voice warned John not to move.

John tried to blink open his eyes, but the light made his head pound even harder.

The voices around him buzzed in a sharp, rapid pace. He knew some Spanish—enough to know he was in trouble.

Again, John tried to open his eyes, and this time he was able to keep them cracked open just a bit.

The vast blue sky yawned bright overhead while the tops of the leafless trees reached toward the heavens.

"*Vamos a matarlo,*" one man said impatiently, ready to kill John.

"*No. Vamos a hacerle algunas preguntas,*" said another, wanting to ask him questions instead.

"*¿Hablas usted Ingles?*" The first soldier asked the other if he spoke English.

"*Si,*" said the second.

John tried to lift his head to see which of the Spaniards was speaking, but it hurt too much.

The men moved into John's line of vision, looking down at him with dark pointed beards. The sun reflected off their metal helmets and glinted in John's eyes.

"You are English?" one of them asked John, a scowl on his face.

It would not pay to stay silent. He was at their mercy.

"Aye," John said on a moan.

Two other soldiers came up behind John and lifted him under the arms, pulling him into a sitting position. The movement made his head spin, and he was afraid he might vomit.

"What is your name?" the man asked John, squatting to look him in the eye.

"John Layton."

Three men stood around John in a semicircle, with the fourth one interrogating him. Nothing looked familiar, which suggested that he was no longer near his men. He'd only endanger himself further if he tried to call for help.

But how far had they taken him?

"You are soldier?" the man asked.

John was not a soldier, but he'd been trained in the militia—and the last thing he wanted was for these men to think he was unskilled in fighting. "Aye."

The tallest man in the group, who looked to be the leader, said something in Spanish to the one questioning John. He then produced a piece of paper, which he shoved in John's face.

It was a drawing of James Fort, complete with the three bulwarks and a cross in the center, which he imagined represented the church.

"How many men are in fort?" the interrogator asked.

All four men watched John carefully. He had heard that Spain had a network of spies keeping an eye on the progress at James

Fort, but he had not realized they had come so close—at least, close enough to draw an accurate map.

He had no intention of telling them anything that might put the fort in danger—including how many men—or women—were inside.

"I do not know," John said.

The interrogator spoke quickly in Spanish to the others. Whatever he said seemed to anger the leader, who shook the map in John's face.

"What weapons are inside fort?" the soldier tried again.

John kept his mouth shut. The weapons inside James Fort were an abomination. Most were antiquated, and those that were more modern were cast-offs from the British military, many of them damaged from the Nine Years' War.

Without warning, the leader struck John across the head. He fell, hitting the ground hard. His breath rushed out of his lungs and he gasped, trying to breathe. The pain in his head was nearly unbearable.

Dust filled his nostrils as he finally managed to take in a lungful of air.

The Spaniards argued around him, and John could only surmise that they were having a disagreement about what should be done with him.

As the interrogator pummeled him with questions that he would not answer, John knew he was digging his own grave. If he was not useful to them, they would have no trouble killing him. But he could not put the fort—or Anne—in danger just to save his own life.

The pain was so intense, John felt numb from shock. He no longer understood the questions nor knew what he was saying as he groaned and mumbled his hatred at the men torturing him. They continued to beat him each time he refused to answer.

Suddenly sweet, pain-free darkness engulfed him and he no longer worried about the fort, or the Spaniards or the Powhatans. He didn't think about President Smith's absence or Edward Caldwell's selfishness. He wasn't concerned about starving or freezing or wretched disease.

All John could think about was Anne and how much he would miss her.

Chapter 8

By day, Anne braced herself with the hope that John was alive, keeping her fears masked behind a stalwart face. But at night, when no one was watching and darkness swelled around her like crashing waves in a storm, she wept bitterly.

Though the weather had turned frigid and the sky had filled with menacing clouds, Anne spent many hours outdoors, watching the gates for signs of John. Three days had passed since his men had entered the fort with news that he'd gone missing.

Three days since they'd found traces of blood and signs of a struggle.

Speculation had run rampant among the men. It had not been an Indian attack. From the clues left at the scene, the men suspected that the attackers were Spaniards. But why had they taken John, if in fact, they had? But if they hadn't, where was he?

With two active enemies, Master Caldwell had finally ordered the men to stay within the confines of the fort and wait for reinforcements. Anne had begged him to send out a search party, but he refused, saying it was too dangerous. Several men had been abducted and gone unaccounted for in the years they'd been in Virginia.

What was one more?

As Anne knelt on the hard wooden floor of the church, beseeching God to return her beloved to James Fort, she kept one ear attuned to the sounds of the colony. Any little noise that was out of the ordinary made her sit up straighter, her heart racing with hope that John had come home.

The morning dragged on as she remained in the church, and when she felt she might go mad from uncertainty and fear, she heard a commotion. It was quiet at first, and then it built until several men were cheering.

With aching legs, Anne rose to her feet, her pulse racing.

Had John finally returned?

She stepped into the fort yard, casting her eyes to the east, but it was to the west and the river that everyone was moving.

Turning in that direction, she finally saw what had caused the stir.

Captain Newport and President Smith were securing their barge to the wooden pier on the banks of the James River.

Anne's excitement quickly turned to disappointment, but then it was replaced with hope once again. Perhaps now that President Smith was back, he'd send someone to search for John.

She longed to run to the river to make her request but waited as patiently as possible for Captain Newport and President Smith to enter the fort. Over a hundred men disembarked, a festive air surrounding them.

But Anne did not enjoy their celebration. Her only thought was for John. If he had been in the fort, he would be speaking with the priest now about a wedding ceremony, and he'd be asking President

Smith about the use of his quarters.

Instead, Anne was waiting to speak to them about finding her fiancé.

The moment the men entered the western gate, Anne approached them.

"Anne Burras," Captain Newport said with a smile. "How have you fared in James Fort?"

"Not well, I'm afraid." Anne had been shy and hesitant to speak to Captain Newport on the voyage over, but now she stood before him with confidence and desperation born of love. "John Layton has been missing for three days."

"What's this?" President Smith asked, overhearing her statement. "Layton is missing?"

"He was cutting trees to the east," William Cole said as he approached the men. "And we believe he was overtaken by Spaniards. It was the fourth attack by our enemies since you departed, so Master Caldwell has ordered that we remain within the palisade. No one has gone looking for him."

Master Caldwell's door opened and the man in question appeared.

"I want ten of our best men sent out immediately," President Smith ordered, "to search for Goodman Layton." He nodded at Master Caldwell and William Cole. "And I'd like to see you two in my quarters to hear all the news."

Gratefulness overwhelmed Anne, and her knees became weak. She had no guarantee they would find John, or that he would be alive if they did, but at least they would search for him.

"Powhatans approaching from the north!" one of the guards called out from the bulwark.

"Arm yourself, men!" President Smith called as he rushed toward the bulwark and spied over the palisade wall.

Anne's heart raced as she stood motionless, unsure what to do. Should she rush to her room? Stay and fight? Drop to her knees and pray again?

A horrified minute passed while commotion and chaos ensued, and then President Smith lifted his hand. "Stand down," he called to his men. "They come in peace."

Anne's heart began to settle, but she remained where she'd been standing, clutching her apron.

"Pocahontas approaches," President Smith said as he leapt down from the bulwark and went to the gate. Pulling it open, he bowed to Pocahontas as she led a group of four men into the fort.

In their arms, they held John.

Crying out in both fear and sweet relief, Anne raced to John's side.

"Take him to my quarters," President Smith called to the men.

"John," Anne cried. "John, can you hear me?" He did not stir, and Anne looked up at Pocahontas, whose eyes were filled with sadness. "Is he dead?" she asked.

Pocahontas shook her head, but she did not look hopeful.

Anne walked alongside John as he was carried to the president's quarters. She took his hand. "John?"

He was motionless, his face swollen and bruised, almost beyond recognition. Who had done this to him, and why?

William ran ahead and opened the door to President Smith's home. He led the Powhatan men to a room in the back where they laid John on a four-poster bed.

He did not stir or make a sound as he lay there.

"Thank you," Anne said to the men, though she didn't know if they understood.

Pocahontas had stayed outside, as had the others. When the Indians left, it was just Anne and William.

"What should I do?" he asked.

"I need hot water and rags." Desperation made her voice sound tight. "Please have someone make him broth as well."

William nodded and ran out of the room.

"Hurry!" Anne called after him.

She took John's hand in her own and pressed it to her cheek, as he'd done with her when she was sick. "John, my beloved. Wake up."

He was motionless, lying on the grand bed, life seeping from his body. The pulse in his neck was weak and the rise and fall of his chest was so shallow, she feared each breath would be his last. Dark blood matted his hair, dried and crusted. A deep wound on his forehead would need to be stitched, and he was in want of a good wash.

"Do not die," she pleaded. "The priest has returned and he will marry us, just as we planned." Tears streamed down her cheeks. "Please wake up."

Doctor Prescott entered the room, his small eyes hidden behind round spectacles. He had made the crossing with them on the *Mary Margaret*, seeing to Mistress Forest during her illness. He was an older gentleman with white hair and a long, thin face.

The doctor took in the scene without a word and went to the table on the other side of the bed to set down his medicine box.

"Will he live?" Anne asked.

"Only time will tell, my dear." The doctor opened his medicine chest and removed a dark vial of liquid. "After we've cleaned his wounds, I'll stitch those that are gaping and we'll apply some ointment to help them heal."

"And then he'll be well?"

The doctor lowered his chin and looked at her over the top of his spectacles. "I believe his internal wounds are probably more dangerous than his external ones. I can only treat those I can see." He turned back to his box and removed a needle and thread. "The Lord will have to treat those I cannot."

"What can I do to help?" she asked, desperate to do something—to feel as if she could control the outcome.

He looked back at her, compassion and understanding in his kind face. "You can pray—and love him—just as you're doing."

With President Smith's return to James Fort, things began to change immediately, though Anne took little notice as she spent every waking moment by John's side. The noise outside the president's quarters had increased with the additional men, yet so had the sickness that had invaded the fort—even with the doctor's presence. The second day, Daniel came to tell Anne that three more men had died and another five were ill.

When John's unconsciousness was compounded by a fever and delirium, she feared that he had also contracted the disease in his weakened state. Doctor Prescott confirmed her suspicions when he came to examine John later that evening.

Anne had thought John's disappearance was the hardest thing she'd ever faced—yet the uncertainty in the days following his return were even worse. The man who had stood taller and stronger than anyone else in all of Virginia was now as weak and vulnerable as a newborn babe.

"Would you like me to sit with him?" Daniel asked as he came into President Smith's bedchamber on the third morning.

Anne lifted her head off her chest, embarrassed that she had fallen asleep in the rocking chair by John's bedside. Standing, she went to him and laid her hand on his brow. It was still burning and coated in a sheen of sweat.

"I could use fresh water," she said to the boy. The water he had brought to her the night before was now tepid.

Outside, the sun shone once again, and the air was unseasonably warm. Perhaps she should get some fresh air. It wouldn't do for her to become sick again.

Daniel reached for the pail of old water, but Anne grabbed it before him. "I'll go," she said gently, "if you would like to sit with John."

Nodding, Daniel took the seat Anne had just occupied. Life had made the boy older than his years, and Anne was so thankful for his kindness.

She left the bedchamber and found President Smith's front room empty. Since his arrival back at the fort, he had held many meetings in his home. Anne had paid little attention to the men coming and going. She was just thankful for the use of the president's bedchamber for John's comfort.

Stepping outside, she inhaled a deep breath and marveled at the activity in the fort. Construction on the palisade addition had resumed, as had the production of shingles. From where she stood, she could see at least a dozen men hauling the shingles to the waiting *Mary Margaret*. No doubt Captain Newport was anxious to be on his way.

The sudden realization hit Anne, and she leaned against the doorframe of the president's quarters. What if the captain planned to leave before John became well again? How could they marry if John was still unconscious? Worse, how could she leave him without knowing whether he'd survive?

A dark figure stepped into Anne's line of sight and slowly moved toward her.

Master Forest.

Anne swallowed the anxiety that rose in her throat at the sight of him.

He moved slowly, as if in pain, and stopped in front of her. "Is Goodman Layton still unconscious?" he asked.

"Aye." She lowered her eyes, not wanting to show him her fear.

"Is this more of your devilry?" he asked.

"No, sir." Tears gathered in her eyes, and her newfound confidence resurfaced. She lifted her gaze. "I love him."

Master Forest stared at her, anger in his glare. "I have seen you on your knees in the chapel, chanting incantations on several occasions. The doctor claims he did not get sick until he was in your care."

Panic squeezed Anne's chest as she dropped her gaze again. She'd been praying to God, asking Him to return John to her—but no matter what she would say, Master Forest would believe what he wanted.

She pushed past him, unable to stand in his presence any longer.

"If he dies," Master Forest called out to her, "I'll tell everyone what you are."

Anne walked across the fort yard, wiping at the tears that had begun to fall. Men stopped in their paths to watch her, though none approached. She didn't try to hide her tears and prayed they would keep the men away. She didn't want to be bothered—didn't want the attention. She simply wanted to be left alone and return to John's side.

She quickly filled the water pail and then walked back to the president's quarters.

When she stepped into the front room, she was surprised to find that President Smith and Captain Newport had returned. Their faces were grim as they both looked up at her arrival.

"Anne," Captain Newport said, "we'd like a word with you."

A lump grew in her throat as she set down the pail of water. What did they have to say to her? Had John died? Had Master Forest made his accusations?

"Would you take a seat?" President Smith asked from behind his desk.

Captain Newport held out a chair for Anne, and she gladly took it, afraid her legs would hold her no longer.

The captain took the seat next to her, though he sat on the edge and faced her.

Anne didn't want to look at either man, but she couldn't stop herself. She looked from one to the next, feeling as if she might leap out of her skin.

"We've made an important decision," President Smith said, "and it concerns you."

"After our visit to Chief Powhatan, we took several weeks to explore the area west of the James River, seeking a route to the Pacific Ocean," Captain Newport said. "And it delayed our return to James Fort, which has delayed my departure to England."

"It's getting far too late in the season for a sea voyage," the president continued, "but it is imperative that Captain Newport return with our cargo and with news from the colony."

The captain took a deep breath. "I've decided to set sail at first light tomorrow morning."

Anne stared at him, dread sinking to the bottom of her stomach.

"Goodman Cole is a friend of John's," President Smith told Anne. "He shared that you and John had plans to marry as soon as we returned, and that John wished for you to travel back to England on the *Mary Margaret* and await him there."

"Aye." Anne nodded as she played with a loose thread on her apron.

Captain Newport watched Anne, his gentle countenance unhurried. "Do you still wish to return with me tomorrow?"

Just beyond the closed door, John lay unconscious. If he was awake, what would he have Anne do? Would he be angry to learn she left before they could be married? Would he be angry if she stayed and broke her promise to him?

And then there was the threat of Master Forest. What if she stayed, only to have him make his accusations? Would the others hang her, as they had her mother? Even if he hinted at her being a witch, there was no telling how the rumor might grow and twist until it consumed the whole fort.

What would John do if that happened?

"How will I know if John survives?" Anne asked.

"When I return in the spring," Captain Newport promised, "I will check on John and then personally bring a report to you in England."

"It could take a year before I'll know his fate." Anne fought back the tears at the idea of not knowing what would become of John for that long. Even if he survived this, something else might go wrong. If Captain Newport was lost at sea, then who would provide Anne with information? And what about her marriage? If she was not married to John when she left here, she'd be at the mercy of society upon her return to England. She'd have no support and no one to ask for help.

Yet she'd made a promise to John, and the thought of breaking that promise filled her with such dread, she couldn't lift her head to meet the direct gazes of the men before her. John wanted her back in England—of that, she was most certain. Shouldn't she honor his request? He'd be angry if she was forced to remain for the winter.

"You do not need to make your decision now," President Smith informed her. "But we will need to know some time this evening."

Anne swallowed her fear and misgivings and finally lifted her chin to meet the president's gaze. "There is no need to wait. I've made my decision."

She loved John and could not dishonor him by going against his wishes. Somehow, someway, God would protect her, come what may.

"I will depart on the *Mary Margaret* in the morning."

Captain Newport nodded. "As you wish."

It was not what she wished, but it was what she knew she must do—to honor John.

Chapter 9

John lifted his eyelids and lay for a moment in the warmth of the sunshine pouring through the open window. At first all seemed calm and peaceful as he inhaled a lungful of fresh air—but then his chest tightened, and he coughed so deeply his lungs burned and his muscles tensed. Every fiber of his being ached with pain, and as he gained complete consciousness, he realized with sudden clarity that he had no idea where he was or why he was in such distress.

"Anne?" he called into the unfamiliar room.

The boy, Daniel, appeared at John's side, a smile on his thin face. "You're alive."

The pain made it clear that he was very much alive, but what happened? And where was he? "Water," he said through dry, parched lips.

Daniel took a cup and held it to John's lips as he braced the back of John's head. The simple pressure felt like a knife stabbing into his skull.

"Down," John said to the boy, needing his head to rest on the bed again. "Where am I?"

"You're in President Smith's quarters." Daniel set the cup on a nearby table. "You've been here for a week now."

"A week?" Had he become ill with the disease that had killed so many others? But why did he feel as if he'd been beaten as well? "What happened?"

"Pocahontas brought you into the fort. She found you about a mile west of the cedar grove." Daniel took up another cup, this one steaming.

A mile west of the cedar grove? The Spaniards! Details began to return in bits and pieces.

"President Smith had you placed in his room."

John frowned. "President Smith?"

"Aye. He and Captain Newport returned the same day you were found."

A week ago. Did that mean?

John's heart pounded hard and sweat broke out on his brow. "Did Captain Newport return to England?"

"Aye. Four days ago now."

John tried to sit up, but he was too weak and in too much pain. "Four days ago?" He fell back against the mattress, breathing heavily, hating his weakness. "Did anyone return with him?"

"Aye." Daniel brought the steaming cup to John's lips. "Would you like some broth?"

"Who went back?" John asked, pushing aside the broth.

"Master Forest," Daniel said, setting the broth down again. "He hated being here without his wife."

"And Anne?" John's heart thudded in his chest. Had Anne left before he could make her his bride? How could he provide for her if she was not married to him? She must be miserable now, not knowing whether he had lived or died.

"She was relieved to see Master Forest board the ship."

"No." John tried again to sit up, and this time Daniel helped him. His head pounded and his throat was raw, but he wanted to be up, to face whatever lay ahead. Dread filled his heart as he finally asked what he wanted to know more than anything. "Did Anne return to England?"

The bedchamber door creaked open, and Anne stepped into the room with an armful of wood. Her white cap was clean and crisp on her dark hair, and her burgundy gown fit her a bit loosely, but he'd never seen anyone so beautiful in all his life.

"Anne."

She looked up at the sound of his voice and promptly dropped the wood there in the doorway. "John." She rushed to the side of his bed and took his face in her hands. She kissed his cheeks, his chin, his nose, his forehead, and then his mouth, laughing breathlessly the whole time. "You're alive," she finally said as she pulled back to look him over.

Daniel had quietly slipped out of the room and closed the door, leaving John and Anne alone to revel in the moment.

"I thought you left," he said, just as breathlessly as her.

She sat on the edge of the bed and took his hands in hers. "I tried." Tears gathered in her eyes, shame tinting the edges. "I know I made you a promise, but when I came in here to say goodbye to you, I couldn't bring myself to go through with it." She bowed her head and lifted his hand to her lips. "And then, when I learned Master Forest was returning, I knew I couldn't go."

"What transpired between you?" John asked, needing to know why the man had hurt her. "Whatever it is, you can trust me."

She lowered her eyes. "He never trusted me because he didn't trust my mother."

"Your mother?"

Taking a deep breath, she finally met his gaze. "My mother was accused of being a witch in North Berwick—and hanged to death." Tears filled her eyes. "But I never believed what they said about her."

"Shhh." John tried to reassure her, his chest constricting with the pain she'd carried for so long. "I don't either." He'd always been appalled at witch hunts, knowing that far too many innocent people had died.

Anne leaned down and pressed her forehead to John's chest. "Please forgive me for not going, John."

John lifted his free hand and put it on her head, nudging her to look up at him. "How could I not forgive you?" He ran his thumb over her skin, loving the feel of her under his touch. "When I awoke and thought you had gone, I counted myself a fool for making you promise to leave." He shook his head, mindful of the pain, suddenly recalling the day when he'd been attacked by the Spaniards. All he could think about was Anne and how much he'd miss her when he was gone. "I cannot imagine being away from you again."

"And I cannot imagine it either, my beloved." She leaned forward and kissed his lips again. "When I thought you might die, I realized how precious this life is and how little time we have together. I don't want to spend that time waiting for you in England."

He pulled her against his chest and took off her cap, allowing his hands to run freely through her hair. It was so silky and smooth, he could only marvel that he was so fortunate to have the pleasure.

"I love you, John," she said on a whisper. "I know there are dangers lurking in the shadows here in Virginia, but if it be God's will, we'll shine a light on all those shadows and chase away the darkness together. I do not know what the future will hold, but I do know that each day with you is a gift I will never take for granted."

He wished he was well enough to pull her into his arms and show her how much he loved her. Instead, he simply caressed her hair as it fell down her back. "I love you too, Anne." He kissed the top of her head, thanking God He had spared his life, if for no other reason than to glory in this moment together. "I cannot promise a life without worry or strife, but I can promise to love you and honor you all the days of my life."

She lifted her head and smiled upon him with her beautiful brown eyes. "And that is more than enough for me, John Layton."

He smiled and kissed her again.

"As soon as I'm able to stand on my own two feet, I intend to make you my bride."

Anne smiled, her eyes shining. "And will you marry me in the church you built?"

"I will."

"And will you build me a home where we can grow old together?"

"I'll start the moment our honeymoon is over—and not a second sooner."

Her cheeks turned pink at the mention of their honeymoon.

It was his turn to ask her a few questions. "And will you fill the home with children who will care for us in our old age?"

She placed her hand upon his cheek, gently caressing it, making him sleepy again. "I will," she whispered.

"And will you tell me you love me every day, even when I'm so old, I can no longer hear you?"

"Even when you're old," she promised.

He closed his eyes, her healing touch filling him with renewed strength. "And will you kiss me when I awake, and when I go out, and when I come in, and when I lie down?"

Anne laid her lips upon his in a sweet and gentle kiss. "I will."

John smiled, his eyes still closed, as he drifted off into a restful sleep.

Anne stood in President Smith's bedchamber alone, two months after she'd arrived in Virginia. Master Forest had left his wife's trunk, not wanting the reminder of her to follow him back to England, and President Smith had given her belongings to Anne as a wedding gift. Since Anne had loved her mistress, she counted it an honor to own her things. And today, on the most important day of her life, she stood in her mistress's best gown, awaiting President Smith's call to the church.

The gown was made of silk, the color of burnt orange, with a skirt worn wide at the hips. Long, tight sleeves went down to her fingers, with pointed oversleeves draping to her waist. A high lace collar accentuated Anne's hair, which she'd painstakingly styled in curls. At her throat she wore white pearls. Never in her life had she imagined she'd be so lavishly dressed, but her mistress had been the closest thing Anne had had to a mother, and it felt right to have her things close.

Nerves caused Anne's stomach to burble, and she put her hand over the tight bodice to quell the feeling. She bowed her head and clasped her hands to thank God for the blessing of her marriage.

There was not another woman in James Fort to assist her today, but Anne knew it wouldn't be long before others joined her. At the moment, though, none of that mattered. Her beloved was alive and well and waiting for her at the church. Even if they were all alone in North America, as long as she had him, she would be content.

Thinking of her husband-to-be, Anne smiled. He had gained his strength and vitality back faster than she thought possible, and she surmised his eagerness was due to their impending wedding. Her smile turned to a grin when she thought of his boyish excitement and his heartfelt passion. She longed for the hour when she'd finally be his wife, in mind, body, and spirit.

"Anne?" President Smith knocked at the door. "Are you ready?"

Taking a deep breath, she lifted the hem of her gown and opened the door to greet President Smith.

He stood for a moment, admiration lighting his eyes. "You are lovely."

"Thank you."

President Smith offered his arm, and she took it with gratitude. Her legs were shaking, and her knees felt weak. It would be good to lean on him as they walked to the church.

He led her outside where the men had lined up, shoulder to shoulder, creating a path for her to take to the church. She paused for a moment as her eyes adjusted to the sudden light—and the grand reception.

Everyone in James Fort had come out for the wedding. Some wore the finest clothes she'd ever seen, while others wore mere rags—but every person had the same thing in common: their generous smiles.

Daniel stood in the middle of the walkway of men, a bouquet of pale purple flowers she'd never seen before in his grasp. His ears were as red as apples when he presented the flowers to her. "With my best wishes on your marriage, Anne."

Tears sprang to her eyes as she took the flowers from the boy. "Thank you, Daniel."

He gave a sheepish grin and then stepped aside for her to pass.

"God's blessing on your marriage," called out one man after another. They doffed their caps as she passed. Some she knew by name, others were still strangers to her, but all of them seemed to take pride in being at the first wedding in North America.

The air was cool and crisp and the sky was as blue as a robin's egg, with nary a cloud overhead. Just beyond the palisade walls, the James River sparkled in the sunshine. But it was the church, which stood tall and proud in the center of the fort, that captured Anne's attention.

As they moved past each man, he stepped in behind her, starting with Daniel, and followed her all the way to the church, singing "Come Live with Me." The men's voices and their encouragement strengthened her courage as she came to stand outside the church doors.

"Goodman Layton is waiting for you," President Smith told her as he paused. "Are you ready?"

Anne took a deep breath and nodded. She was more than ready to become John's wife.

Master Caldwell walked forward and opened the door.

Anne clung to the president's arm as she stepped over the threshold and into the chapel. Though Master Caldwell had been a difficult man, he had been good to her, and she would forever be thankful for his taking her into his home.

John stood waiting at the front, William Cole by his side. He turned when the door opened, and his gaze caught on Anne's.

He wore a handsome black suit and a matching cape, with black hose. A white linen shirt and an unstarched white collar looked vibrant against the darker hues. He wore no hat, but at his side he wore his sword. The hilt had been polished to shine, reflecting light from the overhead lanterns.

Admiration shone bright in his eyes, and the smile on his face was as wide and beautiful as anything she'd ever seen.

President Smith led Anne down the aisle to join her beloved, who reached for her when she drew near.

She took his hand in hers and released President Smith, who moved to take a seat at the front of the room. Men poured into the church, quickly filling the space until there was nowhere left to sit or stand. Some had to remain outside, trying to see over the shoulders of those ahead of them.

John continued to smile at Anne as he shook his head in amazement. He leaned down and whispered in her ear, "How is it that I earned your favor, Anne Burras? You could have had anyone at James Fort, but you chose me."

She wanted to nuzzle into him yet knew they had an audience watching their every move. Instead, she squeezed his hand and returned his smile, looking deep into his eyes. "You and I were meant for each other," she said. "There is no one else in this world I would rather stand with before God to pledge my life." And she meant every word. There was not another man in all of James Fort, or all of England for that matter, who had so captured her heart and soul.

"We gather here today to witness the marriage of Anne Burras and John Layton," the priest called out to those in the room. "What God has joined together, let no man put asunder." He smiled at the couple and nodded. "Let us begin."

Quiet had settled upon the fort as John sat near the hearth and watched his wife put away the dishes from their evening meal. She had changed into her burgundy gown and white cap, and though he had loved seeing her in the silk and pearls, it was this version of Anne that he loved the most. This beautiful, genuine, hardworking woman he had pledged his life to that very morning.

Firelight danced upon her features as she closed the cabinet door and let out a contented sigh. The purple flowers she had carried earlier were in the green glass vase, and the furniture John had made was lovingly arranged and polished.

Anne turned. Her brown eyes were alive with anticipation—and a little apprehension.

They had spent the day celebrating their union with their friends, receiving gifts for their new home. For now, John had been given the use of two rooms within the communal quarters, but come spring he would build a small cottage in the fort's new addition.

Instead of using President Smith's quarters for their honeymoon, as John had originally planned when he thought they'd have only one night together, they were well situated in their own personal space. It was almost identical to the rooms Master Caldwell occupied, though these were filled with the gifts of their well-wishers.

John smiled at Anne, still amazed that she was his bride. She stood across the room from him, a shy smile filling her lovely face.

He extended his hand, beckoning her to join him at the table. She moved across the room and took his hand, allowing him to pull her into his arms.

Anne sat on his lap and rested her forearms on his shoulders, clasping her hands behind his neck. John's arms went around her waist, enjoying the privilege of holding her freely.

"Are you happy, my love?" he asked.

"More than ever." She leaned forward and moved one of his curls off his forehead. "And are you happy?"

In answer, he pulled her closer and kissed her like he'd

never kissed her before.

When he was through, she was breathless and flushed, and no longer bashful.

"I cannot believe I was going to let you return to England." He shook his head at his own foolishness as he gently removed her white cap and took out the pins holding her heavy hair in place. Her locks fell over her shoulders and down past her waist in a glorious curtain he couldn't wait to explore. "It seems unfathomable to imagine what it would feel like to put you on a ship tomorrow and say goodbye for a year and a half."

She ran her fingers past his temples and into his hair, massaging his scalp. "So you're not angry that I broke my promise to return to England?"

John closed his eyes and moaned. "No. I'm angry at myself for suggesting such a thing."

Anne leaned her forehead to rest on his. "Let us not talk of what has gone before," she said. "Instead, let's focus on the future."

Without warning, John stood and cradled his bride in his arms to carry her over the threshold and into their bedchamber. "I couldn't agree more."

No longer would they look back. From that day forward, John and Anne Layton would chart a new course and a new destiny for themselves and for all those who would follow in their footsteps.

Historical Note

The story of Anne Burras, as I have written it within this novella, is as accurate as I could make it. Little is known about Anne, but what we do know is that she came to James Fort as a maid to Mistress Forest in 1608 and was the only European woman in the fort when her mistress died shortly after arriving. We also know that Anne was just fourteen! (I took the liberty of making her a tad bit older in my story.) Anne married Goodman John Layton, a carpenter at James Fort who built the chapel and was among the first to arrive in Virginia in 1607. Their wedding took place about two months after Anne arrived, and they went on to have a long, prosperous life together, though they endured unthinkable hardships, including the Starving Time of 1609–10 and the Indian Massacre of 1622. Their oldest daughter, Virginia Layton, was the first child born in Jamestown. After Virginia, they had three more daughters, Alice, Katherine, and Margaret. Eventually they helped to colonize Elizabeth City, which is present-day Newport News, Virginia. Though I do not know Anne and John's true love story, I hope that the one I have presented here has done it justice. Amid their story, I have also included as much accurate history of early James Fort as I could find in my research and my visit to the archaeological dig in Virginia. It's truly a fascinating piece of American history.

Personal Note

For years I knew I had early American ancestors, but it wasn't until I was contracted to write this novella that I began to dig a little deeper into my genealogy to find them. What I discovered were dozens of men and women in my family tree who came to America during the Great Puritan Migration between 1620 and 1640. I also discovered I have at least six ancestors who came directly to Jamestown, Virginia.

The earliest ancestor I found was a man named William Powell who came to James Fort in 1609 with the third supply mission led by Captain Newport. On February 9, 1610, the acting governor sent William and another man to capture or kill, if necessary, Wochinchopunck, the chief of the Paspahegh, a tributary tribe of the Powhatan. The chief had been harassing and killing colonists, even attempting to kill Captain John Smith the previous year. When William and his companion found it impossible to capture the strong Paspahegh chief, William struck him down with his sword. Shortly thereafter, William was appointed a captain and put in charge of the Jamestown defenses and its blockhouses. He was further appointed lieutenant governor of the Virginia colony in 1617. He went on to be a burgess in the Virginia House and was responsible for warning, and thereby saving the lives of, hundreds during the Indian Massacre in 1622. It's believed he died late in 1622 or early 1623 from wounds he received in a retaliation attack on the Powhatan. William is just one of many ancestors I found connected to Jamestown, and though I didn't include him in this novella, his memory resides within the story I have written.

Gabrielle Meyer lives in central Minnesota on the banks of the Mississippi River with her husband and four young children. As an employee of the Minnesota Historical Society, she fell in love with the rich history of her state and enjoys writing fictional stories inspired by real people and events. Gabrielle can be found at www.gabriellemeyer.com, where she writes about her passion for history, Minnesota, and her faith.

Embers of Hope

by Kimberley Woodhouse

Dedication

To my beautiful friend, Cathy Castillo.
You have been a source of great encouragement to me, and I miss you
more than I can say. You are truly beautiful on the inside and out.
For all the smiles, laughter, hugs, Bible studies, shoebox packing, joy-
filled moments, bell practices, and everything in between—thank you.
For being my friend. For praying. For loving on me.

Dear Reader,

Superstitions ran high in the 1600s. The era would usher in more levelheaded thought based on facts, but it took a good deal of time to get to that point. Even those who were believers in Christ struggled with the prevalent culture of superstition. This is a compelling dynamic in Esther's story. And it really made me think. . . *How would I handle a situation in which people's fears and superstitions ruled their decisions and actions?*

The history behind America's forts is fascinating. In fact, it interested me so much that I even bought a used library copy of a massive tome titled *Encyclopedia of Historic Forts*. I know, I know. I'm a history geek. But it was so interesting, and since there's not a lot of documented writings about this period, it was an invaluable resource for this story.

The Castle was the first fortification on Castle Island, dating all the way back to 1634 (but it even had a battery there as early as 1632). That's only twelve to fourteen years after the *Mayflower*! By 1692 it had been replaced by multiple structures and renamed Castle William. Then in 1797 it gained the prestigious name of Fort Independence. It is the oldest military installation in the United States.

Castle Island is actually no longer an island and is attached to the mainland via land reclamation for the port and a narrow strip of land. It is open to visitors.

If you have read my novel *The Mayflower Bride*, you know the true story of John Howland and his infamous trip overboard. It truly was a miracle that the man survived, and he now has more descendants in the United States than any other *Mayflower* passenger. By more than double. So I chose to have our heroine here in *Embers of Hope* be his descendant. For more fascinating information about John Howland and his descendants, I recommend you read *The Mayflower Bride*, also from Barbour Publishing.

While I based this story on the true history and timeline of the fort, all of the characters and events are fictitious. Join me as we head to Castle Island and the early stages of our nation in *Embers of Hope*.

Enjoy the journey,
Kimberley

Chapter 1

Castle Island off the shores of Boston
March 21, 1673

ire!" The cry echoed across the night sky.

"Fire!" Captain Christopher Latham repeated the shout that had come from the tower guard. Not that it was even a tower, but it was the platform built at the point of the island. Racing up the hill, Christopher felt his heart pound in his chest. The colonel had left for Boston, and that meant Christopher was in charge. If anything disastrous happened, *he* was responsible.

Shouting the cry again, he lengthened his stride, hoping that all the men had heard and would rally to help quench the blaze. A fire on their small island could be devastating. He prayed it wasn't bad.

As he crested the man-made hill they used as a fortification, his heart raced and then plummeted with a thud in his chest.

Flames licked at the fifty-foot-long west and south walls of ten-foot-thick pine that surrounded the square-shaped compound. And they were spreading. Fast. Pretty soon the entire structure would be engulfed if they couldn't get the fire under control. The center, a three-story structure which they'd named The Castle, held the nine mounted ordnances. But the brittle bricks it was made out of would burn quickly if the fire made it there. The artillery and gunpowder were stored at the top. The potential explosion of the armaments caused the hair on the back of his neck to stand on end.

Men scrambled around, wooden buckets swinging, as they made a chain to the shore.

Christopher shouted orders. "Remove the powder! Keep the fire from The Castle!"

Water sloshed as the buckets traveled up the line of men to douse the fire. Again and again. But the blaze only grew.

Within minutes flames seemed to almost touch the sky as they ate hungrily at the decaying wooden structure. The fiery beasts roared as they licked at their fuel. The men closest to the flames were pushed back by the scorching heat.

Another row of men headed to the blaze. But Christopher held up his hand to halt them. They could do no more without risking the loss of soldiers to the ferocious flames. He turned to the men he'd ordered to remove the powder, "Did you retrieve it all?"

"Yes, sir." The younger one, out of breath and skinny as a pole, lifted his chin. "But not the ordnance."

Nothing could be done. The fire had already reached the brick structure and devoured it. "Stand back!" All they could do now was watch it burn. He turned to his head lieutenant. "Have you accounted for all the souls on the island?"

"Aye, sir." John's head bobbed up and down. "All except for the washerwoman. No one seems to know where she went."

Christopher placed his hands on his hips and looked around. Maybe she ran when she saw the fire? The men had been neglectful of the old woman from the moment she arrived. Since she wasn't young and beautiful, the soldiers didn't care for her—just threw their laundry her way. Of course, it didn't help that Colonel Brown was a superstitious man and believed that every time there was a mishap, it was because a female was present. She'd only been there a few days, and she'd been blamed many a time.

No matter how much Christopher tried, the rumors that it was bad luck to have a woman at the fort couldn't be stopped. As captain, Christopher had hoped to keep his men from being so irrational, but he couldn't control the gossip any more than he could control an outbreak of disease. With a glance around, he walked through the crowd. No sign of the woman. The men were covered in soot and grime, their faces and hair black and singed. It didn't help that they looked skinny and worn out.

Nothing like a disaster to help him see the reality of the state of his troops.

Ever since a warship had come into the harbor decades ago, they'd kept at least fifty men posted on the island to man the guns and cannons. To be a formidable presence. At least in the eyeglass of an enemy ship's captain. The soldiers trained on their weapons daily and sent out watch parties. Never again did they want to give the notion that they weren't ready to defend their new colony. The first fort back in 1634 had been a sad structure made out of mud walls and oyster shell lime. But when that French ship arrived in '44, it scared them into building a better fort out of timber. But now that was gone.

Of course it could always be rebuilt—this time out of something even sturdier and preferably not so ready to burn. What mattered was that all of his men were accounted for. But where was the old woman?

As he walked through the men whose gazes were fastened on the glowing destruction before them, Christopher looked at each soot-covered face. Maybe she was hiding?

" 'Twas her, I tell ya." A young soldier's voice made Christopher turn. The man swiped at his trousers as he talked to some of the others. "Just like the colonel said. Bad luck for us all."

The words brought Christopher to a halt.

"I saw her stoking her fire under the washin' pot. The old hag tripped over her own feet and fell into the fire, knocking wood and flames every which way."

"She fell into the fire?" Christopher stomped toward them. A dozen or so new men had arrived last week, and he wasn't sure of the integrity of any of them.

The soldiers straightened. "Yes, Cap'n." The one who'd been telling the story lifted his chin. "I saw it with my own two eyes. 'Tis her fault the fire started."

"Did you help her up?" His ire rose along with his voice.

"Uh. . .no, sir."

"Are you telling me that you just left her there?"

The young soldier's eyes widened.

"Well?"

"Yes, Cap'n."

Christopher pointed a finger in the young man's face. "That conduct is unacceptable. Not only for a soldier, but for a man of honor." He couldn't keep the shock from his voice. "Report to me tomorrow. We will discuss this then." Storming off, he headed to what was left of the west wall. The place where the woman— Martha?—had been doing laundry the past few days.

It didn't take him long to find the black cauldron she heated and stirred the wash in. It lay on its side, a mass of burned ash inside and out.

As Christopher moved closer, he swallowed the bile that threatened to choke him. Amid the ash he saw them. Ivory and gray.

Bones.

He swiped a hand down his face and tried to remove the grim picture from his mind. The men would resound the cries of bad luck as their superstitions were refueled.

Would any of them realize what this woman had sacrificed, coming to this island to toil day and night for them? Amid their scorn and gossip?

No. Most certainly not. They would only blame her for the fire that burned down the fort. Christopher doubted that she'd ever been thanked by a single soldier. Of course he hadn't shown her any appreciation either. And now she was gone and it was too late.

He went down on one knee and removed his hat. The colonel probably wouldn't even allow a proper burial. Especially not on the island.

The woman had no kin. That's why she'd come to work here. Skin and bones, she'd slaved away each day, all so she could eat. She'd be forgotten—other than as the woman who had brought devastation to the fort. The thought was intolerable.

God, grant her peace. I pray she knew Thee. His heart twinged. So many had abandoned God and the church for worldly lusts and superstitions. Why hadn't he thought to speak to the woman about her faith?

Probably for the same reason he'd neglected speaking to his men. Guilt wrenched his gut. He took the blessings of life for granted. His comfort. Provisions. Until death brought thoughts of faith and God barreling forward. That shouldn't be the way of things. Was he truly so selfish that he would go about his daily business and forget about people's souls?

As he gazed around at the ruins of the fort, an invisible weight pressed on his chest. His gaze was drawn back to what was left of a life. Neglected. Forlorn. *Oh Lord, what have we done to this woman?*

Six months later

Waves lapped at the sides of the small skiff as Esther Howland watched the shore of Castle Island draw near. She tugged her shawl tighter and tried to disappear into the corner of the little boat. It was really happening. For the foreseeable future, she'd have to live on an island—the only woman among men.

Papa's voice floated to her from the bow of the skiff. His excitement about building the new fort bounced back and forth with her brother's. Stonemasons by trade, they were indeed good at their craft. But had Esther been given a choice, she would have turned down the work. Especially since it meant leaving their home and living on the island for the next year.

But not Papa. Samuel Howland was a proud descendant of John Howland, who had come over on the *Mayflower*, miraculously survived falling overboard during a storm, and was the patriarch of their family.

Those who'd arrived here first were held in high esteem by the many weary travelers who made their way to the New World. And Papa wanted the Howland name to live on in history. By building the new fort, he meant to ensure that. At least that's what he told her every night.

It had been one thing to live in Boston where there were women and children, stores, and church. But now he was taking them into uncharted territory—at least for her. The fort on Castle Island was a legend in and of itself.

The men stationed there took their jobs seriously ever since the French had come into the harbor all those years ago. The legend had grown in exaggerated detail, and Castle Island had become the place where the people of Boston put their trust. Who would dare come against them by sea when The Castle was protecting them with all its armament? The Castle was known for firing its cannons at an incoming vessel until the ship yielded and acknowledged the fort with a raising of its flag.

But what would this mean for her? At seventeen Esther was still unmarried. The past two years she'd taken care of Mother until she passed while all her friends were starting families of their own. Now Papa was taking them to the island. Which was all well and good for Sam—her brother—but what was *she* supposed to do?

Since her closest friends were recently married, it would be unseemly to ask to stay with one of them. So she hadn't asked. Regretting that decision, her mind flew to thoughts of how awful it would be for her to live on an island of men. She'd heard the rumors. Some believed the island was cursed—that if a woman set foot on it, tragedy would follow. The rumors started when that warship came and scared the people with an invasion. A woman had been on the island then. A few years later, a woman had snuck on the island and one of the guards shot her and two other men. And when fire had burned the fort down this past spring—once again, a woman had been there.

This indeed felt like a very bad idea. But Papa had insisted she come with him.

Sam made his way from the bow to the corner where she huddled. At twenty he was strong and handsome. He had his eye on sweet Mary Whitham who was two years Esther's junior. It wouldn't surprise her at all to see them betrothed once the new fort was completed. Having Mary as a sister-in-law would be wonderful. But would there ever be a wedding for Esther?

Her brother put a hand on her shoulder. "Certainly, 'twill not be as bad as you think."

She puzzled at his statement. "Pardon?"

"I can see the storm of doubt on your face. The rumors are not true, of that I am sure. The colonel must be a reasonable man. Even so, you are so quiet, no one will even know a lady is around."

Poking her elbow into his side, she shook her head. "You are quite the uplifter, brother."

"You must know I am teasing. Papa would be overjoyed if a good man here took a fancy to you."

"Hush!" She gasped. "Please tell me that is not why he insisted I come?" Heat rushed to her face.

He chuckled beside her. "No. Again, I jest. My apologies." He nudged her with his shoulder. "You should know how protective Papa is of you. As am I." His tone turned serious. "And the only way to ensure your safety and well-being during the building of the fort is to keep you with us." He leaned in closer. "Besides, you have always been the best at picking the perfect stones for placement. He would not want to do this monumental task without you."

"'Tis true. And do not forget that anytime soon." She allowed a small smile. "But your compliments do not change the fact that I will be the only woman. The thought makes me quite uncomfortable."

"I will be there with you."

"Not at every moment." She crossed her arms over her waist. "Which is what concerns me. What if something terrible happens and they blame it on a woman being present?"

"You worry too much, little sis." He winked at her. "Once you have been there a while, the rumors of a curse will be labeled as nonsense and superstition. The soldiers will be clamoring for your attention. Just wait and see. Nothing bad is going to happen."

Chapter 2

We can't be havin' a woman here! Have ye lost yer mind?" The stout man that greeted them at the shore stood with his hands on his hips, a deep crease in his brow. " 'Tis exactly why the fort burned down to begin with!"

Esther slid behind her brother, hoping to disappear from view. Papa was saying something, but she didn't even want to hear it. It was just as she feared. No one wanted her here. They thought she was a curse. A bad omen. Bad luck.

Heavenly Father, how am I to endure this?

Tears sprang to her eyes, but she lowered her head and blinked them away. How was she supposed to live here for months if this was how the men would react?

More men voiced displeasure in a woman being present. Talk of bad luck and the colonel who believed the island was cursed. She prayed she could stay away from him. Whoever he was.

As the arguing increased, so did the beating of her heart. With a deep breath, she tuned it out and pressed her forehead against

Sam's back. Her mind went back to her scripture reading last night with Papa. They had just started Peter's first epistle, and verse six of the first chapter had stuck out to her. *"Wherein ye greatly rejoice, though now for a season, if need be, ye are in heaviness through manifold temptations."* The words echoed in her mind.

They'd discussed suffering and the apostle's instructions. This verse struck her heart. No matter the trial, she should rejoice. But how? *"For a season"?* How long would that be?

As quiet as she usually was, her mind always spun with questions and thoughts. Probably much more than Papa would approve of. Especially when she questioned scripture. But she simply wanted to understand. Wasn't that good in the sight of God?

Papa's voice was drowned out by several others. Apparently even more soldiers had heard the news and had come to voice their displeasure.

Sam stood firm and still. She felt like a child cowering behind his back, but it hurt too much even to think of showing her face. Couldn't the men just allow them to go to their quarters in peace where she could hide for the next twelve months?

"My daughter is not a curse!" Papa's voice sounded strained—and angry.

"She will be the death of us all!" someone shouted above the din.

"What—by the name of the King—is all this commotion about?" A deep voice silenced all the others.

Esther peeked around her brother's shoulder. A man, about the height of Sam, commanded everyone's attention. His long red coat hung from broad shoulders over his breeches, which were gathered into bands at his knees. Whoever he was, he looked spotless and authoritative compared to the disheveled appearance of the soldiers.

"The stonemason has brought along his *daughter*, Cap'n. A

female." The stout man lifted his chin. "And ya know how the colonel feels about women on the island, sir."

The captain glanced their way. His piercing gaze found hers, and she gasped, hiding behind Sam again as quick as she could. Maybe if she closed her eyes, it would all go away.

"The colonel has made his superstitions well known, but they are just that. Superstitions. Which are not real, gentlemen."

Grumbling sounded through the voices ahead. After several minutes of it, she couldn't keep her eyes closed. She braved another look.

The man in his red coat stood with his hands behind his back. Clearly unhappy. "That is *enough*, gentlemen." His voice was clear and strong. "I believe I have given my orders. Please escort the Howlands to their new accommodations."

"Captain, might I have a word with you?" Her father stepped forward.

"Of course, Mr. Howland." The captain gave a stern look to the soldiers. Probably to keep them quiet.

"The behavior of your men is completely unacceptable." Papa lifted his chin. "While it is an honor to serve the King by building this new fort, I refuse to stay if my family is to be treated in such a manner."

"My deepest apologies." The captain bowed and then raised his eyebrows as he stared down the men and spoke to them in a loud, commanding tone. "There will be no talk of a curse, gentlemen, nor any negative comment about a lady being on the island. Serious repercussions will follow if my orders are not obeyed. Please show our guests to their quarters."

She hid behind Sam again as the captain's gaze traveled her direction.

Footsteps sounded and then stopped. But she dare not look. "*Without* any more of this superstitious nonsense. Mr. Howland is a fine stonemason, and we are grateful to have him—*and* his family—here to help us rebuild. Is that understood?"

"Yes, Captain."

"Yes, Cap'n."

Voices sounded from all around. Albeit hesitant and just a touch whiney.

Esther let out her breath and waited to hear the noise of men shuffling away. After several moments passed, she whispered up to Sam's ear. "Are they gone?"

"Most of them. Except for the ones carrying our belongings."

"I knew this was a bad idea. Me. . .coming here. Did you see how they reacted? Like I was the plague."

"Now, Sis, 'tis not all that bad. Just a little excitement at the beginning. I am certain it will all be taken care of. The captain called it nonsense and gave them orders. 'Twill blow over. He seems like a good man."

She braved taking a step out from behind her brother. "Indeed, I was glad to hear it. But I am not sure that will be enough."

"Come. Let us trust that the good Lord will take care of this, all right?"

With a nod, she picked up her small bag. It wasn't like there was anything else that could be done. Except pray. In abundance. She'd have to leave the matter in God's hands. "Let me walk behind you just in case?"

"Of course."

Following Sam's steps, Esther attempted to ignore the whispers she heard as they made their way through the fort. She kept her head bowed, looking down at her feet so she wouldn't have to see any of the men who thought she was a curse upon them all. Sam was right. Where was her trust? God had brought them here for a purpose. It was her job to rest in that. The longer they walked, the steadier she felt. Papa needed her here. She would just stay out of everyone's way and do her best at whatever task she was given. If she worked hard, perhaps the time would pass quickly, the fort would be completed, and they could return to Boston.

"Daughter." Papa's voice made her lift her chin. The captain's apology apparently made everything better for him, because a big smile lit up his face. "You go on in and get settled. Sam and I will meet the soldiers and see how well they have followed my instructions for digging the foundation." The twinkle in his eye showed Esther how much he loved his work and how excited he was to be in charge of the building. As he walked away, her heart tightened in her chest. She didn't want to be the cause of his displeasure.

If only she could love being here as much and show him her support. Papa had done everything he could to fill the hole left by her mother's death, but it had been difficult on them all. Maybe over time the talk of superstition and curses would die down.

One of the soldiers stared at her.

Or perhaps not.

She turned on her heel as quickly as she could. The sooner she could get inside, the sooner she could shut the door on all the prying eyes and gossiping tongues.

"*Oomph.*"

Esther stepped back. Embarrassment and horror washed over her. "My apologies." Who had she run into?

The captain emerged out of the darkened doorway. "No, Miss Howland. I am the one in your debt. I simply came to check on the cabin the men had built for your family. After the atrocious way in which you were greeted, I wanted to offer my own apology to you personally."

Now that they were in closer proximity, Esther noticed that he was a bit shorter than Sam. Leaner and yet stronger looking. "I am most grateful. But 'twas not necessary." She held his gaze but wished he would leave so she could be in misery alone.

"If you are in need of anything, I shall see to it myself."

"That is very generous of you, but I think we will be fine."

"The last supply ship of the season to Boston will not run for a few more weeks, so keep a list." He stepped away from the doorway, and she was tempted to run inside. "Your father has probably already told you, but your family will eat meals with the rest of the men, thus you will notice that there are no pots or utensils in the cabin."

Wonderful. How could she become invisible when she'd have to be among the others three times a day? She managed a nod and switched hands on her bag.

"The necessary is through the back door. I made sure that a private one was built."

"Thank you. That was very kind." Attached to their cabin and everything. Well, that was at least one pleasant thought for the day. She'd been afraid of how to take care of her needs on an island full of men, and out of embarrassment she hadn't asked Papa.

"I shall let you see to your things. Your father and brother are wanting to see what we have done with the building site, I am most certain." He nodded and bowed. " 'Twas a privilege to meet you, Miss Howland."

"And you as well." She dipped into a curtsy.

He walked away, and she allowed herself a long, deep breath. No matter what all the other men on the island thought, the captain seemed to be honorable and a gentleman. At least there was that bit of encouragement.

She rushed inside the cabin to find a single room. Removing her bonnet so she could smooth her hair, she took a deep breath. The room was dark without any windows, so she lit a candle and glanced around. Indeed, there was a back door. She ventured forward and found that it led to a privy. How thoughtful. They wouldn't have to trudge out into the snow or rain. That was something to be thankful for.

Three small bedsteads were arranged on three walls, with a curtain hanging in one corner. Obviously for her privacy. A simple table with three short stools sat near the fireplace.

Even though their cabin was small, it would be adequate, and the fact that someone had acknowledged that she would be with her father and brother lifted her spirits. Even if the men were superstitious.

She went to the small table and set down the candle.

Placing her hands on her hips, she surveyed the room one more time. The least she could do was organize their small trunks by their beds and put the bedding out.

When dinnertime came, she'd just have to bolster herself and pray that the good captain had spoken with all the soldiers about her presence. Otherwise she might have to hide until the new fort was built.

Chapter 3

Standing on the spot where the Castle had once stood, Christopher gathered all the men for inspection. He watched Samuel Howland and his son, Sam, walk back toward their quarters and waited a moment before he spoke. A hush fell over the group.

"Men. Tomorrow begins the stonework on the new fort. All the stones you have hefted and piled these past months, all the digging and clearing out—it has not been in vain. Now that our stonemason is here, he is satisfied with the foundation work that has been done and is ready to get started."

Cheers sounded from the crowd.

Christopher held up a hand. "But this will be a lengthy task. It will take every ounce of our strength and stamina as we work through the fall and winter months. The work will be grueling. But rewarding. In addition, we must still prepare for any threats that might come to bear against His Majesty's holdings."

"Aye!"

"Long live the King!"

Voices shouted from all over the square in front of him. The excitement in the crowd was contagious. Everyone was ready for the bigger and stronger fort to be built and to show their might. It was the perfect time to broach the subject of the gossip.

"I find the need to address an issue that has come to my attention today." Christopher stood a little straighter and narrowed his eyes as he focused on the men. "The rumors that I hear among you about a curse being on this island need to stop. Henceforth. Immediately."

Shoulders dropped, faces frowned, and many disapproving glances were shot his way.

"Attention!"

Feet snapped together and frames straightened.

"You are soldiers. In service to His Majesty, the King. And in such service, I will not tolerate any foolishness. That includes any talk of curses or bad luck. There is no curse on this island. It is not bad luck to have a woman here. Thusly, Miss Howland will be treated with respect. Is that understood?"

"Yes, sir."

"Yes, sir."

"Yes, sir." The men's voices weren't as loud as they had been, but as least they understood his order.

"Superstition has no place here. Our faith is in the Lord God Almighty."

"Aye!" A single hand shot up with the shout.

Well, at least there was one sane man among them who hadn't succumbed to the idea of the curse.

"To make certain we are clear, I will not abide any ill treatment or hurtful remarks to be said to her. Neither will I allow the gossip and rumors to continue amongst your ranks. Repercussions will be faced by those who participate." He scanned the men's faces. At least they were listening, but Christopher was doubtful it would stop the tide. Those who had served for years under Colonel Brown were steeped in superstition. Christopher prayed the men would take his words to heart. "You are dismissed to your duties."

Whispers and mumbling sounded as the men dispersed. Christopher was certain they would talk among themselves about the curse and the fact that a woman resided on the island with them. But he'd have to remind them—daily if need be—that the rumors would not be tolerated. Neither would any abhorrent behavior toward Miss Howland. But even as the thoughts went through his mind, he realized as many times as he said it or thought it. . .the truth remained to be seen. As much as he'd tried to change the men's thoughts and actions by being a good example to them, he knew he'd failed miserably. And the more he worked it over in his mind, there was no doubt that he needed to work on his own attitude more. To put others first. To be aware of those forgotten and neglected. But it was increasingly difficult. Especially when his men proved trying.

His thoughts went back to Miss Howland. A small woman, she really was a mouse of a thing. While she'd held his gaze for a few moments without timidity, he knew that she had been ready for him to leave. Was it all because of what the men had said, or did she just feel uncomfortable around strangers?

Of course she would feel uncomfortable. She was the only woman among dozens of men. On an island. Away from all that she knew.

He couldn't coddle her while she was here, but he could at least keep his men in line. The colonel would be back to inspect the troops and progress before the next supply ship arrived, but then he would be back in Boston for the winter. Which was a blessing. Because the man was the cause behind most of this chatter about a curse.

Good thing the King wasn't aware of it. As the head of the Church of England, surely he wouldn't abide any such nonsense. Christopher shook his head. What was he thinking? Superstition seemed to reign supreme even among the royals and the church. Where had all the sane thinkers gone?

He clasped his hands behind him and surveyed the trenches that had been dug for the foundation of the new fort. It would be a presence to be sure. The men were already calling it the New Castle—and it really would look like one this time. Not just a brick tower in the center.

Orders had come down that this fort would boast even more armaments. The castle itself would have four bastions with thirty-eight guns and sixteen culverins, and it would even have the addition of a six-gun water battery.

Christopher's chest filled with pride. It had been his dream to command, and the fort would be completely *his* post next year. The colonel had already informed him of it—as long as everything went well with the construction and provided Christopher could keep all the men in line, drilled, and ready for battle.

It was everything he'd ever wanted.

Well, everything except a family. But as a captain in His Majesty's army and commander of the fort on Castle Island, that wasn't a probability anytime in the future. Especially with no women around. Oh, he'd been to Boston several times, but it hadn't been for pleasure. Not that he expected to meet someone he could court in a day. The time for family would simply have to wait.

His parents were back in England and didn't care for the New

World. Letters were few and at times disheartening for Christopher as they made him feel alone and separated from all he'd known, but God had brought him on this journey. For a purpose.

Time to rest in that and do his job to the best of his ability.

The bell rang for supper, and he watched the men hurry off. Most of them were living in tents until the fort was complete. Once winter set in, Christopher hoped they would at least have some walls completed so they could build fires and keep the encampment warm. But his men were sturdy stock. They'd been through worse and could handle a little cold and snow.

The deep blue fabric of Miss Howland's skirts caught his attention out of the corner of his eye. He turned and saw the Howland family heading toward supper as well.

Perhaps he could offer to sit with them and answer any questions they might have.

As he approached, the senior Howland lifted a smile in greeting. "Captain."

"Mr. Howland, Sam, Miss Howland." Christopher bowed. "Might I invite you to join me for the meal?"

"Of course. We would be delighted." The senior Howland returned the bow.

While most of the men sat on stumps and rocks since all of the chairs and tables had burned in the fire, there were two tables and a few chairs that had been constructed for the senior officers. It had taken them all these months to get rid of the debris from the fire and prepare for the new fort. Now that it would get under way, he could put some men in charge of building adequate furniture. They *were* civilized, after all.

He held out a guiding hand. "Please join me at my table."

He snuck a glance at Miss Howland. Her cheeks were rosy

from the heat of the afternoon, and it struck him that she really didn't look mousy after all. Timid maybe, but her eyes held a depth he hadn't seen before. In a man or in a woman.

Curious. Behind the shy exterior, she must be quite intelligent.

"Our cook does a good job feeding the hungry men every day. And 'tis better than just porridge."

"Excellent. I must admit, I am famished." Sam rubbed his hands together. The younger Howland also had keen eyes. "It was exciting to see the area laid out for the fort. I am ready to get to work."

"My men are equally as eager. They have expressed their longing to sleep inside and have furniture again. Although, the first focus must be the protection and armament."

"Of course." Mr. Howland took a chair and leaned back. "We will begin work on the forward bastions tomorrow. My son will be in charge of one, and I the other. Esther has an eye for finding the perfect stones to fit, so I shall leave her to instruct your men at the stone piles."

The comment took him aback. "Miss Howland will be assisting with the building? I am not sure the men will take instruction from a member of the fairer sex."

The object of his remark looked at him, hesitancy in her eyes. "I am certain Papa did not mean that I would instruct them. Only that I would show them the stones I choose for placement. Is that all right with you, Captain?"

"Well. . . That is. . ."

Mr. Howland held up a hand. "She will not be lifting anything, but I need her eye. It will help us move at a faster pace if she can instruct the men to bring the correct stones to us."

Christopher raised his eyebrows. There was that word again— *instruct*. But Howland didn't bat an eye. Utterly unconventional, but the stonemason was in charge. "If you need her to assist you, I will *instruct* my men likewise." As he watched Esther Howland, the look on her face made him curious. Did working among the men make her uncomfortable? How could it not? One, it wasn't a woman's place. Two, she'd experienced the rumors and gossip already.

He might need to keep a close eye on things.

One of the soldiers brought a tray of bowls to their little table. "Fish stew, Cap'n."

"Thank you, James." Christopher offered a bowl to each of his guests. "Something we eat a lot of here on the island with the bounty of fish, but it is hearty and tasty."

Supper passed in rousing conversation with Samuel and Sam. It would be a joy to have them on the island during the building of the fort. While Mr. Howland was his senior by a good many years, his wisdom and wit were good companions. As well as his knowledge of the scriptures. Young Sam was several years younger than Christopher's own nine and twenty, but his keen enjoyment of life and fervor for his work were encouraging.

Christopher couldn't help sneaking glances at Esther. While she was quiet, she was an observer. Watching not only them, but the other men around them. What thoughts could be going through her mind?

"How do you like your quarters?" He looked each one of them in the eye.

"They are quite amenable." Mr. Howland nodded. "Thank you for building it."

"You are most welcome. I apologize for the lack of windows, but as you can imagine, it was difficult to get glass at the last minute."

"Quite all right. We shall not be spending much time there anyway." The younger Howland shrugged.

A slight frown flashed across Miss Howland's face. Then it vanished as she stood from her seat, which initiated all of them standing. "If you will excuse me, I would like to attend to some mending."

"Of course, dear. We will not be long. Tomorrow will be quite demanding, so it is imperative to get plenty of rest." Mr. Howland smiled at his daughter.

"Thank you, Captain Latham. Supper was lovely."

"You are most welcome, Miss Howland." Christopher bowed and watched her closely. Perhaps a window would have been wise. Especially if she wanted to hide away from all the gossip. The thought of her sitting in that dark little cabin by herself did something to Christopher's insides.

A group of soldiers and their raucous laughter moved by, blocking her exit for a moment.

His ears burned when he overheard the word *curse*. Even after his speech this afternoon, the men dared to continue in this folly?

Miss Howland scurried away after they passed. She most certainly heard it herself.

Christopher narrowed his eyes at the group. With a quick glance to Samuel, he spoke through clenched teeth. "Excuse me for a moment, gentlemen."

Chapter 4

The day had warmed considerably, and Esther found herself wishing to be out of the sun in all the layers of her dress. But Papa needed her there, especially since the soldiers hadn't proven to be any good at finding foundation stones. It was a new task to them to be sure, but it was also clear that they didn't appreciate being told what to do by a lady, so they tried in earnest to get better at the job. Only to fail time and again and be sent back to the rock pile for her advice.

She pulled out her fan and waved it briskly. Her cheeks were no doubt pink from the heat. One of the downfalls of having fair skin.

Surveying the pile of stones gathered, she walked around it to find the right one to finish the foundation of Sam's bastion. It needed a good corner but a flatter top. Substantial depth and height as well. The soldiers who didn't seem to mind her presence had helped to lay out the stones so she could see them, while the others voiced their displeasure at heaving the massive rocks and continually asked why one stone wasn't as good as another.

If it were up to them, the walls would be a jumble of rocks of all sizes, which would prove to be unstable and topple over. So she kept at it. She tried not to speak much and let her brother be the one to order the soldiers around. They *were* working quite hard.

"The cap'n's comin'." A whisper-shout echoed from one man to the next.

Esther lowered her brows. Just as the men said, the captain strode toward them, his red coat draped over his arm. She tore her gaze away. While she wasn't surprised by his informality in this heat, the sight of him in his shirt and breeches made her heart pick up its pace.

Captain Latham was a handsome man. And a very strong one. Of that, her eyes were certain.

As soon as she looked back to the pile, she spotted the stone that would be perfect. "That one." She pointed.

The young soldier named Peter gave her a smile. "I shall fetch it straightaway for Mr. Howland, miss."

"Thank you." But Peter wouldn't be able to lift it on his own. It would probably take three men. She opened her mouth to say as much but then snapped it closed. The majority of the men didn't like her giving her opinion.

"Good day, Miss Howland."

She curtsied to the captain but kept her eyes averted. "Good day to you."

"Pardon me." He slipped his coat back on. "I see they are making good progress on the bastions."

Lifting her fan, she whipped it faster than she probably needed. "Yes, Captain Latham. We just chose the last stone for the foundation of the north side."

"My men have told me that you are quite particular." His grin made her feel at ease. "And that is a good thing."

"I wondered what you would hear. Most of them do not appreciate my presence, but the choosing of the stones is of great import for the structure to be stable." The fact that she'd said so many words to him shocked her a bit.

"I can see that." He clasped his hands behind his back and began to walk among the pile. "Would you mind explaining to me how you choose?"

She blinked at him. No one had ever bothered to ask such a question. "I would not mind at all." She cleared her throat and prayed she could make sense and keep her tongue from tying. "We start with the largest stones at the base. I must see the space that we need to fill and then discern the dimensions and shape. Then I simply find a rock that fits." Esther gave a little shrug. She'd been helping Papa so long, it was second nature to her.

"What caused you to take an interest in such a task?"

His questions weren't of the polite sort to keep the conversation going. He genuinely seemed interested, and it lifted Esther's spirits. Perhaps she could survive here with at least one man treating her respectfully. "Papa and Sam needed help one day as they were both down in a trench on their knees. Thankfully, it was a small stone, because I was not much older than ten at the time. It took all of my strength to drag it over, but it was a perfect fit. And it saved them a trip to the rock pile."

"Fascinating."

"Papa says I have an eye for it. I like to help when I can."

"Watch out!" The shout made her jump.

Then a blood-curdling scream followed.

Captain Latham ran toward the sound. Esther followed and put a hand up to shade her eyes so she could see. What happened?

Lord, please let Papa and Sam be all right.

Men scrambled from every corner.

Papa ran toward her from the bastion. "Come with me, Daughter."

"But—"

"Now, Esther. A man's arm is crushed underneath that last foundation stone."

The cook examined the mangled arm. "Cap'n, sorry to say, but he'll lose it. The barber-surgeon in Boston will have to do it. I lack the tools here." He wiped his hands on a rag.

Christopher let out a heavy breath. The colonel had insisted on taking their barber-surgeon with him everywhere he went. That left them on the island with dozens of men and no medical help. Christopher hated for men to get hurt under his command. And he'd done a pretty good job ensuring all was well. But lifting massive stones was sure to create issues. It was a miracle the soldier was still alive. That stone could have crushed him—not just his arm. "I shall have some men get the skiff ready." Turning on his heel, he was thankful the young soldier had passed out from the pain. An amputation was always hard to bear, but even more so if the patient knew about it ahead of time.

"Captain, sir." One of his sergeants stopped him. Steven had been a bit too outspoken about the curse and having a woman on the island. The look on his face said that his chosen topic of conversation would be precisely that.

Christopher narrowed his eyes. "Be quick about it. We need to get this man to Boston."

"Yes, sir." He lifted his chin. "But I saw the whole thing happen.

Miss Howland was the one who instructed—"

"Yes, yes. I know all about that. But she certainly did *not* have anything to do with the accident."

"But sir, she should not be here." Steven lifted his chin.

The ridiculousness of the statement made Christopher want to toss all the superstitious ninnies into the ocean. "This is neither the time nor the place. Is that all, Sergeant?"

A scowl filled the man's face. "Yes, sir."

"Good. You can row this man to shore." His tone was gruff, but the man had overstepped. "Assign three others to go with you. I shall expect you back tonight. No excuses."

"Yes, Captain." Steven stomped off.

He couldn't seem to squelch the rumors, but he could at least try and stave off the worst of it. No one needed to be blaming Miss Howland for this disaster. They'd had plenty of accidents on the island without women around to blame them on.

With a shake of his head, Christopher headed back to the bastions where his men still worked. His legs ate up the distance, but with every step, his dread grew. If Steven was already blaming the lady, how many others would do the same?

The sharp sounds of chisels and hammers hitting rock resounded throughout the work area. He headed straight to Mr. Howland.

The older man had sweat trickling down his temples.

"Mr. Howland."

The man looked up with relief on his face. "Captain. How is the boy?"

"I am afraid he will lose the arm, but other than that, I believe he will be fine."

Howland shook his head. " 'Tis sad to hear. I tried to warn them about the dangers, but these young men believe they are invincible."

"Aye, sir. No one is blaming you."

"But they *are* blaming my daughter." He pointed a finger toward the soldiers. "I have heard it. And she has too. So I allowed her to return to our cabin for a bit of respite." Howland sat on a rock and swiped at the sweat on his face. "I heard tell of what you said to your men, and I appreciate it, Captain Latham. But I will not stand by whilst they say horrible things about my daughter."

"I would not expect you to, sir. I will speak to the men again. Do you know who it was who is spreading the rumors?"

"No, the names of most of them are still unfamiliar to me. But I saw Esther's face when she overheard it. She's a strong and quiet one, but I saw the hint of tears."

"I shall go apologize myself. After I speak to the men. Again." Christopher didn't wait for the man to respond. Pure anger pushed him forward.

"Atten-tion!" His harsh tone caught everyone's attention. The soldiers all moved in to form their lines and ranks.

For the next five minutes, he berated his men for their participation in gossip and superstitious lies. Additional duties were added for everyone. He wanted to deny them all supper as if they were a bunch of careless children, but he couldn't do that.

Silence engulfed the group as Christopher yelled his orders once again. No gossip. No curse. No ill treatment of Miss Howland. Then he ordered that each man apologize to her individually as soon as they saw her next.

Not that it would cure the problem. But he could hope. He stepped away, his ire still growing. But he needed to calm down before he saw Miss Howland. He had to show her that they could be gentlemen. And that he was in charge of his men.

But how? They clearly had no shame in believing in a silly curse.

Even when that defied orders.

The ground crunched beneath his shoes as he approached the small cabin. Would she even answer the door? He hoped so. To his utter consternation, the stonemason's daughter occupied his thoughts all too often of late.

He lifted his hand and knocked.

A shuffling noise sounded. Then the door opened a crack. Her blue eyes peered out. "Captain Latham." She opened the door a bit wider.

"Miss Howland, please allow me to offer my apologies for the men yet again, letting their mouths take off without them. I told you that gossip would not be tolerated, and I am working on that now."

She looked down at her hands, a lacy handkerchief twisted between her fingers. " 'Tis not your fault, Captain. But I appreciate the apology." She moved to close the door.

"Please. Hiding away is not going to make this any better."

Her head tilted as she gazed at him. "I do not see any other appropriate plan, sir."

"Take a walk with me." The words were out before he realized what he'd said.

"Pardon?"

"Forgive me." He swallowed. "Would you care to join me on a walk of the island?"

"I . . ."

"Miss Howland. I know that your time here so far has been nothing but heartache and embarrassment. I am not wishing to cause you any more discomfort, but I do believe that if you hide away, the rumors will only grow. Let the men see that you are not afraid of them and that you have nothing to do with any ridiculous curse." He offered his arm. "Thus, the walk. They will see you in public and will see that I certainly do not believe in any such nonsense."

Much to his surprise, she exited the cabin and closed the door. "Thank you. A walk would be nice."

Her father had said she was strong. But all he'd really seen was the quiet and shy woman. He watched her for a moment. Her hair, plaited and wrapped in a knot at her neck, glistened in the afternoon sunlight. The cap on her head covered too much of it. Why did women always have to cover their hair? Didn't scripture call it a glory?

She turned her head and looked at him. "Is there something wrong, Captain?"

He blinked several times. "No. Not at all. Why do you ask?"

"You have a frown etched on your face." She pulled away. "If you have other duties to attend to, we do not have to go." Her eyes snapped with a fiery light.

He liked it. "I have no desire or need to be elsewhere, Miss Howland." He let a smile emerge. "I admit I was pondering a question, but now I would like nothing more than to show you our island."

A soft smile lifted the corners of her lips and made her whole face light up. "Lead the way, Captain."

Chapter 5

Water sloshed with each rhythmic pull of the oars. Steven watched Castle Island come closer and closer as he plotted his next accident. Captain Latham thought entirely too much of himself. And not enough of the curse.

Steven didn't mind bringing the rumors to the forefront of everyone's minds. It was the only way to dispel the eventual doom of them all. Hadn't they learned anything from the past?

Of course, he hadn't meant for anyone to lose his arm. The kid had tried to be a hero and stop the stone from injuring anyone else. Selfless. Yet stupid.

It didn't matter now. The kid would live. Would return to his family and learn how to live with one arm. What *did* matter was getting everyone's attention. And making sure they were all on his side. The captain couldn't stand against all of them if they banded together.

It wasn't that Steven wasn't fond of women. He was. Very fond. But they had no business being at the fort. It only brought danger and death.

It was his job to stop it.

The island wasn't very large, but it was very interesting. Flat, and for the most part without trees, the island afforded Esther a spectacular view.

Captain Latham had given her the history of the island, including the forts. The first one had been built by the donations of the governor and his council. It had boasted two platforms and had a strategic location to be the first military defense of Boston.

"Was that the one that burned last year?"

"No. That one was built out of timber after the scare of the French warship coming through in '44."

"Ah, yes. I see." She'd never understood why they built so much out of wood when it was an easily burning fuel. Perhaps being the daughter of a stonemason gave her such thoughts.

"Nothing will compare to the fine fort your father is building though."

"He's a master at it, to be sure. What he envisions will serve for decades and stand against any storm." Pride in her father's work rushed to the surface. Papa was the finest stonemason in all of New England.

"The men like to fish off of this point." Christopher led her around the south side of the island to a peninsula that jutted out to the water like an arrow.

Esther took the moment to study the man before her. While his periwig covered his hair, she imagined it to be dark like his eyebrows. His eyes were a shade of green she couldn't name. Striking. Commanding attention.

Taking care of Mother had kept Esther from pining after any

of the young men who'd attempted to get her attention when she was younger. Studying the man before her now, she was thankful she hadn't given her heart to any of the boys her age. Where that thought came from, she didn't know. But she couldn't deny it.

There was something about the captain that she liked. Trusted.

Even though he'd had a man injured and probably needed to attend to a number of other things, he'd taken the time to make her feel comfortable.

It was sweet. And caused her to be bold. "Do you enjoy fishing as well?" It was the first personal question she'd ventured to ask.

"I do. But there's not a lot of time for it, unfortunately."

They stopped their walk and stood in silence for several moments. Seagulls squawked above them, floating on the breeze.

"I cannot help but notice that you are quieter than most women I have had the privilege of having an acquaintance with." The captain turned toward her and quirked one eyebrow.

Esther couldn't stop a slight smile. " 'Tis true, the fairer sex are commonly more talkative. But I have always enjoyed listening more. My mother was the talker of the family."

He tilted his head a bit. "What is it that you listen for?"

"That is a good question. I am not sure. . . I guess, what people *aren't* saying." Lifting her shoulders a bit, she prayed he wouldn't think her odd.

His mouth opened an inch and then closed. "You are a very interesting person, Miss Howland."

"Thank you. I believe." He puzzled her.

A deep chuckle filled the space between them. "I meant no disrespect. It's the first time I have heard a female—or, well, anyone for that matter, speak in such matter-of-fact terms. 'Tis refreshing. Honest."

"I find joy in observing people. Quite simple, really."

"And what do you discover in observing them?"

"If they have a need. Or perhaps they are hurting. Is it not pleasing to God for us to care for one another?"

"Indeed it is, Miss Howland. I simply have not run into anyone of late that actually takes that to heart." He dipped his head with the words.

"Oh, but Captain Latham, that cannot be true."

"Quite true, I assure you. The world has become a selfish place."

"I did not take you to be a pessimist, Captain."

"I never thought to be one. But alas, here we are." He stood a little straighter and seemed to ponder the silence. After several minutes, he took a step back toward the fort. "We should be getting back."

Her heart plummeted. Why was she so disappointed? It's not as if she had reason to take up all the man's time. "I am sure you have much to keep you busy."

"My apologies for not taking you all the way around. Perhaps another time?"

"That would be delightful, but I can always explore it myself too. The island is not very large. But thank you for the invitation."

"You are most welcome, Miss Howland."

The walk back was enjoyable enough. He asked questions about her father and the work he'd done. She answered, but something in their conversation had changed. They were back to the aloof chitchat of society. Perhaps when she'd called him a pessimist he'd taken offense? Best not to say anything. She was already in his debt for attempting to quell the rumors. And she didn't want to wish him any more strife because of her.

When they reached the little cabin, the captain bowed.

"Thank you for the walk." She curtsied.

" 'Twas my pleasure. I hope to see you at supper?" He lifted an eyebrow in question.

"Of course. Until then." Esther went inside and closed the door. As she leaned up against it, the few facts she knew about Captain Latham swirled in her mind. Not that she had any right to be thinking of him at all. Although it did give her something pleasant to ponder.

After a quick use of the necessary, she went straight back out to the bastions where the men worked. The captain was right. Hiding wasn't the answer. She would just have to prove the rumors wrong.

Chapter 6

A strong chill in the air greeted Esther a few mornings later. And it wasn't just from the men. The sweltering heat they'd been enduring in September appeared to be on its way out in a hurry now that October was upon them.

Grabbing another shawl from the cabin to take back to the bastions, she lifted a prayer heavenward. *Lord, I give You this day. I don't know what it will hold, but I pray for safety for the men, for grace toward me, and for many stones to be set.*

Every little mishap that happened had been blamed on her. Whether it was a man tripping, a fly in someone's stew, or the man whose arm was crushed. Apparently everything bad that happened was because of her presence. It had gotten to the point where she dreaded being around the men. But Papa insisted he needed her help. And she remembered the captain's words about hiding. Even though that was what she wanted to do, something inside her also wanted the captain to be proud of her.

When she made it to the rock pile, Peter stood waiting for her.

"Good morning, Peter." She dipped her chin.

"Good morning." He followed her around as she looked at the rocks.

When she turned to head the other way, his nearness made her step back. Roughly around her own age, he seemed eager for. . .something. "May I help you with some task?"

He opened his mouth and then closed it. Then took a deep breath and opened his mouth again. "I would like to learn, Miss Howland. In watching you yesterday, it fascinated me how you were able to see how each rock would fit with the others." He looked at his feet for a moment. "I think maybe I would like to be a stone-mason one day."

"And a fine one you will make." She gave him a smile. "My father and brother are the ones who really know the craft. I am just good at finding the stone." The fact that, as a man, he was even willing to work with her was amazing.

"Can you tell me how ya do it?"

"I can try—"

"Peter, do not be listening to her nonsense, now." A sergeant gripped Peter's shoulder. "If you know what is best for you, you will stay away from her. I think you need to work with Mr. Howland today."

Peter looked from the sergeant back to her. "Uh. . ."

"Get to work." The sergeant stepped closer.

"Yes, sir." Shoulders slumped, the young soldier walked away.

The sergeant's eyes shot daggers in her direction, and he stuck his finger in her face. "You just keep your ideas to yourself. We all know that you have brought the curse down upon us once again." With a glance around him, he straightened his shoulders and smoothed his coat. Then he turned and marched toward the north bastion.

Esther watched the blond-haired man walk away. And then glanced over at Peter. The young man was eager to learn but wouldn't disobey. Would he have the nerve to ask her father for his guidance? She prayed so. Her heart sank at the thought of the encounter she'd just witnessed.

No matter what Captain Latham ordered his men, the rumors of the curse were alive and well. And Esther wouldn't be able to persuade them otherwise. In their minds, a woman shouldn't be here. Especially working with the men.

Was there any way for her to help Papa and Sam without putting the men in an uproar?

She went over to the bastion where Sam was working a pulley system they would use to lift the stones above their heads. Discouragement fought against her good sense, but she shook it away. "What do you need next?"

"The north wall is coming along nicely. The men are getting better at choosing stones for the wall but not for the corners. Papa is getting ahead on his side, so I want to step up the pace."

"I shall work on finding good cornerstones. And staying out of everyone's way."

Sam gave her a sympathetic look. "I am most sorry, Esther." So much was conveyed in those words.

" 'Twill be all right." She headed back to the large rock piles and studied all the stones, looking for just the right ones to be corner pieces.

But it couldn't take her mind off the sergeant's words. It wouldn't be all right. She shouldn't be here. Women had no place working among the men. It was one thing to help her father and quite another to be the object of rumors and gossip. Any determination she'd felt before melted away. She wasn't strong like her brother. Couldn't take the weight of all the men's scorn.

Esther had felt the hatred coming from the sergeant. Did *all* the others feel that way too?

While most of the men stayed away, a few greeted her. Some had even apologized for their behavior. Most likely because Captain Latham had instructed them to do so, but still. . . She'd felt a bit accepted and less of a pariah.

But now?

Things weren't getting any better. If anything, they were getting worse.

Heavenly Father, my soul aches. You know I've tried to have a good heart about being here and how I worried about how the men would react. But it's too hard. Now I fear that it was a grave mistake to come. But what choice did I have? What should I do?

Feeling disrespectful for questioning God, she tried to focus again on the large stones in front of her. But it was no use. She felt the stares of some of the men. As if they were burning holes in her back. Her personality was not to stand and fight. She'd much rather hide.

"Help! Get me down!" The shout pulled her out of her thoughts of self-pity. When she turned around, she saw Peter hanging upside down from the pulley.

Men ran from all directions. But she stayed back so they couldn't blame this on her too.

"Sam!" Papa's voice boomed over the commotion.

Her brother was already running toward their father.

"Hold this rope tight so he does not get caught in the mechanism." Papa handed the rope to Sam. "You, and you!" He pointed at two others. "Get below his head. Once we release the pressure, we do not want him to fall. The rest of you, stand back."

Esther took a few steps forward. Peter dangled a good fifteen feet in the air. How had that happened? Papa was always good at instructing the men on how to stay clear of the ropes.

She held her breath as they maneuvered and then released the pulley. Peter was on his feet on the ground in moments, and she let out a sigh of relief. Before anyone could see, she returned to the stone pile. But out of the corner of her eye, she saw Captain Latham headed their way.

If only she could disappear among the rocks.

Christopher paced in front of Peter, Samuel, and Steven. "Exactly how did you become entangled in the pulley?"

"I am not sure, sir." Peter gripped his hat in his hands. "I did what Mr. Howland said and watched my feet around the ropes. But before I knew it, I was hanging upside down."

Something didn't set right in his mind. Christopher looked to the sergeant. "And you witnessed the event?"

Steven lifted his chin. "I did, sir. I was there to assist."

"What exactly did you see?"

"Peter had trouble with keeping the ropes straight, sir. His feet were in the middle of them. I tried to warn him, sir, but it was too late."

"I see." But he didn't. Could the sergeant be lying? Christopher turned back to the young soldier. "Is this what happened?"

The young man looked to the sergeant and then back at him. A bit of fear flashed across his features. Then he swallowed. "Not that I recall, sir. The ropes were not near my feet. Mr. Howland wanted to test the pulley, and I was straightening the lines."

"Why were you helping with the pulley? Had I not assigned

you to the stone piles?"

Peter glanced at the sergeant again. His face turned red.

"I expect an answer."

"The sergeant told me to, sir."

Now that wasn't surprising in the least. Christopher turned to the sergeant and raised his eyebrows. "Sergeant?"

"With the pulleys going to work today, sir, I saw the need for more hands over at the wall."

"I see. So you decided to supplant my order."

"It was necessary. And if I might add sir, this accident is clearly because of Miss Howland's presence."

Samuel stepped forward. "I say! Esther was not anywhere near—" The older man sputtered. "How dare you blame my daughter!"

Christopher held up a hand. "Sergeant, there is no need for you to bring your superstitions into this matter. We deal in facts. Not gossip. Miss Howland's presence has nothing to do with the matter. More likely it was because *you* were present."

Steven's lip curled.

"Captain, if I might add something." Peter's voice cracked.

"Of course." Christopher took a deep breath to calm himself. Steven was becoming a problem.

"Miss Howland wasn't around. She was still over at the rock piles. So she could not have had anything to do with this."

"But 'tis bad luck to have her here. Are you blind? Have you not seen what all has happened? There's a reason the colonel was vocal about the curse. He believed in it too." Steven's face was hard and full of anger.

"Sergeant. That is enough. There will be no more about a curse." He turned to Peter. "I am most glad you came out of this unscathed. From now on, your orders are to assist at the rock piles."

"Yes, sir." The young man hurried off.

"Mr. Howland, is your pulley system in working order?"

"Yes, Captain."

"Good. I'm glad there wasn't any damage done. My apologies for the sergeant's words." Christopher gave a pointed glance at Steven and then back to Mr. Howland. "I am sorry to have taken your time."

Mr. Howland nodded, but the wariness in his eyes couldn't be mistaken. What man wouldn't be wary? Especially when there seemed to be those bent on blaming his daughter. Christopher was sure the older man had begun to worry for her safety. If Christopher was in his shoes, he most certainly would. With a prayer for wisdom, he turned back to Steven. "Sergeant, you were out of line."

The man squinted at him but didn't say anything.

"Might I remind you, I have already given my orders pertaining to the rumors about a curse *and* the treatment of Miss Howland. You have directly disobeyed both of them. Moreover, you changed Peter's orders without instruction from me."

Steven straightened his shoulders but remained silent.

"This evening after supper you will report back to me. I will have the disciplinary action decided by then."

"Yes, Captain." The sarcastic tone wasn't lost on Christopher.

As the sergeant walked away, Christopher swiped a hand down his face. No matter how much he tried to fix this problem, it only seemed to get worse. The facts were becoming all too clear.

Miss Howland's presence was a problem.

Chapter 7

For two days there'd been nothing but accidents. At least it seemed that way to Christopher. And as much as he tried to speak to Miss Howland and encourage her at mealtimes, there was nothing he could do to lift her spirits. She became quieter—if that was even possible—and avoided all eye contact.

Seeing her spirit crushed in such a way was disheartening. The fairer sex should be treated with respect and dignity. Instead, she'd been labeled, accused, and gossiped about.

It didn't help that all this was a blow to his own ego. No matter what he said to his men, the rumors seemed to spread. He was supposed to be in command here, and yet when it came to this superstitious nonsense, his men saw only one thing—a woman in their presence, the cause of the curse.

Unacceptable. But how could he change it?

It would take an act of God to get them to see her as anything other than the cause of all their problems.

And Christopher didn't have that kind of power.

He'd prayed and prayed for a miracle. For a change of heart for the men. For them to see what a lovely person Miss Howland was. To appreciate her help.

But nothing had changed. Only more accidents had occurred. And no matter how minor, they always blamed the curse. And thus. . .Miss Howland.

The more time he spent around her, the more he realized what a fascinating woman she was. Granted, she was quite young, but her wisdom and maturity in the face of unpleasant circumstances never ceased to amaze him.

The sound of musket fire reached his ears. What on earth? The men shouldn't be attending drills right now. They were all to be working on the fort walls.

Another shot rang out.

Christopher ran toward the sound.

There was no call from the tower guard. No shouts or cries of distress. They couldn't be under attack, could they?

He scanned the horizon.

No ships.

Another shot.

Where was it coming from? It seemed to echo all around him.

Then another.

He turned in a circle. Squinting, he saw men at the point. They were the ones ordered to fish for Cook. Why would they fire a musket?

Running in that direction, Christopher tried to piece it all together. And nothing made sense.

When he reached the peninsula, he saw one of his men helping another to his feet. "What has happened here?"

"I do not know, sir." The soldier's eyes were wild. "We were just fishin'. Like we was supposed to. Then all of a sudden we heard the first shot. Then another. The rocks around us were pinging. Then, before you know it, Robert here was on the ground. Someone shot him in the foot!"

Christopher looked at the wound. "Thankfully, it looks like the musket ball ricocheted off one of the rocks and just grazed him."

Robert's eyes were a bit glassy. "I am fine, sir. I thought it was much worse." He looked down and then away. "I am not too good with the sight of me own blood."

"Get him to Cook. I am certain he can be patched up."

As the two soldiers hobbled away, Christopher scanned the island from the point. A shot could be taken from many different areas to hit this spot. But who would do such a thing? And why? Accuracy with a flintlock musket was difficult at any distance. So could the shooter have been aiming at something else?

What else was out here?

For the next half hour, he looked for signs, any kind of tracks that would give him a hint. But the only thing he found were footprints in the sand at the beach where many of the men bathed. Lots of them. And nothing that pointed to the firing of a musket.

John, his lieutenant, approached from the north. "Captain, I believe we have a problem."

"Go ahead."

"Robert will be fine, but someone has stirred up more rumors."

He let out a sigh. "About Miss Howland?"

"Yes, sir." John looked resigned. "They are saying that no one is safe with her here. And that we did not have accidents and problems when a woman wasn't on the island."

"It's a bunch of nonsense."

"I know, sir. But the younger men are beginning to listen to the superstitions of soldiers who served under the colonel before—Steven in particular. And with Robert getting shot—and no idea who the culprit is—I'm afraid we will soon have a revolt."

"A revolt? You cannot be serious." Christopher shook his head. "In all my years, I've never seen anything like this."

"I would not want word getting to Boston and Colonel Brown, sir."

"Agreed." Christopher shook his head and let out a long breath. The colonel had delayed his trip back to Castle Island several times. As selfish as it sounded, Christopher didn't want to take the chance that the superior officer might rescind the command. What was worse—losing the command or losing Miss Howland? The question instantly surprised him. When had he begun to think of her as part of his life? Or that she would remain a part? But he did think of her often. He cared for her.

Not that he had any right or claim to her.

"Well?" John gave him a pointed look.

"I shall go speak to Miss Howland."

Feeling like a complete failure for being unable to keep his men in check, he headed toward the bastions.

Peter stood next to Miss Howland as she pointed to several large stones.

"Miss Howland, might I have a moment of your time?"

Her serene exterior didn't cover the distress in her eyes. "Yes, Captain."

"My apologies for the interruption."

"I understand why you are here. I have heard nothing but comments from the men since that young man was shot." She clasped her hands in front of her and looked at the ground.

"As much as it pains me to say this, my men haven't been heeding my direction. You see, the colonel who was in charge before me is quite a superstitious man."

"There's really no need to explain."

"But I feel that I must." He paced in front of her. "I do not believe in such things. I do not believe that the island is cursed. And I definitely do not believe that you are the cause of all the accidents. But until I can ascertain what is going on and the cause behind all the mishaps, I need to ask you to stay in your cabin and away from the work area for a few days."

She caught her bottom lip between her teeth. A moment later, she said, "I had a feeling you would say something of the sort." Looking back down at her hands, she smoothed her skirt. "Would you please let Papa know where I have gone?" She lifted her chin enough for him to see a sheen of tears.

But before he could say anything else, she left.

Christopher watched her hurry away. It felt like someone was squeezing his heart. Perhaps he cared more for her than he realized. When had her quiet ways slipped in and gotten ahold of him?

" 'Tis not right." Peter stepped toward him. "I know it's not your fault, Captain, but 'tis not right." The young soldier lifted his chin.

A bold statement from a subordinate. But a truthful one.

Peter continued. "Miss Howland is smart. And nice. I do not know why the men think poorly of her. Like when Sergeant Jones told me to stay away from her and go work somewhere else. It doesn't make sense. Especially since I woulda been safer here."

"Wait. What did you just say?" His mind shifted back to the details of the day.

"Miss Howland is nice. And smart."

"No. After that. What did Sergeant Jones say?"

"It didn't make sense to me that Sergeant Jones told me to stay away from her. He told me to go work somewhere else."

"He specifically told you to stay away from her? Not just to go help with the pulleys? When did he say that?"

"Right before I got hung up in that pulley. When he told me to go work with Mr. Howland." Peter wiped his hands on his breeches. "I had just asked Miss Howland to teach me how she picked out the right stones. It seemed odd for him to be watching like that and then to be so angry about her teaching me anything. Especially since she's so good at it. Not that I have ever seen a woman work, even with her father being—"

"Peter, thank you." He didn't mean to cut off the young man, but the situation had become clear.

Sitting beside the fire, Steven stared into the flames. So far his plan had gone as he hoped. The men believed in the curse, and most of them were scared to death that a female was on the island.

And the captain had relegated her to her cabin. Now if Steven could just get her banned from the island altogether, they would be fine.

One thing was certain. He wasn't willing to die in service to the King just because of some woman. No telling what kind of horrible damage she could cause.

Why weren't more men willing to listen to reason? It wasn't superstition. Curses were real. And if they didn't pay attention, another one—possibly even worse—could come down on them. They could be overrun by some horrible disease. Or. . .they could be attacked!

The witch back in Boston had told the colonel as much. Steven had heard it as he'd eavesdropped through the curtain. The captain was foolish not to heed the same warnings.

But Steven wasn't foolish. He paid attention.

He'd just have to get rid of her. For good.

Chapter 8

Three weeks had passed and Esther hadn't even left the cabin. Ever since Captain Latham spoke to her, she'd insisted that Sam or Papa bring her food so she wouldn't have to be seen. At all. Convincing herself it was best this way, she spent time sewing. And reading Papa's Bible. And hiding.

So far she'd stitched two new shirts for both Papa and Sam and had read through the entire Word from Genesis to Revelation. She'd spent several days just reading and rereading First Peter, clinging to the verses about joy through suffering. Her next project was a new boned bodice she'd hoped to finish over the winter with a lace-edged linen apron to wear over her skirt. But with nothing else to occupy her time, she could probably have both of those finished within the week. Then everything she'd brought with her to stitch over the winter would be done. And the first snow hadn't even fallen yet.

Papa seemed weary from all the hard work, but said at least the mishaps had ceased.

Which didn't help Esther feel any better. She didn't believe in curses, but she was beginning to believe that someone didn't want her here. Why else would the accidents have happened?

It couldn't be a coincidence that bad things occurred when she was around. But why would someone do that?

Putting her hands to her head, she squeezed. All this time alone with her thoughts wasn't prosperous. She'd begged Papa to allow her to return to Boston, but there was no place for her to go. They'd leased their house for the year since they were going to be building the fort. And no one else had room. She'd sent letters, but alas, every answer was no.

A gust of wind shook the small cabin. Winter had come early.

In just a few days, November would be upon them.

If she didn't leave, that meant she'd have to stay all winter. Like this. Locked up in the cabin with no company.

Oh, in the beginning Captain Latham had stopped by every day, but she'd given excuse after excuse about how it didn't help his cause to be seen around the cabin. Eventually he stopped coming by.

Now she missed him. And the fact that it seemed like he cared. She'd always been a quiet sort, but she found herself aching for a companion. Someone to share her thoughts with. She'd never been one to need much company, and the realization startled her. And made her wish the captain would come back. She cared for him more than she had allowed herself to admit.

Papa and Sam were so tired whenever they came in that there wasn't much conversation. Other than talk of the fort. Which walls were progressing and how much longer before all the bastions were done.

She didn't want them feeling sorry for her, but what could be done? There was no other option for her other than to stay and wait for the fort to be finished.

She blew out a breath. Rejoice. Always. With joy inexpressible. She hadn't had much joy of late. Maybe she needed to read First Peter again.

Urgent pounding sounded at the door.

Esther jolted off her stool and put a hand to her chest. At the door she took a breath before opening it, praying that nothing had happened to Papa or Sam.

"Miss Howland? It's Captain Latham." His deep voice came through the heavy wood.

At the sound of it, her heart picked up its pace. She opened the door. "Yes? Is everything all right?"

"I am afraid Cook has died."

"Oh. I am most sorry to hear that." Cold air stung her cheeks, and she realized it was snowing. Quite abundantly.

"Might I speak to you inside?"

"Of course."

Once he was inside, he shook the snow from his clothes. "My apologies for muddying your floor, but I have an urgent request."

"Do not mind the floor." She couldn't keep her gaze from him. "What can I do for you?"

"The harbor is already iced over. We weren't expecting it this early in the winter, and it looks like there are storms coming our way. I know this has been very difficult for you, but I need to ask you to fill in for the cook. It will take weeks, possibly even months, before we can get a replacement, and there's no one else on the island even barely capable."

She couldn't help but stare at him and blink. Cook? For all the men? While it would be wonderful to get out of the cabin, it sounded like a daunting task. And she had no desire to listen to all the rumors start up again and face the nasty looks the men sent her way.

"I know what you are thinking, and I have already assembled and spoken to all the men. While there are a few who still believe you are part of their ridiculous curse, the rest have agreed to let their superstitions die. It seems they would rather eat than think you are bad luck."

"I see." The look in his eyes was different than what she'd seen before. "Does my father think it's a good idea?"

"Yes. He said you are a wonderful cook, and it would help the other men let go of their fears." His eyes had taken on a tender look. "I must admit that I have missed seeing you, Miss Howland."

The words made a blush rush up her neck. "I'd be happy to help you out, Captain Latham. Whatever I can do."

"Thank you." He went to open the door. "Supper has not yet been prepared, so. . ."

"You need me straightaway." She offered a slight smile.

"Yes. If you don't mind."

"Not at all, Captain." She headed to her bed. "Just let me fetch my cape."

She had a new spring in her step. No longer would she have to be cooped up in this little cabin. It didn't even matter that a few of the men still thought she was bad luck. She was needed, and she wouldn't have to be alone any longer.

The men were lined up for inspection before supper. The snow poured down on them so Christopher could barely see. But as soldiers they were trained to deal with the weather no matter what.

"I'll remind you men one last time that there will be no disrespect directed toward Miss Howland. As long as you want to be fed, you will keep this rule." He shot a glare at Sergeant Jones.

"Yes, sir!" Men shouted from their lines.

"Good. Let's eat."

He clasped his hands behind his back and watched the men traipse into the tent. It would be wonderful once the fort was finished and there was a roof over their heads, but until then, this would have to do.

Moving to the open flap of the tent, he watched the men as they went through the serving line.

Miss Howland smiled at each one, and he noticed that many of the men spoke to her. Her face never registered fear, embarrassment, or shock. That was good. Perhaps things could finally settle down.

As he continued to watch, Christopher had an odd sensation in his gut. He wanted Miss Howland to feel wanted and appreciated. And he knew that would be very difficult because the men had been quite ugly to her before. But she had agreed to stay and cook for them until a replacement could be found. That was a step in the right direction, was it not?

While the rest of the men were served, Christopher watched—guarded their new cook—and was ready to pounce as soon as he heard a negative word.

But nothing happened.

In fact, Miss Howland looked quite happy. The smile that lit up her face took his breath away.

"Captain?" Was she speaking to him?

"Pardon?" Getting his thoughts back in check, he stepped forward.

"Are you going to eat?"

"Oh yes. Most certainly. Thank you."

She ladled him a bowl of something creamy looking. A big whiff made his mouth water. "It smells delicious. What is it?"

"Potato soup." The grin she sent him made him want to keep it there forever. Her white cap covered her light brown hair while the blue of her dress brought out the color of her eyes. While he'd thought she was lovely before, there was something different now. And he couldn't put his finger on it.

He went to sit at his table, where Samuel and his son were sitting. "Good evening, gentlemen."

"Good evening." Samuel smiled. "It looks like Esther is doing well."

"Yes, it does." Christopher snuck another glance at her. Not seeing her for a couple of weeks had made him look at her differently. At first he'd thought it would be good to get his mind off the fact that he was drawn to her. But now? He wanted nothing more than to stare at her or go and talk to her. He needed to get his thoughts back in order. He was in command here. "How is the work coming?"

"This snow will slow us down." Sam shook his head. "I wasn't expecting it this early. Especially not in storms like this."

The elder Howland nodded. " 'Tis true. I haven't seen anything like this in many a year. It will make things more difficult."

"But it looks as though the bastions are all almost complete." Christopher offered a smile.

"Yes. Which is good. But I must admit, I was hoping for a bit more progress before the snow piled up." Samuel looked over to his daughter. "It's good to see her smiling. These past few weeks have been very hard on her."

"I'm sure they have." He didn't want to admit how difficult the weeks had been on him. He could only imagine how it had been for her, locked up in the cabin by herself.

Sam nudged him with an elbow.

Christopher blinked and turned his gaze to Miss Howland's brother.

His eyebrows raised and a small smile lifted the corners of his mouth.

Christopher was caught. Oh well, the younger Howland didn't seem to be bothered by it, so Christopher spooned some more soup into his mouth. He wasn't sure how she'd done it, but she'd creamed the potatoes perfectly into a thick and hearty soup. He knew it wasn't very exciting to cook for dozens of men with a limited amount of ingredients, but she had done it well. Several comments from the men around him proved that she was winning them over.

"Papa." Sam tapped his spoon on the table. "I wonder how much effort it would take to get one of the areas between the north and east bastion covered so that there would be a gathering place of sorts for the winter?"

Howland leaned back in his chair. "Hmm. . . We'd have to put off finishing the other two bastions for a time. Then there would be two more walls that would need to be built on the interior before we could put a roof on." The older man nodded. "But it could be done."

"Maybe we should focus on that with the way the weather has turned. It would help the men not catch their death of cold." Sam turned to him. "Captain, would that be acceptable to you?"

"It actually sounds warm at the moment, gentlemen, so yes, that is most acceptable." He finished off his soup. "And as long as the fort is done by next spring, I don't think anyone will complain about which parts get finished first. Especially if it would keep us all from freezing our toes off."

Chapter 9

By the middle of November, Esther's feet were numb most of the time. Not only were they cold, but being on her feet day in and day out had made them ache. Papa told her that morning, however, that they should be able to cook and eat in the new gathering room they'd built between the front bastions by tomorrow. The thought made her want to jump for joy, but she attempted to control herself as she served the men in line. The thought made her want to laugh. What would they do if she started jumping while she served them dinner?

Only three of the men still gave her disapproving looks. But even they couldn't keep her spirits down. The rest of the soldiers and officers spoke to her at every meal. Many complimented her cooking and told her that her sweet disposition lifted their spirits. And why had they ever believed the rumors? Their words did her heart a lot of good.

Lord, thank You for what You've done to change things around here. Thank You for the encouragement, because I know it's only because of You

*that I am receiving it. And thank You for Your provision. Even in the
storms and snow we can rejoice. Just like First Peter says.*

"Miss Howland?" The captain's voice made her open her eyes.

She blinked several times and remembered where she was. "My
apologies, Captain Latham. I was praying."

"Forgive me for intruding." A slight smile lifted the corners of
his mouth as he held his bowl aloft. It made him appear like a
young boy. Even though he definitely was not.

"My apologies." Her stomach did another little turn, as it did
every time she saw him of late. What was that all about? She wasn't
certain. But even with the busyness of their schedules, the highlight
of every day for her was seeing the captain's face.

Why was that?

She shook her head. The answer was all too clear. Probably not
a question she should even answer right now. When she'd come
to Castle Island, their initial acquaintance had not been a pleasant
one. Not because of him, but because of the horrid circumstances.
But somewhere along the line, things had changed.

"Would you care to sit with me by the fire?" The captain was
speaking to her again.

She looked around and saw that all of the men had been served.
It wouldn't hurt for her to get off her feet for a few minutes and eat
her supper. "That would be lovely."

He pulled up two stumps in front of the fire. "It's been quite
chilly of late."

"Yes, my feet haven't thawed out yet." Esther slipped her feet
closer to the fire. Cupping her bowl in her hands, she lifted it to
her face and let the steam fill her senses. Tonight was another fish
stew. A dish she was getter better at every day. At least the men
appreciated the way she tried to change it up. Not that any of them

would complain. The soldiers were looking all too skinny the last week. "Will supplies be coming anytime soon?" The last supply ship hadn't come because the harbor was frozen.

"I've been told they will come across the ice as soon as they know it's safe. But a skiff has to get close enough for them to attempt it. Too many deaths have occurred in the past when they've tried to venture across ice that wasn't solid." He took a bite of his stew. "This is delicious."

"I remember a little boy fell through the ice and died when I was young. It's made me scared of walking on ice ever since. I wouldn't want anyone risking their lives to bring us supplies." Although provisions were getting scarce. But how did she tell him that?

"I can't imagine that we have enough to see us through until spring."

She let out a breath, relieved that he'd brought it up. "No, I don't think we do. But I can get creative for a while. As long as the men don't mind eating a lot of the same thing over and over."

"You need to let me know when things are dire. Perhaps when we can get the message about needing a new cook to Boston, we can let them know about additional supplies as well."

"Have you ever been through a winter as harsh as this one here?"

"No. Not on the island." The captain looked at her intently. "Which I must admit worries me just a little. Especially since we don't have adequate shelter for everyone yet."

His answer made her pause. Would they be all right here? The island wasn't very protected. And it seemed that one storm after another had hit them. Sergeant Jones glared at her from across the tent. Thankfully, Captain Latham had been near every time the sergeant came through the line, but it didn't keep the angry man from giving her looks from time to time. "Captain Latham, might I change the subject for a moment?"

"Of course. Is something wrong?" He looked behind him.

She put her attention back on him. How much should she say? His eyes were kind and he waited patiently for her to speak. Best to be honest. "No. I don't think so. But Sergeant Jones makes me quite uncomfortable."

"Has he said something to you?" The captain straightened, and his congenial expression changed to one of fierce distaste.

"No. But he glares at me whenever he has the chance. His looks seem so. . .hateful."

He shook his head. "I'm sorry. I've written a letter to my superiors about the man's behavior. But nothing has left the island the past week because of the weather."

"Don't worry about it, Captain. I just need to ignore him. I'm sure he means no harm."

"Could we dispense with the 'Captain' title? When it's just you and me, I would prefer your calling me Christopher." His face softened.

She took a moment to glance around. That wouldn't be inappropriate, would it? "Thank you, Christopher."

"As for the sergeant, I will speak with him."

She put a hand on his arm. "No, please. I don't want to get him in any trouble. It will only cause him to despise me even more."

He looked down at her hand and then covered it with his own. "As long as you promise me that if you do not feel safe, you'll let me know."

"I promise." The heat from his hand warmed her whole arm. "And please, call me Esther."

Without the men supporting him and the curse, Steven found himself disliking Miss Howland even more. There had to be some way to get rid of her. If only he could turn the men against her again.

He'd had two allies. Now he was down to one. And he only had him because he'd threatened the young soldier. How had his plan fallen apart so fast? The disciplinary action against him had kept him so busy, he hadn't even had time to set up another "accident." He was too smart to ignore the curse. No man was safe. Why weren't the men more concerned?

They would be. As soon as people started dying. Which was inevitable with her here.

If only the colonel was in charge. He would get rid of the lady the minute he set foot on the island.

But what could Steven do now? Without any way to reach Boston safely, he was stuck with a woman on the island.

A woman who was destined to bring them nothing but trouble.

Chapter 10

*E*sther. . ." As her name rolled off his tongue, Christopher realized he'd longed to say it aloud for some time. The fire in the stone fireplace crackled and the glow from it lit her face.

"Yes?" Her sweet smile was back now that her gaze was off the sergeant.

He took in her features for several moments. The noise from around the room seemed to diminish, and he could *almost* imagine they were alone and not in the midst of dozens of other men. Her eyes held such intelligence, warmth, humor—light. They made him want to sit and gaze into them for hours. Her shy manners were for the most part gone now that they had spent a good deal of time together. Nevertheless, she was still often quiet. But he found that her silence was usually because she was observing others or thinking things through. He found it endearing. Just like everything else about her.

"Did you forget what you were going to say?" A slight teasing in her tone made him laugh at his own distraction.

"No. That is. . . Well, I have been wondering. . .how is it that you are not betrothed to anyone back in Boston?" The question was out, even though he knew it was entirely too forward. But he couldn't help it.

A blush crept up her cheeks. And then her smile turned sad. "Well, my mother became very ill a few years ago. I stayed by her side and did not have time for visitors or courtship. The young men—suitors—who were interested eventually gave up." She gave a little shrug.

"Then they were not worthy of you."

Esther dipped her chin. "That is very gallant of you to say, but everyone needed to go on with their lives. Even though my own felt like time stood still. Sickness and grief will do that."

She kept her eyes cast down.

A sign he'd made her uncomfortable. "Forgive me for being so forward."

Swiping at her skirt, she tilted her head. "The simple chitchat of society exhausts me. So I appreciate your forthrightness, as always. And I must admit it is nice to have someone to talk to. Most of my friends are all married and starting families. Papa and Sam are all I have, and the fort has consumed much of their time." Her gaze caught his. She studied him for several moments until her lips lifted in a slight grin, the hint of humor back in her eyes. "It seems only fair that I ask the same question of you. How is it that such an eligible gentleman is unmarried? I imagine most of your fellow officers are married?"

" 'Tis true. They are. Which has made it quite insufferable when I am around them." He shook his head as he laughed. "I jest. It brings me joy to be around families and children, but my service has kept me here."

"You have been on Castle Island for some time?"

He leaned back and let out a long sigh. "Indeed. I have been serving here on the island for several years, all in hopes of it one day being under my command. My focus has been here, with the protection of Boston and the soldiers' duties. That doesn't allow for much companionship. As you know, there aren't many ladies around to court."

"Yes, I can see that." Amusement filled her gaze. "Forgive me for asking, but I thought you *were* in command."

"Colonel Brown left me in command but will not be turning it over to me officially until the fort is complete. That's why I must oversee every aspect."

"Ah, I see."

He wanted to get back to the topic he'd initiated. As awkward and intimate as it was. "At nine and twenty, my dreams are to command, yes, but I admit I have longed to have a family. My service to the King has been important, and the colony must be protected." Would she understand his interest in pursuing her? His job and what it entailed for the future? How did one go about these things?

"From what I have witnessed, you are an impeccable leader, Captain Latham. . .I mean, Christopher." The pink rushed to her cheeks again.

He found it enchanting. "Thank you, milady." He bowed his head in a dramatic fashion. "I hope to one day be able to command *and* to have a family." He longed to say so much more to her, but social etiquette didn't allow for such. Especially since he'd already crossed the boundaries. *Lord, help me to do better. I find myself wanting to bare my heart to her, and patience is not my strongest suit. But I don't wish to scare her away.*

"I will pray for the Lord to bless you with both." She stared into the large fire and wrapped her arms around her waist. "Have you enjoyed the work you do?"

As much as he wanted to pursue the other conversation, this would have to do for now. Because at least he was getting time with her. "I have. And I do. Some days are better than others. When I really feel like I have accomplished something and the men are listening. Others. . . Well, I feel like I'm trying to get children to do the job of soldiers. Those days are not as enjoyable."

Her light laughter washed over him like a rain shower in spring. Lovely. He took in her form. Her slight frame was attractive. Especially when she wore her blue dress. Of course he liked her in the green one as well, but the blue was his favorite.

She tilted her head again in that very attractive way, her eyes studying him. "Is this what you want to do for the rest of your days?"

The question made him pause and think. While he wasn't getting any younger, he hadn't imagined doing anything else. "I enjoy it. But I also would like to make a greater impact for the Lord. I fear I have wasted much of my time already, but your father was reading to us from the book of John, and it inspired me to do more."

"John is one of my favorite books. Especially since it's by a fisherman. The everyday man and yet the disciple whom Jesus loved."

"Has there been any scripture that has been especially significant since you've been here?" He leaned in, wanting to hear her every word.

"First Peter has been the book that I turn to most." A smile lifted the corners of her mouth. "Although, the weeks I was by myself in the cabin, I read through the entire Word in less than a fortnight."

He laughed along with her. "You must have been very lonely. But that is a noble undertaking."

She shrugged. "I was. And I must apologize for turning you

away. I thought at the time that it was best."

"I missed you." Once again, his words were out before he even realized it. Watching her, he saw a bevy of emotions cross her face.

She tucked her chin and looked down at her hands. "I must admit, I missed you too." She cleared her throat. "But I kept returning to First Peter. Memorized the whole first chapter."

"Truly? That's a good deal of memorization. Why the first chapter?"

Lifting her chin, her eyes danced with delight. "Because I needed to remind myself constantly that I was supposed to be rejoicing. No matter the circumstance. Verse six actually makes me chuckle."

Curious. He furrowed his brow. "Why is that?"

"Because it says, '*Wherein ye greatly rejoice, though now for a season, if need be, ye are in heaviness through manifold temptations.*' I felt like Peter was writing that directly to me—though now for a season, *if* need be. As if he's saying that for a little while now, you—Esther—might need to go through this because you need to learn to be content and joyful. No matter what."

"Was that truly a struggle for you?"

"Indeed. Especially as the time alone increased and I was convinced that you would be swayed by what the men were saying. That thought was almost more than I could bear."

Leaning forward, he wanted to touch her, take her hand in his. But he couldn't. Not here. "That could never happen, Esther. Your faith and beauty shine. No rumors of a curse could ever change how I feel about you."

Chapter 11

*A*s the days faded one into another, Esther found herself longing to see Christopher every moment. But they had both been busy. As she'd been thinking about her feelings, her studies of ancient Roman poetry had come to mind. What had it said? *"Always toward absent lovers love's tide stronger flows."*

Warmth flooded her cheeks as she thought about it. But it was true. When they weren't together, she wanted nothing more than to see him again.

A large fire crackled in the stone fireplace Sam had built in the middle of what everyone called the gathering room. The chimney was at least two stories tall and made for quite an impressive sight. Pride filled Esther's chest. Her father and brother had done an excellent job. There was still much work to be done for the whole fort to be complete, but the winter wouldn't be so long with a place to assemble like this.

Soldiers were gathered, conversing, building chairs, or napping between watches. Since it was the only part of the building with a roof and a place for a fire, most of the men even slept the nights here. She couldn't blame them. At least they were dry and warm.

The past few weeks had been full. Learning to prepare enough food for each meal had been quite interesting. She hated to be wasteful but couldn't bear the thought of not having enough either. It had taken time, but she finally felt comfortable with the job.

Snowstorm after snowstorm had come through the bay. More snow than Esther had seen in her entire life. Half the men had been tasked with shoveling snow each day, while the other half continued the slow and steady work on the walls of the fort. Not a ship had been seen for weeks. That was a good thing, for whenever a ship came into the area, everyone was nervous until the passengers' motives were clear.

That was the job of Castle Island after all—to protect the city of Boston. But even though they all understood that, it was still unsettling. Even a bit scary.

Her feet ached tonight. It was probably time for a new pair of shoes, but she hadn't even thought of that before coming to the island. She'd just have to make do with these through the winter.

Christopher normally came and sat with her each night after supper. Their conversations had started out light and friendly, but after he'd asked her why she wasn't betrothed, things had gone deeper between them. In an exciting way—at least for her. The past couple of nights they'd talked about his family, and she'd told him more about her mother. It had been nice to share with someone from her heart, for that was something she hadn't been able to do for a long time.

But tonight he hadn't come to supper, and he wasn't in the gathering room. Could something have happened to him?

Scanning the room, she checked all the faces. Granted, there were a few men out on watch, but she'd gotten pretty good at recognizing them all. Other than Christopher, there seemed to be several other men absent.

Maybe he had some special training mission for them?

"How's my little sister doing?" The sound of Sam's voice instantly brought a smile to her face.

"Other than my feet hurting, I'm doing quite well. Thank you for asking. How about you? I can't believe how much work you've accomplished on the walls in the midst of all the snow!"

"Every bone in my body seems to ache. But I see Papa continuing on without complaint, so I know that I should as well."

"You don't think he's working too hard, do you?" Their father had always seemed invincible in her mind, but he'd seemed to age after Mother's passing.

"I *know* he's working too hard. But we all are." Sam shrugged. "Where's the captain? I've noticed he normally talks with you in the evenings."

"I'm not sure where he is tonight." Recently she'd begun to think that perhaps she cared for Christopher as more than just a friend. She longed to share that with Sam, but would he approve? What if he teased her? He'd been known to tease her mercilessly when they were younger. Especially when it came to boys. Best to change the subject. "Do you know where Papa is?"

"He's over there with a few of the men. He's been meeting with them for a few nights, talking about scripture and God."

"You don't sound too excited about it." She lowered her brows.

"Some of these men are pretty superstitious. The things they've been taught are a bit scary."

"What do you mean?"

"I've heard some of them talk about sacrificing animals and

chanting incantations. Or visiting witches." Sam looked at her wide-eyed. "I'm sorry, Esther. I never should have mentioned that to you."

She swallowed back her discomfort. "That's all right. I shouldn't have asked." No wonder the men had gotten so caught up in the superstition of the curse.

Christopher's red coat caught her attention from across the room. A smile filled his face. "I have good news." He bowed as he approached. "A skiff made it through this afternoon. We have some supplies, and they took word back to Boston that we need another cook." He sat on the floor by the fire and swiped the snow off his coat. "They won't be trying to return here anytime soon though. Not with the weather the way it's been. The poor fellows couldn't unload fast enough so they could row back while it was still light."

"I can imagine." Sam leaned forward. "Was there any news?"

"None of import." Christopher looked back to her. "But there were ten crates full of supplies. It took us many trips to haul it up here—the skiff could only make it out to about a hundred yards off the point, so we had to be cautious of thin ice. And the crates are heavy."

"Can we go see them now?" Excitement filled her stomach.

"Now?" Christopher blinked at her.

"Is that too much trouble?"

"Not at all." A smile made lines at the corners of his eyes appear. "What's a little more snow?"

Christopher pried open another crate and watched Esther "ooh" and "aah" over everything. She acted like each item, from potatoes to sacks of grain, was the greatest of gifts.

She held up a large sack of potatoes and examined it.

"What exactly are you looking for?"

"Nothing. I just had an idea." Her brows knit together.

Christopher crossed his arms over his chest. "An idea about potatoes?" It made him chuckle. "Of course, if the idea is as good as your potato soup, then I shouldn't tease."

"Thank you, kind sir." She analyzed the sack again and then put it back. "If only we had some goose feathers."

Now he was really puzzled. "Goose feathers?" What could she make that would be edible out of goose feathers and potatoes?

"Yes." She looked at his face and started to laugh. "Not to eat, Captain Latham." Shaking her head, she waved a hand at him. "Honestly." She looked at all the crates and pointed to each bag. "There's at least one hundred sacks here. Potatoes and grains."

"Is that not enough to get us through the winter?"

Tilting her head back and forth, she mumbled for a moment. "I'm not sure. These supplies added to what we have will take us a long way. But I'm not thinking about that. I'm thinking about cushions."

"Cushions." From potatoes to cushions. Now he was really confused.

"Yes. You know, the kind you sit on?"

He raised his eyebrows.

"These sacks?" She pointed. "I was looking for a way to do something nice for the men. I can make cushions out of them. That's why I said it would be nice to have goose feathers." She placed her hands on her hips and twisted her mouth to the side. "But maybe I can stuff them with grass or something else. It will still make a comfortable cushion, wouldn't you agree?"

"A flock of geese is on the island right now, Miss Howland."

Her eyes widened. "Don't tease."

"I'm serious, Esther. They flew in today. Probably starting their journey south a bit late, or perhaps they got caught in one of the storms and it blew them east. But they're here. I saw them when we were bringing the crates up."

"Roasted goose would be awfully tasty, wouldn't you agree?" Her sly grin tugged at his heart.

At that moment he would have agreed to do just about anything to keep a smile on her face.

Including hunting geese.

Chapter 12

There's got to be a way to catch them without scaring them all off with the blast of a gun." Christopher lay on his stomach in the snow and looked to John, his lieutenant. "Even if we were to hit one, a single bird isn't going to feed all the men."

"You're right. But what other choice do we have? I've never heard of setting traps for geese." John laughed at his own joke.

But it made Christopher think. "You've given me a great idea."

"Oh? Do tell."

"A fishing net. We have lots of those. What if we were to spread one out. But we need more hands. Then if we move real slow, we can sneak up on them and throw the net over them."

John shook his head. "Well, it's worth a try. But we'd better get moving while they are still asleep. The sun will be up soon enough."

In less than twenty minutes, they were back and ready to ambush the flock. The temperatures had dipped so low that the geese were tucked all together. Might even be a bit frozen? He prayed it would slow the birds down. With the net spread wide, it appeared that it would cover all the makeshift nests. That is, if they could get it over them without the geese knowing. That would be the trick.

Christopher held up one finger. Then two. Then three. They rushed as quietly as they could and spread the net over the sleeping geese.

A few not quite under the net honked and flew away. But Christopher was surprised. They had almost an entire flock of geese within a fishing net. The cold temperatures had definitely helped, but as soon as the birds realized they were trapped, the commotion grew. Flapping of wings. Honking and screeching. Several birds tried to take off.

"What now?" John shouted as the eight men held down corners of the net.

"I have no idea."

Two hours later, they carried a net full of unmoving geese back to the fort. Several of the soldiers gave them odd looks, but no one said a word.

One look at John and the rest of the men told Christopher that he probably looked just as bad if not worse. His lieutenant was covered in mud and feathers, and his periwig was askew. Their little adventure hunting geese had turned out prosperous but not pretty.

Somewhere in the snow, Christopher had lost his own periwig. His hair was probably a matted mess, but he didn't care. He'd send out one of the men to fetch it later, but at the moment all he wanted was to deliver the geese to Esther and then go take a long nap.

Their arrival caused quite a bit of commotion, because every soldier stopped what he was doing to watch them pass.

By the time they reached the large gathering room, Esther had come out to greet them, her white apron looking crisp and clean in the sunlight, her eyes wide as saucers.

"Your geese, milady." Christopher bowed deeply. "Just as you requested."

Her jaw dropped as they deposited the large net at her feet. Then she started to laugh a light, bell-like laugh that made him want to join in.

Too exhausted from the battle with the birds to appreciate the moment, Christopher bowed again and waved his hand. "I'm looking forward to roast goose for dinner."

It took the entire day for Esther and her helpers to pluck and clean all the geese. They'd brought her more than seventy-five! How they managed to kill that many baffled her, but she refused to ask. Especially after the way Christopher had deposited them this morning. The look on his face told it all. He'd gotten in over his head but still accomplished the request.

But what she'd enjoyed the most was seeing him without his wig on. His dark hair was matted and poked up in different directions, but it made him look so much younger. And more handsome—if that was even possible.

The fact that he'd gone to hunt the geese because of her made her heart pound. After all these weeks together at the fort, she had to admit that she admired him very much. But what if he didn't care for her in the same way?

Perhaps he only treated her with care because she was the only woman around.

It was all too much to think about. Especially without Mother to guide her. Esther didn't have any experience with relationships.

Maybe she just needed to wait and see what he did next. Their friendship had grown as they'd talked with each other in the evenings. There was no need to rush anything, but her heart wanted nothing more than to give itself away to one Captain Christopher Latham.

She shook her head and focused on the task at hand. At this rate, she'd be roasting the geese for the next few days. But the men would surely enjoy the change of fare.

And wouldn't they be surprised when she gave them the cushions? She could hardly wait to get started. But first she had to find a place to store all the grain and potatoes. Then she actually had to make the cushions. She'd dragged the goose feathers by the potato sackful back to the cabin, filling every inch of wall space they had. She'd have to clean them and trim them before they could be stuffed into the cushions, but it would take her awhile to sew the sacks into covers anyway. She had plenty to keep her busy in the evenings for the next few weeks. Surely Papa and Sam could manage with a cabin filled with feathers and cushions for a bit. They were hardly there except to sleep anyway. And perhaps it would help keep the cabin warmer. With a shrug, she debated about when to give the men their gifts. Perhaps for the new year? That would be a nice surprise. But she'd have to get Papa and Sam to keep her secret. Sam in particular was horrible at keeping surprises a secret for very long.

She tapped a finger to her chin and surveyed the room. If she worked on one a night, she wouldn't make it by the New Year. Could she manage two?

Could it be true? December was upon them?

That thought made her smile even more. Winter was such a wonderful season. Her favorite. But here on the island it had been a bit dreadful. Especially with all the storms they'd had, the snow mounding up, and the men not being able to leave and see family.

Surely there was something they could do to make it special for the men since they would be separated from the mainland for the duration of winter. What if she planned a special meal to celebrate the new year and gave them all their cushions as a gift? That might be just the trick to boost spirits.

With new determination and delight putting a spring in her step, she set back out to check on the meal. When the last of the first dozen geese was roasted, she rang the bell for supper. Men scurried in from every corner.

"We've been smelling it all afternoon, Miss Howland." Peter looked at her with a big grin. "I can't wait to taste it." He licked his lips.

Every man that came through the line commented on the delicious smells and thanked her for all her hard work to bring them tasty meals. The more compliments they gave, the more her heart soared. Maybe she'd won them over after all.

Even Sergeant Jones, who never had a kind word or expression for her, mumbled a brief thank-you for the first time ever as he came through the serving line.

His acknowledgment almost made her fall over.

Papa, Sam, and Christopher brought up the rear of the line.

"It smells absolutely divine, Daughter." Papa winked at her. "I heard it was quite an adventure acquiring the geese." He looked back at the captain.

Christopher smiled, his periwig back in place and his coat looking clean and new. "It will be my secret that I shall take to my grave. But when Miss Howland made the request, how could I deny her?" He sent a long look to her.

She couldn't look away. Something in his eyes told her what she yearned to hear.

"Well, the men thank you, Sis, or Captain Latham, whoever is responsible for such a fine meal." Sam held his plate up to his nose and took a big whiff. "I shall sleep well tonight with a belly full of roast goose!"

Several of the men cheered.

Christopher leaned a bit closer as she filled his plate. "It seems the geese are winning you even more friends."

"I hope so. I'd hate to think that after all this they would imagine I was still bad luck."

As they sat by the fire in the gathering room, Esther noticed that more and more men gathered each night around her father. He'd told her that all he was doing was sharing the scriptures with them in the simplest way he knew how. The exciting thing was that the men were listening. Asking questions.

Just the night before, she'd encouraged Papa by telling him that he was fulfilling the part at the end of Matthew 28 where Jesus had commanded his disciples to go and teach all nations. By teaching those around him, Papa was doing exactly that.

She was proud that Papa had such a knack for explaining the scriptures.

"Your father is doing a very good work." Christopher's voice pulled her gaze up to his face while she stitched the edge of a potato sack.

"Isn't the fort coming along nicely?" She took a glance around.

"No. I mean, yes, the fort is looking great. But I was talking about what he's doing with those soldiers. They needed someone to look up to, someone they could trust and ask questions of. It's hard when I'm their commanding officer. Some of them don't feel like they can approach me like that. But with your father here, they have their own father figure, someone they look up to but who isn't their commander."

She hadn't thought of it that way. "The good Lord is so gracious to supply all our needs. Even if it's in the shape of a stonemason instead of a preacher."

"Or the stonemason's beautiful daughter."

His words touched a place deep in her heart. Never had a man, other than her own father, told her she was beautiful. As she looked into Christopher's eyes, she wished she understood all that his eyes were saying. But it was enough to hear those words from him. She heard the beating of her heart in her ears and felt heat rush to her face. "Thank you."

"I've been wanting to tell you that for some time now." His eyes went back to the fire. "But I always seem to get nervous before I can say it."

Her mouth went dry and she pushed the needle and thread through the seam faster.

"Perhaps. . .I could ask your father about the proper way to court you?"

Chapter 13

The next day flew by as the skies cleared and the sun warmed their backs. Not wanting to waste the good weather, Christopher ordered all the men to work on the walls while they had the chance. Only two were left on watch. All others changed duties to help with the construction.

Esther's father smiled to have so many willing workers and busy hands. The past few weeks had been difficult on them all. Especially when the men complained of frozen fingers and toes. The cold had slowed their progress considerably.

As Christopher watched their stonemasons at work, he thanked the Lord for giving them such a fine day. Perhaps it would keep Mr. Howland in a good mood for when Christopher wanted to ask to court Esther.

But as the day went by, he found himself pulled in many different directions. Every time he headed toward Samuel, someone would interrupt needing his attention.

Christopher finished up with his lieutenant, straightened his coat, and determined that this time nothing would stop him from speaking with Esther's father. But as he got closer, doubts filled his mind. What if Mr. Howland didn't think that being a captain's wife was a good thing for his daughter? What if he didn't want her living on the island permanently and away from her family? What if he didn't approve?

Swallowing his fears, he shook his head. The clanking of the tools against rock filled his ears. It was a sound he'd gotten used to of late. The scent of roasted goose floated over to him. It would be fine to eat such a nice meal again. Esther had once again done a wonderful job.

His mouth watered just thinking about it.

And then he was only steps away.

Samuel Howland instructed one of the men to set a rock in the pulley system so it could be hefted up to the men above.

This was the time. Deep breath. "Mr. Howland, might I have a word?"

"Of course, Captain." The older man smiled. "Let me ensure this stone gets placed correctly, and I'll be right with you."

Christopher nodded and clasped his hands behind his back. Taking a few steps away, he thought about what he was going to say. And yet everything he'd rehearsed before disappeared. His mind had gone blank.

"How can I be of service?" Mr. Howland's voice made Christopher turn around.

"Sir, it is I who wish to be of service to you."

"Oh?"

"I find myself. . . That is to say. . . I would like ask your permission. . ."

Samuel lifted his brows. "Yes?"

"To court your daughter."

The older man's eyes sparkled. He pointed a finger at Christopher. "I was wondering if you had begun to fancy her. She's lovely, isn't she?"

"Yes, sir. I know this is a bit unorthodox, since she is the only lady on the island and it's not exactly as proper society would have it, but I wanted you to know I am in earnest."

Samuel put a hand on Christopher's shoulder. "I would be honored, Captain Latham."

"Thank you, sir."

"You're a fine man. Will you continue with your duties in service to the King if you marry?"

"I was planning to, sir. Are you in agreement with that?"

"Of course. What you do is of the highest integrity and import. But it will take some time adjusting to the idea of being separated from Esther. That is, if you remain on Castle Island. With the loss of her mother—God rest her soul—still quite recent, I hadn't put thought into her moving away where I wouldn't see her."

Christopher had feared as much. "I assure you that we would make the effort to visit Boston often." Was it too presumptuous even to be speaking of such things?

"There's plenty of time for us to discuss these things. I can see by the look on your face that I've overwhelmed you." Samuel chuckled. "I remember all too well speaking to my sweet wife's father. I was a jumble of nerves."

Even as the captain and commander of the troops on the island, he had to admit that he'd been nervous. More nervous about this conversation than anything else in recent months. "Thank you, sir. Do you mind if I speak with your daughter this evening?"

"Be my guest. You have my approval."

Esther's eyes roamed the room. She couldn't help it. All day she'd longed to hear if Christopher had spoken to Papa. And she hadn't seen Christopher since luncheon. The wait was doing funny things to her insides.

The roasted geese were out for supper again. This batch had been roasting all day, and she loved the aroma. The men were all smiles as they came through the serving line. Probably some because of the warmer weather and sunshine, but most had nothing but wonderful things to say about her food. And that boosted her spirits even more.

Now, if only she could speak to Christopher, her heart might calm down and settle into a slower rhythm. Theirs had been a friendship that was quite uncommon. Simple moments talking together. Sharing by the fire. It wasn't how it would be done in Boston, but what did that matter? It was natural and real. And that was what she loved.

Lively chatter filled the large room. More chairs had been assembled each day, so fewer men had to sit on stumps, rocks, or the hard floor. It really was looking more and more like a fort every day.

As horrible as life had been the first few weeks here, now it was difficult to think about leaving. And the more progress that was made on the fort, the sooner that would be.

Her heart sank with the thought. She still had many months left, best to focus on that.

"Good evening, Miss Howland." The familiar voice brought her head up. Christopher.

Allowing a smile to fill her face, she gave a tiny curtsy. "Good evening, Captain Latham. How was your day?"

"Quite full. Much better now that I get to see you."

She felt a blush rise up her neck.

"Could we perhaps sit by the fire and talk?"

"I would love that." Even though that's what they did almost every evening, she had a feeling that tonight would be different.

"I'll have a chair waiting for you."

"Thank—"

Boom!

The sound of the cannon firing made the entire room go silent.

Christopher dropped his plate on the table in front of her and ran out of the room followed by several of his men.

If the watch had fired a cannon, that must mean that a ship they didn't recognize was getting close.

Boom!

Another round.

Esther stood behind the table and closed her eyes. *Lord, please let it be a friendly ship. Please let them raise their flag.*

She repeated the prayer over and over. No one would be prepared for an attack in the middle of winter. Who would be bold enough to mount one?

Although Boston was a prime settlement in the harbor, another country wouldn't come against England's territories—would they?

Boom!

With every fire of the cannon, Esther felt her nerves tighten. Did they even have adequate shelter here if an incoming ship attacked? The island was out in the open, its sole purpose to guard and protect Boston. But who would protect *them*?

When she looked around the room, she noticed almost all of the men had left the gathering room, except for a few that stood guard at the doors, muskets at the ready.

Papa strode toward her. "I'm sorry I wasn't in here when they fired. I was still working on the west wall. Are you all right? Your face is white as a sheet." He took her elbows in his hands.

"Yes, I'm fine. I just wasn't expecting it." She wiped her hands on her apron. "I'm sure it's just a precaution." Deep breath. "Would you like something to eat?"

Boom! Crash!

This time, it wasn't their cannon firing. A ship was firing on them!

Papa grabbed her arm and dragged her over to the corner. "Sit here." Then he covered her with his body, sheltering her. "We're under attack!"

Chapter 14

Something warm trickled down the side of Christopher's face. He'd barely missed getting crushed by the wall that had fallen from the blast. He reached up his hand and then pulled it away to see red. Blood.

Looking around him, he didn't see any prone forms. "Is everyone all right? Sound off in your ranks!"

"All here, Captain!"

"Aye, all here as well!"

"Here!"

Voices sounded from all around him, some weaker than others. Some full of fear.

An eerie silence surrounded them. The ship had only fired once. What could that mean?

"Should I fire again, Cap'n?" The voice called down from the bastion that housed the forward cannon.

Christopher held up his hand. "Not yet." Not until he understood what they were facing. "But ready all the cannon."

"Yes, sir."

Standing up from his crouched position, he held out his hand to John. "The glass, please."

"Here, sir."

The cool of the metal hit his hand. Christopher extended the glass and peered through. It took him a moment to focus in the dark, but he saw figures scrambling to the mast. A flag was going up.

The French!

His heart pounded. Why would they attack? Were there more ships coming? It didn't appear to be a ship of war—

Then a man at the bow jumped up and down, his arms frantically waving two white flags. What?

"John, they're waving white flags. It's the French."

"What do you think it means, sir?"

"I'm not sure. Why would they fire on us and then wave a white flag?"

"Should I light the torch to acknowledge?"

Christopher put the eyeglass down for a moment. Was it some sort of trap? His mind spun. As commander, he was responsible for all the souls not only on the island but in Boston as well. If he chose wrong, there could be dire consequences. Raising the glass back up to his eye, he watched the ship lay anchor.

"Light the torch."

"Yes, sir."

Once the torch was lit and waved, Christopher watched the ship closely. Several men got into a skiff. After several moments passed, they began to row toward shore.

"Lieutenant!"

"Yes, Captain?"

"Prepare a welcome party at the shore. Muskets at the ready."

"Yes, sir."

Peter ran into the gathering room and shouted, "It's the French! They fired upon us and then waved a white flag. They're coming to shore!" Then he ran out.

Papa lifted her to her feet. "Perhaps it would be safer for you back at our cabin. I wouldn't want them to know a woman is here. In case they are unsavory. . .or hostile."

Hostile? This couldn't be happening. *Oh Lord, save us!*

Sergeant Jones stomped toward them. "It's the curse, I tell you." His voice rose in volume. Then he pointed at Esther and yelled, "All because we have a woman here."

"Utter nonsense." Papa shook his head and then turned back to her. "Ignore him, Esther. Let's get you to the cabin."

Her head bobbed up and down, but not because she wanted it to. Merely in habitual response to Papa's instructions. Her mind wasn't on her own safety but on a certain gentleman who would surely be at the forefront of it all.

What was happening? Why would the French fire on them and then wave a white flag?

In the cover of darkness, they scurried to their little cabin. Her feet felt like they were plodding along, as if ten stones were strapped to them, weighing them down. They entered the cold cabin and nothing seemed right. Like the world had tilted and she was upside down.

A shiver raced up her spine. Blinking away the strangeness of the moment, she stoked the fire and wrapped a blanket around her shoulders. Was Christopher all right? What if he was hurt?

"I'm going to go find your brother. Stay here. Understood?"

"Yes, Papa." She stared into the flames.

What had started out as a beautiful day had crumbled before her. She'd been so excited to see Christopher, to hear if he'd spoken to Papa. Thoughts of the future had scrolled through her mind like a dream. This was what all her friends had spoken of. The joy of courtship. The knowledge of a future with a gentleman.

But what if the men were correct? What if she was bad luck and this was all her fault?

What if there would be no future for her and Captain Latham?

"Captain, I demand to speak with you!" Steven wasn't going to hold his tongue any longer.

"Sergeant, I'm a bit busy at the moment." The captain didn't even look at him. He just watched the skiff as it rowed toward the shore.

"This is all because of Miss Howland, and you know it. She's bad luck! The curse is upon us. The French are going to attack. Why are you allowing them ashore? Please, I beg you to listen."

"Your superstitions are unfounded, Sergeant Jones, and I must insist that—"

"If you won't listen to me, then I will take care of this myself." Imbeciles. If they couldn't see the writing on the wall, then he would have to save them. Steven grabbed a musket another soldier had just loaded and aimed it at the skiff.

"Stop him!" The captain yelled.

But the words didn't deter him. He focused. Took a breath. . .

Oomph!

Three soldiers tackled him. He tried to fire but couldn't. They were too strong. "This is insanity! You'll be the death of us all!"

Chapter 15

*M*ake sure they are good and tight." Christopher looked at John as his lieutenant tied Steven's hands and feet. "Remove him from the premises. I don't want to start a war because one man is out of his mind."

Steven spit at the ground. "You, sir, are the one who's out of his mind."

"Gag him while you're at it!" Christopher commanded and then turned back to watch the Frenchmen's progress. The skiff was close to shore. This was no time to take risks. If the French saw a rogue officer attempting to fire at them, it could be disastrous for them all.

"With me, the rest of you." Christopher headed down to the shore to greet the boat.

Much to his surprise, it appeared to be the captain of the ship at the bow. As his men dragged the boat to shore, the French captain kept a stern face.

Then he stepped out and walked toward them. "Are you

the commander of the fort?" The man's English was good even though his accent was thick.

It brought a great deal of relief to Christopher. His French was quite unpracticed. "I am." He held out a hand in greeting. "Captain Latham."

"Captain Fontaine." They shook hands. "My deepest apologies, Captain. It appears one of my men was nervous and accidentally fired on the fort." He dipped his chin. The pride on his face was evident, but the humility of their circumstances became all too apparent. "The lack of food has made many of the men delirious and weak. We are not here as enemies."

Christopher took in the sight of the men before him. While they held themselves up in posture, it was easy to see they were malnourished. "I am grateful to hear that, Captain Fontaine, but sorry for your situation. How can we help?"

"We are in great need of supplies."

Starvation made men desperate. Is that why the captain came? "I can send word to Boston tomorrow morning." Christopher held his ground, showing the French captain that it would be unwise to raid their camp. "But I can have food brought to your men tonight."

The man's face relaxed. "We would be in your debt."

Christopher nodded. "My men will stay with you here at shore, and I will make the arrangements." He turned to his men, "Light a fire. Keep our guests warm."

"*Merci beaucoup*, Captain Latham." The man practically wilted to a sitting position on a rock. His men followed suit.

As he took long strides back to the fort, Christopher allowed himself to relax a bit. The French didn't have enough strength to do anything, no matter how desperate they might be. As long as his men kept their guard up and sent food with them back to the ship, all should be well. His thoughts returned to Esther. What a relief. He hadn't realized how much he'd worried about her safety until it was all over.

He was met in the gathering room by a group of soldiers.

"Is it true, Cap'n? Have the French attacked?"

"It's all because of the lady, isn't it?"

"We should have listened to Sergeant Jones!"

Questions flew at him from every side. He lowered his brows. "No. The French have not attacked. It was an accidental firing. Their men are malnourished and half-crazed because of it."

"So we're not at war?" Robert's face looked pained.

"No. We most certainly are not at war. And there is *no* curse." He stomped over to the table where Esther had been serving their food. "Where is Miss Howland?"

"I took her to our cabin, Captain." Samuel walked up to him. "How can I help?"

"We need to get some food ready to take to the waiting ship. It appears they have been without sustenance for some time. Tomorrow I'll have to send word for supplies to be purchased from Boston."

"Sam and I can get the food together right now." Esther's father nodded to him.

"Thank you." Christopher turned on his heel to find Peter in front of him.

"Captain, I need to speak with you."

"Go on. But make it quick."

The young soldier cleared his throat. " 'Twas the sergeant, sir."

"What has he done now?"

"He's gone mad. Says that since we're not paying attention to the curse, he hopes that we all die because of it."

Christopher shook his head. "I am afraid I do not understand."

"He caused all the accidents. All of 'em. Once Miss Howland arrived."

Another soldier approached, his hat in his hands, head bowed. Face crimson. He raised a hand. "I can attest that the sergeant set up all the mishaps, Cap'n. He wanted to prove to you that the lady was bad luck."

"How do you know this?" Christopher's ire grew.

"Because I helped him, sir. But only for a little bit. . . Then I told him he had to tell the truth and I wouldn't help him no more. I'm sorry, sir."

Christopher glanced back to the soldiers guarding Sergeant Jones. To imagine that all the upheaval, all the rumors, all the accidents had been instigated by one man made his chest tighten with anger. And then his anger turned to pity. Such a shame. The man would face dire consequences when he was taken to Boston. And once Colonel Brown heard, there were sure to be more repercussions. Christopher wouldn't want to be in the sergeant's place for anything.

But now? Now he could put all the rumors of a curse to rest. The men would finally be able to see the truth and prayerfully put their superstitious natures behind them. Especially since Mr. Howland was doing such an outstanding job teaching them in the evenings. The Lord was doing a mighty work in their little fort.

These realizations spurred Christopher on, and he was filled with new purpose. He saw a way to serve God and do his job well all at the same time. And he wanted nothing more than to share all this with Esther.

His mind put aside everything else as he looked to Esther's

father. "Would you meet me at the shore in about twenty minutes? There's someone I need to speak to."

A grin split Samuel's face. "Yes, sir. I'm sure she'll be glad to see you."

Esther paced in front of the fire. The fort had been quiet for a long time. Too quiet. But she couldn't risk leaving the cabin. At least not yet. Papa said he'd come back and let her know what was going on as soon as he could. But she couldn't seem to stop worrying about Christopher. What if something happened to him? She hadn't even told him anything about how she felt. What if he was killed? The thought of losing him before he knew what their friendship had come to mean to her. . .

All these years she'd been quiet. Kept to herself. Shared her feelings with no one since Mama died. And yet she'd begun to feel different these past few weeks. Like she was a flower beginning to bloom for the first time. Oh, she would probably still be quiet and observing, but she felt complete for the first time in a long time. What did it all mean?

Her closest friends were married. Most of them hadn't known their husbands very well before their unions. The shy and tentative expressions on their faces had changed after time though. Esther often found herself longing to know what the secret looks exchanged between husband and wife meant. How they could communicate by just connecting gazes.

If only Mother were still alive. There were so many things she wished she could discuss. So many questions. So many feelings.

Tap, tap!

Was that a knock? She went to the door.

"Miss Howland. . .Esther? I didn't want to scare you. It's me, Christopher."

Joy rushed through every bone in her body. She yanked open the door. "I'm so glad to see you!" She wrapped her arms around him. As soon as she felt his warmth against her, she realized what she'd done. "Goodness. I'm sorry." She pulled back, and heat rushed up her neck.

"That's quite all right. I enjoyed it." A roguish grin filled his face. He took off his hat and stepped over the threshold. "I need to get back down to the shore, but I couldn't wait to see you."

"Is everything all right?"

"Yes. It's a French ship, and they accidentally fired. The captain is waiting for me at the shore. I don't think his men have eaten for several days, so I offered them some of your good food."

"I am glad I roasted the rest of the geese today." She went to grab her apron. "Do you need my assistance?"

He held out a hand to stop her. Then he set his hat on the table and stepped toward her, reaching for her hands. As he wrapped her hands in his, a shiver raced up her arms.

"Your father and brother are taking care of it. I just couldn't go another minute without speaking to you."

"Oh?" Her voice cracked.

"Yes," He cleared his throat. "I have wanted to express to you my feelings."

She offered him a smile while her heart pounded in her chest.

"My intention was to court you and see the fort finished. . . I even asked for your father's permission today, but. . ."

"But?" Her heart raced.

"I don't want to do that anymore."

The abrupt sinking of her heart felt like it hit her shoes. "Oh. . ."

She pulled her hands away.

"No. That is not what I meant." He took her hands again. "Forgive me for fumbling with my words. What I meant to say is that I do not wish to wait. Would you consider marrying me now? Without a courtship?"

All the air left her lungs. She blinked several times to see if she was dreaming. Had he really just said what she thought she heard?

"My apologies, Esther. Is that inappropriate?" His eyes searched hers.

Esther took a deep breath and found her tongue. "No. It took me by surprise." This man before her. The handsome captain. The man she. . .loved.

It didn't matter that they hadn't courted. It didn't matter that there weren't any parties or get-togethers with family. She'd spent hours with this man talking, laughing, and enjoying each other's company.

"Well?"

Her stomach flipped. She swallowed. "Yes. I would be honored to be your wife, Captain Latham, and be at your side for the rest of my life. That is, as long as you speak with my father."

"I will love you with everything that is within me. I promise." Taking a step closer, his breath fanned her face. "I will speak to your father immediately. Even though there is much we do not know about one another, I do love you, Esther."

"And I, you."

Christopher reached up a hand and cupped her cheek. "I want to spend the rest of my days getting to know every thought that goes through that mind of yours."

Another shiver raced up her arms. She placed her hand over his.

Then his lips met hers in the tenderest kiss. A kiss that promised a future and ignited a passion within her breast that she'd never known could exist.

His arms wrapped around her waist, and he pulled her closer. The embers within her heart fanned into a flame of faith, hope, and love.

Let the French wait. This was where she wanted to be. Forever.

Kimberley Woodhouse is an award-winning and bestselling author of more than twenty fiction and nonfiction books. A popular speaker and teacher, she has shared her theme of "Joy through Trials" with more than half a million people across the country at more than two thousand events. Kim and her husband of twenty-five-plus years have two adult children. She's passionate about music and Bible study and loves the gift of story.

You can connect with Kimberley at www.kimberleywoodhouse.com and www.facebook.com/KimberleyWoodhouseAuthor.

A Treaty of Tulips

by Angie Dicken

Dedication

*To the men and women of Meredith Drive Reformed Church—
You not only inspired me to explore the history of Dutch settlers
in our country, but mostly, you have shared with me the richness
of Christ's love with open arms and abundant hope.
I am thankful to call you my church family!*

Dear Reader,

This story begins when the British Fort Burnet is under expansion during the fur trade of 1741. Eventually, the fort's location is moved to the eastern side of the Oswego river and named Fort Ontario, a beautiful fort that remains today.

Research for *A Treaty of Tulips* gave me a deep appreciation for the rich culture and customs of the Iroquois, as well as the bravery of many European settlers who explored the land peacefully. My most valuable sources of research were actual journal entries and letters from officers and visitors to the area during the same time period.

I delved into the words of men whose matters included French and British arguments over trade routes, their alliances with natives, and attempted plots to thwart peaceful relationships. Yet, as with any conflict, I was pleased to hear of men who wanted nothing but to show respect to the natives, and natives who wanted nothing less than peace among men.

I hope you enjoy Sabine and Jacob's story on the shores of Lake Ontario. Be sure to connect with me at my website www.angiedicken.com.

Sincerely,
Angie Dicken

Chapter 1

Fort Burnet, Oswego
Fall 1740

$\int$ abine clutched the feathered tick beneath her, begging the pounding in her ears to still so she could listen. Her slumber had been interrupted by a loud clap of thunder, and this past hour she'd tossed about, trying to sleep again. Rain never fell after the sky drummed. Now an unnatural disturbance sounded on the nearby Oswego River.

Holding her breath, she waited. No moon shone tonight, and darkness was thick in her corner of the house. Ears strained, she disregarded the soft snores of Papa and the gentle breaths of her sleeping mother, trying to hear beyond the wall of timber. Again—a splash and a rumble of voices. She thrust herself up and tiptoed blindly to the door, avoiding Moeder's loom to her right and the board table to her left. A distant yell had her freeze at the door handle. Frantically searching along the wall with trembling fingers, Sabine at last stumbled upon the hook with her cloak and cap.

She prayed 'twas only a squabble among the garrison and not worse.

Uneasy talk about their poor defenses had seeded itself in her heart. An unwelcomed nuisance by the light of day.

But at night?

Moeder's nightmares had marred most peaceful evenings. For Sabine, night was just as uninvited as the complaints among soldiers.

A cool breeze from Lake Ontario rushed through the doorway, and Sabine quickly slid out and closed the door so as not to disturb her parents. Her heart thudded against her nightgown as she covered her head and her shoulders. Slipping on her wooden shoes that sat on the swept porch, she began to inch toward the tall grasses at the opposite edge of her garden, several yards from the river.

"I sent him back." The old lieutenant's voice shook. "Had furs and a wampum belt in his canoe. Said he lost his way along the lake. I doubt it."

"There is no easy way here from Canada. Did he mosey on around falls and shallows and just happen upon us at this midnight hour?" A soldier dramatized, his voice rising and falling as if he told a long tale. "Coming this way is nothing but a calculated feat."

"A spy, for sure. I've never seen a lost innocent as smug as that Frenchman. And to mention the Treaty of Utrecht? A twenty-seven-year-old argument." The lieutenant's words seemed forced between his teeth.

"We are sitting ducks." The soldier grunted with some sort of effort, then quick, acute plucks of water disrupted the peace of the steady river flow. Throwing stones? How inconsiderate at this hour.

"I shall press the governor to send reinforcements. Trade will get us little if the French continue to manipulate the alliance between us and the Indians. How far will they go to hoard all power over the commerce of the Six Nations?"

Sabine sprang up from her position, unable to keep quiet any longer. "Sirs, forgive my interruption," she called through the night, the movement of their dark figures against an inky horizon signaling where they stood at the mouth of the river.

"Miss Van Der Berg," exclaimed the lieutenant. "What are you—"

Sabine strode forward, still several paces away from them. "You must remember our deep friendship with the nearby Iroquois village. Apenimon is the chief's son and has shown only loyalty these many years."

"We are but twentysome men, a few traders, and your small family against the Six Nations and a French bully."

"Six Nations are not against us. You are wrong." Sabine puffed out her chest. "We have never met danger here, and one Frenchman is hardly worth an outcry for reinforcements."

"My dear, you have crept from a dreamworld into the reality of this night. I urge you to go back to your slumber and keep such romantic exclamations to yourself. Our position in this trade has either expired or demands a seriousness that has not yet been given." The two men moved along the bank. "I bid you good night," the lieutenant called out, less as a pleasantry and more as a prompt ending to this conversation.

Sabine knew that no good would come from pressing the issue. And she realized more why fear gripped her in the still of the night. Moeder's terrors were unnerving, but the concerns of their British neighbors at Fort Burnet grew like unwanted vines in her consciousness. She would harvest and prune the validity of such concerns and demand that nothing need change.

Life was full here where the Oswego met Lake Ontario.

Spring 1741

If she could gather the edges of Lake Ontario into a bouquet of its bounty and shimmer, she'd trade every tulip ever grown for such a gift. But for now Sabine was content with her basket of flowers on one arm and her other arm bent in a salute to the vast greatness of water—or rather propping her hand up to shade her eyes—as she pushed through the tall grasses toward the shore.

Her footsteps found a steady cadence in silent harmony with the rhythm of Apenimon's rowing as he led several others inching along the western edge of her sight. Today was a fine trading day— her very favorite of the year.

"Sabine, have you left already?" Moeder's voice snagged Sabine's next step. Turning her back on the glory of the morning, she drank in a different sight. The log cabin squatted as a gatehouse of the wood, with the trading post, Fort Burnet, to the east. Moeder clung to the frame of the door, daring to venture out from the dark haven onto a precarious path—for her.

What was Sabine's delight was Moeder's dread.

"Please, wait!" Sabine left her basket amid the waving grass. She inspected her swept path as she approached and flicked aside any fallen debris from last night's wind. "I thought you were sleeping." Snatching the large walking stick resting against the wall, she wrapped Moeder's hand around it. "Here. I should have left it beside your bed. Come, Papa is down by the trading place."

"And you've collected all of them?" Her words were a test. For ten years Sabine had taken Moeder's place beside Papa at the annual spring trade, but 364 days were plenty of time to forget her daughter's competence.

"Of course not, Moeder." Sabine assisted her mother down the path, the stick waving back and forth, knocking against the stones lining the way. "We always save the best for further negotiating," she recited. "And then the white ones are not for sale. They are beautiful this year, Moeder. A sure example of redemption. If only they had been in bloom for our Easter celebration—"

"We'd still leave them be."

"Of course." Sabine perused the swath of white lining the eastern side of their home. "We could have had a lovely picnic beside them though."

"True." Moeder shrugged. "But I made a promise a long time ago. They are an offering, in a way. My offering." Sabine had heard the story each year during this special week. "Just after that first spring those tulips bloomed without color."

"Papa said your sister must have added to our bulbs."

"Perhaps. But after that valley I walked, the surprise of those white flowers marked a season of forgiveness." Her mother's lips trembled, and a tear slid down her cheek. Every year Sabine heard the story, and every year her mother cried.

Papa had told Sabine that Moeder was repentant for turning her back on God out of anger after she lost her sight. She'd entered a valley of spiritual darkness at the onset of physical blindness.

Father compared her to Job. But Sabine often wondered if she was more like the Savior's friend, Mary—weeping because Jesus showed up too late.

When Moeder was at her lowest, a new flower bloomed among their colorful tulip patch. A white variety. Father was perplexed by this new crop, but Moeder took it as a sign. She realized the beauty wasn't in the seeing but in the knowing—not just appreciating His creation by sight, but knowing Him fully in her heart.

They began to wade through wild grain. Sabine grabbed her waiting basket without letting go of her mother's arm. "I believe Apenimon's child is due soon. Perhaps the best tulips will go today as well."

"What are their colors?" Moeder turned her attention to Sabine's face, her glazed eyes unable to hold steady on any one point.

Sabine glanced away with a sweeping intake of the masterpiece of their world. "They are the pinks, Moeder. Full and perfect, with identical petals."

"Ah, that *is* perfect. A sure sign for our friend Apenimon." Moeder squeezed her arm. "Pink is a color of health. Like your cheeks as a child. Full of health when I'd watch you on the shore, Sabine."

"Ho, there!" Papa called out across the water, his usual greeting when the canoe reached the shore. He splashed into the lapping waters and assisted Apenimon with his vessel. The familiar rumble of conversation mixed with hearty laughs stirred anticipation in Sabine's heart.

"This is the best day, Moeder."

"It used to be better." Moeder stabbed the ground with her stick.

"Do not worry. I shall tell you everything, as I always do."

Once they reached the trading place, smoke from the large crackling fire shrouded the Wyatt brothers' cart filled with powder, cloth, and various wares from Albany.

"I smell the roast," Moeder whispered, breathing in deeply as if it were her only chance to savor the scent.

"Everyone is here. Apenimon's friends are just now arriving

around the bend." Three more canoes crawled along the peaceful waters.

They exchanged goods as the waters lapped like an ocean under a cloudless sky. Once the vermillion sheen splayed from a hidden horizon past the bend, their trade business melted into merriment. Meat roasted, and a whistling flute played a jovial tune—happy enough that Sabine's serious mother tapped her hand on the top of her guiding stick.

Beyond the flame of the roasting fire, a man strode toward them.

"He's wearing the British uniform. Perhaps from Albany." Papa waved as he went out to meet the man.

Apenimon adjusted his red covering over his shoulder after he placed his final wares in his canoe. "I must return soon."

"Come, I will show you the flowers." Sabine scooped up her empty basket.

"One day I would like the white ones, Sabine." Apenimon's usual comment during this time of year. "White is a color of peace. My tribe's greatest value."

"You will have to take that up with Moeder." Sabine repeated herself with the same suggestion every year also.

"Such a waste to let them sit without being seen."

"Ah, but she sees them in her heart." Sabine laid her hand on her own beating heart. Apenimon chuckled, and she raced ahead, keeping a sideways glance in the direction of the stranger. The man removed his hat, releasing a wave of chestnut locks as he nodded to her father and then hesitated, spying Sabine across the rippling plain. She diverted her attention to her clogs as she traipsed toward her garden. Apenimon trailed behind her.

"That man is staring at you," he sniggered.

"Perhaps he's staring at *you*," she retorted with a playful smirk.

But her gaze crashed into the man's line of sight. He tipped his hat in her direction.

She pressed her hand to the laces of her bodice involuntarily, trying to contain a frenzy of unexpected flutters. She'd never experienced this feeling before. How could the attention of one man bring about such a disturbance within her?

Had Sabine discovered a layer to her flesh she'd never known? She looked away from the handsome stranger, uncertain that she could allow him to have such an uninvited effect on her.

An exhilarating current rushed through Lieutenant Jacob Bennington's veins. Even if the longstanding Lieutenant Wilson of Fort Burnet did not appreciate an equal peer, Jacob was glad to be in this territory. He was one step closer to life with his little girl.

This evening, Jacob could not keep his eyes off of the exchange between the Dutchman's daughter and that native. There seemed to be some kinship between them. Mr. Van Der Berg offered him a roasted turkey leg and a mug of ale.

"Your daughter speaks their language?"

"Aye. Apenimon also knows English. Sabine began learning his language not long after she learned our own. And any French she knows is also from Apenimon." His face was lit with some sort of admiration. A father's pride. Jacob knew that feeling well, and his heart ached for little Amelia.

As he ate his dinner, he listened more than spoke. He was there for a purpose and soon wondered at this odd family settled in the shadow of Fort Burnet. They seemed more allied to the natives than even the twenty men who'd been stationed under Governor Clark's appointment. Perhaps they would be key in solidifying a secure loyalty to the British.

After they said farewell to the natives, Jacob was able to find a moment to speak with the trader's daughter.

"It seems that my crew and I are here for such a time as this," he exclaimed, holding out his hand to help escort her around the dying fire. Her father gathered up their newly traded furs. Her mother gripped tightly to her father's arm. The blind woman seemed to scowl more than smile. But her daughter held a different expression of neither bitterness nor joy. Her eyes flashed with skepticism in the silvery moonlight.

"Such a time as this?" Her hand slipped away as soon as she was steady on her feet and she retrieved her lamp. "There is nothing we need, sir. All is well for us. What is it that you speak of?"

"You do have quite a life here, one that is nothing like the stories told in Albany of the ruthless savages and the reckless adventurers of this wild place."

She examined her parents. Her father began to douse the fire. "Why yes, civilized gentleman, we are reckless indeed." By her own lamplight he saw her eyes roll and her disapproval grow deep in the tweaked corner of her mouth. "What exactly is your business here, besides spying on what Governor Clark believes is his reach?"

Jacob resisted a guffaw at such an ornery attitude in this woman. "Progress." He pulled his shoulders back and surveyed the broad shore and the dark canopy of sky above. "Do not worry about my business. It is an inevitable task to which I am assigned. Once it is complete, my life shall begin." He laid his eyes upon her. "But until then, Miss Van Der Berg, your work is much more intriguing to me." He nodded toward the sound of distant lapping of oars on the water. "Tell me, how difficult was learning to speak those men's language?"

"To me, it is no more trying than leading a blind soul along this land. You listen, learn, and adapt. Do you care to speak with them?"

"They are important as to why I am here."

"Ah, as am I, so you say. It seems like you are more in the business of depending too much on strangers than doing what you will to get on with your life." She held up her light, and its sheen bounced weakly off the neat logs of their cabin in the distance. "Do not depend on us, sir. We are settled. I pray your business here is swift and we can all return to life as we have lived it."

Chapter 2

The morning light seeped above the eastern edge of their world. Sabine placed a fur on Moeder's lap. The woman sat on the porch, erect like a soldier.

"What do you hear?" Sabine knew well the posture of her mother's listening. Their early morning watches mostly began this way—Moeder propped in her rocker, waiting for the hot spiced tea Sabine prepared over the fire. Unless the porch was piled with snow in the winter, they hardly missed a sunrise.

"I hear the sandpiper. The heat must be coming."

Sabine wrapped Moeder's fingers around the wooden mug then sat on the stool next to her, cradling her own mug in her lap. "A good morning for such a prediction. The milkweed is in full bloom, the sky is clear, and the sun is bright."

"What else?"

"A mirror to the heavens. Not one crease or stain."

"Perfect, is it?"

"Aye. Like your first day."

"My first day." Whimsical tones bleated from her scratchy throat. "I walked beside the cart, my back sore from sitting. You were curled up on the floor between the bags of flour and sacks of bulbs. The vastness of the green and the towering trees along the crest whispered home to me. Untouched, with no filth in the streets or crowds of people. Purely God's garden. The only place I'd choose to see for the last time."

And she had. The greens and silvers and tall trees guarding the western edge of civilization colored her final views.

"The painting in your mind has not one flaw, Moeder. All is the same, all is—"

The loud bellow of men shook the quiet morning.

"Is that the men from Albany?"

"I shall see."

Sabine set her mug on her stool and stepped into the early light. She snaked around the water barrel and approached the corner of their square home. On the riverbank several men dragged their batoes and canoes toward the existing fort.

Lieutenant Bennington appeared at the entrance, adjusting his coat and straightening his hat. He waved a hand to the men, then took long, confident strides toward the Van Der Bergs's garden.

Sabine matched his gait and met him at the corner.

"Good morning, sir." She curtsied. Pushing open the knee-high gate, she planted herself between the remaining blooms of tulips and the curious lieutenant. "The garden is a fine place to start for breakfast, but Father will have fish roasting in no time."

Lieutenant Bennington rubbed his jaw. " 'Tis a fine morning. And this is a fine garden." "Fine" seemed an understatement to Sabine. The garden stretched twice the width of their home and marched along the wooded border with towering blackberry shrubs, rows upon rows of corn, all guided by the hand of Apenimon's mother. The garden was a world in itself—a broad and established covenant between the Van Der Bergs and their friends, the Iroquois. "You are right, Miss Van Der Berg—I believe your father's bounty will be far more satisfying than what the soil might provide." He studied the entire length of the western fence and then turned his attention to the span of the northern fence—the pickets that bordered all four varieties of colorful tulips, now lining the barren ground after their trade. "I wonder, how attached are you to this plot?"

"Excuse me?"

"We are staking out our walls to expand the fort, Miss Van Der Berg. It makes the most sense that our western wall sit right about—" He narrowed his eyes in the direction of their cabin. "Here." His chopping hand sliced the air above their garden fence.

Sabine's mouth fell, and she only stared at him.

"The cabin will be safe within our walls."

She clamped her mouth shut, her mind whirring against his audacity. "Sir, we have lived a peaceful life. There is no need to be walled up against—"

"Walled up? Nay, only protecting you. This cabin is in quite a vulnerable position."

His charming smile and puffed chest appeared to express an undercurrent of heroism—a trait that Sabine recalled from Moeder's bedtime tales. Yet Sabine was often perplexed by the simple ending of being swept off one's feet by another human being. She preferred Apenimon's true stories about peace treaties among the tribes, where each member was cared for and caring for the other.

"Sir, we have not had one encounter that would require help from you, the governor, or even the King himself. I beg you to reconsider swallowing up our plot." She choked back a strained tone of panic. "My mother—she has come to terms with her blindness because nothing her eyes have once seen has changed. There is great comfort in that. She is content in her mind's eye." Sabine's heart clouded with the memory of gloomy bouts of Moeder deep in agony over her lost sight. "That has not always been the case."

Lieutenant Bennington's eyes glazed. "There is nothing in this life but change." The low rumble of men's voices carried from beyond the old fort, and Moeder's rocking chair creaked in the distance. But all the sounds were fading against the loud pounding in Sabine's ears.

"This is not negotiable, sir." Sabine crossed her arms. "We will not be part of your—"

"Sabine!" Apenimon called from the forest's edge. He stared at the lieutenant but waved his hand for Sabine to come closer.

"Pardon me." She lifted her hem, stepped around the bean plants, and exited through the far western gate. Her conversation with Lieutenant Bennington clawed at her as she hurried toward her friend. She had turned her back on the first danger she'd ever known.

"What does that man speak with you about?" Apenimon continued to stare beyond her. He was her good watch.

"They come to build a fortress."

"Here? With Niagra just beyond the bend?"

"The British must match the French, I guess."

Apenimon now shifted his gaze to Sabine. Ashen circles encompassed his brown eyes, and while he searched hers for an explanation, she blinked several times and concerned herself with his visit. "Is anything the matter?"

A dance of sunlight seemed to brighten his face, and he hooked his thumbs on his leather belt adorned with shells. "He has come."

Sabine's heart leapt. "He has?"

"Yes!" Apenimon tossed his long ebony braid behind his shoulder and laughed toward the heavens. "Come, come." He retreated into the wood, skipping between the hickory trees, casting a longing in Sabine's direction that she could not resist. She turned around, waved a hand at Lieutenant Bennington, and added, "Please wait, and we shall settle the matter soon," then ran up to the lean-to and traded her wooden shoes for her moccasins. Gathering her skirt in one hand so it would not catch on any fallen branches or block her view of any forest creatures, she began running after Apenimon.

Only when they came to the walls of the village did she realize they were being followed.

Jacob caught Miss Van Der Berg's eye as she approached a tall timber palisade atop a terrace. The entrance was flanked by tulips—her tulips. Smoke snaked beyond the fortification, and the sounds of drums and voices mingled with birdsong and forest rustling.

"Miss Van Der Berg?"

She paused. "You followed me."

Several native women appeared from rows of crops at the southern edge of the palisade. Miss Van Der Berg waved to them, and they returned to their work. Yet their heads turned his way more than once, and their scrutiny burned like the scorching sun.

He scrambled up the terrace. "Perhaps your aversion to protection has given you a reckless abandon, Miss Van Der Berg. I warn you that this type of behavior will not sit well once we are built up."

She ran her hand along the wooden wall. "Sir, there is no danger here. These are our friends. Lieutenant Wilson should have informed you."

Her friend Apenimon, who'd appeared earlier, now stood at the entrance. He wore a hide draped on one shoulder, and the other was muscular and bare. His words to Miss Van Der Berg were unintelligible to Jacob. The woman replied with the same tongue, then signaled for Jacob to follow.

A rush of excitement burst in his chest. The simple task of expanding their presence in this region was unexpectedly cast aside in Jacob's loyal heart to Albany. He would mingle among the men he'd only heard about from traders who bragged about their expeditions. Before his arrival to America, he'd heard tall tales of these people from sea captains. Witnessing the secure alliance with the Iroquois among the settlers of Oswego would be a prized account in his first letter to the governor.

When he stepped inside their fortress, the wafting smell of roasting meat warmed his nostrils. Miss Van Der Berg and the native crossed a clearing flanked with lines of beaver skins and dyed textiles. They approached a long, narrow dwelling that spanned the entire width of the clearing. The roof was curved, and neat rows upon rows of bark and sticks deemed the structure securely built. A child appeared in the doorway and ran up to Miss Van Der Berg. The young woman held out her hand, and the child took it, swinging her arm back and forth.

With eyes only upon the boy, she said, "You should wait outside the longhouse, Lieutenant. I will tell the clan mother that you are a friend."

A sweaty film coated the back of Jacob's neck. Clan mother? He wondered where the chief might be and if he should have a proper introduction so as not to stir up unnecessary hostility. But Apenimon very nearly ignored his presence. When Miss Van Der Berg disappeared inside the building with the child, Apenimon just stood at the entrance, his eyes diverted to the ground just beyond Jacob's boots.

He was being guarded.

During the next half hour, men brought fish to a central fire, speaking to Apenimon at the entrance of the longhouse. They stared at Jacob with arms crossed, and then each man spoke a word—Jacob assumed their names, and his assumption was confirmed when Apenimon spoke his also. He studied Sabine's friend, wondering if he would speak English. Mr. Van Der Berg had mentioned that he knew English, and French, but all he spoke was his name. The men looked at each other, smiled, then offered the same cordial expressions to Jacob. He returned the pleasantry but felt nervous in his vulnerable position. Miss Van Der Berg appeared again, her face red with elation, demystifying his anxiety. Apenimon relaxed, and the two conversed. She signaled for Jacob to follow her once again, and they left the settlement. Two men nearly plowed into them. They were both adorned in a mix of native hide and the blasted French uniform. One approached the palisade and conversed with a young man at the entrance. The other tipped his hat to Miss Van Der Berg and said, "*Bonjour, mademoiselle.*" He eyed Jacob. "*Il est votre ami?*"

"*Je m'appelle* Jacob Bennington." Jacob removed his hat and gave a curt bow—not too low to this encroaching Frenchman.

Miss Van Der Berg explained that Jacob was from Albany. The man made a snide remark about the overcrowding of the shores of Ontario. He gave a quick "*Au revoir*" and followed his friend into the palisade.

Miss Van Der Berg continued down the terrace and entered the forest again. Jacob hurried after her. "Do the French also trade with this village?"

"They try to," she remarked. "They offer expensive wares. We have become close friends to the village. Apenimon considers the French a nuisance."

"I see." Jacob hooked his thumb in the buttonhole of his jacket, his chest rising with satisfaction that they were indeed in an advantageous position on this front.

"I'd not seem so smug, sir. You are the most foreign of us all." She eyed his hat and his coat and his boots. "We do not see ourselves as Dutch or British versus French, but friend versus foe. Respect is expected. Those Frenchmen follow the native customs, even if Apenimon has all but cast them off." She avoided a bramble and skirted around a birch.

"Then you can teach me their customs."

"Why would I do that?"

"You are under the same King as I, are you not?"

"That means little to me."

"You might take care of treasonous words such as those."

"Pardon me, but you are the guest here."

"And as your guest, I would appreciate your guidance with our neighbors."

She studied him with large emerald eyes, vibrant like the young wheat fields back in England. "Perhaps you and I might make a trade of sorts."

"A trade?"

"Aye, sir. I shall teach you the ways of this land and the kindness to its people if you do me one favor in return."

"What is that, my lady?"

"Leave my garden alone." Sabine flicked her reddish-gold braid behind her shoulder and planted her fists on her hips. "Build your wall elsewhere."

Chapter 3

"He was perfect, Moeder." Sabine hung their linens on a line from the porch pole to the wooden stake at the edge of their cleared ground. "His eyes were as black as coal, and his skin was so soft—but turned the color of a radish when he wailed." She giggled. "Was I really ever that small?"

"Aye, child." Moeder held a winsome smile while her eyes fluttered closed, no doubt peering backward and inward to a long-buried memory. "I do wish that we had made our way here as soon as I found out about your existence. I remember the fear of disease as much as the joy of your arrival."

An eagle's shadow trailed along the ground and skimmed the linen apron hanging from Sabine's fingers. She thrust her head back and spied the female soaring in a blue sky.

Lord, You are ever faithful.

" 'Twas an eagle that welcomed us here, was it not?"

"Yes, Papa's first catch was made after he spied the majestic bird."

"We are blessed, Moeder, in this place."

"Aye, 'tis why I regret not arriving earlier. Perhaps I would still—"

"Do not speak such things. His plan is perfect. You have told me that since I could speak."

The men beyond their plot were calling out and creating a disturbance. Sabine shook off tension that wormed its way along her shoulders.

"Speaking of a plan, have you considered Papa's suggestion?"

"Of course not." Sabine could not shake off this ill feeling now. "There is no rush. If God wants a husband for me, He shall provide one."

"Do you believe that?"

"Why would I not?"

"Because if there is one thing I have failed in doing, it is encouraging you to embrace your womanly duty."

"You mean my duty to a man? Or my duty to my God? I am a woman, and God is my Master. Why must I be dutiful to anyone else—besides my parents, of course?"

"Daughter, it is good to marry. If I hadn't, you would not be here." She smiled a rare broad grin. Sabine's chest warmed with affection for her mother. Her smile was perfect acceptance.

Papa bounded into view with a string of fish hanging from his fist. "The river current gives us plenty this morning."

"Papa, we need another Sabine running around, don't we?" Moeder jested.

Her father's sun-kissed brow and turned-up nose seemed forever painted with a jovial pink hue. "I have said that a thousand times. But a grandson would be even better, would it not?"

"You two have schemed against me." Sabine gave a playful pout.

"Daughter, you have seen the masterpiece of newborn life just this morning." Moeder began to rock in her chair. "I foresee God's plan for you will be just as full."

"Not with those scrawny soldiers sitting idly by at the command of some far-off governor."

Papa cast a curious look in Moeder's direction. He cleared his throat and muttered, "That Lieutenant Bennington seems an interesting fellow."

"Papa! Since when do you scout out possible matches?" Her cheeks flushed with heat.

"Since I cannot see past my lashes," her mother snapped, and then cocked her head thoughtfully. "From what your father says, he seems a very dependable and handsome man."

Papa gave all his attention to cleaning his fish at the far edge of the porch.

"Funny that Papa would make that observation. I had not given the man's looks a second thought. He's a boring soldier. Same as the rest." A twist of her gut pinched apart the truth from the lie. She hadn't failed to notice Lieutenant Bennington's handsome features.

And contrary to the other men, the lieutenant was not boring at all. If she could strip away the differences of a king's command and her heart for this land, she and the lieutenant were alike in a way. Much like Sabine's own passion, Lieutenant Bennington had a determination to continue his work. Dutiful, proud, and willing to learn—honoring her request to keep away from her own land and desiring to dig deep in the treasures of what he could learn from this place. Sabine lifted her chest with a full, glorious breath. She plucked a cloth from the line to offer Papa as he plunged his hands into a washbasin.

He took it with a grateful nod, then walked over to Moeder.

"Tonight is the night for the white ones." Papa tenderly helped her from the chair.

"Is the raft ready?"

"Aye." He kissed her cheek. "Let us go prepare dinner." They disappeared inside.

Sabine craned her neck around to look past the cabin toward the small fort. Men moseyed about the land, setting stakes and unloading canoes. She could not find the lieutenant this bright shiny day.

But he had found her in Oswego.

What might come from God's plan for a soldier to discover a new way of life at the guidance of a Dutchman's daughter?

"We've got but five hundred pounds, Michael. Let us be wise in our efforts," Jacob urged.

"It would be wisest to stake out this stretch for the western wall." Michael pointed toward the Van Der Bergs's garden.

"That will not be necessary."

"What do you propose then?"

"What say you about a sort of triangular enclosure?"

"Pardon?"

"Perhaps we can avoid disturbing what already exists."

"Preposterous."

"I do believe I am the officer to answer to the governor." Jacob diverted his eyes away from Michael's gawking to the near-glowing tulips. "This is the best way."

Michael folded his lips together and scratched the back of his head. He spoke quietly. "And quickest, right, sir?"

Sir? They had been friends for quite some time. But Jacob *had* just implied his higher rank, hadn't he? Jacob cleared his throat. "There is nothing wrong with efficiency alongside duty." The earlier they completed this task, the quicker he would unite with his daughter at long last.

"Of course not." Michael sighed and landed his hand on Jacob's shoulder. "But I do wonder if your hurry has to do with obligations in Albany more than the hopes of a secure fortification."

He ground his teeth. The man knew him too well, and their rank difference was now cast aside for the truth of the matter. Although Michael knew about Jacob's daughter, he was unaware of the promise Jacob had made to the Dutchman's daughter. Jacob's heart longed for the reunion with the child who'd suffered much, but his heart beat a new rhythm for Sabine Van Der Berg. One of admiration and slight fear. How could the girl be so confident in this wild place and so resistant to his protection?

The one time he failed to protect another's heart ended in destruction. He mustn't grow attached to this daring Sabine. He was too weary from the last time he tried to offer his loyalty to a woman.

"It will do you good to remember that once this is complete, my obligation will carry me elsewhere." Jacob placed his hands behind his back and rocked on his heels. "But only if my assignment is done well. These next several weeks, I guarantee my diligence in making this fort nothing less than dutifully secure."

After dinner, Jacob made sure the stakes were set in the exact placement they had discussed. He was taken aback when he saw Mr. Van Der Berg carrying two large baskets of the white tulips that had adorned the eastern side of their garden.

"Good evening, sir." Jacob approached the man, eyeing the now completely barren corner of the garden. "Are the natives coming this evening?"

"What?" Mr. Van Der Berg looked back toward the lakeshore and then scanned the woods.

"To trade for the tulips, sir." Jacob nodded toward the basket. The flowers were stacked upon each other like plump sheep sleeping tightly together in a shepherd's care.

"Ah," he exclaimed. His rounded belly lifted and dropped with a deep, hearty laugh. "I can see why you'd think so. These would be a fine trade indeed. However, we never trade the white ones. They are an offering. We take them on the lake and—" He hesitated, smacked his lips together, then said, "Would you like to come with us, Lieutenant? It is a beautiful tradition."

"Where do you go?"

"Not far. You'll see." He'd already continued to head toward the shore. Sabine and her mother waited beside a large flat raft. Sabine held two oars upright in one hand and a lantern in the other. Her mother's arms were wrapped around a wool blanket. He followed close behind Mr. Van Der Berg.

"The lieutenant will join us this evening," Mr. Van Der Berg announced.

"Papa, what do you mean?" Although Sabine spoke in a hushed tone, probably not wanting Jacob to hear, her words were clear in the quiet evening.

Jacob took a step back. "Sir, I do not need to intrude—"

"Not intruding at all. I'll put you to work." Mr. Van Der Berg set the baskets on the raft then relieved Sabine of the oars, handing one to Jacob. "You take starboard."

Sabine gave him a weak smile and helped her mother onto the

raft. The two women sat on two barrels in the very center, beneath a sail. Jacob positioned himself on the starboard side, and her father untied the raft and hopped aboard before pushing away from the pebbled beach.

Mr. Van Der Berg went to the portside and began to row. "Lieutenant, my daughter thanks you for taking up the oar."

Sabine nodded, then fired a glare at her father. " 'Tis kind of you, but I can manage the oar just fine."

Jacob wondered why he'd agreed to come on this—journey. This rite? He'd no idea what this was about. The sun was low in the west, bleeding its final color across the horizon. Pink glitter scattered on the surface of the vast water ahead. He did his part and worked his oar in rhythm with Mr. Van Der Berg's. The slap of the wood on the water was the only sound for several minutes.

"That's enough." Mrs. Van Der Berg spoke for the first time since they had left shore. Mr. Van Der Berg gave Jacob a signal to stop with his oar up and out ahead of him. "Begin, Sabine."

Sabine stood from her barrel, steadying herself with the tips of her fingers on the seat. Jacob offered his hand to help her, but she either didn't see it or chose to ignore him. She shuffled over to one of the large baskets and gathered up an armful of tulips then placed them on her mother's lap.

The woman was beautiful like her daughter. Her age showed in the deep crease between her eyebrows. Although, it might not be from age but trial. Around her face the reddish-blond hair grayed.

She brushed her fingertips along the whole length of the flowers, caressing the tulips. "Lieutenant, this is our tradition since the fourth spring after we arrived on this land." She reached out a hand to Sabine, who helped her mother stand. "We all have valleys in which we walk. Mine was dark and desolate—a stubborn journey with my back to the Lord. These blooms were my comfort, my reminder that forgiveness is near."

With her stems in one arm and her hand clutching her daughter's, she sang a psalm:

"The Lord is my shepherd; I shall not want.
He maketh me to lie down in green pastures:
he leadeth me beside the still waters.
He restoreth my soul."

Her voice chimed over the waters like birdsong. Jacob allowed his heart to be moved. He'd not been in church in many weeks. Life had its way with him in his own trials of an abandoned marriage and neglected child. But with the breeze off the water and the solemn company, his soul was quieter than ever before.

Daughter and mother alike took the blooms and tossed them out into the water. Her mother continued to sing:

"He leadeth me in the paths of righteousness
for his name's sake.
Yea, though I walk through the valley
of the shadow of . . ."

Jacob turned his attention to the tulips—floating sheep now, bobbing up against the raft's edge. The two women carefully rounded the barrels where they sat. When Sabine passed him, she glanced at him with flushed cheeks and a scrunched nose. Her father led her mother to the next basket, while Sabine whispered to Jacob, "This might be strange to you, but it's comforting to her. I am not sure why my father invited you."

"I am glad he did." He held her gaze, hoping she believed him.

She tilted her head, studied him for a moment, then slipped past, clutching at her mother's elbow. They neared the edge of the other side of the raft, and the song continued. This time, Jacob joined in,

> *"I will fear no evil,*
> *for thou are with me;*
> *thy rod and thy staff,*
> *they comfort me."*

The tulips splattered into the water, and every Van Der Berg kept their head bowed. Mr. Van Der Berg began a prayer of thanksgiving for the valleys left behind and God's faithfulness on the other side of those valleys. Jacob bowed his head as well, praying that this was the last of his own valley.

He was still praying when the raft shifted beneath him. His head shot up. The women were coming back around to their seats.

"Did you fall asleep?" Sabine smirked as she passed him.

"Of course not." He straightened his shoulders and offered a hand to them. Sabine was no longer paying him attention but staring across the water toward the land. He followed her gaze. Along the shore, a canoe dipped up and down beneath budding trees. He could just make out a person with dark hair and bare skin.

"Is that your friend?" Jacob asked.

"Nay." She waved her hand at the man, and he returned the gesture. "I do not recognize him."

Her mother questioned her, and she explained that they had an audience along the lake's edge.

"He doesn't know not to touch these flowers, Sabine." Her mother lowered to her barrel.

"I am sure he is concerned more with fishing than flowers, Moeder."

"That Apenimon jests often about them though—"

"Is he with others?" Sabine narrowed her eyes and leaned forward. Jacob quickly took her arm for fear she would fall in. "Do you see?"

At first Jacob could see only one man in the canoe, but as he stared, a movement in the wood behind the man caught his attention. "There, I just saw something move."

She stared a moment longer and then pulled away from him. "Perhaps they are hunting this evening. Strange. I've never seen those carvings on a canoe before."

"Do you think he wants my flowers?"

"Oh Moeder, that is ridiculous."

"Well, they've been offered. He may not touch them. You should let him know that."

"Moeder, do not worry."

When Sabine settled on her seat and her father directed them to start back to shore, Jacob continued to watch the canoe. As they drew closer to the shore by the cabin, the canoe disappeared around the western bend.

They tied up the raft. Mr. Van Der Berg took his wife and led her home while Sabine gathered up the empty baskets.

A commotion from the other side of Fort Burnet melted away any unease stirred up by the watching man across the water. Men swarmed from the banks of the river.

"It seems the rest of our crew has arrived to build." He smiled.

But Sabine's scowl dampened his jolt of excitement. "Pardon me, but this *is* why I am here. And I am anxious to be reunited with my daughter."

Her face softened. "Daughter? Is she young?" She took long strides up through the grasses. He stayed beside her.

"She is. Only eight. I've been apart from her more than I have been near to her."

"Is she with her mother?"

"Nay, her mother left us two years ago." He did not want to speak further on this. "I must go settle the men. We have a long day ahead." He did not look back at the woman when he left her behind. Just like the wife who'd done the same to him—leaving without a backward glance.

Chapter 4

The next afternoon Sabine planted some bean seeds she had received from the trade. The sun beat on her neck just beneath the cap containing her coiled braid. She flinched at every sound the men made as they prepared to excavate dirt for the wretched walls they'd build. How could Papa be so welcoming to that Lieutenant Bennington, enough to include him on their special evening last night?

When she questioned him, he only shrugged her off, stating that he was wise enough to know a suitable match for his daughter. Moeder declared that the man proved worthy in his singing the psalm in a heartfelt way. Sabine refused to agree that he was anything more than a nuisance to them all. Today, with the ruckus of his garrison, her own words rang the truest among the Van Der Bergs.

"Sabine!" Moeder called in a shaky voice from the window. "It is coming on."

The seeds fell from Sabine's apron as she sprang up and ran to the window. "Moeder, you must catch your breath." The tiny woman was fanning herself with the wicker trivet Father had made to protect the board table from hot dishes and pans. Her face was blanched, and she sucked in air in quick short breaths. Sabine reached through the window and grabbed her shoulders. During these episodes, Moeder calmed more quickly if she was held in place—instead of falling into the abyss of her dark world.

"I cannot manage with the noise. It is all changing, it is." She whined like a child. Her mouth sagged in a defeated frown.

Sabine clenched her teeth. "Moeder, nothing has changed on our property. Do not be concerned by these men. I've saved our garden. There's nothing else to be done." A convulsion of shaking overcame her mother and she sank to the stool beneath the window. "Please, Moeder, all will be well."

But Sabine feared it wouldn't be. Over her shoulder, men crawled along the sweeping land, building a defense because of a different fear—one that involved greed and entitlement.

Lieutenant Bennington appeared from the riverbank, his shirtsleeves rolled up above his elbows and a large spade slung across his shoulders. Wisps of his shoulder-length hair fell from the tied locks gathered at his neck. He did not look like a superior to these men, but a strapping hard worker, charging the ground with each powerful step.

Sabine captured her amazement of this creature and swallowed it back, allowing objection to coat her tongue instead. "I shall return shortly." She stormed across the garden and flung open the gate. All the while, Lieutenant Bennington continued forward on the disturbed land with focus and strength.

"Excuse me, sir." Sabine planted herself on higher ground.

The lieutenant plunged his spade into the earth beside a mound of loose soil, then glanced up at her, one eye closed against the bright sun and the other eye narrowed but gleaming. "Miss Van Der Berg, it looks like we are both hard at work this day." He smiled and studied her face then her apron.

Aware that he was referring to her disheveled appearance, she wiped her cheek with the back of her hand. A grainy film smeared across her skin. How might she appear to him? But a loud call from one of the men atop a batoe dissolved any insecurity about how she looked.

"Lieutenant Bennington, must your men be so loud and unruly as they work?"

"There is not much to be done about that, Miss Van Der Berg."

"If I came beside your very home and made an ungodly ruckus, you would certainly not appreciate such inconsideration." She ground her fists into her hips. "I expect you to have some sort of care during this upheaval of our peace."

"Do you expect us to whisper?" His face beamed with jest.

"I. . .I. . ." A fire spread up her neck—a mix of humiliation and fury. "I believe you could try to. . .to take more care in your work. . .for the sake of—" Her lip began to quiver. All the anger puddled into sorrow for the poor blind woman whose darkness became darker with every unknown.

Lieutenant Bennington approached her square-on, dropping his tool from his hand and discarding his cheeky expression. "For the sake of?" His voice lowered. Sabine tugged at the turned-up wings of her cap, trying to calm the storm inside her—tears bubbling, throat burning. He lifted a hand and cupped Sabine's elbow. "I apologize if I've upset you."

"You do not realize the toll this takes on Moeder. She has lived in a place that is constant, untouched. The noise, the destruction—" She refused to weep in front of this man. She backed away.

"Miss Van Der Berg, I cannot—" He lunged and wrapped his arm around her, pushing her behind him.

"What is it?" She swiveled around and gripped his arm so as not to fall back by his force.

"Something flew from the wood." He lifted his hand to his brow. Sabine peered over his shoulder, his soft shirt cool against her cheek. He glanced down at her. His mouth was so close to her forehead that she could feel his warm breath. She was lost in his bright brown eyes for but a second, until he turned his whole body toward her and took her by both arms. "You must stay here while I inspect what I saw." His grasp was firm. She tried to squirm and demand he let her go, but she could only nod, derailed by the stampede unleashed in her chest.

He marched toward the patch of clover between her garden and the southern bend of the forest. "Hallo there!" he called into the thick of trees.

Everything became silent around Sabine. The men behind her, the beat of her heart, the trapped breath in her throat. Only the birdsong and the river current imposed themselves amid the alarmed crowd.

Lieutenant Bennington inspected the ground around him with his chin only slightly dipped. His shoulders were square and his posture upright. His hands were clenched by his thighs, as if he were at attention. He was a soldier, after all. And he maintained cautious surveillance as he investigated a disturbance he no doubt imagined.

Sabine's senses came about, and she considered interrupting the search. Gathering her skirt, she stepped forward. The lieutenant broke his stance and crouched, grabbed at something, then swiftly rose again. She paused.

He turned around and barreled toward the work site with whatever he'd discovered held behind his back.

"Lieutenant Bennington, what is it?"

"It is exactly what I feared, and why we are called here."

"I do wonder if you are reading into things." Sabine could not think of one thing that would prove the need for a fortress. Not after years of peaceful trade with the Iroquois. Even the disputes with the French were said to be only heated in the form of handwritten aggression between the Kings' men.

"But you see, Miss Van Der Berg." The bright sunshine shone on his flinching jaw. "This is hardly something to read into." He presented an arrow from behind his back. Hanging limp and ragged from beyond the flint head was a piece of the British flag. "What else might it declare except hostility?"

Sabine snatched it from him.

"Are you certain those Frenchmen hold no persuasion over your. . .friends?" His eyebrow hooked over a questioning countenance.

"Perhaps another tribe has found fault against you, but Apenimon's tribe is nearly family to my own."

The man tried to take the arrow away from her, but Sabine held her arm out to the side. "If you please, I shall seek answers about this. . .this signal." She shoveled in a jagged breath. "I will get to the bottom of this myself."

"I shall come with you, Sabine."

Her breath caught as he spoke her name.

His bright eyes rounded with regret. "Forgive me, Miss Van—"

"Sir, I do not need your protection."

Before he could say anything more, she edged around him and started toward home. "I shall return this to you once I find the truth of its story," she called out, waving the arrow above her head.

Dread filled her with every step away from the handsome lieutenant. He'd caught her off guard with his casual use of her name, his obvious concern for her safety, and his towering presence among the other men. But mostly her anxiety ran deep because this arrow was not strange or unfamiliar—it was indeed the same design of those arrows Sabine had been taught to shoot by her Iroquois friends.

The distant thumps of drums traveled through the birch, elm, and hickory stands, landing on Jacob's ears like soft heartbeats. He took the last swig of his drink then tossed his wooden mug into the pail at the edge of their fire. Tonight the men did not eat on the shore with the Van Der Bergs. They had chosen to dine in a central gathering place within the walls of the fort. His men's tents sat between the lake and the new construction.

Jacob stood up and stretched his arms above his head.

Lieutenant Wilson approached him. "Good evening, Bennington." They'd barely spoken. The man was clear that although they were equal in rank, Jacob was to direct only his men. "It appears that your men work quickly. I fear for the quality of the job."

"They are strong and capable, Lieutenant Wilson. The very best for efficiency."

"I do wonder on the material. Clay?"

"Aye. I was concerned at first, but my mason is confident in his work. He promised it would save the colony money in the long run." Michael was a trusted friend, one who'd seen him at his worst when his wife left. Even if the doubts from the older lieutenant resonated with Jacob's own, his allegiance was to the head mason above all else.

"Surely five hundred pounds would have provided stone." The

old lieutenant strode alongside the newly dug trenches for the foundation. "We wonder if the trade is worth this. We've been here a long time. Our patience wanes. More and more, we discover the French edging in on our territory, compromising our good relations with the Iroquois. They bribe them and take advantage of the native people. We are aware of the well-equipped French forts to the north and west—a seemingly grand legion compared to our speck of British presence on this southern shore."

"Ah, but you do receive our help now. We are here to grow that speck." Jacob patted the man's shoulder, trying to show some camaraderie. "And the Van Der Bergs are close to the nearby Iroquois. I believe that adds to our security."

"You know little of that tribe. Although they are loyal traders with us, French blood has mixed with theirs. The daughter of a clan mother married one of the Frenchmen at Niagra. They do not care as much for French goods as they care to keep diplomacy with the French." Lieutenant Wilson hung his head and kicked at a rock. "We use them for their furs, and they use us for our inexpensive goods. But can we be certain that they aren't swayed by the giant?"

"That is not to be of concern, Lieutenant Wilson." Sabine appeared in the dusk, the strawberry tint of her hair shining bright in the firelight. She bit her lip then gave a quick curtsy. "I beg your pardon for the intrusion, but we are their allies. As the whole confederacy of the Iroquois are ours."

Jacob tipped his hat to the lady. "Miss Van Der Berg, I trust you have assuring news about the recent discovery we made this afternoon."

She retrieved the piece of the British flag from her apron pocket. "Here you are, sir."

He took the flimsy material and held it up between them. "Well?" The hair stood on the back of his neck. The desecrated flag, with a hole ripped in its center by an arrowhead, flapped in the breeze. The skepticism of the old lieutenant began to crawl into Jacob's own senses.

Sabine pursed her lips, and her nostrils flared. "Of course, there is nothing to worry about. A young boy was practicing and accidently caught this piece that had been tangled in the branches of a tree from earlier expeditions." She shook her head, a strand of hair brushing her nose.

"Is that so, Miss Van Der Berg?"

Why was she not looking directly at him, but at his shaven chin?

"Yes." She crossed her arms, bouncing a look between both lieutenants. "Apenimon explained so himself."

Lieutenant Wilson grunted and swatted his hand. "You and that Apenimon. He is but one man among thousands. I will be satisfied only when our walls are built up. Until then, I will prepare for the worst." He trudged toward the fort.

"It seems that Lieutenant Wilson does not trust your friend." Jacob sidestepped into Sabine's line of sight.

Her eyes widened, taking him in with a curious look. "*Apenimon* means 'worthy of trust', and he has proven himself as such, always. The old lieutenant is getting his way, isn't he? He wanted your walls."

"My walls—the governor's walls, more like it." He rubbed his shoulder, the soreness from a day's work pulsating beneath his coat. "We have started our work. When will you stand up to your end of the bargain?"

"Did I not already?" She snatched the piece of flag from his fingers and waved it about. "I am at your beck and call, it seems." She gave a dramatic curtsy.

He chuckled. The laughter strained his aching muscles but lightened his mood. "Well, if I recall, the bargain was that you would help teach me the ways of this land, not act as my errand girl."

"Errand girl? I should hope not." Her mouth dropped open. "When might you learn anything while working all day?"

He shrugged and began to walk toward her cabin. He paused, offering her his elbow.

She considered, then slipped her hand onto his arm. "I believe the first thing you must learn is not to listen to that old man. He will just scare you into building your walls even higher."

He laughed again. "Very well. Have you any ideas for our first lesson?"

"Learning the language is a good place to start. 'The words of a man's mouth are as deep waters, and the wellspring of wisdom as a flowing brook.' "

"Proverbs. Yes, that is a wise place to start." He slipped his hand over hers. Her fingers flinched. He pulled his hand away, and she spun toward him. "Forgive me." He grimaced. She was a young woman, wise to this land, but lived a life secluded from flirtatious gestures, no doubt. He should not confuse her with such forwardness.

She studied him. "Will you have time to learn, Lieutenant? Your daughter waits for you, after all."

"I hope to go to her, then bring her here." He glanced around the place. "You've proven that a girl can grow to be a woman here."

"I have. And there is no other place I would rather have spent my childhood." Her chest lifted with a full breath. "This is home to me."

Home? His was far away, in England. But the bad memories destroyed it.

"Well then, Miss Sabine Van Der Berg," he said, holding his elbow out again. "I hope you do not mind teaching me the language of your old home—and my. . .new one." He forced a smile, even though his throat was tight with the heartache of loss and distance from his daughter.

She smiled back and took his arm.

Even though this woman was unlike any other woman he'd met before, for the first time in a long while, he was content amid everything that remained unfinished.

Chapter 5

Summer 1741

$\int$ abine wiped the back of her neck with a handkerchief, tempted to cast off her bonnet and dip her head in the cool shallows of the river. After Saturday's midday meal, they'd journeyed south to their favorite fishing spot. With Lieutenant Bennington by her side for his fishing lesson, she knew best to attain a certain propriety, enduring the heat with her thin cap clinging to her sweaty hair. Moeder often said, "We might be far from the etiquette of a fine society, but we are still part of such, and you, Sabine, will remain a lady."

Sabine discreetly glanced over at the wood, down the river, and back again. There was nothing to be afraid of—she knew that. But ever since Apenimon's guarded response about the arrow and the flag, she wondered if the lieutenant's concern held any validity. Of course she had relayed what Apenimon had guessed at what might have occurred—a young boy piercing the flag during archery practice—but she omitted that it had only been a guess.

However, a month passed without another incident, at least of the suspicious kind. Each Saturday Sabine sat with Lieutenant

Bennington and taught him the native language, usually over a meal, with men about. And after each lesson, she found herself in an unsettling routine—a regrettable stroll home laced with a giddy eagerness for the next lesson to begin.

She was a misguided arrow now, scouting briefly for any foul play but plummeting gleefully to focus only on this sunny afternoon reserved for the lieutenant's fishing lesson.

The strapping man standing beside her, his sleeves once again rolled up, possessed an unreserved demeanor, nothing like the gentlemen Moeder spoke about. The corner of his mouth inched upward into a lopsided grin as he admired the sharp stick her father had fashioned for him. He seemed to thoroughly enjoy himself.

She couldn't restrain a snicker.

He turned to her, his eyes widened with a mixture of amusement and embarrassment. "Do you find me entertaining?"

Sabine straightened her shoulders and twirled her own stick between her fingers. "I find you—" She cocked her head. "Pleased with yourself."

"I am." He chuckled. "I've come from the hills of East Anglia to this wild countryside, using my bare hands to capture dinner."

"Ha!" Sabine's father blurted. "You might not be so pleased when you discover the skill it takes. If only the men had not left on their annual hunting trip. Apenimon would be your perfect teacher."

"Papa, you are skilled as well." Sabine waded through the water, her sopped hem weighted against the surface. The shimmering scales of a large trout caught her eye. Holding her breath, she leaned over, lifted her spear, and brought it down with controlled force as she'd been taught as a young girl. The fish sped away and her stick landed clumsily in the muddy bottom, thrusting her whole body forward.

Her father caught her by the elbow and helped her to stand upright. "Very close, Daughter."

She pulled her cap in place and wiped her brow with the back of her hand. The lieutenant studied her with less embarrassment and more amusement than before.

"What?" The word was clipped, just like her pride. "It is not as easy as you may think."

"I commend you on your effort, Miss Van Der Berg." He gave a playful bow with one arm across his waist, and the other opening wide as he grasped his spear. "Now, tell me what you did wrong so I can get it right." His posture crumbled with boyish laughter, his dark hair falling forward along his sunburnt brow, and his eyes danced like they welcomed her to join in.

What? At her expense?

But he bounded toward her in the current, winked, and gave her a slight nudge with his elbow, whispering, "I am quite impressed, truly." Aware of his nearness in this sincere gesture, she stepped back, knocking into her father.

"Steady, Sabine." His deep laugh echoed across the river.

The lieutenant's bright smile was ever shining in Sabine's direction. He reached out his hand to her, and she begrudgingly accepted it.

"There you are," he said as she became steady again, allowing her hand to fall away from his. Her cheeks burned with humiliation, even though delight rolled within her unlike anything she'd ever known.

"Thank you," she offered meekly.

He began to wade away, searching the waters with a bent head. "So, you just spy one and catch it?"

"Something like that."

Sabine had never been made the center of such lighthearted attention.

Her father was only mildly encouraging of their merriment. A good Dutchman, he held work like fishing in high regard and pursued it with diligence. He'd employed child's play only when Sabine was a girl. They had splashed about these very waters and held jumping contests on occasion. Whoever jumped farthest from the bank into the water triumphed.

A nostalgic rush of such a time invaded Sabine. Lieutenant Bennington seemingly fished out the rare lighter side of Papa on this summer day. This did not bode well for her persistence that no match should be made. She wondered if Papa's choice for her might bring joy not only in a marriage but to her entire family.

Her nerves frazzled with what she had just considered. While the fort might change the land she loved, marriage would change every ounce of her life. Much of that change was cloaked in the unknown. She knew very little of matrimony.

Sabine laid her eyes on her father, trying to surrender her thoughts to the simple pleasure of his cheeriness. While her frayed nerves settled, Sabine contemplated one of the strategies she learned from her father—never leave a challenge without a good rebuttal.

Perhaps the handsome man's merry play was in dire need of being reciprocated.

Sabine would, of course, return the favor.

She lowered, dipping her hand into the moving waters, wiggling her fingers against the cool drink. "Oh look, Lieutenant."

He swiveled around with his spear raised. As swift as an oar, her hand paddled the water up and splashed him, giving him such a start that he stumbled backward and landed on his backside, knees poking up on either side of his face and his mouth screwed up as droplets trailed like tears down his cheeks.

Father howled. "I think she's gotten the last laugh, sir." He helped the soaked fellow to his feet.

The flash of a dare from the lieutenant's bright eyes set off a drumroll in Sabine's chest. His good nature shone through his chagrin, and their smiles grew in unison.

"The water is refreshing." Lieutenant Bennington licked a droplet from his lip. "Perhaps I shall go for a swim after my catch."

"If we catch any at all," Sabine interjected. "You've gone and scared all the fish away." She pretend pouted, then dragged her skirts through the current upstream. The skies darkened, and thunder roared from several miles away. "I'll find a better spot—" She halted. Beyond the last stand of white pine, a canoe traveled downstream. "Someone is here." Sabine began walking toward the bank, and her father came around her side—his usual defensive move when they were visited by strangers. The lieutenant's reflection appeared from behind, just beside her own.

A man with a golden beard and a broad-brimmed hat sat between two native men. "Ho there!" the man shouted with a raised hand when they neared. "Is this Oswego?"

Mr. Van Der Berg dipped his chin. "It is."

"Wonderful." His face nearly burst with a sort of relief. "My guides have been ever patient with my apprehension in this wilderness." He gave an apologetic smile at both of the men beside him then continued, "I have news for a Lieutenant Bennington."

Jacob's heart plummeted. "I am he." He stepped around Miss Van Der Berg as the two native men jumped out of the canoe and brought it to the bank, placing it upside down on solid ground. A foreboding clap of thunder shook the sky.

"We are an hour away from the post." Mr. Van Der Berg surveyed the heavens. "I do not think we will outrun the storm."

"There is no shelter nearby?" The tallest of the two guides spoke English well.

Sabine reached the river's edge. "Come, there are good trees yonder." She lifted her drenched hem, found her clogs, and began up the bank. "We can use our fishing spears." The two guides fell into step with the woman and marched off to the wood.

Jacob cast an unsettled glance at Mr. Van Der Berg. "Does she know those men?"

"I am not certain," Mr. Van Der Berg replied. "But she knows the custom for an exposed moment such as this." He looked upward again, scrunching his nose. "I felt a drop." He did not express one ounce of concern as his daughter left with strangers.

They jogged over to the stand of trees where Sabine stalked around the littered floor beneath the canopies. The guides cut the bark of a tree. They sliced it several feet up and around the trunk, then dragged their daggers downward. The tallest man unwrapped the bark like the swaddling clothes from an infant—carefully so. They moved on to another tree. Sabine emerged from the wood and found an open area, tossing two stout sticks to the side and sticking two fishing spears in the earth. The shorter guide took the two sticks that Sabine had found and placed them opposite each spear, about five feet away. Securing the bark across the poles, they ushered everyone beneath the shelter just as the thunder cracked, releasing a downpour.

There was hardly room for everyone. They sat side by side, Sabine between Jacob and her father, and the messenger on Jacob's other side. The two guides faced them cross-legged, their backs surely grazed by the rain.

"Please, tell me your message." Jacob spoke in a low voice to the man who introduced himself as Mr. Clive Kimble.

"Sir, it is in my pack, which is beneath the canoe."

"Who sends you?"

"A Mr. Davis."

Jacob's chest tightened. Mr. Davis was his uncle who cared for his daughter. Was it now time? The wall was not secure, and the bastions—nonexistent. He lowered his head and began to pray.

Sabine leaned into him and muttered, "Is something the matter?"

He clamped his teeth, as if he could crush the welling fear with his jaw. If only he could. "My daughter. She is in—" Her hand cupped over his forearm. He met her concerned gaze. Large eyes, swimming like green seas, captured his panic and tossed it away for a brief breath, until he continued, "Danger."

"Danger?"

"Yes." He bounced a look to each person beneath the crude shelter. The rain thrummed like tiny Iroquois drums above them, and anticipation shook in everyone's stare. "My uncle promised to send word once it was time. I fear the time is now. If I do not help my daughter, her mother will steal her away."

Chapter 6

*O*nce the rain subsided, the messenger joined Sabine, her father, and Jacob while the guides disappeared to hunt in the wood. The lieutenant's shocking situation clung to the air like thick humidity. Jacob fell behind, reading the letter of his daughter's strange predicament of being unsafe in her mother's care. Yet he did not explain further, seemingly overcome and unwilling to divulge any details.

Sabine and Moeder prepared the meal without fish that evening since the guides promised venison.

"That Mr. Kimble seems too timid to want to claim his part as a trader. I could tell by his feeble laugh." Moeder ground the cornmeal at the board table while Sabine peeled some squash.

"I do worry more for Lieutenant Bennington. He refused to speak the rest of the way."

"To warn a father that the mother is after his child? How strange." Moeder clicked her tongue. "I am sad to say, you were right, Daughter, to resist a match to that man. He seems a poor match, indeed, what with such a soiled past."

Sabine was conflicted by her own resistance, not to the match, but to her mother's newly stated opposition. Sabine should be relieved, but she was not. Her heart had entertained the match during their fishing escapade, and now it skipped a beat at the thought of secretly entertaining it again.

The knife nearly scraped her finger as she halfheartedly peeled the squash. Shaking her head, she turned the conversation away from the lieutenant. "Mr. Kimble might be a weak sort of fellow, but he did bring several sacks of flour, wanting a more than fair price for them. And enough rum for the entire British army, I suspect."

"It is a shame that the precious furs are traded for such stuff." Moeder's knuckles were white as she pressed down on the pestle. She stopped and pinched the meal, rubbing it between her fingers. "Feels right."

"Looks right too, Moeder," Sabine confirmed.

When they continued their preparation by the fire, the guides arrived, offering a hunted doe for the feast. The newest men to Oswego, the wall builders, circled close as they observed the tallest guide clean the creature in methodical, steadfast movements. The other guide gathered the portions and placed them on a spit. Then he crouched beside the fire and began to slowly turn the spit.

Conversation rumbled, but Sabine and her mother sat without a word, ready to serve their basket of corn biscuits and pot of boiled squash. Finally, they feasted, Sabine keeping a discreet watch on the officers' blockhouse. Would the lieutenant join them?

"I am concerned, Moeder. I do hope that he is not sick with worry," she muttered above her barely touched venison. The guide spied her from across the clearing, and she managed a bite with a smile. 'Twas perfectly cooked.

"Perhaps you should make him a plate," Moeder suggested.

"But do not stay long. I want to return home before they smoke."

Sabine ate with more fervor to be sure to compliment the cook with an empty plate. She crossed to the other side of the fire and curtsied to Lieutenant Wilson. His attention remained beyond the clearing, toward the mouth of the river. "Excuse me, sir, is Lieutenant Bennington not well?"

He acknowledged her with a blank stare, smacked his lips together, then shrugged. "I am not his keeper."

The older man's demeanor had declined over the past several months. The aftershock of that midnight disturbance this past autumn skirted up Sabine's spine. She prayed for his peace. This was a friendly land and was secure with or without a fortification—as long as their neighboring French would leave them alone. Maybe the fort was necessary, not as a defense, but at least as a permanent presence in this place.

Sabine carried a plate down to the blockhouse and knocked on the door.

Jacob answered. "Good evening, Miss Van Der Berg."

"I thought you might be hungry." She could hardly make out his features with the lamp lit within and the darkness of night falling around her.

"That is kind of you." He joined her in the cool night, standing so close to her that she stepped back to give him room. He took the plate, brushing her fingertips.

Sabine ignored her tingling skin and folded her hands at her waist. A low hollow tone floated toward them, followed by a cascade of notes from a flute. The familiar sound of a feast danced around Sabine's heart. The guides offered music not so different than the nearby village.

While her mind ignited with the soulful ballad, her heart

twisted about, trying to root her to this very spot. "I must return. Moeder does not care to be around the pipe smoke." Her mind won the battle. "However, I am sorry about your news today."

He shoveled in a jagged breath, observing the fire. A fragile dust of pink light shone upon his chiseled profile. "It must seem strange to you. I never thought I would be part of such a scandal."

Scandal? Even here, beyond all the streets and buildings and disease Moeder had described, Sabine understood the word *scandal*, and could not fathom the lieutenant being part of one.

"Sir, you have further plucked my curiosity—"

"Or is it disappointment?" He fired a gaze at her through the fast approaching darkness.

"Disappointment?" She balled her fists, only to keep them from slamming against her flaming cheeks. Disappointment met her most because of her mother's new disapproval, therefore proving Sabine's affection for the man.

He strode over and sat on a barrel amid a pile of crates, trunks, and tools, and cradled the plate in his lap.

Straining her eyes, Sabine could make out that Moeder remained near the festivities, and much to her relief, Papa sat beside her. She was not alone, nor had she stood up to leave. Together her parents appeared to enjoy the melody.

"Miss Van Der Berg, will you join me?" Jacob's voice was warbled, as if he spoke around a bubble that threatened to burst into a magnitude of weeping. She understood this. She'd heard such phenomena during Moeder's lowest returns to the valley. "Please, I must explain."

Sabine drew near to him. He rummaged in a trunk at his feet and found a candle and lit it. In the soft glow, Sabine found another barrel to sit on and lowered herself to his eye level, their knees nearly touching. She gazed up at the glitter in the sky, scorning the turbulence in her stomach. She prodded, "Your daughter is in danger?"

If ever a groan was loud enough to summon a wild bear to the party, it was this outburst in her mind. Her heart defeated her good notion to keep silent.

"I fear that is so." His serious tone sliced through her humiliation.

"Your former—"

"Former wife? Yes. You see, the woman ran off to America with another man. I granted her the divorce she sought, against every fiber in my heart. Whatever was left of it."

"And your daughter?"

"Ah, my sweet Amelia. She was a young thing. Clinging more to her nurse than her mother. And, the shame of it all, her mother hardly cared."

The music turned happier, accompanied by hollering. The men were up and about, following in the stomping steps of the tallest guide.

She leaned on her elbows, feeling stuck in a contrast of merriment and sorrow. "I am so sorry, sir." Could she even comfort such a man as this? She knew nothing of love, and even less about falling out of it.

"Please, call me Jacob"—he pushed the food around with a small knife—"at least when my men are out of earshot." A soft laugh puffed from his lips. "The letter today claimed that Amelia's mother would like to take her back to England because she's found a household position for her while the household's master awaits her coming of age to marry." His voice held no jest.

"She's but a girl," Sabine blurted.

"She is. That is why I must protect her." Jacob's words were gruff, slicing.

The shuffling around the fire grew louder, the flute was a high-pitched pulse, abounding but incomplete without a beating drum. Surely they would end the unbalanced song. She did not want to remember the dismay on Jacob's face every time she listened to the familiar instrument.

The music faded, and the men took seats around the fire. Pipe smoke rose up to dance with the flames licking an empty spit. The peaceful night tugged at Jacob's desire to creep out of his misery and only indulge in the next breath with the beautiful Sabine beside him. They sat in silence, allowing the confession of his tragedy to buzz and fade from their ears.

"Are there many nights this festive in Oswego?" Jacob asked.

"Yes, many." Sabine fiddled with her apron's hem. "I cannot imagine any other life."

"How long have you lived here, Sabine?"

"Since I was four years of age. My papa wanted his own land while weaving his baskets and making a homestead. And Moeder despised the disease and walled-in life of the colony." She lowered her head and entwined her fingers. "The irony of all of it—Moeder did not escape disease. An early tradesman came down with a fever his first day at the trading post. Moeder tended to him out of her own goodwill. The same illness stole her sight away."

"That is terribly ironic."

"I remember the day she recovered enough to walk. Papa tried to help, but she refused, caught her hip on the table, and crumpled to the ground." Sabine's shoulders straightened, her hands now grabbing at her knees. "Her sobbing accompanied many of my hours.

So many that I escaped outdoors and spent time with the children of the native tradesmen during trade days. Papa and I learned much from them, and they became our next of kin in a way." She smiled. The candlelight revealed moisture glistening on her cheeks. "Trade days were a bright reunion, the light toward which I walked in a seemingly bleak in-between."

"If I did not hear the words from your mouth, I would hardly believe your suffering. You are a strong person. One who has captured my—" His compliment was too forward. Much too transparent. He continued, "My respect."

"Sir. . .I mean, Jacob—" Anticipation hummed between them as she tested the use of his name on her tongue. A roar of excitement woke up delight he'd not felt in a very long time. She dropped her gaze and admitted, "I must be strong. I fear that if I'm not, we'd slip backwards again."

"Your fear is ironic too." He leaned onto his lap, nudging his plate with his elbow, resisting the urge to hold her hand. "I have hardly seen fear produce such strength."

"I do what I must do. It is nothing strange or extraordinary."

"You are the strength of this place, Sabine Van Der Berg." He was certain she'd laugh at his serious tone and assessment. His way with words had been scorned by the practical woman back in England.

But this woman before him was different. Sabine did not realize her effect on him. He had borrowed her fearlessness to lessen his own fright from their very first encounter. When the guides came today, she did not wait for them to ask for help. Sabine Van Der Berg cleaved to their mission and offered a capable hand.

How many times had Jacob sat back with skepticism, waiting

for a clear sign that it was indeed safe to proceed?

His wife had destroyed his trust. So how could a near stranger be his safe space? What made him want to share his story with her? Self-pity? Perhaps. He'd kept his private life buried so deep for so long that he thought it might be a figment of his imagination—or a skewed perspective of some truth that would point to him as the one at fault for the death of his marriage.

Across from him sat a young woman who grew from hardship yet had been untouched by foiled love. How could he imagine himself becoming anything more to her than a friend? He was not just the man who would impose a permanent disturbance on this peaceful land, but one who had already failed at love and marriage. As he drew in air, his self-pity was burned away by anger at himself. He should not have been so open and tender with Sabine Van Der Berg this night.

She deserved someone standing on the brink of life, not soiled by the muck of it.

"I must retire now." He rose, and she stood quickly before him. Her eyes were round and questioning. "Forgive my brevity. I am exhausted."

She reached out a hand to his arm. "Jacob, I do not know what arrangement your daughter might face, but I can tell—" She glanced over her shoulder then back again. Her face shone a pure loveliness in the moonlit evening. "Your daughter is well loved by her father. There is something very special that grows from such a gift. A strength indeed."

"Sabine!" Her father's voice rumbled like thunder—low and firm.

She hurried toward him. "I am coming, Papa."

Jacob watched her father's lantern bob up and down as the small family headed to their home, and when the light disappeared, he waited until the glow filled the eastern window. Surely that lamp, secure in the refuge of the Van Der Bergs's home, was the brightest place in this frontier. If only it were bright enough to extinguish the gloom in Jacob's heart.

Chapter 7

Sabine couldn't shake the feeling that she was being carefully considered by Jacob. A sudden awareness grew that at any moment she'd find him staring in her direction—or truthfully, she hoped she would. Was this how Apenimon felt around his wife, Talise? Often Sabine admired his loving look for Talise, suspecting it was an outpouring of something deeper felt, something unknown to a tradesman's daughter in remote America. Sabine was certain the whirl inside her stomach at every encounter with Lieutenant Bennington matched the same adoration she'd seen when her friend looked upon his bride.

A bloom unfurled in her chest, welcoming pursuit by the handsome lieutenant. Sabine often brushed aside her mother's fairy tales when she would rather run through the grasses and fish for their supper. On this plain, beneath the grand blue sky, she longed for the chance to play a part in her own fairy tale—one forbidden by the very mother who introduced her to such stories.

As she shucked the corn this crisp morning, she was in perfect view of the prince of her fancy. He sat with his shoulders stooped, hovering over a mug he cradled in his lap in the middle of a quiet work site. She wasn't a lady in need of a handsome knight to save her; rather, the kind soldier was distressed, and Sabine longed to save him.

"We have returned, friend." Apenimon appeared at the wooded edge beside her fence. Sabine parted the cornstalks and stepped through.

"Ah, did your hunt go well?"

"It did. We will have much to trade. I see those white men have continued with their castle."

She followed his gaze. The walls were well under way, producing a troubling change in the scenery that Moeder held so dear.

"They hope to have it finished by the first freeze."

"Their work does not seem solid. Nothing like Niagra."

Sabine smirked. "Are you favoring the Frenchmen now?"

"No." His expression was serious. A deep ridge shadowed his dark eyes. "Have any new men arrived for trade?"

"Only a messenger from Albany—"

"No, I mean a tribesman? Perhaps from the northern shore?"

"No. But I did notice a man watching Moeder's tulip offering. He sat in a canoe at the bend."

Apenimon's eyes simmered as he examined the far-off spot that Sabine mentioned.

"That was over a month ago. Is anything the matter?" She stepped closer.

"We are making sure that the peace is kept by all—even strangers." He ran his hand along his belt adorned with wampum. The pearly shells were sewn close together, as if they were a pebbled shore organized in tightly knit rows. All tension left him and he grinned. "Tell the men to be ready for a plentiful trade tomorrow." He bade her farewell and ran down the tree line, disappearing toward the bank of the river.

She returned to her basket of corn and began shucking the next ear. Now Jacob was nowhere to be seen. Men began to emerge from beneath the shadow of the existing fort and the many canvas tents dotted about the place.

After she finished, she lugged the corn across the garden and over to the fire pit. She left her produce to be boiled for the noon meal. Voices carried from the dock at the river's mouth. Both lieutenants stood with their backs to her, their attention toward the glassy waters of Lake Ontario.

"You cannot leave your post, Jacob." Lieutenant Wilson's words were punctuated with authority.

Jacob slid his fingers around the back of his neck, his curls flipped up against his whitened knuckles. "I might lose her forever."

The long profile of the older lieutenant was outlined against the shimmering waters beyond. He laid a heavy hand on Jacob's shoulder. "I do not think the King's men will pardon that excuse. I am sorry, son." He hung his head as if commiserating with Jacob. A lump formed in Sabine's throat. "Do you not believe the bastions will be finished in time?"

"I do not know whether she has minutes or months left on this continent." Jacob spoke through his teeth.

"Then send for her."

Jacob surveyed the land to the east then the west. Sabine stepped back, fearing he might notice her listening. "An unfinished fort is not secure for a young girl."

"What about the Dutchman's—" Both men turned and caught her staring.

"Speak of the—" The older man hissed then tipped his hat. "Miss Sabine, good morning to you."

She curtsied, then spoke directly to Jacob. "Sir, your daughter would be safe here." Sabine considered the blind woman who sat far off in the distance, rocking on the porch of their square cabin. "A child would be a welcome change, even for Moeder. She may stay with us until quarters are built." Perhaps the young child would soften her parents' impression of Jacob. The arrival of Apenimon's child had sparked their initial matchmaking scheme. This morning Sabine's prayers had been first for the safety of the little girl and second for her parents' to have a favorable impression of Jacob once again. Sabine was hopeful that both prayers would be answered—and she was willing to help them along.

"That is kind of you." Jacob's brow was drawn upward with creases of worry, and his eyes were pink, as if he'd sat in the smoky cloud around the fire much too long. Had he slept at all?

"Well then, that would be a fine solution." The old lieutenant's happy declaration surprised Sabine. The man's usual forlorn demeanor was only matched by Moeder's. "Tomorrow is trade day. We will find a trader heading back to Albany and send a summons for her to journey—"

"I had hoped to be the one to go for her—to take leave after the job was done and bring her myself."

"That is not possible though, is it?" The usual leeriness eclipsed the old officer's expression. A jolt stabbed Sabine's stomach as she recalled his past discontentment. Lieutenant Wilson didn't see the fort as an unsightly disruption to their home but as a secure addition.

Jacob abandoned the man and approached Sabine. "Are you certain that your parents would not mind?"

She smiled wide, plunging into the warmth of Jacob's attention. "Surely she'd not take up too much room?"

His lips quirked up and his brown eyes danced at her humor. "Just waist high," he mused.

"Ah, that is nothing. My friends in the village have twice as many bodies in half the size of our cabin. She will make it cozy in the winter."

He cupped his palm beneath her elbow and stepped closer, blocking all view of the other lieutenant, the lake, and any control of her senses.

"I am forever grateful for you Miss. . .Sabine."

Who'd have imagined that all her daydreaming about saving this prince would become reality by an offer of hospitality? And who'd have believed how quickly God changed her heart from resenting this man's mission to helping him secure it? She had also prayed for him continuously this morning.

When Jacob left her side and joined Lieutenant Wilson to inspect the building efforts, Sabine cradled her elbow as she crossed the plain, unable to stop smiling.

"Sabine?" Papa crossed the ground with long strides.

"Yes?" Her smile faded.

His cheeks were red, his nose was red, his brow, beaded with sweat, was red. "You do not need to spend so much time with that lieutenant. He is not for you."

"Papa, I was just offering him some help."

"With what?"

"His daughter needs a safe place to stay." Her stomach flipped. "She can stay here."

"Here?" Moeder screeched.

"It is the least we can do for a child in such a horrible

predicament." Sabine tried to push aside the thought of a young girl betrothed to an older man. The horror of it sent ice through her veins. She reached out and took her father's hand, tears welling in her eyes. "I cannot imagine such a thing, Papa. Let us be good neighbors—and friends. He needs a safe place for his daughter."

"And as your father, it is my duty to protect you also, Sabine." He squeezed her hand. "You deserve someone untarnished by lovers' quarrels."

"It is not his fault—"

"Sabine," Moeder warned.

Papa kissed her forehead and brushed past her. "Daughter, our home is open to the girl. But remember that Bennington is no match for you, and you mustn't give him reason to believe otherwise."

Jacob's hope kindled after Sabine's generous offer. He had a hard time imagining his child in this place, but now he could see her in the tender care of the Van Der Bergs.

The sun was a distraction this day, burning down on his neck and forearms while they constructed the forms of the fortification. By the midday meal, two traders arrived by way of the river, and as some men helped them unload their wares, the rest filled their bellies.

Jacob retrieved his satchel from his quarters and stole away down the riverbank to find a secluded spot to pen his letter to his uncle. His fingers shook with the anticipation of securing a safe escape for Amelia. Had her mother arrived early? Where was she when she wrote the letter to his uncle? Last Jacob knew, his former wife had returned to England this past October. He'd never thought she'd succumb to such a horrific practice of giving her daughter for servitude then for marriage to a man three times her age. What sum of money had been offered for such a scheme? What man would agree to such a bride? Tears blurred Jacob's vision, and he curled his fist so tight that the parchment beneath it creased under the pressure.

"Lord, be swift with Your protection. Bring my daughter here safely." He spoke the prayer along a choppy breath. Wiping his eyes with the back of his hand, he filled his lungs with air and continued with his quill. Despite the peaceful rustle of leaves above and the gentle flow of the river ahead of him, anxiety coursed through his fingertips as he attempted controlled strokes. As the holler of men signaled a return to work, Jacob finished the letter.

Now to find that messenger.

At the turn of the river, Sabine was bent over scrubbing pots, with her dress sleeves rolled up to her elbows. Her skirt was tied in a knot at her shins, and water flowed around her ankles. Wild strands of reddish-gold hair whipped through the breeze from beneath her cap, and her braid snaked down her back. She hummed a pretty tune that outmatched any nearby fowl, and for the first time this day, Jacob found some joy.

"Hallo!" He made his presence known so as not to startle her.

She popped up from her chore and raised her hand to shade her eyes. "Lieutenant, I did not see you at the meal."

He jogged along the bank and approached the water's edge. Slightly out of breath, he said, "Jacob, remember?" He allowed himself to smile, even if he'd try to resist the admiration stirred up by this young woman.

"Yes, of course." Her cheeks' pink shade deepened and she gave him a shy grin. "Jacob, you must be famished."

"Do not worry over me, I have had some dried beef and ale this day. Besides, the heat steals away my appetite."

"I see." She lifted her foot from the water, her toes grazing the surface as she found dry ground. With careful steps she slipped on her clogs then unknotted her skirt. Her attention fell on the letter in his hand. "Will you send for your daughter then?"

"I shall."

"That is good." Sabine gathered up her pots and placed them in a basket. She then tucked it on her hip and turned, her brow furrowed as if she was perplexed. "I must return home."

"Let me carry that for you." He rushed over to her, placing the folded letter in his front pocket and trying to lift the basket from her arms. But her grip was like a vise.

"That is not necessary. I can manage just fine."

"Sabine, it is customary for a gentleman to give assistance to a woman."

"Is it?" She cocked an eyebrow and her lips wobbled with an audacious smirk. "Customs are different here in Oswego."

He clasped the basket's rim and tugged, but she gave nothing, only a petite step toward him. "It is my duty," he muttered, now mesmerized by her determined glare, her ruby lips, and the sprinkle of light freckles along her nose.

"And my duty is to carry this home." Her emerald eyes rounded and searched his face. What did she see? A man who was weak among these strong men of Oswego, knowing little about living off the land and weathering the elements? Or perhaps a broken fellow defiled by a loveless marriage, unworthy of a woman as pure and strong as Sabine?

"Jacob, you do not need to prove yourself to me." Her gentle retaliation vibrated the current around his heart. Had she read his thoughts?

He pulled at the basket again, and she took another step closer to him. Now her arm rested against his, and his nose skimmed the lace brim of her cap. "Do you mean that?"

She turned her face up to him, a mixture of wonder and uncertainty watering her pretty eyes. "Of course. I do not care for the bounds of society if they are lost in etiquette. That does not make a man—" Her breath caught, and her teeth rested on her glistening lip. He swallowed hard, mustering up words to fill this space that he so wanted to obliterate with a final tug and a delicate kiss.

"Sabine?"

"Yes?" Her grip on the basket lessened, and he felt the weight of it in his hands. Her shoulders slumped. Was she retreating? No, not in this moment, not when he savored her words, her scent of wildflowers, and her glowing beauty amid the even wilder land.

Before she could leave him alone, he leaned forward and whispered, "Please, tell me what makes a man?"

The weight of the basket was fully in his grip now, and her hand reached up and cupped his jaw. "His heart. I see yours—for your daughter, in your attempt to save our property, in your care that harm stays far away." She spoke into his soul like no other human. How did she see him this way?

"Sabine, you are too kind." He set the basket down, his eyes stayed on her gaze. Her eyes were steady, wide, piercing, radiating the fullness of an abundant life. He wanted that—he wanted her to show him how to live so fearlessly.

One curtsy of her lashes and her attention fell on his mouth, welcoming him to lean in. His lips grazed hers, and her eyes closed, hiding the glorious green.

"Jacob," she sighed as he pulled away, her hand clutching at his chest. She was bright, her cheeks as red as her lips, and her eyes intense with the thrill of a new adventure. "I have never—" Her fingertips brushed along her mouth. She dropped her hand quickly. "I hope it wasn't—"

What was this? The courageous woman seemed to teeter with doubt. If he could reveal the fierce storm lashing about in his heart, she'd have no doubt in herself.

He brushed his finger along her cheek. "I have never been so overcome with. . .with. . ." *Awe? Intrigue? Completeness?* "Certainty. That I am exactly where I should be."

She held him in a sort of trance, her sparkling wonder filling his confidence like a waterfall spills with unstoppable force.

Her father shouted from beyond the bend.

"Papa calls." She dropped down and snatched up the basket. "We must ready for the trade tomorrow." She turned to him with a shy smile, and he beamed.

Only when Sabine left him did he remember the letter at his heart.

Could this remote assignment be used by God not only to become a safe haven for his kin but to provide an opportunity for him to love a woman like Sabine Van Der Berg?

Chapter 8

Autumn 1741

*T*he flaming colors of autumn were dull in comparison to the fire ever present in Sabine's heart. She prepared the soil to replant the dormant bulbs. Her eyes and hands focused on her duties, but her mind whirred with anticipation. She could not help but hope for the next encounter with Jacob. She tried to honor her parents and stay clear of moments alone with the man—at first, anyway. But they only saw him for his circumstance, and she was certain that she'd glimpsed his heart.

If one person was undeserving of another, it was Sabine. While Sabine was quick to show off her skills when Papa taught Jacob to use a bow, Jacob was careful and calculated, a perfect student. Sabine took care to remind Papa about every good quality of the lieutenant, and her father agreed. Yet no word about a match was ever mentioned again.

As the fort progressed, so did her affection for Jacob, and her resistance to change became nearly forgotten. She found herself absorbing Jacob's anxiety for word on his daughter. After a stolen kiss or a secret meeting, Sabine would spend hours in her own thoughts, rehearsing a confession to her parents—one that always included her ever-mounting proof that Jacob was a worthy suitor.

When might she have the courage to reveal her secret love to her parents? What might they say? She prayed for their blessing by the first bloom of the white ones—a promise of more than forgiveness, but of peace for the match.

That evening, after the final embers of the cooking fire died, and Papa and Moeder retired for the night, Sabine lingered among the bare tulip patches, waiting.

"Sabine?" His low whisper burst delight in her soul.

"I am here, Jacob."

She could barely make out his broad figure drawing close. He held out his arms, his fingertips brushing her shoulders, and she clasped his hands in hers. The cool night air was snuffed out as she pulled close to his chest, his warm breath mixing with her own. Their foreheads gently pressed against each other.

"Pray for us." His usual request. The distress of his words always washed away Sabine's delight and exposed her own concern for his dilemma.

"Oh, heavenly Father, have mercy on us," she began. "Let our ways be pure and our hearts be centered on You." Sabine squeezed Jacob's hands, and he squeezed back. He pressed her so close that her shoe thumped against his. On a jagged breath, she continued, "Give us peace as You work all things for our good—for the good of Amelia and the heart of her father." A soft sound rumbled from Jacob. Sabine comforted him with her palm against his cheek. "Lord, You are perfect in all Your ways, and tonight, as with every night, we beg You to be swift in the fullness of Your plan for little Amelia and Jacob. Let them reunite quickly."

She bit her lip. The sound of the flowing river and the quiet call of an owl accompanied her prayers upward. Most nights Jacob would finish their prayer. But Sabine knew that tonight he'd not speak a word. His shuddering chest and the tears pooling against her hand on his cheek nearly cut off her own ability to speak. She must remain strong for him. She had plenty of practice with Moeder's need for borrowed strength. Sabine could not deny the hunch that she'd grown up through her hardship for such a time as this—for such a man as Jacob.

"Holy Spirit, You know our prayer without these words. Wash us in Your peace as we wait. Keep sweet Amelia safe. Amen." She slid her hand away from his cheek, wiping his tears with her thumb. "My dear Jacob, it will be soon, I am sure of it."

He lifted his head up to the starry sky. "My greatest prayer is that the letter arrived in time." He snaked his arm across her shoulder and pulled her close to his side as they walked to the door of her cabin. "I did not dream in a million winks that I would have someone speaking for me when I cannot." He spun her toward him. "Sabine Van Der Berg, I do not deserve you."

Her pulse thrummed as he bent down and kissed her. The fairy tales never mentioned the depth and effect of such a gesture from the prince.

She was glad for that.

Sabine savored this devotion meant only for her, like a secret hidden away in her dreams.

Yet her dreams were now in her everyday walking and breathing—and in loving this Jacob Bennington.

No word came before the first snowstorm of the season. Sabine spent many hours at her window, cursing the nearly finished wall that blocked her view of the man she'd longed to see again.

"How many inches do you suppose have fallen?" Moeder clung to Papa's arm as he put on his winter coat of beaver fur.

"At least five inches." He grabbed his spade and began to unlatch the door. Sabine sprang up from beneath her own pelt and stood with her mother. When Papa opened the door, a knee-high wall of snow began to crumble into the house. "Perhaps more than five." He chuckled then peered out. "The sky is clear. I will begin to move the snow."

Distant drums traveled from within the wood near the lake's shore. "They are preparing for tomorrow," Papa noted, peering across the powdery plain.

Sabine lifted on her toes to see the lake in the distance. She could barely make out one man, shrouded in a dark brown fur, raising his chisel and piercing the ice. Then another arrived, and together they began to construct the wood frames for their fishing tents.

Joy bubbled up inside Sabine as shivers crawled on her skin from the wintry air. While her mother might never step foot outside during these winter months for fear of the unpredictable change of snow cover and icy patches, Sabine spent many long mornings spearing fish from beneath her hide-covered poles. During the winter fishing season, she often visited Apenimon's longhouse, staying warm by their small fire as the chief shared stories and legends and the young men carved fishing lures for the next day's catch.

"Papa, I will prepare our shoes!" Sabine swept the crumbled snow back outside and then began to close the door.

Papa gave a sideways glance over his shoulder. "I do believe that Lieutenant Bennington would be interested in joining us tomorrow morn. Might be more successful than the last fishing lesson."

Sabine's face heated at the thought of their first playful encounter in the river and the overwhelming change of her heart later that day. "Yes, Papa. We are obligated to show him the way of ice fishing."

"I want you to fish beside me though, Sabine. We can each have our own tent."

"Yes, you do not need to be too casual with such a worldly sort of fellow," Moeder chimed in.

"Papa, has not Jacob been an ideal student, a perfect gentleman?" She borrowed her words from the practiced speech in her mind.

"He is a good friend to us," Papa admitted.

"He is kind. I believe him when he says the end of his marriage was not his choice." Her pulse drummed inside her ears. Was this her chance to defend the man who had her heart? "Is there no redemption for an abandoned husband?"

"Ah, there is." Papa nodded thoughtfully. "Perhaps he will find an abandoned wife to care for."

Moeder laughed. "I am glad you are interested in what it takes for a marriage, Sabine. At least you are not as resistant as you used to be." If only they knew that she had forsaken her resistance to find love long ago. Love had found her. "There is a match out there for you. A deserving one."

Jacob's words pierced her soul. *"I do not deserve you."*

"Grace is a funny thing, isn't it?" she muttered to herself.

"What was that?" Papa inquired.

Sabine opened her mouth to speak but then clamped it shut. "Oh nothing. Let us go to the officers' quarters after my chores."

She closed the door, ignoring Moeder's complaint about the icy air trapped inside now, and bustled about, frenzied by all that lay ahead this winter. None of the chill that Moeder mentioned caused

Sabine discomfort. All she could consider was the small, snug fishing tent on the ice. If only Jacob could stay beside her as they waited for the next catch.

By the time Sabine had restrung the snowshoes with new netting and gathered their ice chisels from beneath the lean-to, Papa had cleared the usual path between their cabin to the fort blockhouse. However, the path now led to a temporary entrance between the frames of two of the clay walls.

Wrapping herself in her winter cloak, Sabine pressed as much of her face as she could into its warmth and followed Papa, mindful of any slick patches along the way.

The chimney of the officers' quarters puffed against the silvery-blue sky, and conversation carried through the door. After Papa and Sabine were ushered inside, Jacob rose from the table, leaving Lieutenant Wilson with a disgruntled expression on his scruffy face.

Jacob greeted Papa with a firm shake. "Mr. Van Der Berg." His eyes glimmered in Sabine's direction. "Miss Van Der Berg." His smile held back a treasure trove of affirmations, sweet considerations, and of course the intimate use of her name.

"Lieutenant." She spoke each syllable with a precise pronunciation. "I pray that you have heard from your daughter?"

The smile fell. "Nay. I fear with this treacherous weather, not one messenger from Albany will find us until spring."

"That is a sad but true observation," Papa declared, placing his hand on Jacob's shoulder. "But we would like to offer you a chance to make use of your waiting time. Let us teach you to fish."

"Fish? Again?" Jacob bounced a stare between each of them. "I fear that I'd catch my death standing in the icy river now."

"Ah, no, we will fish on the lake. Through the ice." Papa approached the table where some traders sat. "I say, do you plan to join us? I've not seen any preparations made."

"Come, see the new spears we have carved. You'll be pleased, Josef." A trader rose as he chewed a piece of jerky. Papa followed him into the back room. Sabine and Jacob exchanged knowing glances, and she bit back a smile with all these men sitting about.

"Apenimon and his men have begun building their tents already," Sabine blurted to end the trance Jacob had on her.

"The villagers will join us in fishing?" Jacob questioned.

"Aye. They taught us our first winter here."

Jacob then addressed Lieutenant Wilson who had a quill in hand above a fresh piece of parchment. "Sir, it sounds like another opportunity to maintain a relationship with the natives. Do you also join in?"

The older gentleman nodded thoughtfully. "I have. Mostly the traders and some of the other men take to the ice better. I do wonder if our welcome is wearing thin these days."

"All the better then. Let us continue to show them our appreciation for the ways they've taught us." Jacob winked at Sabine.

Sabine shifted from one foot to the other. How could Lieutenant Wilson be so uneasy about Apenimon and his men? She would not stand here and listen to this nonsense that they needed to prove themselves friends with the village.

"Jac—Lieutenant Bennington. If you decide to join us, bring your fishing spear and a heavy coat to the shore. If not, well, you'll need to be sure to have much to trade with the village to keep somewhat nourished." She spun on her heel, reached for the door, and thrust herself into the biting cold.

Jacob joined her in the crisp morning. "Sabine, what is this?" After he closed the door, he slid his bare hand across her shoulder, turning her around.

She gladly faced him but tried to keep her seriousness. "I grow weary of that superstitious officer and his belief that the relationship with the Iroquois is so fragile." She crossed her arms beneath her cloak.

Jacob's nose began to pink in the elements, and his eyes watered in the breeze. "Why is that your concern? They are like your kin. You are secure."

"Ah, but we are just Dutchmen living off the land. We have no control over what a British servant of the King might impose to appease his ridiculous fear." She nodded to the nearly finished wall.

"I see." Jacob laughed and rubbed his hands together then lifted them to his mouth and blew into them. "You are right. Fear is what brought me here to secure this place for the British. This frigid, unforgiving place." His teeth chattered.

"It is not that bad if you are prepared." Sabine drew close to him, gathered his hands in her own, and wrapped them around her waist, allowing the folds of her cloak to drape over his arms. "See, a little warmth is all you need." Could he feel her heartbeat ricocheting in her chest?

"Sabine, we must tell your parents about our courtship." His voice was a rumble, scratchy and low. "I do not know that they would approve—of me."

Her heart skipped a beat and her stomach rolled. She could not bear to affirm the very truth of his concern.

"They know you to be a good man." Her words barely escaped the back of her throat, threatened to be squished by a lump forming as rapidly as the ice across the lake. "Please, do not worry. The time will come to tell them."

"And do not concern yourself with the query of an old officer. I will make sure nothing drastic happens to this place." He kissed her.

His lips were cold, and she was tempted to warm them up also. But the door began to open behind him, and she pulled away, stepping back several feet.

Papa stared at each of them for a moment, then began past them down toward their cabin. "Come, Sabine. We must get the tent poles in the ice so they can freeze by morning. Lieutenant, join us if you choose."

Sabine gaped at Jacob, who did the same at her. *That was close. And foolish,* she thought, as they continued through the snow in silence. Her heart barely quieted its stampede though. Not because of the refreshing kiss from Jacob, but because of the stifling truth of his words.

What if she could not convince her parents to agree to bless their courtship? Might she bring heartache to the father who always provided and the mother who'd lost so much?

Their daughter was in love, and ever foolish.

Beneath the darkened early morning sky, Jacob's boots crunched through the snow. His lantern shone a dim halo on the pure white land ahead of him. Not until he was at the very edge of the shore was he aware of the transition from snow-mounded earth to snow-laden ice. He cast his lantern ahead, observing the three tents he had erected with the Van Der Bergs yesterday. Just a few yards away were the Iroquois tents. Along the far bend of shore, the fishermen began to emerge from the tree line.

From the corner of his eye, he saw Sabine and her father approach. They greeted him with hushed voices. Carefully, they walked to their tents, and after her father entered his, Sabine blew Jacob a kiss from her gloved hand.

"Perhaps I need assistance," he whispered across the short distance of ice.

"'Twas not my idea to put up three instead of two." Her bottom lip poked out. Oh, might Amelia arrive quickly so they could gain approval from her parents to marry. The secret was bursting at his seams, and he wanted to divulge the love growing inside him.

He lay as flat as he could on the ice and readied his spear above the hole but only chased the fish about with his lure. Once he attempted to plunge his spear into their flesh, they escaped.

He was still not successful by the eight o'clock hour. His companions and the Iroquois, however, secured a large enough load of fish for a feast. The sun crawled above the lake as they sat around a small fire on the shore and cooked their freshly caught breakfast.

"Do not worry, son." Mr. Van Der Berg patted Jacob's back. "With practice comes perfection."

Sabine sat across from him, the heat of the fire shimmering before her face, creating the illusion that she was—an illusion. He wanted to be near her and entwine his fingers with her own, but the space between them must remain just as vast as the ice sheet before them. She spoke with Apenimon, anyway. Together they laughed and carried on.

A shorter man, with a face framed in the fur of his hood and his long black hair fanning out down his coat, crouched beside Apenimon. "Look what Pierre left behind." His English was good. He must have been an Iroquois interpreter. He twirled a shiny goblet between his fingers by its stem and flicked Sabine's more simply-made mug. "We give away much to the east, but I do wonder if our Huron brothers have the greater trade."

Apenimon's nostrils flared, and he said something in a foreign tongue. The man made a clicking sound, shook his head, and moved over to another fire where more villagers cooked their food. A couple of the traders exchanged glances then landed timid stares in Jacob's direction.

He tightened his jaw. Sabine whispered with Apenimon and continued to eat. No matter how long Jacob stared at her, she did not look up from her plate.

Once they had finished the meal and the rest of the men retreated to their tents, Jacob approached her as she gathered up the utensils. "What did you talk about with Apenimon?"

"His son." She still did not look at him. "He is growing quickly. I must visit him soon." She gave a complacent smile.

"Sabine, what was said when that man spoke of the French?" His voice was sterner than he meant it to be, but it did the trick.

She looked up. Her intense glare pierced through him. "There is nothing to fear. He is kin to the woman who married a Frenchman. He's always teasing about allegiances." Her mouth's corners drooped. She licked her lips quickly and returned her attention to her chore. Why did she seem uncertain?

"Is that all?"

"Of course."

"Then why won't you look at me?"

"Apenimon is not happy with his friend. He reminds him of their treaty with the British. Yet his friend entertains the Frenchmen often."

"I see."

Sabine shot another heated look at him. "Is it wrong for them to be allies with both of us? Why must we make them choose on land that is their right?"

Jacob glanced around. "You should not express such ideas without knowing who might be listening."

"I have seen the French wares." Sabine spoke in a hushed tone. "They are appealing. The quality is impeccable."

"Enough, Sabine."

"There is nothing to be afraid of, Jacob. You are as pale as a ghost. I am speaking of trade, not war."

"Do not be naive, Miss Van Der Berg. With the French worming their way into our trade relationship, there is always the possibility of—"

Sabine sprang toward him, placing her fingers on his lips. Her emerald eyes darted with nothing less than fear itself—a look he'd not seen from this woman before. "Do not say it," she warned. "You will not bring such ugly ideas to the peaceful day." Her eyes filled, and before a drop spilled, she made her way back to her tent.

After their fishing expedition, Jacob waited by the garden fence in the cold night. But Sabine did not come. He noticed a rolled parchment threaded through the gate's hook. Unrolling it, he held up his lamp and read through the puffs of breath in the icy air:

> *Jacob,*
> *I have been careless not to respect my parents' wishes. You and I are different in many ways. What might life be like with one of us dedicated to peace and the other siding with the throne at any cost? Perhaps it is best to part ways, if not on each side of the fort's walls, on matters of the heart.*
>
> *Sabine*

Jacob twisted the parchment in his fists. The brave soul he was falling in love with was scared. And he understood why.

What would change her world more drastically than war?

Chapter 9

Spring 1742

*T*was not difficult to avoid the man—what with the harshness of winter delaying any gatherings among the men and traders. If only she had not received a scolding from her father that same first day of ice fishing, she might have enjoyed a shameless distance from Jacob. Yet guilt niggled at her as often as the nipping cold.

"Sabine, you have grown up too strong-headed," Papa had counseled when he asked her about the argument he'd seen from a distance. "Have I not instilled some reverence for the government by which we live and breathe?"

"But Papa, they do nothing for us—"

"Do they not? What gives you the flour and fabrics and seeds for your garden? We are grateful for the chance to live as we please, with the provisions from Albany and the security of the men at the fort."

"Security?"

"We have allies. Everyone needs them."

"Yes, they are Iroquois."

"And British. You must be more forgiving of our friends. They only wish to protect us."

Sabine knew it to be true. But her father's reprimand reminded her of the fact that her secret courtship was far worse than her foolish talk. Could she bear to disappoint her father further? No. This was only a foreshadowing of the devastation her secrecy might bring.

She promised herself that just as they waited on the white flowers to bloom, she would wait on the snow to melt before testing her heart by giving it away to such a loyal soldier as Jacob.

During Christmastide and the rest of the wintry months, she clung to Moeder more. Even sleeping in during fishing days and tending only to the indoor chores when she could. The fort walls were a good barrier after all. Sabine preferred to seek her social company in the village longhouse among her dear friends, especially with the chance to help with Apenimon's child as his wife battled a lung infection most of the season.

Only in the evening, while she curled up by the fire before bed, did regret threaten to shatter her strength. Her heart sought Jacob at every step outside of the cabin, with every careful glance toward the fort's entrance, but her mind built up its own defense—he would be sympathetic to destroying the peace here if it meant British presence was threatened.

How could she love a man whose bottom line was at the mercy of his King's desire?

On this day though, with the snowmelt complete at last, she ran to the garden to see if the time had come.

And it had.

The small purple crocus was in bloom, its sunshiny center identical to the gentle light in the sky warming Sabine's face. Only one more month, the tulips would be ready, and the trade day of the year would be here.

She worked about the garden, getting rid of the deadened leaves and raking away the mulch that protected the tulip bulbs in the winter. As always, she prayed that God would shield the tiny bulbs from a late spring frost and that she might be aware of its coming so she could cover them if needed. For now though, the bare ground needed any warmth the sun offered.

Sabine stood, tightening the wool shawl around her arms. Might her heart need to shed its own barrier, which she had placed on it? What risk would she take if she allowed herself to love Jacob? Besides having to convince her parents of his worthiness, would she be able to survive the threat of change if he was in full support of it? That type of change was more than just a late frost to her tulips. It would disrupt the only life she'd ever known. It would crush the woman who'd lived and breathed for these white tulips to faithfully grow in remembrance of beauty from ashes. Moeder had weathered the most devastating change of all, yet hadn't God continued to give them good things—a life of prosperity?

He leads me beside quiet waters, He refreshes my soul. Even amid the valleys—and changes.

Sabine Van Der Berg stood among dormant tulips and blooming crocuses yet felt like a selfish weed greedily wanting to keep all the soil for herself. What life did not have change in it? And her God had always provided after change, hadn't He?

Sabine prayed, "Might the white tulips be for me, Lord? Have I truly been unforgiving and unfair to Jacob?" She hardly considered it for a moment longer before she declared it to be true—God's provision had also been found in the love that grew for the man.

Jacob stood at the river's inlet, observing the work he'd come to do. The new fort at Oswego was nearly finished. His foreman, Michael, headed toward him, "See, it is sturdy, and we're saving a bit of money for the colony." His smile was broad as he swept his arm across the view.

"The governor will be glad," he assured his man. Although gladness was nowhere near his own countenance. The completion of this task was supposed to end in the reunion with his daughter.

But no word had come.

And the sure place of comfort and hope—Sabine Van Der Berg—had remained cool and distant. *As she should,* he continued to tell himself. She was too contrary to British loyalty. Even if they were a world away from Albany—so it seemed—his first priority had to be British interest. And with the French weaving their allegiances in with British allies, he mustn't let her distract him any longer.

"Jacob!" Sabine's call shattered the defense around his heart. "Lieutenant Bennington!" she corrected herself.

"What is this?"

She ran alongside the riverbank, waving one arm above her and pressing her cap to her head with the other.

"Does she warn us?" Michael gripped his pistol at his waist.

"I do not know." Jacob began to jog toward her, trying to keep his senses at the sight of her bright red cheeks and dazzling green eyes. He must question her frantic state for the sake of his post, not the whir of desire this woman so quickly unleashed in his chest.

They nearly collided once they met. Sabine stumbled forward as she slowed down, and Jacob caught her by the hand.

Excitement flared in her lively features, and his senses were indeed overwhelmed—the scent of her sunbaked linen bodice, the feel of her smooth skin in his palm, and the sound of her breath catching as he carefully stepped closer. Oh, how foolish he was to suppress his heart from this woman.

She was the most alive creature on the frontier.

"What is it, my love?" His words spilled out unashamedly.

She slipped her hand away, and his heart deflated. "I come to share great tidings with you." Her teeth grazed her lip as she eyed his hand. In one swift movement, she gathered it up in both of hers. "Oh Jacob, there is no time for propriety at such a time as this." Her joy was a contagion.

He couldn't help but match her smile. "What is it, Sabine?"

"Come." She tugged and began to walk back along the bank. "They could not keep up with me, so I ran ahead to find you."

"Who—" A raised canoe bobbed up and down above the black hair of a native man in the distance, and a tall fellow in a British uniform walked alongside Mr. Van Der Berg.

Jacob squinted in the bright daylight. His heart raced as they drew closer. From behind the men, a scarlet cape flapped about. A tiny figure, waist high to the men, skipped around and continued to skip beside them.

Amelia!

"Thank the good Lord!" Jacob grabbed his mouth as he choked back a sob. He released Sabine's hand and began to run toward his daughter.

"Father!" she squealed and ran up to him as his vision blurred. Amelia leapt into his arms, her dark curls sticking to his moistened cheeks.

"Oh my daughter!" he exclaimed. The nightmare of her mother's plan fizzled in the heat of this day. "You are safe with me."

Amelia pulled away, placed her small hands on his cheeks. Her large brown eyes were just as he remembered them. Curious and warm. "No, Father, you are safe with me!"

Sabine tended to the tulip beds while she tried to spy inside the fortress now blocking her view of the river. The men continued work on the bastions, and while they passed by back and forth, she was most interested in catching a glimpse of Jacob's little girl.

A month had passed since she'd arrived, and much to Sabine's distress, Jacob decided to keep Amelia with him in the fort instead of allowing her to stay with the Van Der Bergs.

Sabine's throat ached with disappointment. On that day of Amelia's arrival, she'd reveled in Jacob's familiar admiration. Even if he carried skepticism and orders from a far-off kingdom aggravating the peace of this place, he was a man who'd leapt into her heart and gave her a taste of what love might be.

"Good morning, Sabine." Apenimon and Talise entered through the garden gate. In a small sling, the baby slept soundly against his mother's shoulder blade.

"Good morning." She stood from kneeling and stepped beside the sprouting rows of white flowers. "Are you ready for the trade tomorrow? I do think the tulips will be some of the best this year. The weather has been perfect." She ran a finger on the dangling arm of the sleeping child. "In time for this little one's birthday."

"Perhaps," Apenimon said, crouching down and caressing a white tulip. "Have you considered giving one to your love?" He squinted as he looked up at her, then over at Talise, who folded her lips in a knowing smile. "I do believe I've rarely seen you so conflicted, friend."

Sabine huffed. "Our distance is nothing a flower can lessen. We are too different. Part of me wishes they'd never come here."

"And the other part?" Talise questioned in her soft voice.

"Could I ever forgive him for bringing strife to this place?"

"He hasn't brought anything but that ugly palisade." Apenimon chuckled and threw a pebble in the direction of the fort wall.

Sabine smiled. She grabbed the reaching hand of the child who was now awake.

"You feel the same for him as I feel for Talise," Apenimon continued, winking at his wife. "Differences are sometimes needed to complete the whole."

Papa came from the back of the cabin. "What do you speak of, Apenimon?"

"You should tell him," Apenimon whispered.

"There is nothing to tell." *Now.* Sabine gritted her teeth.

"Sabine, what is this you whisper about?" Papa towered over her, exchanging looks between the three of them.

"Jacob Bennington. He is a good man," Apenimon said.

"Aye. The poor soul has dealt with much, or so I've learned." Papa rubbed the back of his neck. "His former wife did not deserve such a man as he."

"Papa, what is this?" Sabine queried.

He cast a look of sympathy in her direction. "The man who brought his daughter here shed some light on Bennington's situation, that is all." He motioned for Apenimon to come to the lean-to. "I have some new baskets to show you."

Sabine offered the child a pink tulip to play with, her own cheeks no doubt deeper in color while she thought about all that was just said. Talise began to sing a song to the child. Sabine joined in as he fiddled with the flower.

Apenimon returned shortly. "Come, Talise, let us go prepare for tomorrow."

Moeder called from inside in Dutch, "You tell him he may not have a white one!"

A sly, knowing look flashed on Apenimon's face. Moeder's warnings spurted out nearly every time she heard his voice. Apenimon rubbed his hands together, lifting an eyebrow at the swath of pure ivories.

"Moeder, remember, *Apenimon* means 'worthy of trust'. After so many years, does he not live up to his name?" Sabine brushed the young child's ebony locks from his eyes. Her dear friend and his sweet family were worthy of trust. Over the years they had taught her much about the land and friendship and peace. And today they shared a bit about love too.

Sabine's countenance had given away her heart, according to Apenimon and his wife. She had not been careful. Most of her life, she'd been able to tamp down her weaker emotions with courage and dependability. Her friend had just exposed a side of Sabine Van Der Berg that she did not know herself. A ball rolled in the pit of her stomach as she considered a change she did not expect but one that she might never outrun.

Every moment forward would be measured by her last encounter with Jacob Bennington, and every thought of the past was dim in light of their first kiss by the river.

Life had changed since Jacob arrived, but it wasn't the change of the landscape or Moeder's peace, as Sabine had feared. It was a deeper, more insufferable change. One within Sabine. A terrible, delightful shift.

Papa passed through the garden again.

"What did you hear about the lieutenant?" she asked.

"Only good things, Sabine." He pushed his chin up. "The man has suffered more than anyone should." He wagged his head and disappeared around the corner.

Were her prayers being answered, even amid her stubborn separation from Jacob? Was Papa's opinion about Jacob softening and Apenimon's wisdom ringing true for a providence she'd longed for?

Sabine Van Der Berg was certain of one thing. Regardless of what happened next, life would never be the same—and she was hopeful for the change. She brushed her hands along the white tulips once more. She would dream up a peace treaty of her own—one that offered Jacob Bennington her heart in full.

Chapter 10

Sleep escaped Jacob most of the night. He'd watched Sabine with her friends for a good long while yesterday. His heart twisted at the sight of her gentle way with Apenimon's little child, and he wondered if he was being foolish in keeping his daughter here, among gruff men, when she could be in the tender care of the Van Der Bergs. But he wasn't certain he could maintain the distance his heart needed from Sabine to insure his outward loyalty to his post.

Did he have to choose one over the other though?

Last night the Iroquois joined the Van Der Bergs for a feast. The dancing and music and laughter were nothing short of peace. The Van Der Bergs were aligned with these people, and Sabine grounded herself firmly in that assurance.

But Jacob heard the concerns from the older officer and his men. They had encountered the French finding ways to poke about this place. Jacob had encountered the French in the Iroquois village his first days here. Their trade items had been revered by that Iroquois man from the northern shore.

Jacob had been trained to stay alert, bury trust for safety, and protect his post at all costs. This training applied not only to his service to the throne, but also to the protection of his daughter from a woman who'd destroyed most of his heart. Nevertheless, Sabine was proof that something of that beating vessel remained. She'd shown him a strength in courage and purity unlike the bullish force of deceit he'd wrestled with in his marriage.

Jacob climbed up the newly finished stairs to take watch above the fort. Another man was assigned such a position, but Jacob enjoyed the calm of sitting in silence, looking out on the dawning day. The lake was a silvery plane against a rounding horizon. Below his line of sight perched the Dutchman's cabin, with the sleeping Sabine.

Her tulips were waiting gems, and her mother's white tulips nearly glowed in the graying light. He bent his head and prayed the same psalm from their day on the lake, begging God to bring him the comfort of a sheep well guarded by his Shepherd, and asking for assurance that beneath that roof, sleeping soundly, was the goodness he'd been given for the rest of his life.

Jacob did not want. Not now. Everything he treasured was right here.

In Oswego.

"I can only count on these. Perfect jewels from home." Moeder lowered to her knees and buried her face in the abundant blooms. "So much has changed, Sabine."

Sabine's stomach flipped at the thought of all that had changed for the better. A year ago she'd never have imagined falling in love. "It has, Moeder, but much is the same."

Papa carried several baskets from the lean-to to the front porch.

"Papa, please come here." She must share what had changed the most. Now, before one more day apart from Jacob. She would not reconcile with him until she had been forthcoming with her parents. "There is something I must tell you—and I beg you to listen."

Papa leaned an elbow on the windowsill. "Don't we always?"

"Yes, you do." Sabine reached over and gathered her mother's hand in her own. "Much has changed, you are right, Moeder. Not just the fort or the British garrison. But something I believe you've always wanted."

"What is that, Daughter?"

"I have fallen in love."

"What?" Moeder squeezed her hand, and Father pushed himself upright. "As much as we've spoken about marriage. . .you've found someone?" Glee spread across her face as bright and sunny as the garden.

Papa only stared at her—waiting. "Sabine, there is only one man that I have seen you spend time with."

Moeder's smile faded.

"I know, Papa. I am in love with Jacob Bennington."

Moeder gasped, and Papa's jaw twitched.

"Please, listen. He is loyal, kind—a good man, a good father—"

"Daughter." Papa raised his hand and drew near. "Do you want a man tarnished by a wayward marriage?"

"You said so yourself—he did not deserve such a hardship."

"Does this man take advantage of your innocence, Sabine?" Moeder interjected.

"No, Moeder! Jacob has not one speck of deceit. Just like your circumstance was unavoidable, Jacob had no fault in his own."

"You are in love with him," Papa said in a low tone. "Does he feel the same as you, daughter?"

"I believe so." She grimaced. "He once told me so, months ago. But we have seen little of each other this past winter. Our differences set us apart after we argued the first day of ice fishing. But Apenimon helped me see that perhaps our differences should not separate us but complement each other."

Papa's chest rose with a deep breath. "I believe Jacob should talk to me about his part in this. You are my only daughter."

"I know, Papa. We had planned on telling you. But now I am not sure what he feels anymore. I've ruined it with my fear of change. I cut it off after we argued on the ice, but I feel wretched letting my fear stop what my heart wants the most."

"Fear keeps us from love," Moeder said wistfully. "I know that well."

"Let us pray on this, Sabine." Papa hooked his thumbs on his suspenders. "And if Jacob is worthy at all, may he come ask our permission on his own."

Papa helped Moeder stand, and he escorted her through the gate.

Sabine glanced over her shoulder at the sparkling lake against the dark sky. "Tomorrow's trading day will be successful, I know it."

"Please, Sabine, cut the best and bring them to our own table," Moeder said.

"Are you sure, Moeder? We always have a good trade with all the flowers."

"Yes, I am certain."

"Very well." Sabine began to cut the large patch of violet tulips—they were this year's fullest. She was careful with each stem and each petal, although her hands were shaking after all she'd just admitted. She stood with an armful of tulips, trying to calm herself.

A loud snap made her jump.

"Hello?" Sabine called across the garden to the darkening wood. A rustle met her ears. A long drawn-out silence filled in the next few breaths.

Perhaps it was an animal. Sabine stayed a moment longer then turned to go inside. Before she rounded the corner, she peered into the wood again.

Nothing was there. She sighed and released the last of her trepidation. By the time she entered her cozy home, her hands had stopped shaking and her parents were busy preparing the meal.

Nothing more was mentioned about her greatest confession.

Sabine's usual excitement for this special trade day was ever present as she gathered up her armfuls of cut stems. She kept eyeing the white ones though, tempted to offer one to Jacob as Apenimon suggested. She wanted to speak with Jacob at dinner, but he tended to his daughter as a good father should, and they retired before Sabine could make her way to their side of the fire.

Nonetheless, this day would be a happy one regardless of the changed Sabine. A weight had been lifted now that her parents knew her secret. Oddly, she felt like herself before the arrival of Jacob and his men, and she'd not linger on her feelings any longer.

As she neatly placed the reds and pinks and purples into large baskets, another rustling came from behind the lean-to.

"Hello?" Sabine called out. Perhaps she would be able to see the cause of the disturbance in the light of day. She strode past the young vegetable plants and stepped outside the back gate.

Amelia peered into the wood, her arms wrapped around a birch trunk. "I saw a man with a belt of shells and a large bow," she said.

"I want to learn how to shoot."

"Oh, do you mean yesterday, when Apenimon came by?" Although she did not recall him carrying his bow. "They do not come by foot on trade day. Their canoes are packed with pelts."

"Not yesterday." She ran to the corner of the lean-to, her attention focused on the dappled shade of the wood. "Today. Just a moment ago. He ran back into the shrubbery."

Sabine's heart skipped a beat. She lifted her skirt and traipsed toward the edge of the wood. She queried in Iroquois. Nobody responded. The only sounds she could hear were the distant conversation at the fort entrance and the continuous knocking of a woodpecker.

"I believe you are just as excited as your father to learn the ways of the Iroquois. Perhaps you've dreamed up an archer to follow— but I can introduce you to a real one today."

The little girl shook her head in protest, but before she could speak, her father's voice rumbled from behind. "Amelia."

Sabine and Amelia spun around. Jacob stood at the corner of the white tulip patch with his knuckles pressed at his hips. His face was still and expressionless, as if molded from the same solid clay bricks as the wall that rose beyond him.

He pressed forward, reprimanding his daughter. "You are not to leave the walls of the fort without my permission, Amelia." As he drew near, his expression softened with the same concern Sabine witnessed on the night they spoke about his daughter's fate.

"I am sorry, Jacob. She was curious." Sabine reached out and placed her hand gently on his arm. "I can see that her disappearing would cause you worry."

His lips parted, and he searched Sabine's eyes. "I thank you for understanding. . .Miss Van Der Berg." His eyebrows cinched for a moment, then he gave a smile. "She might have caught the same courage that runs rampant on this frontier." He winked at her, sending a flurry of flutters in her chest. She dipped her chin and peeked at Amelia, mostly to hide the sure blush that bloomed on her cheeks. Jacob reached out his hand to his daughter. "Come, Amelia. You can help me stand watch for the first arrivals this morning."

Amelia twirled, tugging on the strap of her bonnet, and cast her large brown eyes up at Sabine. "Do you think I can help you with the flowers?" She turned to her father and gave a quick curtsy. "I'd rather do that, Father, if you do not mind."

Sabine glanced up at Jacob to gauge his response. He hadn't trusted her to keep his daughter under their roof. Would he allow her to be in Sabine's care this trade day, with all the different men about?

Jacob pressed his lips together and hooked his chin with a finger. "Hmm, I can see why you'd prefer such a task." The corner of his mouth tweaked, and he cast his full attention on Sabine. If ever an embrace could be found in a look, it was now. How she wanted to stay locked in his regard indefinitely. Forever. Heat buzzed around her collar and she swallowed past a lump in her throat. "Sabine— Miss Van Der Berg—would that be any trouble to you?"

"No, of course not," she spoke, hushed. Weakness flooded over her unlike any strength she might have been credited with. No, Jacob Bennington captured her heart's longing, and she had no control over the surrender coaxed out by his kindness.

Amelia yelped with glee and rushed over to the baskets at the other end of the garden. She carefully straightened the tulips on the very top of the pile.

Jacob looked over his shoulder, down toward the shore, then

faced Sabine again. He was close enough to block out her view of the blue sky above. She would cast off the color blue forever if it meant gazing into his umber eyes and feeling the tickle of his warm breath on her nose.

"Sabine, once again, I've let my fear cripple me."

"You have?" She tried to gather whatever strength had not melted away. With a hard swallow, she admitted, "I've not been fair to you. My stubbornness is the ugly side of courage, I suppose." She glimpsed the white flowers just beyond his elbow. "You have your duty here."

"Yes, but you have shown me that peace is abundant too. I chose to believe one side, in spite of your diligence to show the other."

"It seems we are both guilty of choosing sides."

He smirked, then cupped her elbow, sending a current from her head to her toes. "Perhaps, we should stand together, right here, in the middle of it all."

"I could agree with that." She fiddled with the brass button at his chest.

He tipped her chin up. "Forgive me, Sabine?"

"I do. And I promise to be more considerate, Jacob. You have great responsibility."

His eyes narrowed with a broad smile—yes, the blue sky was nothing compared to this. She raised on her toes, and for the first time, she kissed him first. His lips were ready though, and he immediately returned a gentle caress. Her chin trembled with his tender touch.

'Twas ever true that the first kiss had opened wide the continual longing for the next. She pressed into him, completely satisfied but never fully satiated.

With a regrettable sigh, Jacob pulled away but squeezed her

close before standing apart from her. "We mustn't get caught—"

"I told my parents," she interjected.

"You did? What did they say?"

"Not much. They were guarded, but not against you."

"That is good. I need as many allies as I can get in this place."

"You have me." *Completely.* She could not think of life without this man by her side.

"I do?" He waggled his eyebrows. "What can I do to keep you?"

"The one kiss was all you needed." She lowered her lashes at such vulnerability. He pressed his nose to hers and stole another kiss. "Well, maybe a few more." They laughed together.

"I will spend the rest of my life keeping you," Jacob whispered. "But first, I'd like for a proper announcement to be made."

"Announcement?"

Before he could explain, he dashed across the garden. Men began to wheel wares down to the shore. Jacob kissed his daughter on the head and shouted, "See you both at the trade. Don't be long." He tipped his hat at Sabine and then joined the others.

The blue sky was a vibrant shade today. And too vast and open for Sabine's liking. She'd rather every corner of her sight fill up with the handsome Jacob Bennington.

The excitement from the traders buzzed through the air like the docks of Albany when a new vessel appeared from England. Even the man from the northern shore who bragged on the French during ice fishing appeared content as he bargained beside Apenimon.

As far as Jacob could tell, each party was satisfied with their exchange, and all seemed well on the shore of Ontario.

Yes, all was extremely well with Sabine in the mix, her hair with a copper shine as it caught the sunlight just so and her knowing smile finding him across the crowd.

Not only did her confidence boost Jacob's admiration of her, but her tenderness with his daughter nearly burst his spirit. How could a woman be so bold yet so gentle?

As the trade went on, he became more anxious for it to be over. This day would close on the brink of a brighter tomorrow—a day when Jacob would forget his past heartache at last and vow his heart completely to Sabine Van Der Berg. First he had to speak with Mr. Van Der Berg. But there was hardly a chance to do so.

At dusk the fire blazed, and the savory scent of roasting salmon distracted him as his stomach rumbled. Not long after the meal was served, Sabine's parents departed from the group, her mother complaining of a headache.

Perhaps this was Jacob's chance.

While Sabine and Amelia admired a necklace Apenimon had offered in the exchange, Jacob bounded across the tall grasses and toward the cabin. When he approached the door though, a low unintelligible voice carried from the garden.

He crept around toward the east then froze midstep, clutching at the timbered corner of the cabin. To his surprise, the man from the northern shore crouched down among the white tulips. He spoke with someone out of Jacob's view. A familiar wave of suspicion frenzied the blood in his chest, sending a drumming pulse in his ears.

But what harm could they do in a flower patch?

Jacob opened his mouth to make himself known.

"Hello, Jacob," Mr. Van Der Berg called out from the porch.

Jacob spun toward him.

"You seem rather focused on my wife's tulips." He lodged his thumb under his suspender. "They aren't for trade."

"Oh no, that is not what I was—" Jacob looked back at the garden. The man had disappeared. Jacob leapt over the short fence and ran down and around the cabin. He could barely see anything in the fading light, nor among the dark shadows of the wood.

"What is the matter, Lieutenant?" Sabine's father called out.

Jacob darted back through the garden, hurried out of the gate, and ran toward the edge of the Van Der Berg property. He searched the crowded shore for Apenimon's red covering. If Sabine's friend accompanied that man, he would not worry. Searching the circle of men by the fire and the traders gathered by the canoes, he was relieved not to find Apenimon among the crowd. Amelia and Sabine were now by the edge of the lake, skipping rocks.

All seemed well.

Jacob swiveled around. Sabine's father looked as defensive on the outside as Jacob had felt on the inside. His arms were crossed. Jacob was certain he probably scowled, though the light was too dim for him to be certain. "Pardon me, sir. I saw an Iroquois man in your garden. He spoke to someone in a hushed tone."

"They are our friends, son." The man dropped his arms and began to walk toward the feast again. "Who did he speak with?"

"I believe it to be Apenimon." Jacob joined Mr. Van Der Berg as they strode through the grasses.

"You know that Apenimon adores the white tulips." Mr. Van Der Berg chuckled. "I am sure he was showing off to his friend."

"Of course," Jacob replied. But why would they disappear so quickly? No, he need not worry.

Jacob shook away the last ounce of doubt, practicing his newfound trust on this frontier, and stopped in his tracks. "Uh, sir—" He rubbed his hands together, heat creeping along his shoulders and up his neck.

Mr. Van Der Berg continued for a few steps then faced him. "Yes, Lieutenant?"

"There is something I must ask you." Jacob cleared his throat, his stomach as topsy-turvy as his crossing from England.

"What is it?"

The first sprinkling of stars in the indigo sky shone above the great lake ahead. A dull glitter compared to his treasures below. Sabine and Amelia ran toward the fire from the shore again. He borrowed the courage he believed was forever aflame within the woman he loved.

Drawing a breath of the cool night air into his lungs, Jacob began, "I am in love with your daughter, and I would like to ask for your blessing."

Chapter 11

This morning was different than every other morning. Although Jacob missed out on sleep again, it was only because he anticipated his proposal to Sabine. Her father had given his blessing. Yet with little Amelia ever present and the Iroquois sharing their stories and music well into the evening, Jacob did not have one moment alone with Sabine.

He climbed the stairs to his morning watch, waiting for Sabine to wake. Perhaps he would steal his chance in the garden among her mother's tulips. That setting would be nothing short of perfect.

He leaned his elbows on the square window of the bastion and breathed in the crisp morning air. No candlelight shone from the cabin windows. Jacob was awake while peace fell sleepily around him. His lids grew heavy, and he leaned his chin on his crossed arms. Something moved in the garden. He rubbed his eyes and peered down to the Van Der Berg place.

In the gray light, Apenimon slipped onto the property from the far west side. Even though Jacob couldn't make out his face, he recognized the red covering draped across one shoulder. Apenimon kept his head lowered as he bent forward and slinked across the dirt path lined with mounding plants. Jacob rose as the man continued toward the far patch of white tulips.

What was he doing? He knew the sacredness of those flowers. Sabine's parents had mentioned Apenimon's fascination with them.

Jacob left his watch and bumbled down the stairs, talking his heart out of suspicion once again. This man was a friend—nearly kin—to Sabine. Jacob would only go to him as a friend, paving the same foundation of trust for himself with this ally.

When he left the walls of the fort, the man was in the thick of the white tulip patch, hunched over like a crimson boulder. The muscles in his bare shoulder worked. Jacob hastened. A tulip head flew to the dirt beside the cabin wall.

"Apenimon?" he called out. The man turned his head with his nose and mouth hidden by his arm. He leapt up. The crimson covering crumpled to the ground as he ran across the garden and toward the wood again. Jacob sprinted around the fenced area, panicked at the trail of tulip heads splayed across the garden path. What act of deceit had just occurred? And by someone whom Sabine had considered family? How could he?

The man's long ebony hair whipped behind him as he rushed through the tall birch trees and wild shrubbery. Jacob ran faster. He could not lose him. "Apenimon! I see you, man!" Jacob waved his arm in front of him to slap away the brush. The man dipped down and disappeared.

Agitation crawled along Jacob's spine as he considered the magnitude of such an ally-disguised vandal. He opened his mouth to call out again. Before a sound escaped, a blinding force hit the back of his head. Pain radiated from his crown to the back of his neck and everything grew dark.

Sabine woke with a start. Dawn's pale light shone through her window. She closed her eyes, but they only fluttered like her overactive heart. Perhaps she dreamed. She could not recall anything. Slipping her dress on quietly, she crept across the main room, unlatched the door, and slid out into the cool morning while her parents slept soundly.

Anticipation overwhelmed her as she considered the chance of finding Jacob out and about this day. They'd hardly spoken yesterday, but she'd enjoyed accompanying his daughter. What gentle words of affirmation and sweet embrace would she encounter next? She entered the garden and couldn't help but laugh to herself. How amused the Lord must be at their match—one loyal to the throne, the other to the land. Their love was a treaty in itself.

Cupping a white tulip in her palm as she eyed the fort entrance, a swath of crimson in the middle of the tulip patch caught her eye. Apenimon's covering lay crumpled amid the white flowers. Where was he? She retrieved the covering and looked around. As she called his name, a memory hit her. She'd awakened to a man's voice calling the same name in her sleep.

Was it a dream? Or was it—

Sabine gasped. Flower petals splayed across the ground, headless stems poked up between the untouched tulips. The covering fell from her hands. At least twenty stems had been massacred.

What had Apenimon done?

He'd teased her about desiring the white tulips, or she had assumed it was only in jest. Where was he now though? Her lip trembled and she stumbled backward out of the patch, her clog crushing something beneath it.

"No," she whimpered as she knelt down and gathered the smashed flower head. "Why would he waste such a gift?" Her peace was ambushed.

More petals were strewn along the path. Sabine gathered them in her apron, tears streaming down her face. A high-pitched cry cut through the air. The flowers tumbled to the ground again. As she turned the corner, Amelia emerged from the wood. The girl fell to her knees as her body shook with sobs.

"Amelia!" Sabine called out, running toward the back gate. She crushed another tulip beneath her foot. Panic rattled every bone in her body.

The child scrambled to her feet, casting a look of desperation in Sabine's direction.

"Miss Sabine!" she cried with her arms opened wide. Amelia crashed into her, wrapping her waist in a fierce, trembling hug. "They took him! They took my father!"

The blood pumping in Sabine's ears now drained from her face. She gripped Amelia by the shoulders and bent down eye level. "Who took him?"

"A man hit him over the head and took him off into the wood."

"What man?"

"He–he wore a belt, and paint on his face. Was it your friend?"

No! Not Apenimon.

Sabine's heart plummeted to her stomach, and she stumbled back in the garden. All the fear and skepticism Jacob brought with him now threatened to expose roots of truth.

"Come, Amelia. We must notify my father. Surely there is some misunderstanding."

"Why would he hit him, Miss Sabine? What had he done wrong?"

"I do not know."

When they passed through the garden again, her father was kneeling beside the fallen beauties. Her mother gripped the fence, whimpering.

"Papa, Apenimon took Jacob." Sabine's words shook.

"Jacob must have caught him defiling Moeder's garden." Papa's face was dark. He clenched a white tulip in his fist. "This will not bode well for our alliance."

A wave of anguish drenched Sabine's soul. Had God sent Jacob, not to borrow her bravery, but to reveal the paper-thin friendship she'd so counted on these many years?

Amelia tugged at Sabine's hand, blubbering and twisting back and forth as she looked at the wood then the fort. "Please, my father!"

"I will alert the men to find him, Papa—"

"No, do not tell one soul," Moeder sharply demanded. She carefully stepped closer without letting go of the gatepost. "If Apenimon wants the flowers, give them to him."

"Love, what is this?" Papa wrapped his arm around her shoulder. "These are yours to keep, not his to take."

"They are not precious enough to cause one to sin." She pressed her lips together as she considered in silence. "Let us give them all to Apenimon if he wants them. Jacob is worthy of such an offering."

"Moeder, you say this now, but you've said otherwise about him in the past."

"Do you think you are not convincing, Daughter?" Moeder prodded. "I hear the love in your voice. If I had to choose, no man would be worthy of your hand. But I cannot always have control, can I?"

"But, Wife—"

"God has forgiven much. And He sacrificed much as well. These flowers have reminded me of that. Now is the time to forgive, no matter the sacrifice. For the sake of peace."

Sabine guided Amelia around the fallen flowers and to her mother. "Moeder, this is a great sacrifice, I know it."

"I only believe it because of you, Sabine." Her mother reached out her hand, and Sabine leaned forward, allowing Moeder's palm to find her cheek. "You are strong and courageous in this land. And loved by all. God has shown us that above all else, love must prevail. This is your time to offer up what is needed."

Tears streamed down Sabine's face, and Moeder wiped them away with her hand. "Go, Daughter, save your love."

Her heart leapt. "I do love him, Moeder," she whispered.

"And he loves you, Sabine, greatly," Papa interjected, a knowing flash in his eyes.

Sabine gulped in the morning air, turned to Amelia with all the determination she could muster, and focused on her big brown eyes once again. "I will find your father. Do not worry."

"Please, Miss Sabine. I—I need him."

"I know you do." Sabine kissed her forehead. "I need him too."

Her parents took little Amelia into the cabin. Sabine began to work toward forgiving Apenimon in the very act of cutting down the white beauties to offer him. With each stem she prayed forgiveness and safety for Jacob. While Apenimon spoke often of peace, this morning destroyed her assurance that his words were true.

She laid out the crimson covering and placed eighty tulips carefully on top then folded the corners and slung the bundle behind one shoulder. As she traipsed past the heads of the defiled tulips along the ground and exchanged her clogs for moccasins beneath the lean-to, she begged for God to accept this offering. Not as a symbol, but as a very real exchange for the man she loved.

Chapter 12

*J*acob's wrists burned with the twine cutting his flesh. Sweat dribbled down his temple as he sat in a sunny clearing somewhere in the wood near the Iroquois palisade. If his mouth was free of the gag tied tightly at the back of his head, he could try and reason with these men.

But he awoke in this position, sitting against a dead tree, bound with his hands behind his back and his legs tied at the ankles. His head throbbed from the blow.

Three men gathered at a small fire, seemingly collaborating in hushed voices. He recognized two—the Frenchman who'd visited the village when Apenimon's son was born and the northern shore native. But the third man stood between the seated two, his back to Jacob.

Behind Jacob, a man breathed heavily, and a low scratching sound continued in rhythm. The man's shadow on the littered floor proved his existence. The scratching sound grew deep and forceful. Was the man trying to set himself free by cutting through his own bindings?

Jacob's pulse froze at the hope of being set free, but then it pounded in double time when Sabine marched through the trees at the far end of the clearing, the early light dappling her cap and shoulders. Jacob squirmed wildly. A fierce urge unleashed within him. He must warn her. He shook his head and groaned.

"Quiet, man!" The Frenchman, wearing native paint on his face, tossed a stone in Jacob's direction. The standing man turned around.

"Michael?" Jacob spoke the garbled word with the gag in his mouth.

His friend stepped back, a fierce glare upon the Frenchman. "You talked too long. I did not want to be seen."

"Does it matter? You'll find safety behind Fort Niagra's walls. The money you contributed by building the cheaper clay fortification is as good as spent."

Jacob nearly gagged on the cloth in his mouth. His friend had convinced Jacob to use clay. All because of an agreement with the enemy?

Michael wrung his hands and trod toward him. "I am sorry, Jacob. The French are convincing—and have promised me quite a sum of my own." He grimaced. "Nonetheless, the governor will be pleased with the fort." He lowered his head as he pulled his broad-brimmed hat down over his brow. "You have led well. Forgive me—" He clamped his mouth shut, lifted his shoulders, and trudged away, disappearing into the western tree stand without another glance back at Jacob.

Again Jacob had been betrayed. And again he suffered the repercussions from the deceit of someone near to him.

Oh Michael, what have you done?

He laid his eyes on Sabine, praying God's rod and staff would pull her away from this darkening valley. Yet the brave beauty stepped into the clearing with a large bundle hanging from one shoulder. "Where is Apenimon?" she bellowed.

The two captors rose to their feet, blocking Jacob's view. "You must leave, woman," the Frenchman barked. "There is nobody of your concern here."

"Jacob!" Sabine began to run toward him. The man from the northern shore lunged out and caught her by the arm. "Leave me be!" she cried, the bundle falling to the ground. It unfolded and revealed a mass of white tulips.

"Do you bring us flowers?" The Frenchman guffawed, kicking at the stems.

"I bring you nothing," Sabine seethed, attempting to jerk her arm away from the other man. He only tugged harder. The two men escorted Sabine across the clearing, their backs to Jacob.

"We have a message for the fort." The Frenchman spoke through gritted teeth as he took Sabine's other arm. "The treaty is null and void. The British are no longer in alliance with the village yonder, or any other. If they do not leave, the lieutenant will perish by Iroquois hands."

"This man is not from the village," Sabine rebuked, still trying to pull away.

"Ah, but your friend is—and, as I see, you've found the cloak he left behind. Those flowers were a prize he could not resist. And it seems he's helped us in our plot by leaving it behind. The Iroquois will soon choose the French over your cheap wares and poorly packed goods."

Jacob heard a groan from whoever was behind him. "I did not help them." A scraping whisper crawled around the tree. "They stole my covering when they captured me." Apenimon's profile came into view as he leaned around the trunk. His dark eyes stared across the clearing. "Do not make a sound. We will take them. For now, let them squabble." He began to work on Jacob's bound wrists.

Jacob considered their predicament while Apenimon worked. Sabine's friend had been framed. All along, Lieutenant Wilson had been right that trouble was brewing. Yet 'twas in the actual building of a fort where trouble occurred. Even though their treaty was strong and secure with the Iroquois, peace was threatened from the outside.

As his wrists and ankles were set free and Apenimon untied the gag in his mouth, Jacob prayed for strength to save Sabine and preservation of the peace at the new Fort Oswego.

He followed Apenimon, crawling around the far side of the fire. Signaling with a click of his tongue, Apenimon took off in a sprint toward the two men. Jacob ran as best as he could with his pounding head. The men swiveled around and ran toward them. Sabine cried out as Jacob lunged at the Frenchman, grabbing him by the neck and thrusting him to the ground. The man ripped away Jacob's fingers and then tried to wrestle Jacob beneath him, but the man did not succeed. Everything important to Jacob depended on capturing this troublemaker.

"You shall not get away with this," Jacob roared. He secured the man's wrists behind his back and anchored his knee firmly on the man's thigh.

Apenimon held the other man secure with hands tied behind him.

Sabine wept on her knees beside the fallen flowers.

They quickly secured the men to the same tree where Jacob and Apenimon had been held captive and then hurried to tend to Sabine.

"It is over my love, all will be well." Jacob gathered her in his arms, and she clutched him close. "Do not fear." He kissed her forehead.

"Jacob, I am so thankful you are safe." She pulled away, searching his eyes. "What would have happened—" She shook her head. Her face blanched. A nightmare must have unfolded in her mind.

"You have a good friend in Apenimon," he assured her. The man crouched down beside them.

"They stole my cloak, Sabine." Apenimon picked up a flower, twirled it about, then handed it to her.

"I brought these as a treaty of sorts." She shook her head. "Now they are a bribe for forgiveness. Please, Apenimon, forgive me for not trusting you."

"My friend, there is nothing to forgive. Those men have crept about, spying on us. They knew how precious these tulips are and assumed it to be a weakness." He clapped a hand on Jacob's shoulder. "I am sorry your friend betrayed you."

Jacob's stomach was like lead. He said, "He is a fool. The governor will be glad that we've captured Michael's accomplices. And I am sure the French would rather turn Michael over than start a larger conflict. Unfortunate for him." He shook his head but could not linger on the traitor for long. All was not lost. "No matter stone or clay, the fort is secure, regardless of his foolishness."

Sabine squeezed his hand.

Apenimon continued, "He was fooled by darkness. Yet Sabine offered the most powerful weapon of all—a sacrifice of peace." He smiled widely. "And you even returned my covering. I thank you." A long hearty laugh burst from the kind man, and both Jacob and Sabine joined in.

For the last time, Jacob relinquished his skepticism of this place. He may never be able to avoid trials, but he could remain strong and courageous to face hardship when it came. No matter the discord around them, he'd follow Sabine's persistent desire to courageously follow peace.

"Moeder gave these flowers to me," Sabine said. "I believe that they've transformed from forgiveness to peace."

"A treaty of tulips." Apenimon winked.

"Yes. A gift you've longed for," she teased.

He began to gather up the corners of his covering, careful that no flower would escape. "But friend, I want you to have them."

"Moeder will not want them back." Her mother might not always like change, but once she'd decided on something, she was determined to follow through. Sabine's strength was an inherited trait. "What would you have me do with them, Apenimon?"

"I have an idea," Jacob interjected. He gathered Sabine's hands and helped her up to standing. She gave him a curious look.

Apenimon handed Jacob the bundle and nodded in the direction of the captives. "My men and I will take care of these fools. "You go ahead."

Jacob held the bundle with one arm and twined his fingers in Sabine's hand. Her arms prickled with gooseflesh, and thanksgiving poured from her heart as they moved beneath the shade of the trees.

"What is your idea, Jacob?" Sabine nudged him with her elbow.

He turned and faced her. His moistened hair clung to his temple, and his disheveled shirt was loose around his tanned skin. He appeared to be more a frontiersman than a soldier. Sabine melted into his firm embrace. He did not speak. His searching brown pools swam with such familiarity, she could hardly remember life without him.

"You must tell me your idea, Jacob," she insisted, overcome with the same love he so clearly beamed with in this moment.

"Well it is up to you to make it come true." He slowly leaned in, his lips positioned just above hers, but with a catch of his breath, he kissed her cheek instead. She reveled in his playfulness but longed for something more than a simple kiss on the cheek.

"How can I make it true?" she whispered. The same glorious stampede must be racing within him. She could feel his wild rhythm against her chest.

He stepped back, placed the flower bundle between them, and lowered to his knee. "I believe these flowers would be best used at a wedding feast. Don't you?"

Her smile grew wide as tears spilled down her cheeks.

"Your father was kind and gave us his blessing. And, I believe, your mother's blessing is here, in her offering." He patted the bundle. "But the only person I care to receive a blessing from is you, Sabine Van Der Berg. And I'd be mightily blessed if you'd become my wife."

Sabine sank down in front of him, drinking in his excited gaze. She locked away this happily-ever-after in her heart. The fairy tales she'd been told were nothing compared to this.

"I will happily become your wife, Jacob Bennington," she affirmed in the strongest of voices, leaning in and receiving her lieutenant's kiss.

With a treaty of tulips between them and a bright future promised on the shore of Lake Ontario, Sabine Van Der Berg was certain—together they had found middle ground, rooted in peace, abounding in love.

Angie Dicken credits her love of story to reading British literature during her time as a military kid in England. Now living in the US heartland, she is a member of American Christian Fiction Writers, sharing about author life with her fellow Alley Cats on *The Writer's Alley* blog and Facebook page. Besides writing, she is a busy mom of four and works in adult ministry. Angie enjoys eclectic new restaurants, authentic conversation with friends, and date nights with her Texas Aggie husband. Connect with her online at www.angiedicken.com.

A Promise for Tomorrow

by Amanda Barratt

Dedication

To my frontier-loving sis. You encouraged me to write this story, and your excitement for this project buoyed me every step of the way. Thanks for talking all things Boone and fangirling over Silas. I love you more every day!
And to the One whose unfailing love carries us through all storms.

Chapter 1

Kentucke Territory
July 1778

*P*eace was a thing too fragile to be left unbroken.

A shudder heaved through Rosina Whiting's body as her gaze took in the scene. Smoke rose from the desecrated remains of the once-proud cabin, ashes floating downward as if tossed from the sky by God Himself. The acrid stench of smoke mingled with the metallic odor of. . .blood.

Her stomach churned. She clamped a sweaty palm against her mouth in an attempt to stave off rising bile.

For there, on the blood-soaked grass, lay the prone body of Jeremiah Whiting.

Her husband.

Arrows riddled his body, their feathered tufts and long straight shafts sticking up from the blood soaking his fine linen shirt. He'd been brutally scalped, his fine blond queue hacked in an act that could be termed nothing but savage. His brown eyes stared skyward. Empty. Glassy. Rolled back into his head with stark terror.

Rosina bent double and retched into the grass, just inches from where her husband's body lay. Bile burned her throat. She fought for breath.

Almighty God, deliver me. . .

She straightened, wiping a hand across her mouth. Sweat dribbled down her back, dampened her brow. Forgotten, on the grass a few feet away, lay the basket of yarrow she'd set off to gather, her rifle and powder horn beside it.

The former now unimportant. The latter useless.

She shivered, the sticky summer air no match for the chill driving into her bones. A chill that had nary a thing to with the weather and everything to do with the danger that, even now, might still lurk within the dense foliage.

Whoever had slaughtered her husband might still seek to quench their thirst for bloodshed with her.

She needed to flee.

Her limbs trembled, her mind swam. She crossed the grass and snatched up the rifle, its wood and metal pressing into her fingers, then slung the powder horn over her shoulder.

Could her weapon thwart the arrow of an Indian?

She wouldn't linger over what little remained of their cabin— the two-room structure that had been complete with real glass windows and puncheon floors, a lace coverlet to cloak their bed.

Jeremiah had been able to purchase most anything with his money.

Except exemption from death.

Everything in the cabin was either burned beyond repair, smashed, or stolen. The rifle and her life were the only prizes she'd be lucky to escape with.

She turned away from the smoldering remains. Her gaze fell

once more on the body of her husband. Now wasn't the time to relive the sixteen months of their marriage, nor regret the past. She steeled herself, bent, and laid a hand against his unsullied right shoulder, his flesh strange and cold beneath her fingers. His eyes seemed to follow her. Possessive, even still.

She jerked away, straightened.

"Rest in peace, Jeremiah Whiting." Her fractured whisper emerged from dry lips.

She didn't look back again. Just let the forest swallow her, trusting the path would lead to safe harbor.

If she survived the journey.

An eerie stillness dogged her steps. She'd learned to be fleet and silent of foot, walking in such a way that her worn moccasins made nary a rustle.

Her gaze slid downward to her middle, rounded beneath her indigo skirt.

She'd carried the child nigh on six months, as far as she could reckon. Doubtless she sounded like a lumbering buffalo as she trod the trace.

Onward she walked in the late afternoon heat, feet aching and throat crying out for water. Her slender arms ached from the weight of the rifle. Her sweaty bodice clung to her skin.

Kentucke. A place of beauty, some might call it. Those of Boone's ilk, who lusted for adventure and craved the satisfaction that came with carving out a life against all obstacles and odds.

But her heart did not thrill to the task.

To her, every tree sheltered some attacker, every sunrise bespoke another day of uncertainty. The high call of a bird might not be a bird at all, but a warrior's prelude to attack.

To her, the wilderness of Kentucke meant death.

It was a five-hour walk from her cabin to Fort Boonesborough, if she kept a steady pace. Darkness would set in by then. Would hide the trace, the trees wide of girth and dark of foliage, the swirl of clouds in the sky that now owned the blue of turquoise trade beads.

Darkness. A friend to those who sought to harm her. The Indians who slipped through the forest, owning the land and all its secrets in ways the settlers did not.

A persistent kick beneath her rib cage assured her of the child's safety. She paused, freed one hand from around the rifle, and placed it against the swell of her growing babe. Part of herself and encompassing the whole of her heart.

Rosina lifted her chin.

She must survive. For the life within, if not for herself.

Guide my steps, almighty God.

The hours dragged by, blurring together in a haze of putting one weary foot in front of the other, keeping to the trace, and praying her sense of direction wouldn't fail her. Her breath came in jagged gasps. She wet her lips, tasting salt.

She must needs make it to Boonesborough.

Finally, *finally*, her head aching near to bursting, limbs scarce holding her, she glimpsed the fort.

The fortification bearing the name of the great Daniel Boone was anything but grand. She could make out little of it in the twilight fast turning ebony, save for the stout picket walls in the stages of completion and the nearby cornfields—though few settlers felt brave enough to risk leaving the safety of fort gates to till the land that would bring them needful sustenance.

Grand or not, the fort gates beckoned her as darkness claimed the sky. A footsore, bedraggled girl of nineteen, bearing nothing but a rifle, an unborn child, and a tale of tragedy.

She hastened her steps, the sounds of baying dogs and lowing cattle welcome as any music, luring her toward the gates, toward the Kentons and Callaways and Boones—friends all. The stark aloneness haunting her since she'd first emerged into the clearing and witnessed the devastation of her husband's life would ease. Dissipate like an unwelcome downpour in their presence, though all may not welcome her.

Aye, Fort Boonesborough spelled safety, a thing both bitter and sweet. Sweet, because it meant security for her babe. Bitter, because it also meant her fight for survival would lapse, leaving her long hours to think.

Right now she'd rather not dwell on the space Jeremiah Whiting had occupied in her life.

Right now? Mayhap never.

Twilight was a chancy time. One could never be sure just what brewed.

Safety or danger?

Captain Silas Longridge rolled his shoulders, easing out the kinks, and strode from the blockhouse, leaving men sitting among stubby candles, tepid mugs of coffee, and talk of rebellion. He didn't want to listen. What good did words do? Words were leaves, flung into the air to flutter down weightless. Action—now action was lead, heavy and powerful.

The familiar stock of his rifle resting against his shoulder, he made his way through the shadows, scanning the distance. He knew the fort, with its encirclement of cabins, picket walls in final stages of repair, scents of cooking smoke, and settlers busy at their evening tasks, as well as he knew the grooves of his own hands. Better, mayhap.

He climbed the crude ladder to the upper level, pausing to speak with a couple of the men who stood guard, swatting mosquitoes and keeping an eye out for anything that might give cause for concern. They greeted him with smiles easing across their leathery faces.

"See anything?" he asked Zeke Wainwright, who stood within viewing distance of the fort gate.

"Nay, sir." Zeke rubbed a hand marked with mosquito welts through his grizzled beard. "Pretty quiet this evening."

A rustle, faint enough to be a squirrel, even a field mouse. Silas's gaze sharpened, closing in on the clearing swathed in purple twilight. His heart kicked against his rib cage, his muscles tensing.

"Then you haven't looked close enough," he muttered.

Someone approached the fort, a sure sign of danger or unrest. A tilting of the kilter of Boonesborough life. At least they came alone. He made out the cadence of one step, not two. Not an Indian party. . .

The figure emerged from within fast-lengthening shadows.

But a woman.

Silas stilled.

Nay. It couldn't be. He sucked in a breath. Feminine faces were enough of a rarity to make each one stand out as something distinct. But not like this.

Hers was a face that had long dwelt in hushed remembrance within his heart, encompassing so large a space he could not decipher its beginnings or its end.

Rosina.

She came toward the fort, trudging under the weight of a

rifle. . .and the burden of an unborn babe.

But no husband walked at her side.

Need drove him toward her. Need to ascertain if this was a fiction of his overworked mind, or reality. To relieve her of the load she struggled under, chest heaving with shallow breaths, steps stumbling.

And to discover the whereabouts of Jeremiah Whiting.

"Remain at your post." He flung the order over his shoulder at Zeke as he climbed down the ladder and strode toward the front gates. The other guards had noted the new arrival, and their low ripple of voices turned into a tide. The stout log gates moaned open.

His strides ate up the distance between them as he brushed past the men on guard duty, past a cadre of fort dogs near the entrance, and past a trio of women carrying water pails.

He knew the moment their gazes met when her eyes—blue as the indigo dress she wore—widened. They'd closed the front gates after she entered, and he met her just inside them.

"Mistress Whiting." The words emerged steady, a stark contrast to the melee of emotions churning through him.

"Captain Longridge." At this proximity, no detail of her person escaped his notice. Haggard shadows lined her delicate cheekbones, a streak of something dark spotting the right side of her oval face. Her thick mahogany hair straggled down her back, wrinkles and dirt marring her gown.

And her eyes. . .her eyes told a tale all their own. Twin pools of mingled relief and misery.

She ducked her chin, hiding her gaze from his view. Despite her rounded middle, her slight shoulders gave her the appearance of something fragile on the point of breaking.

So he did the only thing he could. Placed a hand on her shoulder and led her away, heedless of whoever stood by and watched. Which was doubtless half the fort. Mutely, she let him, keeping her eyes on her dusty moccasins as they crossed the parade ground.

No doubt madness besieged him when he guided her toward his cabin. 'Twas the only place he could think to take her where they could talk privately. Unseemly or nay, he needed to hear what had happened, because he was one of the commanding officers at the fort and because. . .

Try as he might, struggle though he did, he'd been unable to disentangle his heart from hers since that day when her summer-sweet smile had first lured him to join the dancing at a fort frolic. Not even when, in spite of that day, more than a year ago, he'd entered the Boone cabin and found her standing by the fireplace speaking vows to another man. Forcing him to consign their hoped-for future to a grave in his heart.

They entered the cabin, and he propped his rifle near the door. It was a goodly cabin, as far as fort homes went. He'd constructed it himself and striven to make it a home. Suddenly self-conscious, he wished he could hide the worn sheets flung haphazardly over the straw tick mattress, the socks drying near the fire, the crumbs on the puncheon floor.

But as Rosina sank, nay, collapsed, into a chair without invitation, housekeeping worries fled his mind. She leaned her rifle against the table, set her powder horn on it, and gripped both hands together in her lap.

He pulled the other chair close to her side, the legs scraping against the floor, and sat.

She looked up, her gaze piercing his.

"My husband is dead."

He swallowed, absorbing the news. Jeremiah Whiting dead?

Jeremiah, with his acreage and kingly cabin, bounty aplenty, and pride to match.

"How? By whose hand?"

"Indians. I don't know. . .didn't see them. I left the cabin to gather some yarrow to dry. I must have wandered farther than I realized. I started home an hour later. 'Twasn't long before I noticed the smoke, so I ran. When I entered the clearing, I found him." She shuddered, eyes falling closed, lashes dark against her ashen skin.

He almost reached out to touch her, to comfort her with a hand on her shoulder. But she opened her eyes, sucking in a tremulous breath, and continued. "He'd been scalped. Shot with arrows also, three or four. The cabin burned. Ashes are all that's left."

Silas had seen more than one mutilated victim of an Indian attack. 'Twas a grisly sight for a frontiersman, let alone for a solitary young woman to come upon. Especially when the target was her husband.

He didn't want to contemplate the outcome had she not decided to gather yarrow. A curl brushed her delicate cheek. A shiver spidered down his spine.

"What then?" he asked. Talking was better than letting the memories boil inside her chest. One of the many lessons experience had taught him.

"There was precious little left, so I took the rifle and fled here. I knew I couldn't stop till I reached the fort."

"You did right." Had she paused, had her sense of direction failed her, Heaven knew what or whom she'd have come upon on the trail. 'Twas a miracle she'd arrived at all.

He stood, moving to the makeshift cupboard against one wall, pulling out a tin plate and mug. He bent in front of the fire's dying remains and scooped out the last piece of corn bread—the leavings from his evening meal. Grateful there was coffee left in the pot, albeit lukewarm, he filled the mug and placed both before her.

She turned her head, giving him a look of thanks over her shoulder, then set upon the meal, gulping down the liquid with little decorum. As she picked up the corn bread, he took the empty cup from beside her elbow and moved to the fireplace to make a fresh pot.

He stoked the fire, coaxing a flame. By rote, his hands moved as he fixed the coffee, leaving his mind to turn.

Unrest hung over the fort, a smolder tindered by a blaze of Shawnee anger after Boone escaped his Indian captors. They'd taken him in February, along with several other men who'd gone out one frigid day to the springs at the Lower Blue Licks to gather salt—a dear commodity and one they'd been precious low on at the time. Daniel's face filled Silas's mind, the sinewy frontiersman clad in a hunting shirt and fur-lined moccasins, his breath clouding in the bitter air as he instructed Silas.

"Remain at the fort. Someone needs to."

Silas had wanted to join Daniel and the others on the salt expedition, but he'd stayed behind, following Boone's orders. When news reached the fort of the capture of Boone and the other men, Silas had been pressed with heavy guilt. . .and ruled by the need to provide for the starving settlers, many who feared to leave the fort walls lest they be ambushed. Months passed. No one knew whether Boone and the others were even alive. Mistress Boone, accustomed to fending for herself during her husband's many absences and supposing him dead, packed up and returned to her kin in North Carolina. Only their daughter Jemima remained behind, steadfastly waiting for her father to come home. In late June, Boone managed to escape from the Shawnee and return to the fort. He'd greeted

Silas warmly, thanked him for his service, and spoken of his time with the Shawnees. Some of the settlers, Richard Callaway especially, had been chary of Boone upon his return.

But Silas trusted him. Would trust him with his life, if need be. He reckoned Boone felt the same.

With the relations between settlers and Indians growing in turbulence, his own life might be at the top of the list of things Silas would be required to forfeit in defense of the fort.

He turned, the steaming mug of coffee warming his hand. He expected to find Rosina watching him with her large, expressive eyes.

Instead, she slept, head pillowed on her elbows on the table, eyes closed in exhausted slumber.

He placed the mug on the opposite end of the table and moved behind her chair.

Gently, he placed a hand on her bowed shoulder, letting his fingers settle on the soft fabric of her dress, the warmth of her skin beneath.

Looking up to the rafters, Silas breathed a prayer heavenward. For strength. For wisdom.

And for the woman he'd once loved with every fiber of his soul, every beat of his heart.

Chapter 2

*R*osina turned on the mattress, supporting her growing babe with one hand. She pressed her face into the pillow, scooting over to the middle of the bed. Funny. Usually 'twas all she could do to cling to one side, Jeremiah's bulky frame taking up most of the space.

What was different about today? The quiet?

She'd listened to Jeremiah's ponderous snoring long enough to scarce heed it.

Until silence took its place.

Her eyes flew open. Remnants of yesterday flooded her. The morning, busy at her tasks, trying to keep out of Jeremiah's way lest he fling harshness upon her in either word or deed. Gathering yarrow in the woods, both fearful and fearless at once.

The return to the cabin. Jeremiah's broken and bloodied body.

With a start, she sat up, her heart a drumbeat in her ears. Where was she? She glanced down. In place of her dress, she wore a loose cotton shift. Sunlight filtered through the cracks in the cabin, rivulets of light streaming from the sole window. Not half as large or fine as the one now reduced to ashes. Nor as tidy.

Then she remembered. Fort Boonesborough.

And Silas Longridge.

How well she recalled both the latter and the former. Ah, what sweet memories. Arriving at the fort with her father, being welcomed into the circle of Boone and Callaway girls, families large and happy and brimming with life. The fort frolic when she'd overcome her shyness to bestow a smile upon the quiet, steady frontiersman so often at Captain Boone's side.

One dance in the firelight. 'Twas all it had taken for her heart to cease to be her own. For three months they'd spent some part of nearly every day together. He'd made her laugh with his stories of life on the trace with Boone. Thrilled her with his dreams of what the wilderness of Kentucke might someday be. When he'd dared to hold her hand, it had been a reverent gesture, as if he cherished every part of her and could scarce believe she'd bestow her love upon him.

Then, one afternoon, her father had announced she was to wed Jeremiah Whiting, a recent arrival in Kentucke from a prosperous Virginia family. Not *asked*, but announced. Silas had been away on a hunting trip, and her father urged the marriage forward.

She wouldn't dwell on her marriage to Jeremiah.

Some memories one had to possess more strength to relive than endure.

The cabin door opened, bringing in morning sunlight and a tall, auburn-haired girl.

"Jemima? Jemima Boone?" Rosina gasped.

Jemima shut the cabin door with a laugh. "Jemima Callaway now, thank you very much."

"You've married?"

She nodded. Though she couldn't have been above sixteen, Boone's daughter had the look of a woman about her, from her height to her womanly curves hugged by a rust-colored gown and striped petticoat. But the smattering of freckles across her fair skin and the sparkle in her blue eyes brought back remembrances of the days before Jeremiah, when Rosina had joined Jemima and the Callaway girls in the choring and rollicking that went on among the fort's young inhabitants.

"To Flanders Callaway, Richard Callaway's nephew. Don't you remember him?"

Rosina had a vague recollection of a well-built, dark-haired man who'd been part of the rescue party that pursued Jemima and the two Callaway girls after they'd been captured by Indians two summers prior.

"I can see by your eyes that he's made you very happy." Rosina swung her legs over the bed, supporting her midsection with one hand. Where were her clothes?

"Aye." Jemima smiled, something soft in it. "Happier than a gal has a right to be." She leaned against the cabin door, crossing one bare foot atop the other. Her expression sobered. "The whole fort knows about your husband. I'm sorry, Rosina. Truly I am."

Rosina shook her head with a wan smile. " 'Twas bound to happen sooner or later. Jeremiah was stubborn, refusing to fort up with the rest. He and your father never did get on well."

"A blessing you survived. You"—Jemima's gaze fell upon Rosina's middle, visible through the thin shift—"and your babe. When do you expect?"

Rosina shrugged. Her own mother had passed when she was but ten. With her death went any knowledge of childbearing that might have been handed down. "In a couple of months, I suppose." She rubbed a hand along where her child rested, her fingers greeted with a firm kick.

"Well, Ma unfortunately isn't here. Fort midwife or no, she went back to the Yadkin and the family farm after Pa got captured by the Shawnee. I'm the only one that stayed on. 'Course, I wouldn't have left Flanders. But"—Jemima rested a sun-browned hand on Rosina's shoulder—"I'm here, and Ma taught me most everything she knows. And Granny Anderson is a right fine midwife too. You'll be in good hands. Long as you're planning on staying at the fort, that is."

"I haven't pondered on it." Rosina tapped her foot along the rough boards of the cabin floor. "Everything happened so fast. I. . ." A flush warmed her cheeks. "Where are my clothes?"

"On the line outside my cabin. I washed and dried them." Jemima grinned. "When Silas. . .Captain Longridge, that is, found you asleep, he came straight to me, and I put you to bed. There aren't many of us womenfolk left at the fort, but enough that we still try for some decency. Captain Longridge spent the night on the floor in our cabin. Though I doubt he got much sleep. He was right concerned about you. Said you looked weary to the bone." She scrutinized Rosina's features, head tilted. "You look a mite better this morning."

Rosina glanced at the tangled sheets atop the mattress of the rope bedstead, realization dawning as to where she'd spent the night. Silas's bed. She'd slept well, considering yesterday. But the notion of slumbering atop the same mattress where Silas's frame usually rested brought a flush to her cheeks that had nothing to do with the mid-morning heat.

"Could you fetch my clothes, please? I'm sure Captain

Longridge wants his cabin back."

"Right away." Jemima nodded, swinging around and opening the door. "Be right back." She shut it behind her, leaving Rosina alone again.

Sinking down on the mattress, Rosina ran her fingers across the faded quilt.

What in heaven's name was she to do now? Her father had contracted a fever and passed on at Harrod's Fort some months ago. After his quarrel with Captain Boone he'd made himself scarce at Boonesborough. Thus, Rosina also hadn't returned since her wedding to Jeremiah.

Now her husband was dead, and he'd no kin in Kentucke. She could return to his relatives in Virginia, but to make such a journey in her current state would not be wise.

Life on the frontier often left one with choices that could scarce be called by so generous a name. In her case, as a widowed woman soon to become a mother, she'd options few and far between. Remaining at the fort for the foreseeable future would be best. Surely she could find someone with space in their cabin in exchange for help with chores.

That is, if anyone would have her as the widow of Jeremiah Whiting, a man who'd succeeded in making enemies at every turn. From a wealthy Virginia family, he'd never learned to take direction from another. He did what he chose when he chose, without so much as a by-your-leave. That had not changed with their marriage, a union orchestrated by her father once he'd learned of Jeremiah's prosperous relatives.

No wonder Boone had never gotten on well with her husband.

Rosina blew out a sigh, curling her fingers into fists.

All she could do was survive, taking each day as it confronted her.

No more. No less.

He wasn't watching for her.

Then why did his gaze turn toward any skirt that passed and his mind refuse to keep itself fixed on his task?

Silas wiped his forehead, uncurling his fingers from around the carving knife and setting it on the grass.

Liar.

'Twould be a falsehood to deny he'd chosen this spot, in front of the Callaway cabin in full view of fort grounds, to repair one of the Callaways' hickory chairs. Also a falsehood to delude himself into believing the reason he'd tossed and turned on Jemima's hard plank floor was because he'd grown accustomed to the comfort of his rope bed, instead of giving credence to the truth. That he'd stared up at the rafters, seeing not their solid beams, but the face and form of the woman asleep in his cabin, the vision of her head bent on his table searing his heart like a brand.

He'd left her last night in Jemima's capable hands. But where was Rosina now? 'Twas going on nine. Surely she'd not sleep that long.

Fort sounds surrounded him, as familiar as his favorite quilt. The baying of dogs, the footsteps of men, murmured conversations. He itched for the day when this unrest would cease and there'd be safety enough to claim his own land, build a stout cabin in some secluded spot, and be peacefully, blissfully, alone.

But the time was surely not now. Too much danger. Jeremiah Whiting almost deserved what had come to him, so addlebrained he'd been to remain on his land with the Shawnees traipsing the Warrior's Path. Especially since he'd not only himself to care for, but a young woman and babe on the way.

Though from what Silas had known of Jeremiah, selfishness ran through the man's veins like lifeblood.

Why had Rosina wed him? Had she loved the man? Nay. The look on her face when he'd entered Squire Boone's cabin and witnessed the end of the nuptials had not been one of love. Fear, aye. Misery, aye. But nothing like the appearance of a besotted bride.

As if thoughts of her name conjured her up, she appeared from within his cabin, walking beside Jemima. The two neared where Silas sat, skirts swinging, heads bent in conversation. He grabbed the knife from its discarded spot on the grass, feigning occupation in carving a new leg for the chair. But he couldn't pull his gaze away from the sight of them.

Jemima was the image of her father, same reddish hair, full build, and confident stride. Beside her, Rosina, even with her rounded middle, appeared slight and fragile. Her indigo gown had been washed and pressed, her dark mahogany hair tied in a loose braid that dangled over her shoulder as she walked. Of a sudden, their eyes met.

He tamped down the ridiculous yearning for her smile. She'd lost her husband only yesterday. Such a gesture couldn't be expected of her.

"Morning, Captain Longridge." Jemima waved before sashaying past him and into her own cabin.

Leaving Rosina and him alone.

"I trust you slept well." The words sounded awkward, even to his own ears.

She nodded. Cleared her throat. "Thank you for lending me your cabin. I hope I didn't put you to too much trouble."

He offered a small smile, the knife and chair loose in his hands. Sunlight dappled her hair, framing every slight, feminine inch of her. To look at her, one wouldn't think she belonged in this untamed wilderness. But he knew her better. She thrilled to this life, as he did. Or at least she once had. "Not a bit of it. You know there's nothing I wouldn't do for you."

She nodded, the barest hint of a flush in her fair cheeks. "I know. And I thank you for it. Truly, I do. I doubt there will be many in Boonesborough who will welcome me, as the wife of Jeremiah Whiting."

At least she was honest about the way folk viewed her husband. "You are not him. Around here we try and take things on a case-by-case basis."

She smiled then, but it chided him, as if she knew he'd only said such to reassure her. Which may have been partly true.

Lately, even Boone was under suspicion at the fort due to his actions while with the Shawnees. At the Lower Blue Licks, surrounded by Shawnees determined to march on Boonesborough, Boone had surrendered his men to their captors with the caveat that they would not be tortured, knowing it was the only way to save their lives. He also told the Shawnees that in the spring he would take them to the fort to collect the women, children, and livestock, and then they would all go live in peace together in the Shawnee villages. Silas firmly believed, as did some of the men who were there, that had Boone not spoken as he did, the men would have been massacred. But when Andrew Johnson, one of the captives, managed to escape and make his way back to the fort, he spun a tale that painted Boone as someone glad to surrender his men and lead the Indians to Boonesborough come spring. Of course, that couldn't have been further from the truth, but not everyone agreed, and resentment ran deep.

"What will you do?" Silas asked.

Her smile faded, replaced by lines of careworn tension. "Stay here, if the fort will have me."

"With whom?" The fort was crowded, all cabins claimed. And even on the frontier, where propriety did not hold the weight it did in a Virginia drawing room, 'twould be unseemly for him to invite her to lodge with him.

"Jemima, most likely. At least until after the babe comes. 'Twould be unwise to try and travel before then. The fort is safe, is it not?" A flicker of fear entered her gaze, and her hand went to her middle, as if she sought to shelter her child more than herself.

She'd know if he didn't speak plain. "In a manner of speaking, aye. We've almost finished construction of the walls. A good amount of rotted wood needed to be replaced. It's near as strong as we can make it. But your husband's death is only another reminder of the unsettledness brewing. The Shawnee have already attacked other forts. Many have closed down, folks returned back east. I've no doubt they'll try for Boonesborough sooner rather than later. They're likely vexed Boone gave them the slip."

"Are we prepared?" She lifted her chin. Her father had been a weakling, her husband little better. Both men sought the frontier of adventure novels rather than the reality that daily faced them. Not Rosina. She understood the dangers and confronted them without letting them deter her.

Once, he'd loved her for her strength. For many things.

"Not as well as we could be. We need reinforcements. For now, we wait. And live, best as we can."

She nodded, fearlessness in her gaze. "And when the day comes?" A breeze blew a strand of hair against her cheek. He ached to capture it and rub it between his fingers, its softness like a melody against his calloused skin.

He shoved away the thoughts and smiled slowly. "Why, Mistress Whiting, we face them and fight."

Chapter 3

F ace them and fight. Aye, Longridge. That we will."

Rosina spun. She'd scarce known someone had come up behind her. But that was Captain Boone's way. He had the stealth to rival a panther, most said.

Her stomach tightened. Last she'd laid eyes on the captain, he'd been none too pleased with her husband and made no secret of it.

Somehow the men in her life always found ways to irk the ones she held in high esteem. Her father, then Jeremiah. Both angered Boone with their foolhardy ways.

'Twas a difficult place to be. Betwixt and between the ties of blood and those one chose for oneself.

She tried a tentative smile, shyness overpowering her. Boone possessed a presence that made one stop and stare, a little in awe. He was a handsome man with russet hair and strong jaw, tall height and commanding presence. The children revered him, loving nothing better than to follow him about and listen to his tales. As a friend of Jemima's, she'd always been a bit wary in his company, perchance due to the behavior of her own father.

Captain Boone's face eased into a kind, almost fatherly smile. "Miss Rosina." Perhaps 'twas because of his lingering dislike of Jeremiah that Captain Boone chose to address her by her girlhood title.

"Captain Boone, 'tis good to see you again." She glanced behind to where Silas sat, watching them and carving away at a chair leg. He and Boone were alike, in both manner and attire. Both wore fringed, belted hunting shirts, leggings, and Boone, his favorite broad-brimmed black felt hat. But while Boone's hair was a shade between red and brown, Silas's matched the color of fresh coal. Both men were tall, but had they stood side by side, Rosina guessed Silas would have bested Captain Boone by scant inches.

"I heard about the unfortunate circumstances surrounding your husband's end. Consider Boonesborough your home for as long as you wish."

"Thank you," Rosina murmured. "That is very kind."

"Jemima will be glad to have you. She's been lonesome since her mother and sisters returned to the Yadkin."

Listening to Boone's voice, a cadence she'd not heard in over a year, brought an oft-turned memory to the surface.

Her marrying day. An occasion she'd feared more than anticipated. Dreaded more than delighted in. Since she wedded a man of wealth, hers was a grander celebration than that of other young couples on the frontier. A dress of butter-yellow silk. Leather shoes. Flowers interwoven through her dark curls.

Squire Boone—Captain Boone's brother—was a preacher, and therefore all was done proper and legal.

The front room in Squire Boone's cabin had been cleared, flowers adorning the mantel above the fireplace. She'd entered the cabin, adjusting from morning sunlight to indoor dimness, all the while begging, praying, *longing* to break free. All the while knowing she couldn't.

A compromised woman could not wed another. Nay, she must give herself to the one who'd taken her virtue by force, a thing hushed up, a truth known only by her, her father, and Jeremiah Whiting. 'Twas the way of things. She must be married to avoid a scandal.

And married she would be.

Jeremiah stood next to Squire Boone, dressed in a suit of fine broadcloth. He eyed her as one would a tantalizing delicacy that had been sampled and then denied, but would no longer be after today. Some might call his a congenial smile. But the look of it made her skin crawl.

Jemima would have stood up with her, but Rosina hadn't asked. She had to do it alone. So Jemima sat on one of the plank benches beside her sisters and mother. Captain Boone stood behind his wife, half hidden by shadows, hair combed and broad-brimmed hat, for once, doffed. His features wore the look of one attending a burying rather than a marriage ceremony. He'd spoken to her father about her marriage to Jeremiah, cautioned him about wedding his still-youthful daughter to such a one—a man who'd been sent to the wilderness of Kentucke because his well-bred family wearied of his degenerate ways. Rosina had not known that until Captain Boone related it to her father. But her father had been immovable in his decision.

Squire Boone began, but Rosina could scarce hear the solemn words above the ringing in her ears. Her hand in Jeremiah's trembled like a windblown leaf. She tried to heed the vows. After all, they were sacred, uttered before God. But what could be sacred about a girl no longer chaste, wed to the man who'd been her ruination?

The ceremony drew to a close, the seconds dragging.

Suddenly the cabin door groaned open.

In the doorway, framed by sunlight, stood Silas Longridge, begrimed by the trail, rifle in hand, the scruff of days on his jaw. She turned, hand still caught in Jeremiah's. Silas's gaze pierced her, ripping her heart like a flint-tipped arrow. First, shock. Then. . .anguish.

When he'd left to conduct a party of settlers back to Virginia, she'd been whole. His.

He'd returned to find her broken. And another's wife.

The memory dissipated. Rosina looked into Captain Boone's tanned face, smiling today, then back at Silas. He followed her with his moss-colored eyes in that cherishing way of old, as if he hoped the past between them might rekindle anew.

But he didn't know *her* past. Not the ugly darkness of it. Doubtless he already mistrusted her. Had they not promised themselves to each other, not so much with spoken words as with those left unuttered? He'd come back to find her wed to Jeremiah and had every right to think her a promise breaker and to be angered by her faithlessness. Only he didn't seem angry, at least not in deed. His kindness to her last night, the way he'd hastened to feed and care for her. . .

Nay. She'd not allow herself the slightest hope of a future with Silas Longridge. Too much had separated them, her own betrayal foremost.

After a bridge had been broken, 'twas foolishness to try crossing it again.

"You still fancy Mistress Whiting then?"

The question, issued from Boone's lips in a calm, matter-of-fact manner, threw Silas off-kilter. They sat in Boone's cabin—the one he'd occupied with Rebecca before Mistress Boone returned to North Carolina—cleaning their rifles. Boone took great pride in his, naming it as one would a faithful hound. Tick-Licker, named thus because Boone said it could shoot a tick off a bear's snout at one hundred yards.

Silas focused on the methodical movements of cleaning and polishing, avoiding Boone's sharp gaze in the meager light. Did he fancy her? He could scarce sift through the soil of his heart without producing some remembrance of her. Some sweet moment the two of them had shared before. . .

Before he'd returned on her marrying day, the very hour she spoke vows to another.

"You need a wife," Boone continued. "When Miss Rosina, as she was then, came across the trace with her pa in '76, I didn't think much of her. She seemed too genteel to survive in a life such as we live here. But seeing her again, I believe she'd do well for you, Silas. A fitting helpmeet. And with a child on the way, she'll need a man's protection. In the months ahead, particularly."

"I'll ponder the matter," Silas said quietly. Aye, he'd ponder it all right. More than he'd a right to. Boone wasn't mistaken. Rosina had changed since her marriage. Her face was still that of a girl, but her eyes bespoke a soberness that went beyond her nineteen years.

But the question remained, burrowing under his skin like an unwelcome tick.

Why had she wed Jeremiah Whiting when Silas had been a hairsbreadth away from asking for her hand?

'Twould take time to retrieve that answer. Rosina was the only one who could truthfully give it.

Yet with the threat of attack looming large each day, another query begged response.

How much time did they have?

He forced the thought away and turned to Boone with a question of his own. "What of Mistress Boone? Do you not wonder what's become of her?"

A shadow passed over the frontiersman's face. He set aside his tools and folded his hands atop the plank table. Rebecca had done her best to make their cabin behind fort walls a family home, but it had suffered in her absence. Jemima had a husband and home of her own to tend, leaving her father's residence dusty and unkempt, the bed made haplessly, the dried herbs hanging from the rafters whittled down to a few scant bunches.

"She's with her father's family. I sent a letter thataway a few days after my return. This isn't the first time she's thought me dead. She's a fine woman, Rebecca. I trust—"

"Captain Boone!" Zeke Wainwright burst into the cabin, gulping like a fish. "You'd best come outside."

Instantly, Boone and Silas were on their feet, following Zeke outside. Evening shadows snaked across the sky. Silas's heart drummed in his chest. What was the matter? No shouts pierced the air, no warriors emerged decked in paint bearing tomahawks and British rifles.

A throng clustered around something in the center of the fort. As Boone and Silas approached, the crowd stepped aside to let them through. The few women in attendance wore aghast expressions. Silas spotted Rosina standing beside Jemima.

Not something. *Someone.* Someone Silas never expected to see again.

William Hancock, a member of the salt-boiling party captured along with Boone February last. Wearing only his small clothes, gaunt and filthy, Hancock gulped greedily from a water gourd, liquid trickling down his scruffy face. His dark hair was still plucked like a Shawnee, as Boone's had been upon his return. His wife, Molly, knelt at his side, sobbing quietly.

Boone crouched beside Hancock. Silas turned to the gaping onlookers.

"All who aren't outside for guard duty, return to your cabins." Silas took in the assemblage with a single look. "Give the man some room. Captain Boone and I will speak to him."

A ripple of protest swirled through the group, but they nonetheless dispersed, drifting toward their homes in small clusters. Silas watched Rosina walking beside Jemima as the two women turned in the direction of Jemima's cabin. She glanced over her shoulder, meeting his gaze, her eyes wide, a strand of dark hair brushing her cheek. He nodded, then joined Boone beside Hancock.

"I took the chance, and escaped," Hancock mumbled around greedy bites of corn cake, heedless of his state of undress. "By heaven, what a journey! I thought my sense of direction would prove me right, but the deeper I wandered, the more lost I became."

Face glistening, Molly Hancock listened to her husband's tale, passing him pieces of dried buffalo meat and corn cake at intervals.

"Finally, after I don't know how many days, I gave up. Figured myself beyond all hope, my escape for nothing."

At this, Molly emitted a little sob.

"I lay down to die, praying my Maker would see to it that my end came swift. Then I looked up and saw a tree nearby, carved with my own initials. I recalled I'd been in that very spot hunting only last autumn, so I gathered what remained of my strength and found my way here. Back to you and the least 'uns." He turned toward his wife with a faint smile.

"What of the Shawnee? Blackfish?" Boone asked, referring to the Shawnee chief who'd adopted him during his time in their village.

Hancock guzzled more water, wiping his mouth with a filthy hand. "He's postponed the raid on the fort till he can gather a larger force of British and French soldiers. And at least four hundred Shawnee."

Four hundred? The number sliced the air like a tomahawk's blade. Fort Boonesborough, as it stood now, was comprised of roughly fifty able-bodied men, along with about forty women and children.

Fifty—and that was being generous—against four hundred? Silas and Boone exchanged glances. They'd known the scales wouldn't be tipped in their favor but never imagined coming against so large a force.

The war between King George of England and the American colonists had exacted a heavy price from the settlers in Kentucke. From the sound of things, it was only going to get worse.

"Anything else?" Silas asked. The furrow marking Boone's forehead had deepened as Hancock unspooled his tale. Even for him, fearless as he was, this news came as a shock. They'd expected a march on Boonesborough since June. Today marked July 17, and the absence of any activity held an eerie silence. Worse than aught else was the waiting. Give him a fight any day of the week.

"Nay. Save that I'm weary to the bone and thankful to be home. Not all of us adapt to the Shawnee ways like Daniel Boone." A note of bitterness edged Hancock's tone. Boone had spoken of Hancock's sulking during his months with the Shawnee. Boone, who always made the best of things, wasn't one to let depression beat him.

"You'd best see to your husband, Mistress Hancock." Silas stood, dusting off his knees. "We'll speak again in the morning."

Molly nodded, helped her husband to his feet, and led him toward his cabin and, hopefully, a bath.

Boone stood with a grunt. At over two score, he nonetheless bore the appearance of a hale and hearty man ten years younger. Tonight though, Silas noted the haggard hollows in his cheeks, the gray threading his russet hair.

"We'll send word to Colonel Campbell, asking for reinforcements. With any luck, they'll arrive before the siege. I'll compose a letter tomorrow, first thing." The men exchanged a long look in the fading daylight.

And if the militia reinforcements didn't arrive? Silas didn't voice the question. After all, he already knew the answer.

They'd pray to Heaven the fort held and, if it did not, sell their lives as dearly as they could.

Chapter 4

*T*he news of Hancock's return and the grim report he brought spread through the fort like smallpox—rampant and deadly. Rosina loosed a sigh.

There was little sense pondering what would become of them all. Only their Maker knew. Days passed. Life went on in unbroken monotony. Animals were tended, meals prepared, crops cared for. A semblance of normalcy, a bid for the future, shone through in the announcement that young Peggy Nelson was to wed her sweet-heart, Aaron Winter, on the coming Saturday. There'd be a frolic following the service. Though some protested against the noise dancing and fiddling would make, Boone had agreed to the festivities, promising to station extra guards where needed.

Sitting in the semidarkness of Jemima's cabin, mending one of Flanders Callaway's hunting shirts—Jemima had always hated stitching, even her own husband's garments—Rosina pondered the coming frolic. She'd not attended one since her own wedding, and she remembered little of that, the hours lost in a haze of misery. Of fear at what would follow later, after she and Jeremiah retired to their private quarters.

Her fears had not been unwarranted.

Of course, she'd not dance at this frolic, heavy with child as she was. She'd nothing fine to wear, no dress at all, save the one she'd fled to the fort in. Of course, few boasted finery, with provisions scarce as they were. Peggy was wearing Jemima's best gown to be wed in, and Rosina's next task, after finishing Flanders's shirt, was altering it to fit the girl's slighter frame.

A small figure appeared in the cabin doorway. Rosina smiled and beckoned Chloe Stuart to where she sat by the hearth. Wee Shadow, Rosina sometimes called her. Three years old, the only one to survive an attack of fever that swept her family last winter, the child had latched onto Rosina for some inexplicable reason. Chloe now lived with the Nelsons, but though Mistress Nelson doubtless tried to look after the girl, her own passel of seven least'uns left her little time to tend another's child.

"Come, Chloe."

Little Chloe stepped inside, clutching a small cornhusk doll in her chubby fists. Her curly blond hair hung in a mass of unkempt tangles down her back. Her bare feet made dusty prints on the puncheon floor.

She held up her arms in a silent plea.

"In a moment." Rosina smiled, laying aside the mended shirt and crossing to the chest at the foot of Jemima's bed. She lifted the lid and pulled out a comb. Chloe followed her movements with wide eyes as Rosina dipped a rag into the bucket near the fireplace.

"First, let's tidy you up a bit." Chloe submitted as Rosina wiped dirt and who knew what else from her cheeks, then proceeded to comb the snarls from her hair. "We must have you looking pretty for the party tomorrow night." Perhaps she might dance after all. Rosina smiled at the thought of twirling little Chloe as the fiddlers played. Goodness knew, the girl needed some joy in her young life after the loss of her father and mother, stricken along with Chloe's older brother.

The sun shone plentifully enough outside the cabin. What they needed was a bit more of it inside all their hearts. Her own, weary and bruised after the long months of marriage to Jeremiah, and then his sudden demise. Chloe's, orphaned inside a fort that, at times, seemed like a powder keg ready to explode with the smallest spark.

A knock sounded on the door.

"Come in," Rosina called, focusing on brushing out a particularly nasty tangle as gently as she could.

She didn't expect Silas Longridge's tall frame to fill the doorway. And fill it he did. The man's presence always made postures straighten, gazes turn. He owned command like a mantle, covering his broad shoulders with as much ease as the buckskin shirt he wore.

"Good day to you, Mistress Whiting." He punctuated the sentence with a nod. Unlike Boone, Silas frequently left his broad-brimmed hat behind. Sunlight wove itself through the jet of his hair.

"Good day, Captain Longridge." Rosina's hands stilled from their ministrations to Chloe's hair, and the little sprite took the opportunity to squirm free. She raced toward Silas with a squeal and launched herself at his leg, wrapping her arms around it. Rosina stood with an amused smile.

"Well, well. If it isn't Miss Chloe Stuart." He bent and swung the little girl high. Her high-pitched giggles filled the tiny cabin.

Rosina watched, a sudden wrench in her heart. Who would play with her child as only a father could? Who would provide a man's strength and presence in her child's young life?

Jeremiah would've done the job poorly. But at least it would have been something. Now her babe would have only her.

Could she be enough?

Still holding Chloe, Silas turned to Rosina. The little girl busied herself with the fringe on his buckskin hunting shirt, bare feet dangling.

"How have you been keeping?" The cabin was too small for the both of them. He stood close enough for her to catch the intermingled scents of sunlight and soap and an indefinable fragrance that could only be called. . .*Silas*.

Rosina's cheeks flushed at her mental cataloging of his scent. She hoped the semidarkness of the cabin prevented him from taking notice.

"Fair enough." She rubbed her lower back, easing out a kink. The more her child grew, the easier she wearied. "I've been busy. Helping Jemima. Cleaning, sewing, and suchlike. You?"

"Doing what I can to prepare the fort. Mending rifles. Making gunpowder. Out of all of it, the simple act of waiting is the most wearisome. 'Twould be easier if something, anything, would happen. That I could contend with. But the job of waiting, wondering. . . I must confess, is not my favorite task."

"Nor mine." She smiled, thoughts turning toward the travail of birthing her child. "But God provides ample strength for whatever we must face. Be it the waiting or the acting. Both require a different kind of strength, I think. But 'tis the same God who gives both."

"Aye." Silas nodded. "'Tis true." He held her gaze in that solemn, tender way of his. "Are you going to the frolic?"

Did he ask out of simple curiosity? Or was there more behind his words?

How muddled he always made her feel. As if she could scarce form a reasonable thought, let alone a sufficient answer.

"I'll be there, I suppose. For Chloe's sake," she hastened to add, reaching out and running a hand over the little girl's rumpled skirt.

"Ah." He nodded. "I see." He turned his face toward Chloe, as if in an effort to hide whatever emotion lingered in his eyes. "There'll be ginger cake. Do you like ginger cake, Chloe?"

"Cake! Aye, Mr. Silas."

"Then I'll see to it you get a great big piece." He set her down, turned toward Rosina. "I bid you good day." 'Twas a polite choice of words. Almost too polite. As if she had disappointed him with her answer about the frolic. But what did he expect her to do? Dine and dance like a carefree girl, when she was a widow newly made and an expectant mother to boot?

Before she could return his farewell, he disappeared, the cabin suddenly yawning wide with his absence.

She pulled Chloe close, resting her hand atop the little girl's curly head with a sigh.

She'd do well to put her emotions and Silas Longridge at opposite ends in her mind. 'Twas best they had no cause to meet.

Threat of an impending siege did not lessen the settlers' fondness for a frolic. Perhaps it was partly because there *was* to be a siege that they behaved so. Laughing and living as if this day might be their last. Fiddling and frolicking as if there might never come another summer's eve, another reel.

Silas had stayed out of most of the proceedings. He'd taken a long stretch of guard duty while the young couple said vows. He'd not needed to hear those sacred words again. They'd only dredge up unwanted remnants of the past—of the last wedding he'd unwillingly witnessed.

The early August air held the texture of summer sweetness. A light breeze stirred the trees, a welcome change from the recent heat. Dusk turned the sky shades of peach and dusty blue. The scent of woodsmoke lent its tang to the air, mingling with that of roasted buffalo meat.

Finished with guard duty, Silas made his way to the center of the fort. The fiddler belted out another reel, brawny arm sawing away, forehead glistening with the effort. The newly wedded couple sat on a plank bench, arms twined around each other. The bridegroom leaned toward his new wife to whisper something in her ear. She smiled and blushed.

Silas looked away. After all, he'd not come to the frolic to witness matrimonial happiness.

What, or perhaps more aptly, whom, had he come for?

Childish giggles drew his gaze to the stretch of grass reserved for dancing. Chloe's blond curls bounced in the breeze as she twirled with Rosina.

The mere sight of Rosina made his heart do a thousand foolish things. She wore her dark hair free around her shoulders, save for a few strands at the top pulled back and secured with an indigo ribbon. It suited her, the girlish style, and though she wore the same dress, the bit of ribbon at her throat and the laughter in her eyes made her prettier than he'd ever seen her.

So beautiful it made him want to encircle her in his arms, press his lips against the silk of her hair, and never let go.

Quiet footsteps came up behind him. He turned. Boone stood at his shoulder. He'd donned a fresh hunting shirt and his square jaw bore remnants of a recent shave.

"All work and no play makes dullards of us all," Boone remarked, gaze on the dancers spread across the grass like a colorful, moving patchwork.

"I don't know what you're referring to." Silas looked away from the dancers, focusing instead on the tables of food and drink—not much by most standards, but a bounty of frontier fare.

"If my Rebecca were here, we'd not sit out a single one." His eyes took on a rare softness. "What a dancer that woman is."

"I've had the privilege of partnering Mistress Boone a time or two, and I agree."

"That's not what I meant." Boone's tone held a trace of command. "Stop looking at the woman and go ask her for the next set."

Silas swallowed. "That wouldn't be fitting. Her husband's been gone only weeks."

Boone turned, facing Silas directly, blue eyes flashing in his leathery face. "If we wait for the right time and place, it may never come. We're promised no tomorrows, Longridge. Live today while you still can." He moved away toward his own cabin. Silas watched him go, the tall frontiersman who carried such a weight yet none-theless managed to make it seem light.

His gaze found Rosina again. She tipped her head back, spinning Chloe with one hand.

Ah, but she drew him. Like a helpless moth toward a flame that had singed before, but tempted nonetheless.

Live today.

Straightening his shoulders, he crossed the space between himself and the group of dancers. The reel ended. Chloe, flushed-cheeked, darted toward him, latching onto his leg.

"Mr. Silas! See me dance?"

"Indeed I did. And a prettier sight I've not found in all Kentucke." He gave her a warm smile, patting her sweat-dampened curls.

Chloe beamed.

He turned to Rosina. "Evening, Mistress Whiting."

She nodded, her cheeks bearing evidence of her exertions. "Captain Longridge."

"Can I get a drink?" Chloe looked up at Rosina. "I'm thirsty."

Rosina nodded, motioning to the tables. A couple of middle-aged women stood beside them, assisting with the serving. "It's right over there."

Chloe scampered away with a child's boundless energy. Both watched her go, Rosina with a soft, almost motherly smile on her lips. The dancing had lulled while the fiddler quenched his thirst from a brimming piggin and the guests clustered around the refreshment table. Silas turned to Rosina.

"Enjoying yourself?"

"I suppose." Her tone took on a note of wistfulness. "It's been so long since I've attended something like this. Since I've enjoyed it, even longer."

"But you have enjoyed tonight?" Of a sudden, he wished he'd taken more care with his appearance. He'd washed and shaved that morning, dressed in a clean shirt tucked into a pair of breeches, combed back his unruly black mane. But compared to her feminine self, he could be nothing but rough and unkempt.

"I have. Peggy and her husband seem very happy."

And absent. Silas noted they no longer sat on the bench, no doubt craving the privacy that could now be theirs. He'd have done

the same if he'd married a wife this August eve. What were dancing and feasting when compared to sweet togetherness with one's
beloved?

" 'Tis good they wed today. With things so uncertain, I mean."

"Living each hour as if there would never be another?" She
peered up at him from beneath thick, dark lashes.

He nodded, taking a step closer. The fiddler struck up another
tune, less lively this time. A cadence out of rhythm with his heart,
beating fast at her nearness. The sweetness of her fragrance—sun
and wind and a trace of lavender.

He couldn't resist. Not in light of Boone's words. Nor hers.

"Dance with me." He held out a hand, palm outstretched. "For
old time's sake."

She didn't answer. The soft pressure of her hand placed in his
said more than any words. They didn't join the others in the set, just
stood together as she and Chloe had. Holding hands, he turned a
circle, the steps familiar and simple.

Her dark hair danced in the breeze. Music and laughter filled
the air. Overhead the sun slipped lower, the magic of twilight claiming full reign over the evening.

This was real. This was right. In the months she'd been married
to Jeremiah, he'd missed it. Perhaps he hadn't realized it then, but
there'd been a crack in his heart growing wider each day they'd been
apart. Each step he took with her tonight was one step nearer to
mending that crack, despite the secrets and questions that still lay
between them.

"I haven't danced with you in so long. I thought I'd forgotten
the steps," she whispered, gaze touching his.

Forgotten. 'Twas a word of finality. Of doors closed that could
not be opened. Walls erected that could not be torn down. He'd

closed those doors, erected those walls the day Rosina married Jeremiah Whiting.

Now. . . ?

"You don't forget something like that," he said simply.

As if of one accord, they stopped, her face inches from his, their hands still intertwined. Fading sunlight fell upon her face. Her breath emerged from parted lips. His own went ragged.

He'd always ached to kiss her. Never had, waiting for the day when it would be right and proper and sanctioned by God for him to do so.

That day had not come.

"Nay." She shook her head. "You don't forget. Not something that meant so much." Unshed tears glittered in her dark blue eyes. She brushed past him, darting away in the direction of Jemima's cabin.

Leaving him standing in the middle of a fort full of revelers, wretchedly, completely alone.

Chapter 5

*Y*ou *don't forget something like that."*

Weeks later the words still burned within her mind. That evening of enchantment where, for a few brief moments, the space of time had dissipated, leaving just the two of them.

Silas and Rosina. Nothing changed.

Only everything had. She'd been ruined by another man, then forced to wed him. Now his babe grew within her womb. Dreaming that things were otherwise was nothing more than girlhood foolishness. And there was no time for that.

Bending over the fire in Jemima's cabin, Rosina stirred a bubbling pot of stew. Days wore on, and still no word of the reinforcements Boone had sent for. Despite the way the settlers cast off their cares the evening of Peggy's wedding, the tension behind fort walls grew palpable nonetheless. Mothers kept their children close. Trips to the spring for water were attempted with cautious backward glances, no easy breaths drawn until one was again safe behind fort pickets.

Silas had been absent for more than two weeks. Boone had selected thirty of the fort's best men to join him on a scouting trip north to the Blue Licks to investigate the whereabouts of their would-be invaders. Before his departure, Silas told her Boone's motive for setting out was both to demonstrate his leadership and also to make the Shawnees aware that he had no intention of surrendering the fort. Boone wanted the Shawnees to ponder that if they did attack, lives would be lost on both sides. And loss of both settler and Shawnee life concerned Boone, who valued the tribes as rightful inhabitants of the land. Richard Callaway, however, viewed the Shawnee as worthless savages. Rosina had glimpsed him about the fort, willing to spew his point of view to anyone who would listen. The man was trouble.

Boonesborough without Silas seemed desolate and empty. Ripe for danger. A few days after Boone and his party set out, twelve of the men returned to the fort, announcing it wasn't worth the risk. Silas had not been among them.

On a quilt spread across the cabin floor sat Chloe, playing with her doll. Rosina smiled at her, replacing the lid atop the stew kettle. She kept the little girl close, sheltered her. She'd spoken with Mistress Nelson, and the woman had gratefully given over Chloe's care. Now the child ate her meals at Jemima's table and spent her nights curled up beside Rosina. Goodness knew, a child in the midst of a fort as boiling as the contents of her kettle needed a mother's care.

"That's a pretty dress your doll has on. Does she have a name?"

Chloe nodded, blond curls bobbing. "Rosina." She lisped the word, chin dimpling as she smiled wide.

Rosina smiled. "After me?"

Another nod. "She's pretty." Chloe held up the worn cornhusk doll dressed in a frock Rosina had made from a scrap of calico. "Like you."

"Like me?"

"Mmm-hmm." Chloe held the doll aloft and twirled her in a spinning motion. "See. She's dancing. Like you and Mr. Silas."

Rosina swallowed. "How nice." But the words sounded too bright. Being held by him, wrapped in the strength and safety of his closeness, inhaling his scent, her hands in his large, calloused ones, had awakened emotions she'd long tamped down. Safe and loved. Two things she'd always known with Silas. Would she ever know such again without the measure of guilt and confusion that came with it? Did she even deserve to?

She took a seat in the rocking chair next to the fire, picking up Jemima's petticoat. A puckered tear marked the striped fabric. Since Rosina's arrival at the fort, Jemima hadn't touched a stitch of mending. The arrangement suited them both well. Jemima, ever her father's daughter, preferred the dangerous tasks, striding off into the forests with her rifle to hunt fresh game.

Rosina wished she possessed the Boone courage. Wished she hadn't clenched her hands in a white-knuckled grip as Silas strode out of the fort with Boone and the rest. Wished a day could go by that she did not fear for them. Particularly the man who'd led the procession from the fort, the same hands that had held hers as they'd danced, wrapped around a gleaming rifle.

Boone was a capable leader. He'd keep the men safe.

Like he kept the salt boilers? Captured by Indians and held for months?

Rosina bit down on her lip. Hard. She wouldn't consider that option. Couldn't. Silas had been a part of her since their long-ago meeting. He'd crept into the corners of her heart and settled himself there.

Putting aside her stitching, she stood and paced to the tiny window, staring out at the fort gates, one hand resting on her unborn child. Praying for a return she feared may never come to pass.

The wilderness was a tough master, sapping a person of all reserves.

Every muscle in Silas's body screamed as they continued their trek along the Ohio River. Shawnee country. At every turn, Silas expected to see a group of them emerge from the dense forest, gleaming bodies painted the colors of war, a lust for blood in their dark eyes.

They moved in utter silence, some riding, like Boone, others walking, like Silas. The long unbroken hours did things to a man. There was little to divert one's thoughts away from dwelling on all manner of fears and dangers, though it required constant vigilance to keep one's ears attuned to the faintest sound—the rustle of a leaf, the breaking of a twig—and one's gaze forever scanning the forests around and ahead for the slightest movement. Often it was only a doe or grouse that caused it. But one could never be certain.

They'd set out on this expedition at Boone's command, though some, like Richard Callaway, vehemently opposed the plan, insisting their absence would weaken the defending forces at Boonesborough. Silas stood with Boone, though he did see Callaway's point. The man had a mean way of promoting it though, forever trying to stir unrest and distrust of Boone among the others.

Sweat dripped down Silas's forehead, smudging the paint Boone had instructed them all to apply to better conceal themselves. They'd constructed rafts and crossed the Ohio River a ways back. Now they were smack in the middle of Shawnee territory.

Silas stole a glance behind him, checking the line of men that followed, horses and humans burdened with supplies. He bore his loaded rifle and a light pack on his back, a broad-brimmed hat both sweltering his scalp and shielding his face from the sun. Behind him, Zeke's breath came in labored pants. Though Zeke was one of the best shots in the fort, Silas wished they'd left the man behind. He hadn't learned to heed Boone's art of conducting himself without a trace or sound through the forest.

Silas reached a free hand and swiped at the perspiration trailing across his cheek. His shirt stuck to his chest and his throat ached for a drink. Sweet cider or cool spring water.

For now, he'd have to make do with the lead balls tucked inside his cheek, a method that kept a man from being parched entirely.

Overhead, a redbird trilled from a nearby tree. Silas heeded the sound, listening carefully. Was the sweet music from the throat of a bird? Or that of a Shawnee brave?

Sunlight cut a path through the dense forest, illuminating the cloudless, robin's-egg blue sky, the deep greens and browns of poplar and hickory trees, and the bright red beads of a nearby berry bush. Red. Like Rosina's lips.

He hadn't expected the ache that filled him upon leaving the fort. He'd left her standing with a group of women, her gaze soft and fixed on him, one hand resting on the swell of her babe.

If only he'd been free to part from her with more than a polite farewell. If only her lips had been his for the claiming, the child within her theirs. Would that have made the danger surrounding both of them easier or more difficult to bear?

His gaze snagged on a flicker in the woods. The hair on the back of his neck prickled. He held up a hand, stilling the group. For seconds, total silence fell, save for the rustle of the wind in the trees. Then he spied them. Two warriors, slipping through the forest, carrying British rifles. Both garbed in naught but loincloth and leggings, forearms and biceps adorned with glinting silver bangles, faces painted in black and red. The colors of war.

There was no concealing their party of eighteen men, plus half a dozen horses. Zeke, moving quietly for the first time in his life, stood at Silas's shoulder. Silas caught Boone's gaze. Atop his horse, Boone jerked a nod. A silent command.

Fire at will.

The Shawnees spotted them. In a lightning instant, Zeke raised his gun. Gunfire rent the stillness. Silas aimed, bracing himself for the kick of his rifle. Both Shawnee fell.

Suddenly the woods swarmed with warriors. Tufts of jet hair ablaze with feathers, clutching bows and arrows, a few rifles, descended upon them. Fiendish yells—the war cry—filled the air and chilled the bone.

Astride his horse, Boone galloped up, firing like a general. The acrid stench of powder mingled with the smoke of each shot. Silas reloaded, racing through the motions, as Zeke took an arrow in the shoulder. He aimed at the warrior who'd released it.

Brutality. That was the frontier. Fight or die.

Silas hated it. Always had. The taking of another life should be left to God, not man. But to survive meant to fight. Boone counted on them to stand strong.

He didn't think, blocked out everything beyond shooting and reloading. Over and over and over. For minutes his world was the high whinnies of the animals, war whoops, and angry blasts of gunshot on both sides. A brave raised his rifle, aiming toward Boone, defiance in his gaze. Before Silas could react, young Simon Kenton fired. Two Indians fell almost simultaneously.

Finally, finally, it ended. The Indians slung their wounded over their backs and fled into the depths of the forest. The smoke settled. Alexander Montgomery bent to tend Zeke, who lay on the forest floor moaning.

Silas caught Boone's gaze. Sweat tracked across the ocher paint, giving his features a strange cast. Boone dismounted in a single sweep, as steady as if he'd just spent the past minutes ensconced in a Virginia drawing room instead of battling for life and limb. Silas envied the man his calm.

"We return to Boonesborough." Boone's voice, though low, held command. "As we've seen"—he gave a wry smile—"the Shawnee are already south of the Ohio River. We acquitted ourselves well. But now comes the real challenge. We must return to the fort with all haste. They're on their way, men." In a fluid movement, Boone remounted, sitting tall in the saddle. "And we must beat them there."

Chapter 6

"They're back!" Jemima poked her head inside the cabin door, the news shattering the quiet Sabbath evening. "Pa and the others just came through the fort gates." The words had scarce left her lips before she disappeared with a haste not so much girlish as it was distinctively Boone.

Rosina started to her feet, her mending cast aside. They'd come back.

Silas had returned.

She pressed her hand against her heart to still its pounding. Chloe slept curled in a ball, thumb in her mouth, on the straw tick she and Rosina shared at night, her doll beside her. Rosina ran a hand across her silky curls, the little girl's even breaths evidence she slumbered peacefully, before moving away.

She glanced at the small oval mirror nailed on the plank wall next to Jemima's bed, checking her appearance before grabbing a shawl. Her eyes shone dark and wide, full of emotion. Smoothing a hand down her braid, she started toward the door.

Twilight painted the sky. The ripple of voices sounded from near the fort gates. Rosina sped her pace, hurrying past the line of cabins, the air still pungent with the scent of cooking fires. Dry grass crunched beneath her bare feet, her long skirt swaying.

She'd missed him. Missed him to the point of distraction, and there was no denying it. Truth be told, she didn't want to deny it. Silas Longridge had captured her heart. Though she might later reproach herself, for now Rosina gave in to the sweetness of quenching her longing to see him.

Other women hurried toward the group, spilling out of their cabins with least'uns in their wake, all anxious to quash their anxiety about their menfolk. Rosina scanned the group, noting familiar faces. Zeke Wainwright leaned heavily on a makeshift cane, obviously lame from some injury.

Where was Silas? Boone stood next to Jemima, who had her hand on his arm, and Flanders. All the men looked tired to the bone and begrimed from their travels. But none of the women seemed to heed their unkempt state, throwing arms around husbands, brothers, and sons.

Beneath her fingertips, the babe let out a sharp kick. Rosina scarce noticed. Silas stood, conversing with one of the guards who'd remained behind. Her chest loosened and tightened all at once. A faint smile creased his tanned face as he listened to the guard.

He was whole. Alive.

He'd returned to her.

Only he hadn't. He'd returned. But not to her. He wasn't hers. She wasn't his.

She tucked her chin, steps turning in the direction of Jemima's cabin. She'd witnessed enough of this scene of reunions. Back to the lonely cabin with only her mending and Chloe for company, until

Jemima and Flanders decided to turn in.

"Rosina!"

She spun at the sound of her name. Only one voice could say it like that, lilting over the syllables in a melodic rumble. Silas jogged toward her. His face was unshaven, his raven hair unkempt. In her Virginia girlhood, before coming to Kentucke, she'd never glimpsed a man as wild as he.

Now there was no man she'd rather see.

He stopped a pace away from her. "Mistress Whiting, I mean."

"You've come back then." The statement flew from her lips, sounding ridiculous even to her own ears.

He took a step closer. "Aye. We've come back." A smile angled his stubbled jaw. He reached out, capturing a wisp of hair that had come loose from her braid. She stilled, scarce daring to breathe as he tucked it behind her ear, his calloused fingers brushing the skin along her jawline for a scant instant. Warmth filled her.

Longing overwhelmed her.

He drew his hand away. Cleared his throat.

"How have you been keeping?"

She hastened to fill the silence. "Very well. Caring for Chloe and helping Jemima keeps me busy." Though not enough to stave off worry. "How did the scouting trip go?"

"We accomplished what we set out to do." His hunting shirt had torn at the collar, revealing a slice of his muscled chest. She ought to mend the rip for him. But he might take the offer to mean more than she meant it to. "We made it almost to the Shawnee village when we came across some warriors. There was a skirmish."

"But everyone's all right?"

He nodded. "Other than Zeke, that is. He'll mend right enough, especially with your and Jemima's doctoring to aid him. After the battle, we made for Boonesborough fast as we could, giving wide berth to the British and Shawnee. But after we crossed the Ohio, Boone spotted signs of Blackfish and his army. It's as we feared. Four hundred of them, from various tribes. By my reckoning, they'll reach Boonesborough sometime tomorrow."

"So soon?" Images roiled to the surface. Of Jeremiah's scalped and bloodied body. The burned cabin. Her frantic flight toward safety. Come tomorrow, the fort would no longer offer that.

"I'm afraid so." His eyes grew solemn.

"We've had others arrive from Harrod's and Logan's," Rosina hastened. "Men, coming to help us." A scant number, only as many as could be spared. The other forts were short enough on able bodies to risk sending many to the aid of Boonesborough.

They'd have to make do with what they had, without the hoped-for reinforcements from Virginia. To be sure, they were supposedly on their way, but of no help until they actually arrived.

Silas nodded. "That's fine. We need all the men we can get."

"It will go well for us." Rosina lifted her chin, trying for a smile.

Uncertain words, they were. How could less than one hundred men hold the fort against attack?

Silas's hand settled on her shoulder, its weight warm and comforting. "I promise you, Rosina. I will do my utmost to defend this fort." His words emerged low, determined. A pledge.

And you.

His gaze held hers, as if his eyes spoke the words. As if here and now he offered himself for her safety and that of her child. And he would, she knew, without hesitation.

The promise burrowed deep. Though she needed none. She trusted him unhesitatingly, with her life, with her all. She always had. That, at least, had not changed. In the dying light of evening, broad-shouldered and garbed in the hearty clothes of a frontiers-man, he made a picture of strength and fearlessness. But the stark longing in his gaze directed at her. . .that threatened to undo her.

She nodded, throat dry. "Aye. You and Boone. If it does not go well for us, it will not be because of weak men. Or women," she added, determined to do her part.

His eyes crinkled as he smiled, but 'twas not a mocking gesture. "The brave ladies of Boonesborough will do their finest for us."

Indeed. All she could do was work and pray and stand at Silas's side, as the other frontier wives would do.

Though she, not a wife, merited little place there.

The time of reckoning had arrived.

Blackfish had been sighted, just behind the ridge. Blackfish and his army four hundred strong.

From his post on the fort wall, Silas watched their approach—a sight that would make even the most stalwart settler's blood turn to ice. The Indians made a bedazzling display, faces painted warring colors of red and black, plucked scalp locks adorned with feathered plumage, rifles glinting in the morning sun. Tories marched to the rear of the Indians—their fluttering flags and cocky expressions a stark contrast to the lithe Shawnee. The entire army snaked forward, heading toward the fort in a line that seemed to stretch to infinity.

Silas gripped his rifle. Overhead the sky was a carpet of peerless blue, the air warm with a gentle breeze. Beyond the fort lay the meadow, peach orchard, and cornfields. Beyond that, endless acres of fertile land waiting to be settled.

If they surrendered, they'd be forced to leave all this behind, for the city of Detroit and the whims of Governor Hamilton. They'd go from proud settlers to shamed captives of the blasted Tory government.

Silas ground his jaw. He'd be hanged before he let that happen. To this land, to these brave pioneers.

To Rosina.

God in heaven, keep her safe.

All he could do was pray for her safety and hope she stayed inside the cabins with the other women.

Minutes ticked by. The men of the fort stood above and below, gripping weapons, their eyes on the invaders. The Indian troops constructed a headquarters for their chiefs in the peach orchard outside the fort, an arbor of sorts built with brush, poles, and tent cloth. With great ceremony, the Tories planted the Union Jack near the arbor, the royal flag a slap to the red and white stripes and circlet of stars fluttering high above Boonesborough. Their flag for a country ruled by a government of their own, not by British tyranny. Silas ground his jaw at the sight of the Tory colors.

Boone stood a few paces away on the wall, dressed in his usual hunting shirt and broad-brimmed hat, Tick-Licker almost an extension of his arm. He caught Silas's gaze. Silas read in Boone's lined face what both of them knew.

The events that followed would be their greatest test.

Their stand for the glorious land of Kentucke.

A man approached the fort carrying a flag of truce. Impressive in height and stature, his white teeth a flash against the ebony of his face. Sun gleamed on his bare chest and arms, bedecked with silver bands and beaded necklaces. The white fabric of the flag flapped in the wind. Closer and closer he strode, nearing the fort. Silas's fingers tightened around the stock of his rifle as he peered through a loophole. The air rang with stillness, breaths bated.

"Captain Boone!" the emissary shouted. "Are you in there?"

"Aye." Boone called back, his deep voice carrying over the high fort pickets.

"Chief Blackfish has come to accept the surrender of your Long Knife fort, as you promised him last February. I come bringing letters from Governor Hamilton, promising safe passage to Detroit for every settler behind these walls if they promise to go peacefully."

Letters of safe passage? From Hair Buyer Hamilton, named thus because he paid the Indians handsomely for each white scalp brought to him?

A ripple spread through the fort. Men left their posts and made for Boone, forming a cluster around him—men with lined faces and hard expressions, ready for a fight. Silas stayed near the back.

"Letters." The voices rose, speaking different words but with the same meaning, Richard Callaway's loudest of all. "Demand to see the letters, Boone. Who does he think we are? Half-wits?"

Silas remained silent. Boone could hold two things—his liquor and his composure. He rarely made use of the first, but he was having opportunity aplenty with the second. He nodded and listened for a few minutes. Then Boone, at the center of the circle, held up a hand. The men reluctantly quieted.

"Sheltowee!" Another voice rose strong, borne by the wind, carried from the direction of the peach orchard. "Sheltowee!"

Boone's features tightened. *Sheltowee*—Shawnee for "Big Turtle" —had been Boone's name during his time in their village.

"Come out of the fort," bellowed the emissary. "You must parlay with Chief Blackfish. He wishes to speak to you. Bring no weapons."

"Go out and meet 'em unarmed? Not a chance." Zeke Wainwright's words were soon echoed by others.

"What say you, Captain Longridge?" Boone's voice rose above the cacophony. Unlike the Indians, Boone had not dressed for the occasion. But his gaze, shining out from beneath his black felt hat, held grit and determination. Silas sensed Boone needed another voice of reason. He made his way forward, Flanders Callaway stepping aside. "I—"

"You oughtn't go," Richard Callaway interrupted, crossing his arms over his burly chest, black brows drawing together. Silas caught a whiff of the man. He reeked of sweat and bear grease. "Who knows what the red devils' game is."

"Was I speaking to you, Callaway?" Boone seared his son-in-law's uncle with a look. "Longridge?"

All eyes shifted to Silas. He rubbed the back of his neck. "You're aiming to go?"

Boone nodded, once and firmly.

"You know Blackfish and the Shawnee better than any of us. If you're of a mind to go, none of us ought to stop you." Silas leveled a look at Callaway, whose angular face had turned the shade of a fresh-picked beet. Flanders's lips pressed tight, as if in shame over his uncle's outburst.

"The riflemen will cover me. And the Shawnee won't attack, not like this. Care to join me, Longridge?" Boone gave a sort of half-smile, tone easy, as if he'd asked Silas to accompany him on a fishing trip, instead of heading out to meet a war party determined to see their fort emptied.

Silas drew a deep breath. He'd not refuse, no matter the danger. They'd shared in Boonesborough's success. Who knew what the next hours would bring?

Come what may, there was no better man to stand beside than Daniel Boone.

He nodded once. Without another word, they handed their rifles to Flanders and climbed down the ladder. Toward the fort entrance they strode, two lone men breaking away from the shelter of the fort and heading into only Heaven knew what. Silas tasted grit, his throat dry. Out of thirst or fear?

As the gates groaned open, he glanced behind him.

A flash of indigo caught his eye. Rosina, at Jemima's side, Chloe clinging to her skirt. Jemima crossed her arms, watching the men with a determined stare. But Rosina. . .Rosina smiled. Bidding them onward with a brave upturn of her lips.

If the Indians opened fire on him and Boone, this might be the last glimpse he ever had of her this side of heaven. The woman he'd pledge heart and soul to without a second thought.

Chapter 7

She held her smile in place until the gates closed behind the men as they left the fort and headed straight toward their would-be attackers.

But as the gates shut, shielding them from view, Rosina's smile wobbled. Momentarily.

"What do you think Blackfish will do?" Rosina turned to Jemima.

"Can't rightly say." Jemima shrugged, swiping a strand of rust-colored hair away from her freckled face. "He's a wily one, Blackfish. No doubt he'll put on a great show, fussing about how much he's missed Pa, his adopted son."

"Do you think they're safe?" Rosina hated the waver in her voice. The possibility that this would all end in their being surrendered as Shawnee and British captives was real. One hand went instinctively to the rounded place where her child rested, while her other hand settled atop Chloe's head.

"You want the truth?" Jemima's eyes snapped. She looked even more the fiery frontierswoman than usual, exchanging her dress for a boyish-looking shirt cut to mid-calf, paired with leggings and moccasins. "I trust Pa. But I don't like him going out there. Not one bit." She swung around, striding toward her cabin, clasping her rifle as easily as a genteel lady might clutch a lace fan.

Rosina bit her lip, breath tangling in her chest. She'd already borne witness once to an arrow-riddled body, a fallen man. She'd not opened her heart to that man, so there had been little to grieve. But now. . .

Dear God, what will become of them?

What if her chance for a future with Silas was stolen a second time?

A memory surfaced, timeworn and gossamer.

She'd been seventeen, recently arrived in Boonesborough, after the arduous journey across Boone's Trace. The day had not begun well. Her father had spent nigh on an hour berating her for going barefoot like Jemima and her friends. Finally, she'd fled the cabin and slipped from the fort. Deerlike, she ran, taking deep gulps of spring air. Sunlight drenched the forest, but she'd scarce heeded the beauty, angry tears stinging her eyes and tracking down her cheeks. In that moment, she'd not feared an Indian arrow or a ravaging animal. Freedom from her father was all she sought. From his strict rule over her life, forcing her into the wilderness as an escape from his past in Virginia, one rife with countless gaming debts and cuckolded husbands.

Suddenly she stumbled, tripping over a patch of thick-growing cane. The sharp stalk sliced deep into the tender sole of her foot. She cried out, clutching the injured limb. Blood dripped from the gash, leaving a trail on the forest floor.

Lifting her gaze to the sky, the thick trees rising high, her heart pounded beneath her stays. In her overwrought state, she'd not realized how far she'd traveled. Now she was alone in a place she'd never seen, without any recollection of the path she'd traveled. And wounded in the bargain.

How daft could she be? Jemima would scoff at her if she saw this predicament. Jemima, ever the daughter of the great Boone, as at home in the wilderness as her father.

Wincing, Rosina sat down on the forest floor in an ungainly heap, grabbing her foot again and turning it to assess the damage. With a wry look at her petticoat, she ripped a strip of fabric. Her favorite petticoat too, the one with the little blue flowers.

Sucking in shallow breaths through gritted teeth, she struggled to knot the fabric tightly.

A branch cracked. Footsteps. Her breath clogged her lungs. Her jaw trembled. Even on a good day, she would be no match for a pursuing Indian. Now. . . ?

A tear trickled down her cheek, stinging a scratch where a branch had slapped against the side of her face.

A man appeared from the depths of the forest. Relief flooded through her. Not an Indian, but a settler. She made a hobbling attempt to stand as he approached. She'd noticed him before at Boonesborough. He and Captain Boone seemed always together, about some task. But while Boone was pushing two score, this man looked closer to Rosina's age, perhaps about five and twenty. He'd hair the color of the black pearl necklace her mother, God rest her, had once owned, ebony and shining. It hung, unbound, to his jaw. The width of his shoulders bespoke hard work, the outline of muscle and sinew evident beneath his butternut hunting shirt and buckskin jacket. A gleaming rifle was slung over his back by a strap.

What a sight she must appear. Petticoat torn, curls tangled, cheek scratched and tearstained, foot bloodied.

He nodded, the gesture formal in light of where they stood.

"Miss Rosina, isn't it? I don't recall our being formally introduced."

She shifted, foot aching. "Captain Longridge, I believe."

"I saw you sneak out of the fort. Figured you were running from something, so I thought I'd follow and find out what. Besides, it isn't safe to be traipsing through the wilderness unarmed."

She hung her head at the mild censure in his tone. "My behavior was imprudent. I was angry and discomfited. I didn't stop to cipher the danger before I set off."

He rubbed the back of his neck. "From the looks of things, you didn't stop to cipher much at all. What got you riled?"

She blew out a breath. "Oh. . .I don't know. My father. He's always berating me about some offense or other. No matter how hard I try, I can never seem to please him. I just couldn't endure it another moment." She flipped her hair over her shoulder. "Have you ever felt like that—bursting with vexation until you feel you'll explode if you don't get it out?"

He studied her, empathy in his eyes. "Aye, miss. I know the feeling well. Not with a parent, but with others. I've learned something though. No matter how ireful we become in our minds, taking foolish risks is never justified." His tone wasn't chiding. More as if he meant to counsel, steady her with his words. "Come." He held out a sun-browned hand. "Let's get you home."

She expected him to merely guide her, not swing her into his arms, bloodied foot and all. Didn't expect settling against his broad chest as they continued toward the fort and experiencing a sweep of sensations she'd never before reckoned with. Being cradled in his strong arms made her feel safe. Cherished. As if, after this, she could face anything, even the wrath of her father. He smelled of pine, sun-warmed fabric, and woodsmoke—a curiously alluring blend.

When he'd set her down in front of her father's cabin and nodded farewell, he'd taken a portion of her heart with him. She'd returned to face her father, filled with a glow not even his harsh words could eradicate.

Today, watching Boone and Silas approach Chief Blackfish, she was a much wiser woman than the girl who'd raced headlong into the forest. A widow and a mother-to-be. She was past girlhood hurts, sober, and full of much she wished she hadn't been forced to endure.

One thing remained unaltered. Silas Longridge still carried a piece of her heart. Much as he'd once carried her.

"Well, Boone, I've come to take your fort. If you surrender, you shall be treated well. If not, I will put all the other prisoners to death and reserve the young squaws for wives."

Following along with Blackfish's words, spoken in the Shawnee language, Silas sucked in a quick breath, glancing at Boone. The red-haired captain merely gave a short nod, sitting opposite Chief Blackfish on a blanket spread across the grass. Silas stood behind him, hands behind his back. After the formal greetings, where Blackfish expressed grief over Boone's departure—real or feigned, Silas couldn't tell—and an accusation from another chief, Moluntha, who said Boone was responsible for the murder of his son, which Boone denied, the official business had begun.

The young squaws? That would mean Rosina. Beautiful as she was with her dark hair and deep blue eyes, she'd be a prize among the Indian braves—with child or no.

Did Boone realize how many lives were at stake here? How much depended on his actions? Of course he did. Boone knew these people, had dwelt with them and respected them. If anyone could see them through, 'twould be he.

"I have here a letter from Governor Hamilton." Blackfish held out a folded sheet of paper, the rich stationery creased and wrinkled.

Boone reached out and took it. The Indian forces stood around in a circle, arms folded, eyes buttonholed by the painted designs on their faces.

Silas leaned over Boone's shoulder and quickly scanned the letter's contents. In so many words, it reiterated Boone's promise to surrender Boonesborough without a battle, and stated Governor Hamilton's guarantee of safe passage for all who surrendered and came willingly to Detroit. The British would compensate for lost property and allow those at the fort who held American military rank to receive the equivalent rank in the British forces. But if the settlers did not surrender, they would have the Shawnee to deal with, and whatever happened to them was out of the governor's hands.

A slow burn twisted through Silas. How could they make such a decision? Death by Shawnee hands or surrender to the British?

With admirable calm, Boone handed the letter back to Blackfish. Bedecked in the finery befitting his rank—silver earrings, red ochre painted over the top half of his face, a ruffled shirt of snowy white, and a braided belt of red and black—the tall, muscled chief made a fearsome sight, sitting straight and cross-legged on the colorful blanket.

"And this"—Blackfish held up a belt of multicolored wampum—"is my letter to Boonesborough." He passed the belt into Boone's hands. It was finely worked, containing three trails of beads. "The red represents the warpath." Blackfish pointed to the strand of red. "The white is the path of peace we take together, back to Detroit. And the black"—Blackfish pointed again—"represents the death you will all die if you do not surrender."

Silas stared at the belt. The three paths they must choose from. In color as stark as it was vivid, lay their options.

"You decide." Blackfish jabbed a finger toward the belt. "You decide which path to take."

Boone nodded. He even smiled slightly. "I will surely do that," he answered in fluent Shawnee. "But my decision will take time. I must needs consult with others at the fort. I've only recently returned. While I've been away, others have assumed my command."

Blackfish offered a nod. "Do that. But while you talk, my people are hungry."

Boone gestured to the cattle and corn in the nearby fields. "Take what you need. I only ask that you treat what we have as you would treat what is yours and not waste it."

Blackfish expressed his thanks. Looking around at the group of Indians and British soldiers, Silas wasn't so sure any of them had gratitude on their minds. Blood lust, yes. Victory, yes. But gratitude? Not likely.

Boone stood. As they had upon their arrival, Boone and Blackfish shook hands. The chief motioned to a young Shawnee brave, who strode inside the arbor, returning with a bundle wrapped in deer hide. He handed the bundle to Blackfish, who passed it solemnly to Boone. Silas swatted away a pesky fly as Boone took the bundle.

"Cured buffalo tongues. A delicacy for your women," said Blackfish.

"Many thanks," Boone answered.

The chief turned to Silas, offering his hand. Silas shook it, his fingers enveloped in a grip of steel. His hand ached after Blackfish drew away.

In silence, steps measured and slow, they returned to the fort. Silas sensed the gazes of those in the fort and those in the peach orchard on them, eyeing their journey. The former willing them safe passage. The latter? What thoughts ran through their minds, Silas could not be certain.

Once the gates were barred behind them, Boone faced the swarm of settlers. He passed the bundle of meat to Jemima.

"Take these to my cabin, Daughter. Chief Blackfish was kind enough to offer us a gift of buffalo tongue."

"Chuck it in the fire, girl!" shouted Richard Callaway. "It's likely poisoned."

Chin jutted, Jemima shot him a look as fiery as her hair and strode toward her father's cabin.

"Men, we'll gather in the blockhouse and discuss Blackfish's proposal." Backdropped by the high log walls, Boone spoke in a clear, loud voice, steady in tone and manner despite the fact that not all eyes looked to him favorably. "Meeting will commence in half an hour. We'll determine our course of action and take it from there."

Beside him, Silas faced the crowd of settlers. Young and old, male and female, strong and feeble. Good man and wastrel alike. People who had wagered much to travel to this great frontier, seeking freedom and riches, a parcel of land to call their own, a new beginning. The future rested in their hands.

And God's. Silas sent a silent prayer heavenward that somehow the fort and its inhabitants might be saved.

Rosina stood on the fringes of the group alongside some older women, listening to Boone. Her forehead furrowed in a look more pondering than fearful.

Everything in him wanted to race to her side. If the worst happened, and the men were killed and the women taken captive, he'd not want regrets for her to remember. He'd want her to know how much he still loved her—no matter what had happened between her and Jeremiah. What import was that now?

After the meeting, he'd tell her. Voice the words he'd kept inside his heart. He'd offer them, and himself, to be her own as long as they both had breath in their lungs.

Aye, now was no time to wait for tomorrow.

'Twas today or never.

Chapter 8

The storm was coming. Rosina could sense it. It remained to be seen when the first clap of thunder would strike, the maiden streak of lightning slash the sky.

But it approached. Of that there could be no doubt.

The men had been closeted inside the main blockhouse for over an hour. Rosina kept to Jemima's cabin, watching over Chloe and some of the other children, mindful of the Shawnee only a short distance outside the fort.

She sat in the rocker by the hearth and distractedly read aloud from a storybook while the children listened, clustered on the cabin floor with rapt expressions on their grimy faces. The dim interior of the cabin was stifling with so many bodies cramped within, the odor of sweat permeating the air.

If she couldn't do something different soon, she was going to go crazy.

Blessedly, Peggy arrived. The new bride's cheeks were spots of color against her pale face. Her eyes shone with barely tamped-down terror. Rosina put her to work showing the children how to make a puppet out of an old sock and slipped from the cabin as soon as they were occupied.

A strange kind of stillness hovered over the fort. Most of the men were at the blockhouse meeting, and nary a cabin door was left ajar to let out some of the cloying heat. Moving as quickly as the bulk of her child would allow, Rosina crossed toward the blockhouse. Her breath came in short bursts, strands of hair escaping her hastily woven braid.

As she neared, the door swung open, and the men emerged single file. She stepped back into the midafternoon shadows and tried to read their expressions as they exited. She noted Flanders Callaway, who ducked out the door and clapped his hat atop his head with the expression of one out to vanquish the world.

Minutes passed. Men left and crossed the fort. Still, Rosina waited. Finally, Silas strode from the blockhouse. She stepped forward in his path. He looked up. Their eyes met. She tried to read his.

Weariness. Worry. Fear. But overshadowing them all, another emotion. One she wished did not live in his fathomless eyes.

He approached her. With steadfast bravery, he'd accompanied Boone out of the fort this morning. She'd been close enough to hear the murmurs from those standing by, sentences like "There's the last we'll see of them" and "Fools, the both of them."

"I was just about to go in search of you." A softness that seemed at odds with the harsh reality around them threaded his voice.

"Why?" She wove her fingers together behind her back.

"Can we. . .might we speak privately?"

She drew in a breath. The air held the tang of smoke from the cooking fires of those beyond the fort. Supper for those within

Boonesborough would likely be naught more than a square of cold corn cake. "I. . .I suppose so."

"Thank you." Placing a hand against the small of her back, he started in the direction of his cabin. His touch was not heavy or possessive. More guide than command, the gesture that of a gentleman.

"What happened?" She looked up at him as they walked, his moccasined strides matching hers, the sun high and beating mercilessly.

"Many think Boone is a traitor and that he wishes to surrender fort and settlers without a fight." Bitterness tinged Silas's words. " 'Twas not a peaceable meeting."

They passed several of the men on the way to their cabins. All wore grim expressions.

"What do you think?"

"Boone's aim was to try for a delay. A semblance of peace while we await reinforcements. He tried to talk sense into the men, to explain to them the size of the army we're up against, but it was no good. Boone asked for those who favored surrender to turn out or speak up. Then Callaway vowed he'd kill the first man who agreed to surrender."

Surrender. The word crept down her spine, chilling her. "Did you say anything?"

Silas rubbed a hand across his jaw. "I said we should try and stall for a few more days, but that I'd be prepared to fight if it came down to it. Squire declared he would fight to the death, as did others. There were some pretty speeches." He chuckled, a dry sound. "In the end, when the vote was taken, it was unanimous. Stand our ground and fight. All Boone could get them to promise was to arrange another parlay with Blackfish in an attempt to stall." They'd reached Silas's cabin. He placed a hand on the door, turning back to her.

"Come inside," he said quietly.

She did so, following him in, eyes adjusting to the dimness. The fort gossips hopefully had more pressing matters on their minds than observing a widow and an unmarried man going off alone together. She stood in the center of the cabin, hands knotted at her waist, while Silas lit a stub of a candle, the scent of tallow permeating the air.

Why did he seek her out? For that matter, why did he want anything to do with her at all? By all appearances, she'd forsaken him. Could his goodness truly extend to giving grace for something such as that?

He moved to the mantel and stood, head bent, one hand resting on the wood. She bit her lip. What battle was he fighting? The struggle with Blackfish? Or did something else tear at him?

He looked up. In a single stride, he crossed the distance between them, gathering her hands in his. His scent overwhelmed her. The candle sputtered. A heaviness filled the air between them.

"I know not who will come out victorious in the struggle that lies ahead. Boone is the finest of commanders, but we're outnumbered five to one, if not more." His gaze delved into hers. A strand of hair fell across his forehead as he bent his head toward her. "If. . .if the worst happens, I don't want regrets between us. I don't know why you married Jeremiah when you did. I reckon it's not my place to ask you. But you're here now. Marry me, Rosina. I love you. I believe at times I've half gone off my head for love of you. Please. Let us promise ourselves to each other. If the worst comes, at least we'll have that promise."

Tears burned her eyes. She turned away from him, unable to look him in the face. Nay, he didn't know why she'd become the bride of Jeremiah Whiting. He couldn't know. How would he view her if he did?

She'd allowed herself to treasure thoughts of him in the secret places of her mind, but it could not go beyond that. If she told him the truth, and they survived whatever lay ahead, he'd want nothing to do with her. She was ruined. Forced into marriage because she was no longer chaste. Unworthy to be the wife of a man of honor like Silas Longridge. She was sullied, a piece of linen no longer white. He wouldn't want her. And she wasn't sure if she could live with herself after hearing from his lips that he did not.

She turned back, trembling from head to foot. He regarded her, pain lancing his expression, as if he knew her answer before she spoke it.

"I cannot promise myself to you." Tears sped down her cheeks. She wiped them away with the back of her hand.

"Why not?" He placed a hand on her shoulder. "Do you not care for me?"

"I. . ." The anguish in his gaze made her long to give him something. Perhaps this week would see the destruction of Boonesborough and its inhabitants, and the memory of any words they spoke would vanish along with their earthly selves. In that case, could she not offer him a ray of hope? Just a little one? "I do care for you. But. . .'tis too soon. After Jeremiah."

"You loved him then?" His tone was a hoarse whisper of disbelief. She let silence be her answer.

He rubbed a hand against the back of his neck, chest falling in a weighty sigh. Like a man stricken. Felled by the blow of her words.

Guilt wracked her insides.

"I beg you. Let us not talk of this now," she hastened. "Not when everything is so uncertain. I want to help. Tell me what I can do." She brushed a hand against his forearm. Strength emanated from him, in each muscle and sinew. Strength. . .and a wound that she had caused.

"Do?" His brow furrowed.

For now, the defense of Boonesborough was all that mattered. Best to leave the luxury of woes of the heart until that had passed. The decision emboldened her. "I can aim true. Jemima says that women must don men's garb and man the loopholes. To give the appearance of more men at the fort than what there truly are." Her words tumbled over each other.

He shook his head. "In your condition, you'd best keep to the cabins."

She lifted her chin. "If the fort is taken, my *condition* will matter little to our captors. Let me help. I promise you'll find me a good shot."

He seemed about to refuse, then something in his expression broke, and he gave a grudging nod. "If it comes to an exchange of fire, aye, you can join the rest. But only if you promise to take the place I give you and do exactly as you're told."

Rosina nodded. "I will."

He swallowed, face lined and, right now, aged beyond his years. She forced aside the longing to take him into her arms and hold him close. "For now, let's pray to God it doesn't come to that. For all our sakes."

Monday evening passed in a haze as sticky as the September heat.

Silas and Captain Boone parlayed with Blackfish once more. Rosina had waited in the cabin, relegated to caring for some of the littlest children, to hear the results. Jemima returned and told her that Blackfish requested an answer to Hamilton's letter, but Boone and Silas managed to buy more time for negotiations among the fort inhabitants and gain permission for the women to go outside the fort to collect water without fear of reprisal. In return, the Indians could continue to help themselves to cattle and crops for food. A tidy arrangement.

But the Shawnee and British were running out of patience. They'd come to take Boonesborough, not wait around at the settlers' convenience. Jemima said her pa told her Blackfish's gaze had taken on a cold, calculating gleam. This would be the final delay.

Rosina slept little that Monday night, curled beside Chloe on the cornhusk mattress, the little girl's even breaths a reassuring cadence. Jemima and Flanders didn't come to bed until after midnight. Rosina reckoned they were with Boone, helping to prepare the fort's defenses. She'd offered to help in any way, but over and over Jemima cautioned her to stay inside and watch over the children. Thus, she did, most of Tuesday morning. But the inactivity of the task chafed, despite its needfulness, and she escaped the cabin midmorning. Outside the cabin door, a breeze soothed her flushed cheeks, and she rested one hand against her middle as she took in the sights around her.

'Twas a fortification making ready for battle. Men stood at intervals below and along the walls, eyeing the Indians' encampment. Several young men, Flanders Callaway included, bent their backs to the task of digging a well near the center of the fort. Sweat streamed down their dirty faces. Truly though, water would be of the utmost importance, as the well already within the fort gave little water.

A few women strode purposefully toward the smithy carrying armfuls of metal bowls and utensils to be melted into bullets. Rosina spied two lithe-looking young men carrying rifles. One of them pushed back his broad-brimmed hat, revealing a familiar sunburned face.

Why, 'twas Betsy Callaway, dressed as a boy. And her sister, Fanny. Both of the girls had been good friends of hers and Jemima's, and had been captured along with Jemima in the summer of 1776 and rescued by Boone and a party of other men. Rosina would've been among them by the creek that day had her father not insisted she remain inside that Sabbath afternoon and mend his waistcoat.

Now the girls marched back and forth in front of the gates, likely to make their invaders believe there were a greater number of men within the stockade. Doubtless, Jemima was somewhere in the fort doing the same or some other important task for preparation.

Rosina pressed her lips together. And here she'd been relegated to tending the children, a task that could be performed by the older women too feeble to be of active help.

Well, she wasn't going to stand for it. She'd find Jemima or Silas and demand to be given a task.

Shouting sounded in the distance. Rosina stiffened. A scattering of others headed toward the fort gates as the call came again. She followed them, skirt trailing in the kicked-up dust. Heat baked her head, and she stood pressed up next to an elderly man. His eyes were squints in his liver-spotted face, and he reeked of unwashed skin and garments. As they all likely did.

"Boone!" Rosina recognized the voice of the dark-skinned

man who'd borne the white flag of truce. It rang across the pickets, landing on all ears. Doubtless he stood within fifty yards of the fort entrance. "Chief Blackfish and his warriors wish to see your women."

Footsteps sounded behind her, pressing through the crowd. Captain Boone and Jemima, followed by Silas. The three of them drew near the front gates, slightly apart from the others.

"What's that you say?" Boone called.

"Chief Blackfish has heard you have a very pretty daughter. He and his warriors desire to look upon her."

A gasp went up from inside the fort. Rosina swallowed, throat gritty. Was this some kind of trick? Would they truly attack a defenseless woman?

"Since my daughter's kidnapping, she and the other women are very much fearful of Indians." Though loud, Boone's voice had a guarded edge.

"All she need do is come outside. Blackfish will look upon her from a distance."

Jemima Boone was one of the most fearless people Rosina had ever met. But to leave the fort gates alone and face a party of warriors. . . ?

"Pardon me." Rosina nudged the man beside her. He let her pass. She elbowed her way forward, sidling through, until she reached Jemima and Flanders. Captain Boone had both hands on his daughter's shoulders as he spoke quietly to her. Silas stood slightly to the side, hand resting on the powder horn at his waist. She avoided his gaze.

Before she could speak, Boone turned to her. "Mistress Whiting." Gravity etched itself across his unshaven face. Sweat ringed the collar of his hunting shirt. "Jemima has agreed to go.

Will you go with her?"

"Nay." Silas's voice sliced the air. "I won't permit it."

Boone nodded slowly. "I understand."

"Wait." The boldness of her tone surprised her. Had her father heard her, she'd have gotten a strapping and gone to bed without supper. But Boone paused, looking down at her from beneath his broad-brimmed hat. She cleared her dry throat. "Is it necessary for Jemima to go?"

"Doing as they ask may give us more time."

"Is there danger?"

"Rosina—"

She turned to Silas, leveling him with a look. Surprisingly, he silenced.

Boone drew a weighty breath. "I think not. They would not stoop to attack an unarmed woman, especially my daughter. But I cannot promise anything."

Rosina reached and clasped Jemima's hand. Sweat slicked her friend's calloused palm. Jemima glanced at her. Her blue eyes were steely in her freckled face, but a trace of fear filled their depths.

"I'll go with her." The declaration came out strong. Determined.

Boone nodded. "Fine then. We'll be keeping watch." He slung his rifle from his back and held it in both hands. Flanders's forehead creased as he eyed the two of them, reluctance in his gaze, though he made no move to speak against his wife's decision. Silas stood at his side, motionless, hands fisted around his own weapon. Had their encounter in his cabin gone differently, would he have put up more of an effort to stop her? She shoved aside the question. She didn't want him to stop her. She could face this.

"Are you sure you want to come?" Jemima whispered, her voice sounding suddenly young and scared. "You don't have to."

"I'm coming." She wouldn't let her friend face this alone. Even Daniel Boone's daughter wasn't invincible.

They dropped hands. Jemima turned to Flanders. The two embraced, Flanders whispering something in Jemima's ear before pressing a kiss against her lips. Rosina swallowed, caught by the intimacy of the moment between husband and wife.

Jemima broke away from her husband. "Let's get this over with then." She set her slim jaw.

Shoulders straight, the two women approached the fort gates. The towering pickets creaked open. Behind them, Rosina sensed the gazes of the settlement upon them. Her legs shook. Perspiration slid down her back. Her skirt swished in the warm breeze. Overhead the sky was pale blue, sunlight raining down.

Each step they took carried them away from the strong walls that spelled shelter.

Just keep walking. God help us.

She forced herself to face the assembled Shawnee with lifted chin and unblinking gaze. They eyed her openly, curiously. Beside the interpreter stood a well-built man with plucked and braided hair bedecked in a fine English-style shirt open at the throat, adorned with silver bangles and beaded jewelry. Obviously, this must be Blackfish. The other warriors were dressed in simple buckskin, many bare-chested. A hatchet glinted from the belt of a muscled young warrior.

Jeremiah's bloodied body rose before her mind in a stark flash of memory. Her heart hammered.

Captain Boone thought they would be safe. Permitted his beloved daughter to face them.

There was nothing to be afraid of. She played the statement through her mind as Jemima stood beside her, utterly still.

The chief turned to his interpreter and exchanged a few words.

"Chief Blackfish asks you to let down your hair," the interpreter called.

Rosina glanced at her friend. Jemima quirked a brow, a fleeting gesture of amusement, before lifting her hands to her pinned-up hair. Rosina's fingers fumbled for her braid. She ran them quickly through the thick, dark strands, the ribbon that secured them crumpled in her fist. Jemima pulled out her comb and shook free her lush auburn mane.

Wind played with the strands, pulling them away from Rosina's face. She stared straight ahead at the onlookers. Chief Blackfish watched them, a smile spreading across his lined face. Several of the warriors grinned. Yet they were not lascivious smirks, but gestures of almost boyish enjoyment.

Feet rooted to the grass, the women stood a couple of minutes longer.

"Let's go," Jemima murmured. They turned and made their way toward the fort, the gates opening to receive them. They hastened inside, and the gates shut.

Boone and Flanders waited just inside. Boone pulled his daughter close in a quick embrace. A smile softened Rosina's lips. What would it be like to have such a kind and loving father? She could scarce imagine it.

Silas approached and stopped beside her. "Are you well?"

Her hair still hung unbound about her shoulders. But her hands remained at her waist. Whether weary or unwilling to put herself to rights, she couldn't tell. "I'm fine."

Relief showed in his face. He'd worried about her. The knowledge pooled through her. In a gentler time, she'd have let herself bask in it. But perhaps hours from the start of a siege, this was not that time. They must focus on securing the fort, personal feelings aside.

Thus, she gathered her hair and bound it with the creased, sweat-dampened ribbon. "I'd best go see if Chloe's all right."

He nodded, and she walked away.

Chapter 9

*O*n Wednesday afternoon they held a feast. . .for the enemy. The women of Boonesborough outdid themselves with an array of victuals—venison, buffalo tongue, fresh vegetables, platters of bread and cheese, and pitchers of milk. The spread looked mighty tempting, and they'd dipped into their dwindling supplies to procure it.

It was a pity that Silas couldn't swallow more than a bite, surrounded as he was with a Shawnee brave on each side. The whole affair was to lead up to another parlay, decided among Blackfish and Boone last night, after Blackfish demanded a decision and Boone gave his answer—they refused to surrender. Instead of taking up arms, however, Blackfish said he had no wish to massacre the fort, and asked for another day of talks tomorrow.

So they dined. Nine men from the fort. Twenty Shawnee. Like one of those church socials back east where food was served before a meeting of the congregation.

And what a congregation.

Silas cast a glance at the fort, where riflemen manned each post, instructed to fire at the slightest sign of unrest. Rosina—stubborn woman—along with Jemima, was among those standing guard.

Man, woman, and child alike, they must all do their part. Although Silas would rest a heap easier if Rosina was safe inside her cabin.

Feast eaten—or not, in the case of many of the fort men—Boone invited the group to leave the long plank tables set up outside the fort gates and move to the large elm tree some sixty yards away for their meeting. Silas moved in beside Boone as they walked. Despite the friendly facade Boone had donned during dinner, Silas read the telltale lines of concern mapping the captain's face.

"Most of these men aren't chiefs," Boone whispered, clapping his broad-brimmed hat on his head, "but the finest warriors the Shawnees lay claim to. Best be on your guard, Longridge."

Silas nodded. Despite the cool breeze, perspiration trailed down his back. He'd been in a few skirmishes against seasoned warriors before. But 'twas not a prospect he relished.

After everyone was seated on woven blankets and pelts spread across the ground, the meeting began. Silas glanced at the warrior seated to his left, his angular face painted red and black for war. During his time as a scout, he'd encountered braves who'd shown him kindness, and he'd shared food or the warmth of his fire in return. But the one next to him today had the look of a man who'd rather torch Boonesborough to the ground than sit and listen to negotiations. At Blackfish's right, standing like a hewn marble statue, stood Pompey, the interpreter.

A pause hung in the air. Blackfish sat straight and tall,

cross-legged, beneath the shade of the tree. "I will withdraw my army if the settlers of Kentucke promise to abandon the fort within six weeks."

Boone, seated between a Shawnee brave and Blackfish, looked to the other men of the fort. The air smelled of bear grease, Kentucke wind, and tension. "Nay," Boone said in a firm voice. "That we will not do."

"By whose right did you come and settle here?" Blackfish uttered the words, the demand in his tone overshadowing the lilting language of his people. Pompey quickly translated.

"Richard Henderson purchased this region from the Cherokee through the treaty made at Sycamore Shoals," Boone answered.

"I know nothing of this treaty." Blackfish turned to a warrior dressed in the garb of a Cherokee who stood nearby. "Did your people sell this land to the whites?"

Features stoic, the man paused for a moment, then nodded. "Yes, I believe such a treaty was made."

A flicker of surprise crossed the middle-aged chief's rawboned face. He paused. A fly whined over Silas's head, but he didn't dare make a sharp movement to swat it away.

"I see that what Boone says is true. That alters the case. You must keep this land, and live on it in peace. But for a time, my people and yours must be separate. We will go over the Ohio River and stay on our side. You will not cross the river for a time. Later we may hunt on each other's land and trade and be brothers."

Silas eyed the chief. Sounded reasonable enough.

"You will also take the oath of allegiance to the great King across the sea, King George, and submit yourselves to the British authorities."

Silas tensed. Submit to British tyranny? Lose their hard-fought independence in the midst of a revolution? He'd sooner walk over hot coals. But if it meant the prevention of bloodshed, a play for more time. . . They were ill-equipped to defend the fort without the Virginia militia, and there were women and children within its walls to consider. And if Blackfish withdrew his warriors this time, they might never be able to muster such a large force again.

After a pause, Boone nodded, glancing at Silas and the other men from the settlement. Richard Callaway rubbed the scruff on his chin, looking disgusted.

"Seems fair enough," Silas said.

"We agree to abide by your terms," said Boone. Pompey repeated the sentence to Blackfish, who gave a satisfied nod. Quill and pen were brought, a treaty made and signed. For long minutes, Blackfish spoke to his warriors, explaining the terms. Silas listened carefully. Then Blackfish turned back to Boone.

"We have made a long and lasting treaty, and now we will shake hands and embrace as brothers."

Almost in unison, everyone stood. The hair on the back of Silas's neck prickled. Sun slanted through the leaves of the great elm tree.

Two of them for every one of us.

Blackfish swallowed Boone in an embrace. The Indian who'd been seated next to him turned to Silas and grasped his arm in a nooselike grip, bony fingers crushing painfully. Silas steeled his jaw, keeping his face composed.

Instead of letting go, the brave only tightened his hold. Panic dug beneath Silas's skin. This was no brotherly handshake.

A grunt. A thud. Silas glimpsed the blur of Richard Callaway and a Shawnee tussling on the grass. Another Shawnee warrior to his right tackled Flanders, tomahawk in hand.

Then chaos. Silas grappled the Indian holding him, slamming his knee into the man's gut. The Shawnee staggered backward. Boone struggled with Blackfish, throwing the chief to the ground.

Gunfire erupted from the fort. A Shawnee fell, blood spurting from his chest. Some of Blackfish's warriors sprang from a clump of nearby brush and fired back.

The world was ablaze with bloodcurdling cries, flashing tomahawks, and the brute will to survive. Silas fought as hard as he could, dodging the stream of bullets from both sides, yanking a warrior by the back of his shirt and throwing him off Boone, who'd taken a hit in the back from a tomahawk. Blood seeped, a blooming, growing stain against the fabric of Boone's favorite hunting shirt. Smoke hung in an acrid haze.

Squire clutched his shoulder with a howl. A warrior ran at Silas with a whoop. Silas dodged, ducked, fist slamming into the solid muscle of the man's torso. Bursts of gunfire exploded. Prone bodies of the wounded and dead littered the ground. Boone, despite his wound, butted a charging Indian with his head, and sent him flying.

"Back to the fort, men!" he yelled, voice cutting through the thick smoke.

Silas dodged a warrior, fists pumping, feet pounding. Sixty yards seemed like an eternity. Silas's moccasins scarce touched the ground. Boone and the others kept pace, Richard Callaway half-carrying Squire. Silas's lungs burned. Another volley of shots exploded, bullets whistling inches above his head.

Rosina.

Her name came to him in that suspended moment. Her winsome face. Her tears.

He must survive.

The fort gates opened with their familiar creak that had never seemed so blessed. The last man scrambled inside just as the gates swung closed. Silas bent double, gulping for air and counting heads. Five. . . Six. . . Seven. . .

All nine. Alive. But this was no time to rejoice.

The siege had begun.

Chapter 10

*I*f she lived long enough to recall this day, she'd never forget the stench of burnt gunpowder. Nor the terrified bawling of the cattle, the frantic whinnying of the horses, the shouts of men calling back and forth. The smoke that choked the air in a blinding haze, the bursts of shots. A world of fog and fire.

Dressed in a loose-fitting hunting shirt and a pair of leggings, Rosina ran as fast as she could from one loophole to the next, carrying a water bucket, powder, and balls to the men. Her muscles screamed, but now was no time to acknowledge pain.

All must fight to save the fort.

She glimpsed Silas shouting orders, assigning posts. He stood tall in the center of the compound, figure unmistakable, face a study in strength, smoke clouding the air around him. Just looking at him gave her courage. She hastened up the ladder, movements weighted by the heaviness of her child. Hair straggled from her braid, clinging to her skin.

Squire Boone had instantly taken a position at a loophole and commenced firing, despite the hasty bandage and blood seeping from his shoulder. Rosina passed him a dipperful from the water bucket.

"Drink." Her voice could scarce be heard amid the thunder of shots. The Shawnee and British fought like wild things. So many against so few.

He stared at her, eyes glazed, forehead glistening. "Thank you," he rasped.

"You must rest!" she shouted, sweat streaming down her face. "You'll die if you don't."

She turned. Silas approached their post on the upper level of the wall. In that moment, she ached to fling herself against his strong chest and feel the safety of his arms around her. She'd had that opportunity when he'd asked her to be his. She'd turned it down.

Now it might be too late.

"You must get to your cabin, Squire." Silas kept his gaze beyond fort walls, forehead furrowed.

"Who will man the loophole?" Squire's breath grew heavy. Red bled through his bandage. He had a bullet within that needed to be dug out before infection set in. For him to remain in the thick of the fighting could be fatal.

Rosina spared only a glance at Silas before answering. "I will."

For the first time since his approach, Silas looked at her. A sudden flash of longing leapt into his eyes. But just as quickly, it vanished.

"Aye. Jemima's doing the same on the other side."

With a look of gratitude, Squire stumbled away. In a swift motion, Silas pulled his broad-brimmed hat from atop his head and shoved it onto hers. His calloused palm grazed her cheek. Her eyes burned. Both from the smoke and from everything that lay between them.

"Get to it then," he said in a rough voice, then strode away, as if it cost him everything to leave her there.

Taking up Squire's rifle, she went through the motions of reloading. Peering through the loophole, she sighted. Aimed.

The kick of the rifle nearly threw her backward. But she'd aimed true. Through a haze of powder, she saw the fallen body.

Had she wounded him? Or done worse?

A sudden surge of bile rose up in her throat. Nay. . .nay. She daren't think of that.

Reload. Aim. Fire. Her muscles screamed. Grit and gunpowder coated her throat, slaked only by an occasional drink brought by one of the women. The walls of the fort crackled and thudded with bullets. But still they held.

How long she stood at her post, she didn't know. Hours? Centuries? Her keen eyesight proved her an able shot. Bullets whizzed and whistled all around.

At any moment, one might fell her.

God, deliver us. Deliver my child. Silas. All of us.

Over and over, she repeated the prayer, clinging to it with as much strength as she gripped the rifle.

Finally, she made out a voice behind her from amid the haze. Silas stood near. Sweat soaked his shirt. Powder and exhaustion lined his face. Beside him stood an adolescent youth, excitement sparking in his eyes.

"Ambrose will take your place while you eat and rest. You've been at your post for hours. Come."

Too numb to protest, Rosina let Silas lead her away. She stumbled down the ladder, fingers scraping the raw wood. He followed, jumping down the last few rungs. She wrapped her arm through his, leaning her head on his shoulder as they walked. *Sweetness.* The word rose to mind, as out of place as a minister in a gambling den. But 'twas sweetness, walking at his side, feeling his strength beneath the thin fabric of his shirt.

"You did well." His whisper brushed over her.

"Better than you expected?" She wanted to smile, but her lips were cracked and she couldn't summon the strength.

"Aye." He did smile; she heard it in his words.

"Just a short rest," she mumbled, energy ebbing from her limbs.

He led her into the dim blockhouse. Settling her onto a bench, he returned a few moments later with a mug of water and a plate of corn cakes and dried meat. A candle sputtered on the trestle table, providing a glow of light.

"Chloe?" she asked after she'd taken the first gulp and swiped her mouth with the back of her hand.

He propped his arms on the surface of the table, a mug of his own at hand. His shirtsleeves rode to his elbows, revealing tanned arms dusted with hair and streaked with grime. "Granny Anderson is caring for the youngest children in a safe cabin. They're frightened, but she's doing her best to keep them calm and content."

"And Squire?" Heedless of her filth-stained fingers, she ate with her hands, shoving corn cake into her mouth. The familiar taste eased the gnawing in her stomach.

"Boone cut the bullet from his shoulder. He's resting now, with a draught of spirits to keep him comfortable." Silas drank from his mug, cupping his large, begrimed fingers around the pewter handle.

"I'm. . .glad." She leaned her head on the table, plate forgotten, comforted by her babe's hearty kick. At least no harm had come to the child. And she'd survived. Right now she need not think beyond that. Her eyelids grew heavy. All she wanted was to sleep. Only for a moment.

Just before succumbing to dark oblivion, she felt a familiar hand stroke her hair and a quiet voice whisper something. Something that seemed half dream, half reality.

"I'll never stop loving you, my Rosina. I'll never stop loving you."

All throughout the next day, the siege continued. As Thursday crept toward Friday, bone-deep weariness soaked through Silas. He'd slept little, taken long stretches of duty at the loopholes, and strategized with Boone about the Shawnees' next move. Jemima had suffered a surface graze from a stray bullet and had gone to rest in her cabin.

It was six in the morning, or thereabouts. Morning cool provided blessed relief from the previous day's heat. For now, silence hung like a mist over the weary fort. Silas, standing at his post, overlooking the ridge, turned and looked toward the center of the fort.

Their flag still stood. That proud emblem of colonial freedom high on its pole fluttered grandly, despite its bullet-riddled tatters, the colors of red, white, and blue proclaiming to those on the other side of the ridge that the fort was theirs. The Indians had fired countless bullets at it, trying to tear it down.

But the flag still stood.

Silas rubbed a hand against the back of his neck, fingers finding hard knots of tension. This fight wasn't just about the fate of Boonesborough.

Kentucke. The future of this grand and wild place. The future of their freedom from the iron grip of King George and British rule.

Taking in the lush scenery, the rich green of the trees, the rugged, rolling countryside, and the endless blue sky, a new rush of vigor swept through Silas.

Kentucke would always be his home. There could be no other place first in his affections.

Just like Rosina—the woman he would ever and always love.

As if conjured by his thoughts, he caught a glimpse of his broad-brimmed hat—and the face beneath it. Rosina walked toward him, accompanied by Ambrose, the lad who was to spell him. They changed shifts without breaking silence. Ambrose took his place, keen eyes fresh and missing nothing. Allegiance to Kentucke beat within his breast, tender though his years.

They descended the ladder. Silas turned to Rosina as they crossed the fort grounds. She looked as if she'd slept, the grime washed from her cheeks leaving a pink glow, her long braid swaying as she walked. The swell of her child mounded beneath her loose-fitting hunting shirt. A surge of protectiveness flooded him. She'd fought as hard as the rest, her aim as good as any man's. But she was still a mother-to-be. And the sight of her made him ache to keep her safe.

"You must rest," she said softly. "Leave the watch to others for a while. I've fixed you something to eat. It's in your cabin. Come."

She led the way and he followed. Exhaustion pressed bone deep. She opened the door, motioning him to precede her. He stepped inside. A tin plate sat on the table, filled with corn cakes, meat, and greens. He picked up the mug, quenching his thirst with a blissful drink of hot coffee. Setting down the mug, he turned to her. She hovered in the doorway, her eyes following his every move, hat discarded.

"Thank you." The cabin was lamp lit and coffee scented,

brimming with the bewitching intoxication of her nearness. Weariness forgotten, he let himself look his fill of her, wishing she were his wife, leaving him free to press a kiss against the silk of her hair.

"You're welcome." She smiled, turning to go.

"Wait." That single word held as much power as ten bullets. Why he uttered it, he didn't know. Only. . .he did. He needed her. Loved her.

She stilled. Their gazes met.

Two strides closed the distance between them. Silas settled his hands on her shoulders, looking down at her. Her chin tipped up, breath coming fast. Her eyes held promise, her parted lips beckoning. Call it the privilege of a man who knew not whether this day would bring his end. Call it insanity. Perhaps, 'twas both.

The instant his lips brushed hers, he was a lost man. Drowning in the bliss of cherishing her with his touch. He did not linger long. Just once and gently.

She stared up at him with startled eyes. Regret crashed over him. What kind of man was he? He'd always prided himself on being a man of honor. Then why had he just done something that embodied the opposite definition?

"I'm. . .sorry."

Before the sentence had left his lips, she began to weep. Gulping sobs shook her shoulders. She pressed her hands against her face. He brushed a hand across her shoulder.

"Rosina, I shouldn't have. . .I shouldn't have done that." Remorse tightened his throat.

She looked up, tears shimmering on her cheeks. "Nay," she whispered. " 'Tis not that, Silas. I've wanted to kiss you so long, my heart aches with it. But. . .there are things. Things you don't know about me."

"Nothing matters. It can all wait." His words tripped over each other.

She shook her head. "It matters to me. You've not asked why I wed Jeremiah."

He swallowed, gaze lowered. "It wasn't any of my concern. I figured you'd tell when the time was right."

"I shall do so now." Decision shone through the tear tracks on her face.

She crossed the room with quiet steps, seating herself in a vacant chair. He stood in front of her, hands clasped behind his back.

For long moments, silence fell. She stared into the ashes of the hearth while he waited, giving her time.

"Remember when you left on that scouting trip?"

"I remember we said goodbye." And almost kissed. He'd as good as said he'd wed her upon his return. She'd as good as said yes. Even now, the memory still had the power to rub him raw.

"A few days after you left, Jeremiah came into my cabin when my father was away. For a while, he'd been seeking to court me. I didn't like him. Compared to you, he seemed so insignificant, despite his swagger. That night he proposed. I turned him down, saying I was pledged to another. He. . .he got angry." Pain tightened her face. She pressed her lips together in a thin line. "He compromised me." A shudder shook her slim shoulders.

Silas clenched his fists together, white-hot anger roiling through him. Whiting was fortunate to already be dead. If he'd still lived, Silas wasn't sure he'd be able to answer for the consequences.

He could easily believe Rosina's words. Whiting was the sort that always gained what he wanted. He'd wanted the most beautiful girl in Boonesborough. And he'd used the most treacherous means to capture her.

Silas was grateful the warriors had given him his due.

"After that, he told me no one would want me anymore, but that he'd make it right and marry me. My father discovered what happened and insisted we be wed. I didn't love Jeremiah." Tears choked her voice. She gazed up at him, indigo eyes pleading with him to understand. "Every day of our marriage was a misery. This child is the only good thing he's ever given me." She stood, taking his hand and covering it with both of hers. The strength with which her calloused palm grasped his held the promise of tomorrow. "I *ached* for you. All I've ever wanted was to be yours. But I knew I must tell you the truth about myself before I could ever think of accepting your love. I thought to wait. . .to put you behind me. But I find I cannot. While I've been standing at the loopholes, all I've been thinking is, *What if it's too late?*"

"It's never too late." He pulled her into his arms, encircling her as close as he could. She leaned her head against his chest. No pretense lay between them. No fine clothes or pretty words. Just a man and a woman, clinging together in the midst of a storm-shaken sea. Only God on high knew what the day would bring. But at long last, secrets no longer stood between them. He whispered the words again. "It's never too late."

Chapter 11

September 17, 1778

She dreamed of her wedding day. Not hers and Jeremiah's, but where the groom had hair the color of the night sky and a smile meant for her alone.

Silas.

Rosina sat up with a start, an explosion of gunfire shaking the space between dreamland and reality. Her heart thudded. Another burst sounded.

She clambered out of bed and hurried to the window, bare feet padding against the floor. From Jemima's cabin, empty of sleepers save her, she'd a good view of the fort. Though it was the middle of the night, it scarce seemed so as the sky lit up with another volley of exploding gunpowder. Thankfully, Chloe was with Granny Anderson and the other least'uns in the cabin furthest distant from the fighting.

She should dress and go outside. She'd participated in little of the fighting over the past week, not by choice, but because Silas feared for her safety and that of her child. Many behind fort walls had suffered injury, including Jemima, and she'd occupied herself with tending them. They all were weary, supplies dwindling. In everyone's thoughts, if not on their lips, was how much longer it could go on before either the invaders fled or the fort fell.

A sudden twist seized her midsection, the pressure so tight it made her gasp and clutch her stomach. She'd had twinges all yesterday, but they'd been minor compared to this.

Struggling for breath, she stumbled away from the window and toward the bed. Another pain, even sharper, made her cry out.

Cacophony drowned out the night stillness. Breathless from the pain, Rosina bit her lip. Chilling Shawnee whoops. Shouting. Screams. Rifle fire.

She had to get up. They might be short men at the loopholes, more injuries piling up as the hours passed. She stood, grinding her jaw against another cramp. Wetness trickled down her legs, pooling on the floor.

The babe. Jemima had said something about waters breaking, signaling a woman's time had come.

"Nay," she moaned. "Not now."

She stood. Took a few steps. A sudden burst of light flashed through the cabin, turning it bright as day for an instant.

Rosina stumbled. Fell. A sharp pain jolted through her as she landed on the hard wood, splinters from the floor scraping her bare legs.

Another surge of light. Something whizzed past her, so swift it seemed a blur. The scent of smoke choked the air.

Flames leapt from the cabin wall.

Panic clawed at her. She cried out with another pain, sharper than before. Tears stung her eyes. The sound of crackling fire filled her ears. Red and orange flames licked the cabin wall.

The cabin was burning.

She struggled to move as the flames darted higher. Smoke choked her airways. She couldn't stand. Couldn't breathe. Another contraction noosed her body. She fought to rise, but her legs buckled beneath her, and she fell again. The flames, coming ever closer, seemed to mock her.

She was going to die. Death, that springing panther, was about to pounce. On her.

I don't understand, God. Why? Were these past days of happiness with Silas too much to ask?

Her eyes grew heavy, the cabin a blur of smoke and fire.

Always, she'd deemed herself unworthy. For those few short months in her youth, Silas had changed that. But then her father and Jeremiah had gone right on demeaning her. In their eyes, she'd read that they thought her worthless. Only worth something as long as she was useful.

Did God feel that way too? Mayhap earthly joy was only for the very good, which wasn't her. She'd grasped her chance at happiness with Silas, and now it was being pulled. . .and pulled. . .and taken from her. Was her life even worth praying about?

God, I've never really felt Your love. I've tried to pray, but You never seemed to answer. I begged You to rescue me from Jeremiah, but You didn't.

Fog enveloped her mind.

I want to trust You. And I want to live. Please give me strength to get up. Please. . .send a miracle.

Flaming arrows arced through the air, finding their marks in cabin walls and fort pickets. Manning the loophole, aiming and firing for all he was worth, Silas doubted he'd ever see a sight so fearsome again. An eerie glow shrouded Boonesborough in light. Boone shouted orders, yelling both to the men hauling water to douse the flames and to the ones firing at the enemy. His red hair hung unbound, shirt open at the collar, sweat glistening on his face and neck.

"Longridge!" he called. "Some of the cabins are on fire. Organize the men not covering the walls. We've got to keep the flames from spreading or the fort will burn. Jenkins here will take your place." He shoved a lanky man toward Silas's post.

Jenkins took over, and Silas raced into the crowd of surging men and women, pulling some aside, shouting orders. After days of fighting, all were worn threadbare. Terror filled every face, the scent of smoke and crackle of flames thick and dangerous in the air.

"Come with me. All of you." Silas waved them onward as he circled the fort. Arrows had lodged in several cabin roofs.

"Behold, how great a matter a little fire kindleth!"

The scripture rose to his mind. It wouldn't take long for flames to spread and the blaze to consume Boonesborough, just as the Shawnees intended. Since weapons had failed, they chose to destroy them by flame.

"Get more water." He ordered the few women standing by. "Men, we need to tear off the burning boards from the roofs. Now! Start with those cabins there."

He turned, facing the opposite direction.

His heart thundered in his chest.

Flames sprang from Jemima's—Rosina's—cabin. An angry conflagration bent on destruction.

"Rosina!" Her name roared from his lips. Fists pumping, feet flying, he ran with everything in him toward the fast-burning cabin, pushing past whoever stood in his way. "Rosina!"

Let her not be trapped inside. Let it not be too late.

More a prayer than a thought.

He bludgeoned open the door. Billowing smoke clouded the interior. His eyes burned.

Rosina stumbled through the smoke, fighting her way forward, hands groping blindly. Her chest heaved with hacking coughs.

In an instant, he had her in his arms. Lungs screaming for air, he carried her outside. She crumpled in his grip, head falling back.

He set her on the ground, bending over her. Papery flakes of ash dusted her hair. Her chest rose and fell in shallow breaths, but they were even.

"Rosina. Can you hear me? Answer me, my love."

Footsteps pounded, men shouted, fire and gunpowder illuminated the sky. So bright one could almost believe 'twas day. He scarce heeded any of it. She was too still.

God, please. Please, please, please.

"Rosina! Open your eyes." He spoke louder, gathering her into his arms, slapping her cheek with his palm. "You've got to wake up." He hailed a passing woman. Peggy. "Fetch some water," he shouted. "She's fainted."

Peggy darted away.

What else could he do? He hated such helplessness. Give him a fight any day over this. His hands were tied. He was unable to do the thing he most wanted in the world—save the woman he loved. It was her wedding morn all over again. He'd stood there at the cabin door, completely helpless, as she'd married Jeremiah Whiting. Now, she was on the verge of being his, and he was helpless again.

"God." He lifted his face to the sky. " 'Neither know we what to do: but our eyes are upon Thee.'" The scripture emerged from his throat, as true a prayer as any he himself could have contrived.

"Silas." A whisper so ragged it was barely audible caught his ear. Rosina stared up at him, gaze focusing, face pale against the dark pool of her hair, skin smudged with ash.

"My love." He pressed a hand against her forehead.

She smiled, soft and slow. "Silas. . ." Her face tightened, and she let out a low moan, body tensing upward.

"What? What is it?"

"The baby. . ." She groaned again.

Instantly, he stood, sweeping her into his arms. Urgency sped through him. "Let's go find Granny Anderson." Cradling her close, he strode the length of the fort. Fires still blazed, men working feverishly to extinguish them.

"A miracle," she murmured, looking up at him as he carried her.

"What?"

"I prayed for a miracle. And then you came." She smiled, resting her hand against his stubbled jaw. "God is with us, Silas."

Just as they reached the threshold of Granny Anderson's cabin, the second miracle of the night came, visited upon them through cleansing drops of water from the heavens that drenched the fort and doused the flames.

Rain.

Chapter 12

*T*he fort?" Rosina gasped out between contractions. Hours melded together in a haze of female voices, the pungent scent of herbs, and the pain of bringing a new life into the world.

"It stands." A smile flickered across Jemima's weary face as she pressed a cool cloth to Rosina's forehead. "The Shawnee have retreated. Boonesborough is ours."

Rosina would have thrown her arms around her friend in a celebratory embrace if not for the next seize of agony slicing her body.

"Pant now." Despite being as wrinkled as an old apple and hobbled with rheumatism, Granny Anderson had cared for the youngest children while their parents defended the fort and was now proving an able midwife with Jemima as assistant. "The head is nearly born."

Rosina moaned. Sweat slicked her body, the building pressure within seeming never to end. But pain meant life. She was alive. Alive and ushering life in. The most divine of miracles.

"There. Now one more push, and 'twill all be at an end." Granny bent over Rosina's spread legs.

Every fiber of her being drew inward with concentration as she pushed, rearing up and gripping the sheets in her clenched hands. Release followed as the child slipped from within her.

Spent, she lay back against the bed, eyes closed. A snip. Footsteps. She opened her eyes. Granny and Jemima bent over the table. Silence echoed.

"What? What's happening? Why isn't it crying?" Rosina tried to sit up. Sudden panic clawed at her.

But in the next instant came the sweetest of sounds. The mewling of a babe. Gently rocking, Jemima carried the baby to Rosina.

"Meet your daughter." A smile wreathed Jemima's sunburned face.

Granny Anderson propped her up with pillows and helped her to sit. Rosina took the bundle reverently. She cradled the infant in her arms, marveling at the weight of her. Blue eyes blinked up at her.

"Is she really mine?" She brushed her fingertips gently over the downy hair wreathing the little head. Tears suddenly rose to her eyes.

"Aye." Jemima laughed through a sheen of moisture in her own gaze. "She's really yours."

Rosina pulled back the blanket in awe of the perfection before her. Tiny toes. Little arms and fingers that tucked into fists. A puckered mouth. Nose the size of a button.

Each part nothing less than a miracle.

"Silas." She met Jemima's gaze. "I want to see Silas. And Chloe. Bring them both."

"You can fetch him." Granny Anderson stood on the other side of the bed, looking down at the baby. "But not for half an hour. We've still got to finish, then mother and baby must both be tidied up before any visitors. Those are orders, Mistress Callaway." Yet a smile creased her wrinkled face.

Grinning, Jemima left the cabin, door creaking closed behind her.

While Granny worked, Rosina looked down at her baby nestled in the crook of her arm. Jeremiah's face came suddenly to mind. He'd missed this day. Would miss everything about the child he'd fathered.

A lump rose to her throat.

He'd shown her little in the way of kindness. But he'd come to a miserable end, and doubtless, eternity offered him little better. In her heart, the anger she'd once felt toward him had dissipated, just as the flames engulfing Fort Boonesborough were washed away by cleansing rain.

"Your baby will have a father, Jeremiah," she whispered. "And I can promise you he'll be good and strong and brave."

Finished with tending Rosina, Granny took the baby and carried her to the table to be washed. Rosina lay in bed, fingering the ends of her freshly plaited braid. What a sight she must be. The past ten days had done her no favors, nor had the hours of childbirth.

Thank You, Lord, for a man who sees me for more than the prettiness of my face.

Jemima bustled in just as Granny carried the baby back to Rosina. Bending toward Rosina, Jemima whispered, "He's a fine man, your Silas. A right fine man."

Rosina flushed. Jemima squeezed her shoulder and moved toward the table.

They entered, Silas holding Chloe's hand. The little girl looked as fresh and rested as a summer's morn, while Silas bore marks of another sleepless night. He'd donned a clean shirt, and his face looked newly washed, though unshaven. A smile spread across it.

"Come here, Chloe," Rosina said softly.

Chloe approached the bed, eyes filled with nervous curiosity. "Is it your baby?" A lisp tinged Chloe's words, her smile shy.

Rosina laughed. "Aye. My daughter." She looked up at Silas.

His gaze turned soft as he knelt beside the bed. He reached out a hand and rested it against the babe's head, almost hesitant. "She's perfect."

"Come outside, Chloe. You'd like some tea with sweetening, wouldn't you? Miss Rosina needs to rest." Jemima took Chloe's hand, drawing her away. "You can come back later."

Granny Anderson following, the threesome left the cabin, leaving Silas, Rosina, and her baby alone.

"Here," Rosina said softly. "Hold her."

Silas held out his arms, breath tangled in his chest as Rosina placed the tiny bundle into his arms. He gazed down at the scrunched little face, eyes burning with emotion.

"She's. . .so. . ." He'd spent the past days yelling orders at the top of his lungs, and now the miracle of a babe had left him speechless.

Just as it should be.

"Aye." Propped up with pillows in the middle of the bed, a quilt pulled to her waist, Rosina nodded, eyes soft with maternal love. "Perfect. I know."

"What will you name her?" Silas tucked the infant closer to his chest. She was so fragile. Like fine porcelain. And beautiful. Like her mother.

"I wanted some help with that." A gentle smile spread across Rosina's lips. "I was thinking Faith Miracle. Do you like it?"

"Faith Miracle Whiting." He turned the name on his tongue.

"Nay." She shook her head. "Faith Miracle *Longridge*."

He opened his mouth, but no words came. She couldn't mean. . .

"I want you to be my daughter's father. Chloe's too. If. . .that is, if you'll have us."

Love, tender and precious, swelled through his chest. "There's nothing I'd like more."

"Me too." She leaned forward and softly pressed a kiss against his lips. He kissed her back, her daughter in his arms. His beloved Rosina. His at long last.

She drew away, leaning back against the pillows. Fatigue marked her face, but her expression was peaceful and content. "I heard about the fort."

"Aye. We withstood the siege. Two of the men are dead. Several wounded." The weight that had settled on his chest loosened as he spoke the words. They'd survived and held the fort. The colonial flag would continue to flutter above Boonesborough, and the settlers would remain free.

He'd scarce imagined such a thing could be possible.

"When Jeremiah died, I thought to go east as soon as it was safe." Her braid lay across the pillow like a rich, dark ribbon, and her tone grew low and sleepy. "But I find I've a love for Kentucke too deep to deny. What say you, Captain Longridge? Shall we settle this wild land and watch our children grow up upon its soil?"

He absorbed her words, smiling slowly. 'Twould not be an easy task, and there was no guarantee they'd not encounter danger. But the steps that made history were never trod with gossamer slippers. Strong backs and determined hearts were needed to carve out a future worth having. "Aye. But first you must rest. I'll not have my bride too weary to dance at her wedding frolic." He stood, placing the baby beside her and pressing a kiss against her forehead. "Sleep, my love."

Eyes half closed, arms around her infant, she nestled into the pillows. "A wedding frolic. . . ," she murmured.

With a final kiss, he left her to sleep, trusting that while they were apart God would keep her safe. Only He knew what trials the days ahead would hold, what paths they would walk.

But tomorrow brimmed with the sweet truth of knowing the woman he loved, his to cherish unreservedly, would walk beside him on those paths. For better, for worse. In good times and bad. Till death parted them and sent them homeward to an even better life. But until that day came, they'd live for today.

And for the promise of tomorrow.

"Amen," Silas whispered, closing the cabin door, taking in the walls of the fort, the land he loved, and the song of a redbird soaring high overhead.

So be it, Lord.

Author's Note

Though the main characters in *A Promise for Tomorrow* are fictional, the events surrounding the Siege of Boonesborough are not. In my portrayal of this historical event, I tried my best to stay as close to what we know to have actually occurred, utilizing biographies and documentaries as resources. Of course, any errors are my own.

On the morning of September 18, 1778, eleven days after Chief Blackfish and his army arrived at Fort Boonesborough, the siege ended with the fort in the hands of Daniel Boone and the settlers. On the heels of the grueling winter at Valley Forge and other military losses, the victory at Boonesborough was a much-needed win for the American colonists against the British and their Native American allies in the War for Independence.

Including Daniel Boone in this story was such a treat for my history-loving heart. His bravery in the midst of almost unbeatable odds and his determination to carve out a civilization founded on freedom and independence truly earned him a place among the ranks of great American heroes.

In telling the story from the point of view of Kentucky's white settlers, I have in no way intended to demean or negatively portray the Native Americans who lived during this tumultuous period in history. Daniel Boone himself held the Shawnee people in great respect. Soon after the siege, the militia asked him to guide them to the village where he was held in captivity so harsh reprisals against the Native Americans could be made. Boone refused. Soon after, he left Fort Boonesborough and went home to North Carolina. He never again dwelt within the fortification that bore his name.

Thank you for spending time with Silas and Rosina! It was a joy penning this frontier tale and researching the fascinating history of our forefathers. Most importantly, I hope this story encouraged you to draw closer to the One who holds all our tomorrows.

Blessings,
Amanda

ECPA bestselling author **Amanda Barratt** fell in love with writing in grade school when she wrote her first story—a spinoff of *Jane Eyre*. Now Amanda writes romantic, historical fiction, penning stories of beauty and brokenness set against the backdrop of bygone eras not so very different from our own.

She's the author of several novels and novellas, including *My Dearest Dietrich: A Novel of Dietrich Bonhoeffer's Lost Love*. Two of her novellas have been finalists in the FHL Reader's Choice Awards.

Amanda lives in the woods of Michigan with her fabulous family, where she can be found reading way too many books, plotting her next novel, and jotting down imaginary travel itineraries for her dream vacation to Europe. She loves hearing from readers on Facebook and through her website amandabarratt.net.